WACKO HACKO

WACKO
HACKO

Nasser Hashmi

Matador
9 Priory Business Park
Kibworth Beauchamp
Leicestershire LE8 0RX, UK
Tel: (+44) 116 279 2299
Fax: (+44) 116 279 2277
Email: books@troubador.co.uk
Web: www.troubador.co.uk/matador

ISBN 978 1783064 748

British Library Cataloguing in Publication Data.
A catalogue record for this book is available from the British Library.

Typeset in Palatino by Troubador Publishing Ltd
Printed and bound in the UK by TJ International, Padstow, Cornwall

Matador is an imprint of Troubador Publishing Ltd

To those who forgot about journalism...
... and devoured the grubby jewels

A fellow prisoner said I had a PHD: Phone Hacking Diploma. I laughed but he had a point: if celebrities were too dumb to change their codes it's not up to me educate them.

Danny Love, Former News Editor
Convicted at the Old Bailey, June 2011

1.

She Ain't Curvy She's My Mother

Jamie Parkes heard gasps in the newsroom. He dared not look over his shoulder. His story on Larna Wilson sleeping with the young Prince was bigger than a nuclear bomb going off in London. No, it was. Don't hold the front page, you wimps.

He looked deep into the city from the 21st floor. Only if someone plunged from this gleaming glass tower was he interested. The gasps got louder. Jamie reluctantly walked over to the closest plasma screen which had sub-editors Jenny, Pete and Leo stood around it, huddled together, eyes raised, a solitary hand across the mouth. Even Warren Fitton, the 31-year-old editor, was out there, perched on the corner of newsdesk, hands behind his neck, blue-rimmed glasses, braces so tight they were about to snap. Jamie stopped a few feet behind his three colleagues and looked up at the screen. Was that a plane flying into a tower? Jamie was briefed by Jenny. A terrorist attack? What would happen to his splash now? Jamie took off his waistcoat and blew down his chest. He could see Fitton walking across to the centre of the newsroom, palms together, index fingers on lips, eyes darting out of the glass windows.

'Okay ponies, red top turns to black,' said Fitton. 'Time to get serious.'

There was a hush of silence across the newsroom. Jamie looked at his colleagues and then burst out laughing.

'Fuck that for a game for soldiers,' he said.

Jamie walked back to his desk and heard most of the

1

newsroom behind him joining in the laughter. He felt as tall as the tower he occupied.

Jamie was sat in Pub A looking at black and white photos of Lenny Calvin's leaving party. The retired district reporter had passed his treasured contacts book to Jamie after 35 years of service. Jamie was finally about to find out what the fuss was about: Callum Gordon, the PI, SA (Search Agent), Blagger or Pinger, was about to call him – and give him the keys to the gold mine.

Jamie popped a handful of Skittles into his bottle of Grolsch. He took a swig and savoured the tangy sweets shrinking in his mouth. He glanced up at the pictures on the pub wall: Alexander Graham Bell, Busby the bird and Sam Spade. The picture of Bogart made Jamie want to put a fag in his mouth.

'That other number you were trying to track down,' said Gordon, speaking from a noisy train platform. 'Your bird or something?

'It's private, mate. Have you got it?'

There was a long pause and then a sigh.

'Come back in three months. Requests for my services have gone through the roof...

'Since when?'

'This morning. Regards, Callum Gordon.'

'Hold your horses, what about voicemail? Lenny Calvin's a good mate of mine. He said you like Don Diego's. I'll get you a few more packs.'

Gordon took a deep breath. Jamie had initially wanted his ex-girlfriend Gemma Bamford's number but now he sensed he was about to get more; much more. Gordon spoke for half a minute and then hung up. Jamie finished off his bottle of Grolsch and threw his smudgy Nokia on the table. He swivelled it around with his fingers like a spinning top. He grinned and tapped in a number followed by a one-digit number and then, when prompted, a security code, four digits long. Viva La Vodafone. He pulled out his notebook and raised the phone to his ear. He grabbed his pen and concentrated hard for shorthand mode: eyes down, deep breath, steady without squiggles. But as he scented treasure, he was distracted by a woman crying near the bar area. She was almost hysterical. He never liked Pub A, always too noisy. He cut off the call and put the mobile down. It rang immediately.

'Leg it down to Shepherd's Bush,' said Danny Love, the news editor. 'Man lost his brother in the TT attacks.'

'But I'm just about nail Miss Wilson... '

'Hurry up. Get a pic of the dead guy too. Oh, one more thing...

'Yeah?'

'That bent fireman, he said you made up the quotes... '

'Nah, dodgy subs put some salt on it. They just can't leave stuff alone.'

'Get to the Bush, now.'

Danny hung up. Jamie went to the bar to order another bottle of Grolsch. He threw more Skittles into it and knocked back as many swigs as he could. He flicked back his notebook to look for the shorthand notes on Leyton Stubbs, the fireman with the hot story. They were unreadable. He glanced up at the crying woman by the bar – and left Pub A.

Jamie got off the Metropolitan Line at Amersham at 10.07pm. The death knock with the TT man hadn't gone well: the victim's brother shouted 'hope your editor gets cancer' through the toilet window. Jamie came back after hiring a ladder from a window cleaner (it took a couple of hours) and climbed up it in an effort to talk to the man on the same level. He could hear the man being sick in the sink. The man still didn't respond but Jamie took some pictures through the window with his dicky camera.

Jamie was glad to get home and leave the filthy carriages and big city claustrophobia behind. He stepped out at Amersham station and nipped into Santhi restaurant for a takeaway. A few minutes later, he was in Stanley Hill, fumbling with his keys while his mouth watered with desires of shit-kicking, electric curries. He stepped into the house and could already tell his mother was in the kitchen: radio too loud, singing off key, flimsy door wide open. He walked in and placed the takeaway bag on the kitchen table. His mother was wearing an Afro wig and dancing to Michael Jackson's *Wanna Be Starting Something*. There was a full bottle of gin and a half-open packet of painkillers by its side. Jamie walked over to the radio and turned the volume down.

'Get a grip, mum,' said Jamie. 'Have you finished my packing?'

'This wig's better than chemo; warms me up, good and proper. Where did you get it from?'

'A tribute band wanted a write-up.'

Jamie walked over to the kitchen table and started to unpack the takeaway.

'When are you getting my story in?' asked Tina.

'Massive attack in America. You'll have to wait now.'

'Sorry, I'm listening to Michael. Are they doing well in America?'

'Not the band, mum, the twin towers; they've been attacked by terrorists.' Jamie looked up at his mother and shook his head. He walked over to her and took the Afro wig off her head. 'I know you hate the news, but it pays to keep up sometimes.'

Tina straightened her short, spiky blonde hair and fastened the top button on her blouse. She poured a glass of gin and started drinking it through a straw.

4

'Did you call Gemma?' she asked, grimacing and holding her jaw.

Jamie grabbed a fork and sat down at the kitchen table to eat his takeaway.

'Well, did you?'

'Fuck her.'

'No wonder she dumped you; language like that.' She put the glass down and walked over to the table to pick up the wig again. She felt it between her fingers. 'I'd have understood if they played the race card more often.'

'Has your boss got back to you yet?'

'Forget him. What about the story?'

'Like I said the terrorist attacks are going to dominate. Anyway, what can we write? Boss asks female worker for sex to drop case?'

'Sounds right to me. I've even wrote it down for you.' She turned and walked towards the fridge, picking up a notepad and pen from the top of it. She came back and dipped her fingers into Jamie's Bengal Chicken Massala before licking them and sitting down at the kitchen table. She flicked over to the relevant page and started reading out aloud.

'Headline: Randy MD molested woman in office after she refused sex over wine drama.' She paused and looked up at Jamie. 'What do you think so far?'

Jamie didn't answer and carried on eating.

'Mr Jack Barnstable, 58, was accused of sexually harassing Ms Tina Graves while the duo were discussing the theft of six bottles of wine at the head office of the off licence chain... ' Tina paused and mimicked drinking a wine bottle. '... Barnstable's is a popular off-licence chain throughout the country but it may not be for long because boss Jack Barnstable is a rude man who tried to grope Ms Graves' bottom... '

'Stop right there. Makes me sick hearing about it.' Jamie

5

got his dictaphone out and slid it across the table to his mother. 'Tape it. I need some space.' He picked up his takeaway and headed towards the door. 'Should have taken him to tribunal, anyway.'

'Missed the boat didn't I? Only had three months after I complained. He said I could keep my job so I let things drift. Please get the story in, Jamie, I'll use my maiden name too. No-one'll notice.'

Jamie opened the door and walked down into the hallway.

'You've been all different since you broke up with Gemma,' said Tina, clutching her jaw as she raised her voice. 'What did you move back here for? You should have stayed in London.'

Jamie ran up the stairs and wondered if his mother was right about his flip-flopping. A firm denial was the answer. He wasn't happy in London, Amersham or anywhere else; only the newsroom.

Jamie placed his contacts book, dictaphone and mobile phone on the bedside table. He looked around the tidy room and was grateful for his mother's standards; the rooms in London had been filthy. Nikki was slack with the laundry rota and Rob left dirty plates in the sink. Jamie admitted he had slipped on occasion too, particularly when the microwave wasn't repaired quickly enough, but his hours were more challenging: Nikki was a budding actress and Rob was a teaching assistant; case closed. He smiled as he looked at his fax machine, black speakers, classic red rotary dial phone and Joytel phone recorder. The news lab was still intact.

Jamie could see the musty, yellow-tinged tabloids neatly piled high by the wardrobe. He picked up the whole batch and placed them onto the bed. He took off his River Island suit and kicked off his shoes. He sat up on the bed and picked out the newspaper with a pink wallet of photos popping out of the side. It was marked 'Lido di Jesolo'. He opened it and enjoyed all the photos he wasn't in. In one, Gemma was eating breakfast in the hotel. Jamie liked the shape of her mouth and her poppy-coloured nail varnish. He wanted to call her immediately but knew he would have to wait for Gordon. God knows which animal she was cavorting with now.

Jamie browsed through the papers. He smiled when his byline appeared at the top of a story but there were no splashes. He got more annoyed as another paper went by. He was tired but ploughed on until the early hours. At times, he did wonder whether he should tune into the news or watch *Lock Stock* and *Snatch* again, but he was too lazy to get up from his bed. Jamie put the paper down and looked at the photos again: one of Gemma holding a pool cue bending over a table to take a shot; one of her in a bikini by a pool supping a cocktail; one of her giving two-fingers to Jamie outside the hotel; one of her leaning on the hotel balcony wrapped in nothing but a bed blanket. He straightened his curtain-style hair and got out his mobile. He tapped in Larna Wilson's number and leaned back, still looking down at the photos of Gemma. He didn't expect her to answer and the phone eventually went into voicemail. He tapped in '9' and was asked for a security code; he tapped in '3333'. He reached over to one of his huge speakers, on the bedside table, and connected the phone with one of the wires. He laid the mobile carefully on the bed by the photos and looked down. He took a deep breath and slipped his hand down his trousers.

'Pick up, if you're there,' said the unmistakable voice of the young Prince. 'I want to suck your nipples so much I'd enrol with the anti-monarchists. Give me some cream.'

Jamie looked down at the photos of Gemma but could only see Larna. He closed his eyes and started masturbating.

'There's a do in Kensington tomorrow, can you make, Lar-Lar? Need some minty muff, now.'

How many messages were there? Six, eight? Jamie had lost count. There was one from Larna's sister – and one from a charity – but the rest were from the Prince.

'You're the only active service I need, pussykins. A red carpet rogering for Lar-Lar if she doesn't call back.'

Jamie looked up at the ceiling and disturbed the photos with his damp, wandering leg. He closed his eyes and smiled. This was the only splash that mattered.

2.

Kiss And Tell's Can't Spell But Good At Figures

The Lar-Lar story had been spiked to leave Jamie in a state of sick bewilderment. He felt almost physically paralysed when Danny told him it was off; the toilet mirrors had never seen so much phlegm. As he walked in to the editor's office, he saw reporter Louise Dorrans coming out dressed in an extremely tight Wonder Woman outfit. Jamie walked in and closed the door. He looked up at the framed pictures of the Daisies' best front pages on the walls and knew he had missed out. There were two tub chairs in each corner, a yoga mat, a fish tank and a dartboard. Fitton was lying on his leather couch, headphones on, hands behind his head, eyes fixed on the TV screen hanging off the ceiling. He was eating a chocolate croissant while watching a talk show hosted by David Letterman. A few minutes later, Danny breezed into the editor's office with a rolled-up copy of the Screws hanging out of his back pocket. Fitton finally took his headphones off and got up off the couch. He headed to his desk and slipped the copy of the Screws out of Danny's back pocket. He sat down and started flicking through it.

'Sit down, James... ' said Fitton.

'Jamie.'

'Corrected. Now look, Danny agrees with me on this. I know you're terribly upset about the Larna Wilson story not making any of our pages but the Prince was ready to sue us and our pockets aren't as deep as our competitors. Pity because 'Henry the Filth' would have made a good headline. How long have you been on the paper?'

'About seven months. That was the biggest story of the decade.'

'Steady on,' said Fitton. 'Try telling a New Yorker that, or even an Afghan. How did you get the story anyway?'

'From a good source.'

'Keep it that way. When I was royal reporter and then later on the showbiz desk, we built relationships and worked to a code.'

Danny laughed. 'Yeah, the PCCNoSeeSee.'

'What happened to our new serious tone anyway?' asked Jamie. 'The masthead's gone red again.'

Fitton grinned. 'Business as usual again. Two months is a lifetime in tabloid newspapers.'

'So do you still go riding with the Prince?' asked Jamie.

Danny coughed and got up from his chair. 'What stories are you working on this morning, Jammy?' said Danny. 'Need a couple to take into conference.'

'Got a couple, yeah,' said Jamie. 'Is that it? Can I go now?'

Fitton glanced at Danny. 'Where do you get these whippersnappers from?'

'Who cares as long as they deliver? So what are your stories? I've got something else lined up for you.'

'The Taliban have infiltrated MI5 and a Premier League footballer's driving without insurance.'

'Is that all?' said Danny. 'I've got this showbiz story; they're a bit stretched over there.'

'But I'm a news reporter... '

Fitton threw the copy of the Screws into the bin and slipped his hand underneath his braces.

'We're all showbiz now,' he said.

Jamie didn't make any headway, for the whole day, on Danny's 'showbiz' story. He tried to firm up an allegation that a Hollywood film star was gay but the star's agent didn't return his calls. Other stories were filed: one on an Islamic fundamentalist working at a hospital, another on a pop star addicted to cocaine and a third on a much-loved TV programme which was about to return to air. Jamie also pushed his mother's Jack Barnstable story across with a little note and hoped Danny would run it. He listened to the voicemail on Barnstable's phone while on a lengthy toilet break. The messages were so boring (mainly from his wife) that Jamie nearly fell asleep in the cubicle. No wonder the fat bastard wanted a nibble at his mum. It was while Jamie was doing his pants up, that the call came from a young woman called Hannah Rocheman asking him to meet if he wanted an exclusive. Of course, he wanted a good story but a looker would go down well too. He returned to his desk, made some dead-end calls until his shift ended and then went down to Pub D which was further down the Jubilee Line than he'd hoped. He walked in and knew where Hannah was immediately; as instructed, sat at the table beneath the framed picture of Christine Keeler. He approached her and noticed one of her dress straps was looser than the other leaving a hazy white line on one of her shoulders. She was watching two men playing pool as she took a sip of mineral water. She picked up a slice of lemon from the glass and looked up at Jamie.

'What have you got for us?' said Jamie, pulling up a chair and sitting down.

'Don't you want a drink?'

'Haven't got time,' said Jamie, getting his dictaphone out.

'You can put that away.'

'Said he… ' Jamie smiled and took out his notebook and pen. He picked up Hannah's mineral water and took a sip. 'Trust me, I only needed a mouthful.'

'How much are you offering?'

'Who's it about?'

'The MP Don Leaver… '

11

'Is he Labour or Tory?'

'Aren't you supposed to know that?'

'Just get on with it.'

'Think he switched to Labour after 97. Anyway, he's a bigger rat than I thought.'

'How many times did you have sex?' asked Jamie, eyes down on his notebook, pen at the ready.

'Lost count. We did it at this mingey hotel in Hertfordshire every week for about three years.'

'So that's about 150 sex sessions, what positions?' said Jamie, furiously started to scribble in shorthand.

'Not going into that. He did like whips, though. Napoleon too, he liked wearing a funny hat. How much will I get for this? I'm putting my future on the line.'

'What future?'

'I work in a department store, might be made into a supervisor soon. Also trying to get into the hockey team for the Commonwealth Games.'

Jamie looked up and stopped writing.

'What the fuck are you doing this for then?'

Hannah sighed and noticed her loosened strap, which she pulled over her shoulder.

'My dad was diagnosed with Parkinson's and we were trying to get him moved into suitable accommodation, a bungalow so he didn't need to climb the stairs. My mam too, she would have looked after him. The council were being difficult so I wrote to Don, my MP, and he eventually asked to meet with me. He was very polite but then came on to me. I was stupid because he had a bit of power and let it all happen. He promised he'd help but every time we met, we just did it and went our separate ways. Got a wife and three kids too. He's a fucking bastard – and I want him to pay. I'll use the money to help my dad. If I lose my job, so be it. I don't care.'

Hannah picked up her glass of mineral water and finished

her drink. She wiped her mouth and waited for Jamie to stop writing.

'Is there an 'a' in Leaver?' asked Jamie.

'You're the reporter. I don't think so.'

'There is,' said Jamie, looking up with a smile. 'How do you rate his performance? Did he roam like Napoleon? Could he keep his pecker up all night?'

There was a sturdy envelope on the kitchen table when Jamie got home. Jamie grabbed a can of Groslch and took the envelope upstairs into his bedroom. Jamie hadn't realised but it had already been opened. Annoyed, Jamie sat on his bed and pulled out a four-page letter. It was from the owners of his paper; Coby News. Jamie expected it to be the usual guff about company pensions, some bribery act or a new software system but it was titled 'Newspaper Restructure'. He started reading the letter which stated that 140 staff would be made redundant; Jamie calculated that was about a quarter of the workforce: reporters, editors and sub-editors were all in the firing line. Candidates for voluntary redundancy were asked to come forward. If there weren't enough, a selection criteria based strictly on performance would begin. Jamie threw the letter onto the bed. Was there a recession on? Course not. 9/11? Couldn't be a factor surely. Jamie remembered his three-year stint on the local rag, *The Bucks Chronicle*. Staff left and weren't replaced. There were three subs for the whole paper. Mistakes galore.

Jamie looked at the torn envelope and walked out of his bedroom. He waited in the hallway outside his mother's bedroom and took a deep breath. If she opened his mail again, he'd leave. Yes, he still had sympathy for the cancer cock-up that caused her so much grief but that was six years ago and he'd covered a thousand stories since then. He knocked louder than usual and went in. She was asleep in her bed. She

13

looked so small. He considered waking her up but thought better of it. Tina hadn't had a man around since Jamie's father left to marry medical student Fiona Ashcroft eight years ago. They lived in New Zealand now. She never did become a doctor – and Jamie's father never wrote or called. Some stories should never be filed.

Jamie went back into his bedroom and pulled out the number Callum Gordon had given for Gemma's new mobile. He already had her work number – at Lavendales, a recruitment consultancy, but it always took too long to get hold of her, sometimes half an hour – and that in a reporter's world was much too long. He rang her from his landline. There was a short delay and Jamie took another swig of lager.

'Hello.'

Her voice was met with silence. Jamie put the receiver down on the bed side table and picked up his mobile. He tapped in Gemma's mobile number.

'Hello, who's there?

Jamie enjoyed hearing the desperation in her voice.

'Fucking answer, now, if that's you Julian, don't worry, I know where you are?'

Julian? Who the hell was that? Jamie tapped in the security code. The voicemail was so gripping, he wanted popcorn.

'Hello, lover it's me,' said a deep male voice. 'Can't wait to see you. Train comes in at about noon tomorrow. Meet you at the kiosk at Marylebone, yeah? Call back if stuff changes.'

Jamie put the landline receiver down and listened to more messages, which gradually became less engaging.

'Your dad, here Gems. Got that part you needed for your motor. I'll bring it down in the morning before heading off to work. Don't lie in.'

I'd be the daddy, tomorrow. There were a few more messages from family and friends but Jamie quickly got bored. He ended the call and put his mobile down. He

14

glanced at the 'redundancy' letter and picked up his contacts book from the bed side table. He opened the book and started reading down the list of numbers, which had been boosted nicely by Lenny's generosity in passing up his lifetime's worth of contacts after his retirement. Jamie still didn't know why Lenny had chosen him for this act of kindness but a support of Watford FC probably had something to do with it. As Jamie turned over the pages, he imagined copies of his first splash piled so high they wouldn't even get through the newsagent's door. The stellar names were all there: TV presenter Beth Rogers, British film star Ben Isaacs who'd made it big in Hollywood, Premier League striker Anthony Blake, a former Prime Minister and many more. He rang Beth Rogers first, using the diversion of his landline, followed up with his mobile.

No messages.

What? Does no-one ring the Botox bitch?

Ben Isaacs was next.

'We can't offer more than 12 mill for a Brit. We only have a budget of 140. Call me anyhow.'

Jamie smiled as they kept coming. The movie star was delivering.

'Me again. Got great news. Call me urgently. Aw, fuck it, what the hell. Just been down the hospital. I'm pregnant. Wheeeeeee!!!! Call me, need to hear your voice now. Know you're on set but please. Need to hold you close.'

The jewels kept coming.

'Evening Mr Richard Burton the second, your old man here. How about calling me once in a while? I'm on business in New York so maybe we can patch things up. By the way, did you see Gladiator? Utter bollocks. Sword and Sandals, my arse. Anthony Mann is spinning in his grave. Give me a bell.'

Jamie listened to another 12 messages on Ben Isaacs's phone. Footballer Anthony Blake was next.

'Hello, it's Sheila Lings from last night. You were so hot. Didn't know how big you were. Was it rugby you played again? Let's hook up again. Here's my number and my address again just in case... '

Jamie listened again to ensure he got Sheila Lings address in his notebook. There was a knock on his bedroom door and his mother entered. Jamie carried on listening to the Blake's voicemails as a dishevelled-looking Tina sat on the bed.

'You all right, love?' asked Tina. 'Why have you got the landline receiver off the hook?'

Jamie put his hand up, ordering his mother to wait. After a couple of minutes, Jamie turned off the phone and looked at his mother. He replaced the landline receiver carefully above the dial, closing his eyes for a moment, savouring the sensational conversations he had just heard.

'Why did you open my mail?' asked Jamie.

'I forgot you were back home. You've been sent mail here while you were in London and I opened it all. It was a natural thing to do. Did you get the story in?'

'It's up to Danny,' said Jamie, clearing his bed. 'Might make it in.'

He picked up the envelope and redundancy letter.

'Thought your paper was doing well,' said Tina.

'We are,' said Jamie. 'But some crusty fella at the top's not doing well enough.'

'You'll be safe, though, won't you, love? Kind of need you to be... as I'm not working anymore.'

Jamie turned and looked at his mother. He got up from the bed and walked to the window. He looked outside and tapped in Danny's number. He smiled and gave his mobile a long, lingering kiss.

'Safe as houses, mum.'

Jamie wrote all morning and had never been so excited over a set of stories. He still had plenty of material left over. He almost forgot about the Don Leaver story but filed that too. He got up and walked to the coffee machine for a drink, known around the newsroom as the Daily Rough. Louise was already there, warming up a ready meal in the microwave.

'Got the letter, then?' asked Louise.

'Yeah, I'm not worried.'

'Oooh, confidence,' she said, opening the microwave door. 'None of my stories have made the paper for about six months so I'll be up before the firing squad, defo. Getting married soon too… '

Jamie took a sip of coffee and wondered whether he should hand Louise one of his undoubted scoops.

'Heard you'd moved out of London?' she asked.

'Too big and noisy for me.'

Louise nodded and picked up her ready meal. 'Best city in the world.' She smiled and headed in the direction of her desk.

'Wait,' said Jamie.

'Hurry up, my fingers are burning.'

'… You look good in that Wonder Woman outfit.'

'There's a first and last time for everything.'

She walked back to her desk. Jamie emptied the coffee into the bin and crushed the paper cup.

Jamie got back to his desk but suddenly remembered the noon meeting at Marylebone. He'd had an exhilarating morning and couldn't let this opportunity pass. He told Danny he had to meet a contact near Lords cricket ground and, with the pile of gems Jamie had flung to newsdesk, Danny didn't argue. Danny had his hands full anyway trying to keep a fading pop star entertained while the editor met Christopher Wilmotts, the chairman of the Press Complaints Commission, for lunch.

Jamie took a black cab down to Marylebone; the Tube

would have taken too long. He also snared a few more extra blank receipts from the cabbie to help with future expense claims. At 12.03pm, he walked into Marylebone Station and prayed Gemma and her new Romeo would still be there. He walked past the departure boards and looked down the queue at the kiosk. No recognisable faces. He walked across to the information boards, trying to look busy while peering over his shoulder. Ten minutes passed. He walked into WHSmith but the queue at the counter was so long it put him off. Instead he sat down on the seats outside and ensured he could see all the exits and entrances. A couple of minutes later, Gemma appeared, walking into the station from Marylebone Road in a stripy wool hat, buttoned-up coat, jeans and ankle-length boots. Jamie got up to approach her but thought better of it. He watched her approach the kiosk. She hugged a tall man wearing a bobble hat and then kissed him. Jamie expected the couple to head to the escalators for the Bakerloo Line but they went to the platform for the Chiltern Railways train to Aylesbury instead. It was the only train ready to depart (in seven minutes). Jamie looked at his watch and decided to follow them. He bought a single from the ticket office and walked through the ticket barriers. He got on the train and headed through the carriages until he saw them at a distance, sitting down and canoodling. Jamie sat down about 12 seats away, got out his camera phone and took a picture of Romeo, without him noticing. The train left the platform and Jamie glanced at the couple as each station came and went: Harrow-on-the-Hill, Rickmansworth, Chorleywood, Chalfont and Latimer; were they going all the way to Aylesbury? Jamie knew what the next stop was: it hadn't crossed his mind for a second. Unbelievably, Gemma got off first and stood by the doors. Who the fuck did they think they were walking into Jamie's manor? The couple got off and Jamie followed them out of Amersham station. They walked down the street arm in arm, holding each other so tight that Gemma couldn't have looked over her shoulder if she'd tried. A few minutes later they were in Stanley Hill. Jamie felt sick and his heart was beating faster than ever. He stopped a safe distance away, behind a set of bushes, but not far enough so he couldn't hear. They walked towards his mother's house; his house. Romeo knocked on the door. Tina answered. Gemma unzipped her bag and handed her a bottle of wine.

'Hope we're not too late,' said Gemma.

'Good to see you, love,' said Tina, stroking the bottle of wine. 'Big, big lunch for you this afternoon.'

Jamie nearly threw up in the bush. He never liked long lunches.

Jamie got back to the newsroom and tried to avoid Danny. Jamie could tell the news editor had drunk a fair amount from the way he used his tie to wipe the side of his mouth. Danny also liked to hum Def Leppard songs and persistently touch his red boxing gloves which were hanging from the side of his computer. Jamie was transcribing more quotes from his stories when Danny shouted to him that 'some posh angry bastard' was on the line. Jamie asked to put him through. The end of his shift couldn't come too soon.

'Don Leaver, here, who am I speaking to?'

'Jamie, one of the reporters…'

'I understand you've spoken to this woman. Miss Rocheman? Is that accurate?'

'I can't reveal my sources… '

'Well, let me hand you a major revelation. Whatever tawdry tale you've spun, unspin it. That desperate woman will do anything to destroy my family. You will not run this story or you can forget your so-called career. I'll be speaking to your editor next.'

'Do you deny it happened?'

'I'd stop right there if I were you.'

'Is she lying?'

'Of course, she's lying. And I'll tell you somebody else who lies, yes, maybe you're not too interested in him because he's your boss. You swines are never interested in uncovering your own misdeeds.'

'Who do you mean?'

'Mr Fitton, your editor, he's as corrupt and dirty as they come. My friend in the cabinet knows all about him, oh yes, likes to ensure his paper gets all the juicy stuff first… '

'Sorry, I don't know what you're talking about. So, just to clarify, do you deny ever meeting Miss Rocheman?'

'The arrogance of it. Here I am giving you a story about corruption – and it's not only the cabinet minister, I've heard Mr Fitton pays the police, the army and royals too – and all you can talk about is some two-bit tart who works in a store.'

'You can abuse me, Mr Leaver, but if you've got nothing else to say, I've got piles of work to do.'

'I have got something else to say… '

'What?'

'Court… if you run it.'

Mr Leaver hung up.

3.

Noughts And Crosses On The Celebrity Highway Code

The shiny first editions dropped just before 9pm in the newsroom on Saturday night. Danny ripped open the plastic covering, handing out copies to Louise, Jamie and Chris. Jamie held the paper between his fingers and the bulky supplements fell out. He felt a grudging respect for veteran sub Philip Benson. These nasty fiddlers had butchered many of Jamie's stories but old Benson knew his onions.

Ben Behaving Dadly

Hollywood star to be father after Lisa T confirms pregnancy

Get in. Jamie had arrived; Page 4 lead was his. Page 9, Page 12 and 13. Jamie was a player now. Danny walked round to Jamie's desk.

'Nice one, Jammy,' he said, playfully landing a right hook on Jamie's shoulder. 'Thriller in Manila, Benn and McClennan. You've joined the epics.' Danny started to walk away. 'Redundancy selection starts in a couple of weeks.'

Jamie flicked through the paper and read a story he'd almost forgotten about: a children's TV presenter smoked cannabis while playing on the swings and slides at his local park. Jamie shook his head and smiled. It was frightening how easy these stories were to get. Jamie looked over his shoulder and could see Louise looking at him. She smiled and gave him the thumbs-up. Jamie would have liked to have sat next to Louise but, as ever, things never turned out that way. On his segment of desks, there was only one other staffer, Jimmy Betson, and the other two – Maxine Cort and Will Mackenzie – were like him, still on shifts. Betson was helpful enough, if a little cold, but Jamie found it difficult to penetrate the other two because they already knew each other very well, having conversations about grunge music, all-night drinking benders and their newspaper training in Hastings. When their paths did cross, it was polite enough but Jamie felt no-one should be that pally in a newsroom: it created a lazy environment.

Jamie walked over to the photocopier and made copies of his stories as well as the relevant shorthand notes. He stuffed four copies of the paper into his shoulder bag and went home for the evening. He took one copy of the paper out and acted as though he was reading it on the Tube. He looked up to see if anyone was looking at him and a few people were. Jamie ensured they could see his splash by opening up the paper and reading the inside pages. He got home at 11.15pm and turned on the light in his bedroom. He'd almost forgotten how bare the walls were these days: no posters of Hulk Hogan, The Shamen and Daryl Hannah bearing down on him. That had to change. He grabbed some Blu-Tack and began hanging up all the copies of his stories and shorthand notes on the wall. There were pages of pages of them and they started to look really impressive, covering most of the giant wall opposite the bed. The boost from the stories was expected but the shorthand scrawls gave him a strange, uplifting sensation, as though another language was present in the room. He admired his handiwork and reached down beneath his bed. He pulled out a quarter-full bottle of brandy and poured a glass. First half, Grolsch; second half, brandy – hard and wild. He took a drink and switched on his portable CD player. The Shamen's *Move Any Mountain* came on. Jamie turned up the volume and started dancing around the room with the bottle of brandy in his hand. He ran over to the wall and mimicked boxing moves with some of his stories, particularly the ones with a racy female picture in them. He sang to the chorus with the kind of intensity he hadn't reached since securing his first job on *The Chronicle* six years ago. It felt better now: bigger and more wide-ranging; Mirror, Screws, Mail, People, fuck you, the Daisies have cut you to shreds. Jamie finished the bottle within minutes. He went downstairs for another and sprinted up the stairs to ensure he caught the end of the song. He was singing so loud now that the band didn't exist. He didn't hear the sound of the front door opening. He slumped down beneath the wall where all his stories and shorthand notes were pinned up. His mother walked into the bedroom a few minutes later. She looked around the room and, in particular, the wall above his head. Jamie pointed to the papers by the wardrobe. Tina walked over and picked one up. Jamie was extremely angry with his mother for her secret lunch but that could wait. Nothing could spoil the best day of his life.

'So where's that Jack Barnstable story?' she said, flicking through the pages.

Jamie walked to the newsagent in the morning to see what the Screws and a few of the other Sundays were running. He waited a few minutes to see a person pick up his paper and then paid for his carton of eggs, milk bottles and copy of *Empire* magazine, which he only bought because it was the Lords of the Rings collectors' edition. He got back home and his mother had already prepared breakfast for him: boiled egg, wholemeal toast and cup of tea with three sugars. He sat down at the kitchen table and flicked through the magazine, not speaking for five minutes.

'Seen Gemma lately?'

'I always see her.'

'Made some nice roast potatoes for his boyfriend?'

'Have you been spying on me?'

'I get told things. That's my job.'

Tina washed her hands and wiped them on the towel by the fridge. She walked over and picked up a slice of Jamie's toast, peeling off the crust.

'Gemma's a good girl,' said Tina, putting the toast into her mouth. 'She was there for me when the doctors nearly killed me with their misdiagnosis. I missed our little chats, trips to the cinema, that type of thing. If it wasn't for her, I'd have been driven completely up the wall.'

'… You've got to try and forget about that now. We've all moved on now.'

'Easy for you to say, Jamie.'

'I don't want to talk about this now. Who was the bloke with Gemma? Her new boyfriend? How could you let him in?'

'Gemma wouldn't come without Paul so my hands were tied. He even liked an old Rock Hudson film I showed him.' Tina walked away towards the door. 'I have nothing to apologise for. A son having his mother watched, I'd say that's worth a thousand grovels.' She opened the door and waited. 'No more Snoop Doggy Dogg please.'

'It's Snoop Dogg now.'

Tina put her hands up, mimicked a panting dog and left the room.

Tuesday mornings in the newsroom were low-key, listless affairs but the circulation figures gave everyone a lift. Danny told Jamie the weekend's paper had put on an extra 240,000 copies but Jamie was already working on his story: a meeting in Pub B with a former copper called Bernie 'Peeper' Wallace, a name Callum Gordon had provided. Gordon said Bernie might have a 'minty' story about a celebrity kidnap plot. Jamie was excited and started preparing a list of detailed questions. He hadn't got very far when the phone rang. He waited until the seventh ring to answer.

'Jamie Parkes.'

'Thanks for ditching the story, I'm so grateful,' said Larna Wilson.

'It was a joint decision. We've made our call so it's history now.'

'Just out of interest, what reason did your editor give?'

Jamie paused and wrote another question down for his celebrity kidnap story.

'Why do you want to know?' said Jamie. 'You chickened out anyway.'

'Fitton's the chicken. Such a devious so and so… '

'What do you mean?'

'Doesn't matter.'

'No, what did you mean, devious? I'm interested.'

'Grown up stuff, Jamie. It's not for you.'

Jamie crossed out one of his questions. He clicked his inbox and groaned as 45 new emails came up.

'Are you having it off with the editor,' he asked.

'Te-dious.'

'That's not a denial then?'

'Look, I rung in peace but if you're going to be an arse about it then it's a not so fond farewell.'

'Wait, does he wear braces when he does it?'

Larna hung up. Jamie smiled as he imagined Larna Wilson and Warren Fitton having a wild, exhilarating session. Was it a story? One day, maybe, but not now. Jamie's eye was drawn to the editor's office as he saw Fitton walking in with Grayson Black, the Met Commissioner. Black doffed his cap to the newsroom: a strange but nice gesture. The phone rang again.

'Ben Isaacs's agent here, Cecilia Banks, are you the reporter who wrote that despicable front page?'

'I'm Jamie Parkes.'

'It was an invasion of privacy so I'll be reporting your paper to the PCC. How did you get the material?'

'Can't reveal my sources.'

'Obviously, it's pointless wasting my time with you. Just so you're aware, Ben and the PR company will be withdrawing all promo stuff from you paper for his forthcoming film. Interviews are out of the question. I'll be informing your film critic and showbiz desk in due course. Can you put me through?'

'No.'

Jamie hung up. He took another look at his emails and got up. The phone rang again. He hesitated and didn't want to answer it but a big story was always round the corner so he picked up the receiver.

'Why isn't the Don Leaver story in?' asked Hannah Rocheman.

'Legal have got a few problems with it. Should make it in a few weeks.'

'My dad's really suffering. Got dystonia now too. Will I still be paid?'

'Course, it's just Leaver, he's being niggly.'

'You spoke to him?'

'Yeah, he called. Wants to sue or get an injunction, something like that.'

'I need a favour. How about half of the cash now and the rest when it's published?'

'Not my decision. We have to wait.'

'I know girls who've been paid without the story going in.'

'Not this one.'

'Whose side are you on? You lot are always scratching each other's back.'

'I don't take sides.'

'You will. Bye now.'

Hannah hung up. Jamie got up and headed to the toilet. Danny was on the phone but had his hand across the mouthpiece.

'Oi Jammy, when are you meeting Wallace?'

'Two-ish.'

'Want to see you in the training room before you go.'

Jamie gave the thumbs-up over his shoulder. His mobile phone rang. This one could wait.

Danny stepped into the training room and asked Jamie to wait outside. Jamie's mind was racing with outlandish thoughts. Had he fucked-up a story? Was he about to get sacked? Was he going for special legal training? Danny came out a couple of minutes later with three A5-sized Jiffy bags and asked Jamie to come inside the room. Danny closed the door and offered Jamie a squashed doughnut. Danny picked up a copy of the paper, rolled it up and slipped one of the Jiffy bags inside it so it wasn't visible. He handed it to Jamie and looked him in the eye.

'Old Wallace is a bit old fashioned,' said Danny. 'He likes to feel it between his fingers.'

'Notes?'

'We have to keep them somewhere.'

'Are there any more?'

'Steady on, you're still on shifts. I had to work three years at the Screws before landing a staff job.'

Danny regularly talked about his 'experience' at the Screws. His seven-year stint ended when he felt he was passed over for promotion. Within, two years at the Daisies, he was running newsdesk.

'When's the selection process going to start?' asked Jamie.

'Forget about that,' said Danny, slipping the other Jiffy bags under another rolled-up paper. 'Get some stories because no-one's safe.'

'Not even you?'

Danny opened the door and left the training room.

The missed call Jamie had on his mobile was from Lenny. Jamie was relieved it wasn't story-related but intrigued as to why Lenny would contact him for the first time since his retirement. Jamie was about to call him back when Peeper Wallace walked into Pub B and stood by his table. He was a tall, sturdily-built man with a thick moustache, wearing a curiously incongruous baseball cap and wrist bracelet. He glanced up at the framed pictures of John Thaw in *The Sweeney* and Jack Warner in *Dixon of Dock Green*. He shook his head. Jamie could tell he didn't approve. He laid down a pencil case and asked Jamie to look inside it. Jamie's fingers had been all over a ham sandwich but he eventually obliged and discovered a Sony micro cassette, a Motorola mobile phone and a notebook. Wallace turned the collar up on his coat and put his hands in his coat pockets.

'Lenny not on the paper anymore?' he asked.

'Retired.'

'Shame. Is your mother still breastfeeding you?'

Jamie pushed the stuffed Jiffy bag further into the tabloid paper.

'How many years were you with the Met?'

'More years than you've lived. Now, have you got something for me?'

'Who are the celebrities involved?'

'It's all in the case,' he said. 'Names, dates, locations, numbers, MO. This comes from the very top in the Met. Don't ask me to justify myself to you. I've got a long track record.'

'Is he a footballer, pop star or film star?'

'Don't be sexist now, he might be a she. They're now in charge after all. The story's watertight. Give me the Jiffy or I'll call Danny and he'll get all Southpaw on you.'

Jamie reached inside the tabloid and pulled out the Jiffy bag. He reluctantly handed it to Wallace who smiled as he looked at the front page of paper.

'Is that all you could manage?' said Wallace. 'Shit movie star story about a pregnancy. Standards aren't what they used to be.'

Wallace slipped the Jiffy bag into his pocket and walked out of Pub B.

Jamie walked back into the newsroom and saw Louise sticking a Post-it note on his computer.

'Callum Gordon called,' she said. 'Might have a big story for you. He's got some top clients.'

'I'll give him a bell tomorrow,' said Jamie, slumping wearily in his chair. 'I'm a bit drained right now. Story strike for the rest of the day.'

'Look, we're going to the pub straight after work. Why don't you come down? Matt and Angie are coming too.'

'Who's Matt?'

'Matt Armistead, he sits next to me.'

'Don't really know him.'

'Nor do I – Angie the same.'

Louise confirmed what Jamie had known all along: it was a big newsroom but short on conversation that mattered.

Jamie called it Pub X because he couldn't get Gemma out of his head. It was the first time he'd been 'out' since the break-up and it showed. He sunk four pints of Tennents and a double brandy by the time Matt, Louise and showbiz reporter Angie Octavia had eased into their third round. The pub was packed with drinkers spilling overflowing glasses as they walked back to their table or inches of territory. The sound of SClub7's *Don't Stop Movin'* made him drink even faster. Given these drawbacks, Jamie was thankful it was Matt's round.

Another pint and double brandy was ordered – but Matt got it wrong and came back with a pint of cider. He was a strange sort; quiet and dispassionate. Jamie wouldn't be having a drink with him again.

'I see you reporters have got the Fitton Bug,' said Angie, wiping lipstick off her glass.

'Sorry,' said Louise.

'The stories Jamie got last week. Don't tell me they were all proper quotes and stuff. Lifted from voicemail, yeah Jamie? Don't worry, your secret's safe with us showbiz vampires.'

Louise shook her head. 'Do you know what she's on about, Jamie?'

Jamie raised his tie and waved it from side to side.

'I don't do it, obviously,' said Angie, taking a drink of her vodka and lime. 'But some of the showbiz team have been known to dabble once in a while.'

'The Fitton Buck?' said Jamie. 'Fucker does like his American shows.'

'Bug!' said Angie, laughing and nearly letting the drink escape from her mouth. 'When Mr Ed was on showbiz desk he did nothing else.'

Jamie took out his phone and polished it with his tie. 'This bug's catching… ' He smiled and started tapping in a few codes. 'Who do you want, ponies? A-list only please… '

'Beckham!' said Angie.

'Tom Cruise!' said Louise.

'The Queen!' said Matt.

Everyone laughed as Jamie tried to control his wobbly fingers. Jamie was lord of the ring – and it was a wonderful feeling.

4.

Oh Sweet Rivers Of Blood

Jamie overslept. After Pub X, he only had hazy images of escalators, the Trocadero, vomit on his trousers and the music of Daniel Bedingfield. He got dressed, splashed water on his face and left the house without breakfast. He prayed Danny wouldn't be at his desk but not only was he there, he already had his eyes fixed on Jamie.

'Jammy, what's the SP on this kidnap plot?' he said, stroking the back of his head. 'Does it hold up?'

Jamie pulled his tie up and walked over to Danny's desk.

'Haven't got round to it yet.'

'Well, fuckin' get round to it or I'll get someone more punctual to get round to it for you. Understand? What were you drinking?'

'Er, Tennents and some brandy... '

'You fuckin' puff. We're starting selection interviews in a couple of weeks so nail this kidnap story.'

Jamie nodded and walked to his desk. There were already four Post-it notes stuck on his monitor. He looked over his shoulder at Louise's desk. Angie was standing over it and the two women were laughing. Angie pointed for Jamie to get his phone out. Jamie looked in his pockets but couldn't find it. After a few minutes of sweaty anxiety, Angie held Jamie's mobile up and two women began to laugh again.

It wasn't a 'celebrity' kidnap story at all, but still fascinating. Jamie spent all morning listening to a tape recording of a group of presumed animal rights activists plotting to kidnap the Prime Minister's wife while she was on a business visit to a biotech company in Oxfordshire. It was clear the plotters were under surveillance and, while Jamie was disappointed the 'victim' turned out to be as someone as boring as the PM's wife, it was still a huge story. The sources were watertight: a surveillance tape, quotes from a serving Met Officer, names of the alleged kidnappers, background on the animal rights group, time and dates of PM's wife visit, firm location and, finally, a previous story about the same group vandalising property at the same company. Jamie took a deep breath; he was unaware that Louise was over his shoulder.

'You've had that earpiece on all morning,' said Louise. 'What are you working on?'

'Some dodgy plot to kidnap the PM's wife.'

'Won't last long. They'll get sick of her. Can you firm it up?'

'Looks nailed on.'

'I'd just check again to make sure.'

'If I check any more my head will burst.'

'Thought that had happened already. Anyway, I need the number for this footballer's agent.'

'For what?'

'The Sheila Lings story. Danny handed it to me this morning; said you'd have the details.'

Jamie looked at Louise. The Lings story was his and the humiliation of handing it over only to then see it as the splash was not on his agenda.

'Sorry, I haven't got the number at the moment,' said Jamie, flicking through his contacts book.

'Dog and Duck gobbled it up?'

'No, they fuckin' haven't.'

'Well, when you find it you know where my desk is.' Louise began to walk away. 'Oh, and please don't call me Gemma again. You were doing that all last night.'

*

Lenny rang again and this time Jamie called him back because he was gagging to know what he wanted. The old timer wanted Jamie to join him for a Watford home game at Vicarage Road. Lenny said he had little to do these days and was feeling 'a bit lonely', hence the call. His wife had died many years ago and his three children had long since left home. For the man who gave him the treasured contacts book, the PI tips and the cute simplicity of Pubs A&E, this left Jamie bewildered as to how to react. He told Lenny that he'd think about coming but knew Saturday's and midweek's were difficult to make because of work. Jamie felt he had known and understood Lenny, during their brief time working together, but now he wasn't so sure.

Danny called Jamie over to newsdesk. Jamie was daydreaming about celebrating a goal with Lenny at the Vicarage but quickly snapped out of it and walked towards Danny. He stopped in front of newsdesk, where a shot of anxiety always mysteriously appeared and ended up somewhere around the arse region. Danny was trying, with great difficulty, to eat a heated-up lasagne in a black plastic tray. It was literally burning his mouth as the food swung from one side of his jaw to the other.

'We're running that Barnstable story this week,' he said, finally swallowing a piece of his food. 'Some good stuff in there. Who's the victim anyhow? Do you know her?'

'Er yeah, she's close to home.'

'Get a picture and some quotes. Should be good for Page 5 or 7.'

Danny had a particularly big piece of stringy, cheesy lasagne in his mouth. Jamie wanted to wait for the right moment because he felt he could get a gobful coming his way with the wrong choice of words.

'That footballer story, I did the legwork on it… '

'What, listening to voicemail? We can all do that. Louise's story now. Anything else?'

'The kidnap story. The PM's wife's involved and it all checks out.'

'Sit on it for a couple of weeks.'

'Something wrong with it?'

'Just fuck off back to your desk. Be happy with the couple of page leads and splashes you're getting.'

Jamie smiled and began to walk off. 'About 20 leads a year sounds better.'

'Even Lenny didn't do that. Now write up those stories.'

Jamie walked back to his desk and wondered how a man like Lenny, who could conjure up splashes almost at will, was now prowling around Vicarage Road (even on non-matchdays) with little to say or no-one to talk to. He would never allow it to happen to him. He had to call Gemma immediately.

Jamie reluctantly left the dirty plates in the sink for his mother who had a dentist's appointment. His messy supper of jacket potatoes, cheese and coleslaw had given him indigestion and heartburn. He looked in the cupboard for some Rennies but there weren't any so a drop of brandy, a couple of aspirins and a glass of water had to suffice. Next to the strip of aspirins, however, there was an engraved Zippo lighter with the initials PM: it could only belong to one person, Paul Markham. Hope the dirty bastard didn't light up in this kitchen, he thought. Jamie put the lighter in his pocket and went upstairs to his bedroom. He sat on the bed and called Gemma's mobile number.

'How did you get this number?'

'Could have asked you the same thing. How could you bring that wanker to my house?'

There was a long silence. Jamie thought she'd hung up.

'I wanted to see your mum again. Paul was adamant he wanted to come so I had no option.'

Jamie's landline rang. He wasn't going to answer it but it went to the maximum eight rings.

'Hang on, Gem, I've just got to answer this... '

Jamie placed his mobile carefully on the bed and picked up the receiver from the bed side table.

'Why is your mobile always fuckin' engaged, Jammy,' said Danny. 'Are you on porn lines or something? Anyway, get down to Gerrards Cross, a paedophile's being attacked by a mob... '

'Can't I just put in a couple of calls?'

'GET FUCKING DOWN THERE, NOW!'

'Okay, leaving now... '

Danny hung up and Jamie reached over to pick up his mobile again.

'Gem, are you there?'

The line was dead.

'Fuckin' hell, Gemma, I said 'hang on'!'

Jamie flung his mobile at the front page on his wall and it landed on a mound of socks and underwear. He went to pick it up and was thankful it was still working. He drove to Gerrards Cross but his next story was in his trouser pocket – the engraved lighter.

The Gerrards Cross story ended up as a short, about six paragraphs, but the one Jamie was excited about took a couple of weeks to organise. He remembered a story about lap dancer Holly Rivers (real name, Harriet Smith) having an affair with motor racing star Hayden Mills who was still married at the time. It was a splash in the paper before Jamie started but he managed to fish the story out and get Holly's number from Angie. Holly had since had a poisonous break-up with Mills and was open to another story when Jamie met up with her in

Pub D. The Mills' PR machine had crucified Holly's reputation. She eventually lost her flat and ended up having treatment for clinical depression. Jamie felt a touch sorry for her as he watched her tentatively eat a salad in an old blue Donnay tracksuit – and didn't waste any time in agreeing a small fee (through Danny, who had a joint byline on the previous story with Lenny).

A new story began to emerge. Holly had been hawking herself round the papers for months, trying to get her new career as a fitness instructor off the ground but no-one had been interested. Now, she had an opportunity to plug her new career as well as spin a few new tales. So Jamie tentatively came up with a two-timing story of her and Paul Markham having a one-night stand while Holly was in the middle of the affair with Hayden Mills. She was well up for it. Pictures were arranged: Holly posed with Paul Markham's lighter and Markham's headshot was used. The headline was 'I Two-Timed Speed Demon With Toy Boy'. The story made the paper on Page 11, a few days before Jamie was due to see Danny about redundancy issues. It gave Jamie a strange sense of power, more than any of the other stories combined (even the splash). If he was to be laid off now, he had struck a blow for fairness and respect.

Danny had his arms folded in front of the window as Jamie walked into the conference room. He gestured for Jamie to sit down. As Jamie pulled out a chair, he noticed a familiar Jiffy bag on the table in front of him.

'Why shouldn't I let you go, Jammy?'

'Have I done something wrong?'

'If I look into your eyes, you'll crumble so I'll make it easier for you. You've bent the rules once too often... '

Danny walked forward and picked up the Jiffy bag. He threw it at Jamie who failed to catch it as it fell on the floor.

'Recognise that?'

Jamie looked down and picked it up. 'It's the one you gave me.'

'Open it.'

Jamie was shaking and felt a sharp pain in his stomach. Should have bought those fucking Rennies, he thought. His mind wandered to what kind of jobs he could do if the worst happened: he had worked in a motor insurance firm for six months and a bookies for two months. He'd wanted to work for the Daisies since he was eleven years old: to be carted out after eight months of shifts would be humiliating. His sweaty fingers tried to open the envelope. The door opened behind him. Jamie was too nervous to notice the figure behind him. He looked inside the envelope and a solitary penny coin dropped out. Danny burst out laughing and looked up at Peeper Wallace, who was behind Jamie. Wallace joined in the laughter and stopped by Jamie's side.

'You idiot, Jammy,' said Danny, tightening his folded arms to try and contain his laughter. 'How could you fall for the old Jiffy Bag trick? What did you say to him, Peeps?'

'Give me the Jiffy or I'll call Danny,' said Wallace.

Danny laughed even louder and shook his head. 'Knockout in the first!'

'What are you on about?' asked Jamie, examining the penny coin.

'I was testing you out,' said Danny. 'The PM kidnap plot isn't a real story. It was all made up; names, dates, sources, everything. Peeps, here, was set up to meet to see if you'd take the bait. I wanted to see how far you'd go with the story. You should have listened to Louise and checked again.'

Jamie looked round at a grinning Wallace, seeing him in a different light. 'Well, the story seemed to check out in my eyes.'

'But you got it wrong so now I've got some serious decisions to make... '

'What do you mean?'

Danny freed his arms and walked towards the table. He pulled up a chair and sat directly opposite Jamie.

'Fitton and HR are having an authorised meeting with all staff whose jobs are under threat. Naturally, I've got a big say in the selection process and I just needed a few more days to test a couple of people out to see if they've got the balls to stay in the ring. It's all about mettle; that's what I was testing… '

'Apart from the kidnap story, I've done well, I reckon,' said Jamie. 'Trust me, I can do lots more… '

'Yeah okay,' said Danny, interrupting and raising his hand. 'Some of these stories I like: that film stuff with Ben Isaacs, the Jack Barnstable story, Sheila Lings, some good stuff there, but you need to be producing every week. You started off like a snail. The owner's coming in soon and I can't afford passengers.'

'Course, no problem. I'll get better. I promise you… '

'Promises don't exist in this industry. It's about delivery.'

Jamie nodded and crossed his hands on his lap. There was a moment of silence as Danny looked up at Wallace.

'What do you think, Peeps?'

Wallace looked down at Jamie. 'He doesn't seem a bad sort to me. Tried his best. Bit too impressionable. But he'll do what it takes.'

'I worked with Bernard for seven fruitful years when I worked at the Screws,' said Danny. 'He's a watertight contact. Stick close to him and you'll get stories shining out of your arse.'

Jamie felt incredibly relieved.

'You're getting a staff contract,' said Danny. 'You'll have a pay rise obviously, more holiday and an expenses account. You're now a permanent member of this great newspaper. Make sure you perform. Now, hop it and get me some more juicy ones.'

Jamie got up and shook Wallace's hand. He clenched his fist and walked away towards the door.

'Oh and Jammy,' said Danny.

'Yeah?'

'Listen to Louise, next time.'

Jamie spotted Gemma's name on one of his emails on his home computer and he couldn't open it fast enough. He clicked and read it. She said she was angry and confused about the Holly Rivers/Paul Markham story and couldn't understand how Paul would have done such a thing. It wasn't quite an apology but Jamie knew the door had opened again. He wanted to call her immediately – but it was better to wait. A few minutes later, he got a call on his mobile, to his surprise it was Holly Rivers. She was agitated and speaking quicker than normal. She said she'd been getting death threats after the story had been published. Holly asked if they could meet and, although Jamie didn't want to get involved, he had a desperate urge to get his expenses account going and, to a lesser extent, celebrate his new staff position. He asked Holly to get a cab from where she lived in Morden to Amersham. When she arrived, Jamie didn't invite her in but went out himself and asked the cab to drop them off at the Santhi restaurant. He bought her dinner, a chicken Jalfrezi dish, which she couldn't finish but was grateful to receive. She was still wearing that Donnay tracksuit but the top was only partially done up, the sleeves were rolled up and the bottoms were tucked in to her t-shirt unlike the previous meetings. Jamie had plans for her that evening. He took her back home to try on some of his mother's clothes. Tina was in the kitchen, as they went up the stairs. She noticed them and walked out into the hallway.

'Jamie, who's this lovely girl, you've brought in?'

'Have you got something she can wear?' he said, stopping at the top of the stairs and turning around. 'We're going out.'

Tina walked up the stairs and stopped by Jamie's side. She whispered into his ear. 'Thanks for the Barnstable story. Means a lot to me.'

Tina and Holly walked away into the bedroom while Jamie went downstairs to the kitchen. There was some mail on the kitchen table and Jamie went through it, mostly junk. One envelope, however, was from Don Leaver. What was he doing writing to him at home? Leaver thanked Jamie for not running the story (too soon, of course) but also gave him details of a dossier his colleague – an Independent MP called Michael Trevena – had gathered about corrupt activity on the tabloid press. This time, Leaver did not mention Warren Fitton at all, or any of the payments he'd mentioned in the previous correspondence. Jamie wasn't surprised by this: if it was a straight fight between who told the most lies in relation to the press and MPs, the filthy, fawning politicians would win hands down every time. The public switched off as soon as they saw their posh mugs on TV, at least papers were still read and selling millions of copies. Jamie put the letter back in the envelope and laid it on the kitchen table. He got up and went upstairs to get changed for the night ahead. He put on his light blue Hugo Boss shirt and splashed on some Lynx after shave and deodorant. The Shamen's *Boss Drum* album was playing at full pelt. Half an hour later, Holly was ready, dressed in an awkward-looking mauve dress and high heels. Jamie took Holly to O'Neills in High Wycombe and then onto Winkers nightclub in Chalfont St Peter. By 1am, he wanted Holly badly but was extremely drunk which resulted in a stray kiss on her lips while *Who Let the Dogs Out* by Baha Men was blurting out on the dancefloor. She left soon after and Jamie only remembered wanting to rip his mother's dress off her body. He stayed until closing time and got a cab home – on expenses.

5.

The Oldest Minger In Town

Louise was very vocal after the Queen Mother inconveniently died hours before deadline on Saturday evening. She pulled out all the stops to get a 16-page tribute supplement out for later editions of the paper and, generally, looked to be ordering around some of the more senior staff, which Jamie found amusing. But the bigger shock was that she had volunteered for redundancy. She had been working at the paper for 12 years (so the payout wouldn't be great) but why leave now when the range of stories, from 9/11 to reality TV stars, had never been better? Jamie eventually plucked up the courage to ask her after apologising about his 'silly kidnap story'.

'I'm tired of dressing up as a saucy nurse or Wonder Woman,' she said. 'I'm tired of stories about three-in-a-bed romps and I'd rather not go through people's drawers while they're waiting to be interviewed downstairs.'

'But you've been doing it for ages.'

'Precisely. We all learn from our mistakes.'

Jamie wasn't convinced. The knockabout, flippant culture in relation to stories was part of the appeal. It was fun to stakeout a celebrity and then watch them punch a pap in the face. Why would you want to leave all that behind?

'I haven't got another job,' she said. 'Martin's got more work than he can handle as a linguist so we're getting married and taking stock. I want to write a book anyway so this might be a good time to take the plunge.'

'What's your book about?'

'Something on the women of Afghanistan... '

Jamie nodded but there was an awkward silence.

'You're mad to leave,' he said. 'This is still a great paper. I like all that wild stuff. Gives me a reason to get up in the morning.'

'You like it because you're a bloke.'

Jamie smiled. 'Maybe you're onto something.' He began to walk away. 'Owners are in tomorrow, maybe they'll change your mind.'

'They're even pervier than our readers. Twin brothers as well. Always found that a bit strange.'

Jamie was about to reply when Anne, the editorial assistant, walked towards him carrying six mugs of coffee on a tray.

'Someone down in reception for you, Jamie,' she said. 'Says his name's Paul, didn't give a surname.'

'Didn't you tell him I was busy?'

'You can tell him,' said Anne, lifting the tray as far as she could. 'I've got my hands full.'

Jamie's spot of indigestion returned when he saw Paul Markham sitting down on the tub chair in reception. Paul didn't see him straight away so Jamie thought he could nip back into the newsroom but he eventually caught his eye. Jamie took out his notebook and tentatively approached him. Paul got up quickly and folded his arms.

'Hello, I understand you've got a story for us,' said Jamie, flicking through his notebook to get to a blank page.

'Cut the shit, Jamie, I know what you did,' said Paul. 'I know your name wasn't on the story but your mitts were all over it.'

'Look, I've got to see a source in a couple of minutes... '

Paul walked towards Jamie. He was taller than Jamie remembered, about 6ft 2 with no shoulders and a loping, languid gait. His dark hair and ultra-white teeth completed a certain look: a Page 7 Fella.

'Gemma's ditched me so she's all yours now,' said Paul.

'You're welcome to her moans and groans. I'd still like to break your teeth though – and give you a set like this… ' He tapped his teeth with his index finger. 'But you're not worth it. You'll just spin another story and I won't make any tips anymore. So just give me my lighter.'

'I'll post it to you. Why were you in my house?'

Paul smiled for the first time and then looked at his watch. 'Oh, is that the time. Got some nice pizzas to serve up for some hungry customers.'

'Yeah, go on, you might make supervisor one day.'

'I was in your house for one thing – and one thing only… '

Jamie nodded in that classic journalistic manner which denoted the highest degree of scepticism in a source's lofty claims.

'Your mother, plain and simple, she's got heart that woman,' said Paul, walking away. 'She told me all about those stupid doctors. Never heard a story like it. Been there for her, have you?'

'Got nothing to do with you.'

'A 48-year-old woman, alone, in her house, just wanting her son to be there for her but you can't even do that. What are you good for? Tell you what, she weren't half bad for her age either. We weren't alone very often but, you know, I could imagine breaking her in… '

'FUCK OFF YOU TWAT!'

Paul walked away with a smile on his face. He thanked the receptionist and went through the double doors out into the car park. Jamie followed Paul to his car, a blue Ford Mondeo. Paul got in and Jamie stood outside. Jamie's mobile phone rang. Paul started his car and wound down the window.

'You'd better answer that,' he said. 'If it's your mum tell

her to make sure she's on the pill. I'll send you a free pepperoni pizza tonight. I know the address, see ya!'

Jamie smacked his ringing mobile on Paul's car as he drove off. Jamie cooled down and eventually answered it.

'Hello Jamie, Christy Miles here...'

Christy was one of the sub-editors and she had a habit of being so precise and sceptical about stories that she was given the nickname 'Cautious Christy'.

'It's about that Don Leaver story,' she said.

'So it's finally going in then?'

'Looks like it. Can you check Leaver's age again: you've got it down as 48?'

Jamie was unable to answer for a few seconds as he watched Paul Markham drive out of the car park.

Tina had prepared a special evening meal of roast duck, spinach and boiled potatoes. She had been offered a part-time job at the Rebellion Beer Company in Marlow after going for an interview that Jamie knew nothing about. Jamie wondered if the Jack Barnstable story had helped her get the job but she was adamant that she'd got it off her own back although she did say the management there sympathised with her. Jamie didn't want to disrupt his mother in this form. She was swinging her hips to *The Way You Make Me Feel* and waving her arms from side to side. She laid the steaming plate of roast duck on the table and then took a drink from her bottle of gin. She wiped her hands on the towel and stopped the music. She came and sat down at the table with both hands resting under her chin, looking at Jamie with an intensity he couldn't recall.

'Paul called me,' said Tina. 'He's trying to drive a wedge between us, Jamie. Hope you're not listening to him.'

'Why did you tell him about that private stuff?'

Tina paused and started serving the potatoes.

'Gemma had already told him. He just got a bit more from

me. Not many men in the house these days so I probably just opened up to him.'

'You really do pick them, mum: Dad, those fuckin' doctors and now Paul... '

'You can talk. Look, I've come to the conclusion that's it's better to share what I've been through rather than bottle it up inside. It's not everyday a woman is told she has breast cancer and then, after months of treatment, is told she didn't have it in the first place. That's hard, Jamie, you have to understand that.'

Jamie nodded. Tina handed him a plate filled with too much spinach and not enough potatoes. Jamie remembered the research he had done for a possible story after his mother's misdiagnosis. There were many more cases of breast cancer misdiagnosis than Jamie had expected. Some doctors were too hasty in making judgements on a small number of lesions. The story didn't make *The Chronicle* at the time because his mother wasn't ready to share it. The doctor was struck off and Tina was given a small amount of compensation. That was six years ago – and Jamie wondered how much of that money was spent on bottles of gin and a cocktail of painkillers. She said she had never felt the same since – as though someone had interfered with her and not put her back together again.

'I nearly told Jack Barnstable about all this, that's how shallow I am,' said Tina. 'Thank God, I didn't. He would have even more control over me than before.'

'Too many dodgy men in your life, mum!' said Jamie, with a smile.

'Including you. But at least I've got another job now. Women don't get many opportunities to do anything after a certain age so I'm pleased that employers are still looking me in the eye. Talking of which, Gemma'll be looking you in the eye again. When are you meeting her?'

'Tomorrow.'

'Which means you can start getting out of your bedroom again. I can you hear recording a lot of stuff late at night – and making calls. What are you doing in there anyway?'

Jamie dabbed his fork around the succulent duck, squeezing the juice from its side. He looked up at his mother and smiled.

'Making a name for myself… '

Jamie had a quick meeting with Melvin Moon in Pub E straight after work. The drug dealer (although he claimed never to be a user himself) was wearing a sky blue hooded top, a beanie hat with a red crescent and sunglasses even though it was raining outside. He had a good story about a local TV newsreader using cocaine while being on air – but wanted a high price for the story. Jamie was annoyed that he had to ring Danny again to clear these things and was determined to find out whether he could start arranging things himself. Danny spoke to Melvin direct and a price was agreed. Melvin bought a non-alcoholic cocktail to celebrate. He then offered Jamie a sixteenth of cannabis hastily concealed in a packet of Juicy Fruit chewing gum. Jamie took the only Juicy Fruit left in the pack and refused the drugs. Melvin laughed and claimed Jamie was one of the few 'Fleet Street Dawgs' to refuse the 'food'.

Jamie was in good spirits when he got home. His mother and Gemma were upstairs in a bedroom, going through some of their shopping bags which he could hear rustling with some irritation. He walked into the living room and turned on the TV: Channel 4 were running a boring documentary on local hospitals being shut down around the country. He looked around for the remote to change channels but then MP Mike Trevena popped up on screen to talk about how 'people power' had kept their hospital services in the community, rather than out of town. Trevena had unseated the local

Labour MP solely on this issue at the last general election. The petition to keep hospital services ran to tens of thousands. As Trevena spoke, from a somewhat dilapidated office, Jamie wondered whether this guy was different from the rest. What if he had some major stuff on Warren Fitton and his cushy friends?

Jamie could hear someone coming down the stairs – and hoped it was it Gemma. He remembered the first time he met Gemma after he'd been sent to cover a story about illegal immigrants registering with Lavendales. Gemma took an interest in Jamie because she felt immigrants and asylum seekers were being demonised by his 'paper gang' as she called it. Jamie wasn't that deep into the issue but he was startled by how passionately she felt about it. It was only when Jamie helped her get a good story in the paper about the consultancy that she calmed down and agreed to go for a drink.

'You creeped in quietly?' said Gemma, with a gift bag in her hand.

'It's better if people don't notice us.'

Gemma walked forward and handed the gift bag to Jamie.

'Sorry about everything that happened,' she said. 'Charlotte in the office keeps us up to date with the gossipy stuff and told me about the Holly Rivers story.'

'Come upstairs,' said Jamie, getting up and gently grabbing hold of Gemma's arm.

Gemma was reluctant but eventually followed Jamie upstairs into his bedroom. She went in and was surprised by the number of stories, pages and shorthand notes on the walls.

'Impressive,' she said, walking in and sitting on the edge of the bed. 'Aren't you going to look at your gift?' She hesitated. 'It's a parting gift.'

'What?'

'Look inside.'

Jamie looked inside the bag and pulled out a small, red-topped alarm clock which had the word 'PRESS' written across its display. He pressed down on it – and the display kept changing from one famous masthead of a tabloid newspaper to another.

'What did you mean by 'parting gift'?' he asked.

'Newspapers and time are the most important things in your life, Jamie. I don't want to go back to the way it was. You coming back late, dumping your clothes all over the place and talking about deadlines while we eat dinner or have a conversation. Everything is not a story. There are other things too like helping people get a job or get their lives together. That's real work too. I just want us to be friends now.'

'But it's different now. The local rag worked us like a dog but now I've got a staff job and a bit more spare time. Trust me, we can make it work.'

'Friends or nothing, that's it. I made a big mistake with Paul. I'm not going to make another by diving in again.'

She got up off the bed and walked towards the door.

'Come on, Gem, don't go.'

She stopped by the door and looked up at the some of the stories on the wall.

'Wall to wall,' she said. 'No-one'll ever break through that, Jamie.'

Jamie took up the offer of Melvin Moon's Juicy Fruit. He had smoked cannabis twice before, once at a student party in his days at Amersham and Wycombe College and, again, during a five-month stint at Island News Agency where the pressure to get stories was intense. This time he decided to stick the sixteenth in his inside jacket pocket for future engagements.

Don Leaver didn't help matters. Fitton was in court for a libel case so Leaver harangued deputy editor Ben Fox-Tucker about the Rocheman story and said he was definitely going to fight the paper in court. Jamie had to admit he was nervous of how Fox-Tucker would react but he laughed it off and said it was a good story.

On the same morning, Jamie got a shock in his morning mail. Usually, there were stacks of press releases on charity events and celebrity plugs-ins, with the odd letter from a member of the public with a grudge, but this correspondence was different. The note, written in thick brown felt tip on white paper, was no bigger than the size of Jamie's fingers and it was enclosed in a bright blue envelope with a handwritten address, again in thick brown felt tip.

Sparks
Will Fly
Jamie Parkes
Scum Reporters
Bum Porters
And Die
AB

Jamie ripped up the note and threw it in the bin. It may have been a death threat but it wasn't worth troubling the police. There had been similar, if less threatening, instances in the past: a Z-list celebrity wanted to beat Jamie up because he couldn't get a story into the paper; a race equality advisor wrote a bitter letter saying 'if harms comes to you I won't lose any sleep' and a distraught mother said she'd break Jamie's legs after he turned up on the doorstep asking about her son's cot death. The only thing that interested Jamie about this latest, flimsy piece of correspondence was the AB initials. Who was that? Jamie thought about it for 30 seconds and decided not to waste any more time thinking about losers.

The first wave of redundancies took place without Jamie

noticing until a sizable proportion of the staff started banging on the desks in a sort of hand stampede. Was this a solidarity gesture for their departed colleagues? Jamie lightly tapped his palms on the desk; his sore fingers were needed for important tasks like tapping in security codes. Will and Maxine were part of this cull. They disappeared without a word – so did Chris, the number 2 on newsdesk, who got a job on *The Telegraph*. Many others went too – but Jamie didn't know or speak to any of them. There were leaving do's but he chose not to go. But he did know Louise and, to Jamie's surprise, her voluntary redundancy request was refused. She had been offered the position Chris had vacated but she had rejected it. The madness continued, thought Jamie, how could she refuse such a position? He approached her desk but noticed she was staring into space with her arms folded. The desk by her side, where Matt usually sat, was curiously empty, stripped of its computer, files, stationary, books and all other items.

'Where's Matt?' asked Jamie. 'At least his desk is clean.'

'Sacked,' said Louise, not making eye contact. 'That's why I can't leave. I'm not going to get all Halle Berry over it. It was him that deserved the Oscar.'

'Why was he sacked?'

Louise took a drink from her bottle of mineral water and carefully wiped her mouth with her index finger.

'He was a mole,' she said. 'He worked for the Screws. They were paying him about a grand a week to get our story list from conference so they could act upon it if as something major. He worked for them on a freelance contract. He was obviously raking it in. I didn't have a clue. I had drinks with him, introduced him to Martin and he's been in my kitchen but all the time he was playing us like a fiddle… '

'Jesus, do those of kind of things go on here?'

'Have you been listening? Wake up, or you'll be swallowed up too.'

'Thought there was something funny about him. That night in the pub he just kept talking about work, I got sick of it. At least, something good's come out of it: you're staying.'

Louise didn't answer and just nodded.

'But how could you reject Chris's job? That's insane.'

'I wasn't ready. I just got over the shock of Matt's behaviour and then they told me I couldn't leave. Then Danny threw another grenade in the mix by offering to become his deputy. No chance.'

'Tell him, I'm up for it.'

'What?

'I could do newsdesk.'

'But you've barely been here a year... '

'It'll save the company some more money. Take someone internally, not have to advertise.'

'There are about 30 reporters in here with better credentials than you... '

Jamie smiled and tucked his tie into the top of his trousers.

'Yes, but how many of them are moles? At least, I'm legit and above board.'

Louise burst out laughing which gave a Jamie an incredible rush of adrenalin. He walked away and looked over his shoulder. She was still smiling and shaking her head. It would have been a nice time to get that sixteenth out of his pocket and smoke it all with Louise – on the highest floor of Coby Towers.

6.

Contenders And Benders On The Waterfront

The World Cup sweepstake was won by picture editor Sheena Swift and it got Jamie thinking about Lenny again. So Jamie gave him a call and arranged tickets for the home game against Wimbledon at the start of the following season. Jamie was looking forward to getting a Saturday off because, as expected, he hadn't been considered for the newsdesk job. Danny told him they needed someone more experienced. Jamie couldn't wait to engage Lenny on these matters and would meet him outside the entrance for the Rookery Stand of the stadium at 2pm.

He was ready at noon, in his beanie hat, scarf and trainers, such a nice change from his tie, waistcoat and shoes. But as he walked into the station to catch the Metropolitan Line to Watford, he got a call from Lenny's neighbour Eric Mathieson saying Lenny had been taken into hospital early in the morning with jaundice and vomiting. Jamie went straight to Watford General Hospital and eventually saw Lenny lying awkwardly in a bed on a ward with Eric by his side. Eric got up and shook Jamie's hand. He was in a hurry saying he had to help prepare dinner for the in-laws who were visiting that evening. He put his hand on Lenny's forehead and left. Jamie sat down by Lenny's side and put the flask on the table, close to the clean-looking match tickets. Jamie was surprised to see a copy of his paper there too, his front-page splash on Ben Isaacs and Lisa T.

'I rarely said sorry to anyone while I was on the paper,' said Lenny, attempting a cough without much success. 'But I'm sorry that we couldn't make the game.'

'Don't be stupid. At least you won't be nicking any medical records soon.'

'Oh, stop it,' he said, looking away and trying not to laugh. He managed a much meatier cough this time but coupled with the suppressed laughter, it only made his eyes water. 'Seriously though, you've found some good stories, lately. I must have taught you well.'

'The A&E pubs, definitely, they've been a big help,' said Jamie, with a smile. 'Can't see a bar in here, though...'

'There's one here,' said Lenny, pulling at the bars under the bed. 'Bet you can't remember the names?'

Jamie could only remember the specific names for Pub B (PLODS), Pub D (KATS) and Pub E (DOPES). Lenny soon enlightened him that Pub A was PINS and Pub C was CRIMS. Lenny took extra relish in pointing out that Callum Gordon would never forget any PIN, unlike Jamie. Lenny's desire had been to open a chain of pubs when he'd retired but that dream looked a long way away now. But at least, Jamie thought, he'd helped get the A&E pubs refurbished – with the help of the landlords – with those nice pictures on the walls. Jamie talked to the landlords regularly and they said Lenny had ploughed most of his disposable income into the pubs.

Lenny was in better spirits than Jamie expected. He did look slighter, and more diminished, than Jamie remembered him due to the thinning hair, paleness, unexpected moustache and hospital gown but he could still knock 800 words out in a few minutes if he had to, Jamie was sure of that. In fact, Lenny was reacting so well to Jamie's jokes that it was difficult to curb the banter. But a line had to be drawn at somewhere.

'Spoke to the nurse as I came in,' said Jamie. 'But I want to hear it from you...'

Lenny looked down at his wrist bracelet and moved it up a little.

'Liver trouble...'

Jamie gestured drinking a pint and Lenny managed a weary nod. Jamie looked around the other patients in the ward. Most of them looked over 70. He suddenly felt insecure but not for the reasons expected. These were his tabloid readers, dying out in front of his eyes. Would his paper be around in 20 years? Had they even heard of the internet?

'Redundancies at your place: read about them in Press Gazette,' said Lenny. 'Last round was about eight years ago. I cobbled some stuff down about my time on the paper; turned it into a sort of memoir. Sent it off to one or two agents but… '

'No response?'

'Spend their time arse-licking celebrities; no time for the likes of me.'

'Got a title?'

'… Changed it about six times.'

Jamie moved his chair closer to Lenny. 'Don't you think the internet will kill papers like ours? People'll stop buying it.'

Lenny smiled and shook his head. 'There'll always be a tabloid readership. We don't like unearned success in this country. We like to see those people getting a good kicking: the grubbier the better. Celebrities have infected the front pages and fanzine culture the back; everyone's a loser. A Government minister once said to me you 'manufacture outrage, that's all you do' and he was partly right. We do that, yes, but more than that we relish misfortune. That's our main function: relishing misfortune.'

'Nah, come on, we're better than that.'

Lenny was about to answer but a nurse came over to the bed to check his blood pressure. She awkwardly helped Lenny sit up on the bed. Jamie found it difficult to watch and wondered whether he should go and see his GP for his own indigestion. The thought passed soon enough. Jamie asked the nurse if he was allowed to drink tea and, without speaking, she gave the thumbs-up. Was she exhausted or couldn't she speak English? Jamie picked up the flask and headed to the visitors toilet. He locked himself in the cubicle and got out the battered packet of Juicy Fruit and Paul Markham's lighter. He took the plastic white cup off the flask and unscrewed the cap; the steam almost burnt his nostrils. He took out the cannabis and flicked open the Zippo lighter. He carefully placed the flame beneath the tiny brown block to devour it completely. The cannabis softened and he started to sprinkle it into the flask. He used a plastic spoon (he got from the table by Lenny's bed) to stir into the tea. He screwed the cap back on and shook the flask. He smiled and walked out of the toilet. He walked to Lenny's bed and saw the nurse writing on the clipboard. She replaced the clipboard onto the edge of the bed, offered a mild smile and walked off. Jamie began to unscrew the flask and poured a hot cup of tea, which now a bittier, browner liquid than the one he'd made in the morning.

'When was the last time you skinned up?' asked Jamie.

'Is that what you call it these days? 72, I think, a long time ago. A scab offered me one. Have you been speaking to Melvin Moon? How is that mad midget?'

'Gave me a present.'

'I'd rather have a drink, but I've been warned.'

Jamie picked up the cup and took a drink. He felt refreshed and moved closer to Lenny. He offered him the cup.

'You'll give me another infection, you bleeder,' he said, taking the cup and concentrating hard for a drawn-out, slurpy drink.

'When's the scan, then?'

'Blood tests, first,' said Lenny, handing the cup back to Jamie who poured another one. 'My turn again, don't be greedy.' Jamie smiled and handed Lenny another full cup. Lenny took a drink and held the cup tight, to warm up his cold hands.

'Since the leaving party not one reporter has come to see me,' said Lenny. 'Just a tipple and chinwag would have been nice. They're not as busy as they claim. Young Fitton didn't even come to the leaving do, the snake.'

'He's not that bad... '

'I'm a pipsqueak compared to him. He's got cabinet ministers, Met officers, prison officers and royal secretaries on his payroll – and those are the only ones I know of, there'll be plenty more. If I was still working, I'd be digging into that... '

'Thought we didn't grass our own?'

'We don't. But he's a special case. Talking of grass... ' He looked into the cup. 'This ain't half bad. Who are the Dopes now?'

They both laughed and finished off the tea in minutes.

Hannah sent Jamie a short email to thank him for the Don Leaver story. Most of it was about her father's battle in trying to secure suitable accommodation. But Jamie's mind was on the Coby brothers' visit to the newsroom. The owners finally made an appearance after cancelling a couple of earlier visits. They spent most of their time milling around Warren Fitton's office and hardly got out onto the 'shop floor' at all. Jamie remembered reading an interview with them in a glossy magazine saying they weren't a 'Maxwell or a Murdoch' (although they admired the latter) as they liked to keep a lower profile and let their editors develop their unique newsroom culture. Asked about reporters using illegal methods to secure stories and tabloid culture as a whole, the older one (Richard) said they simply gave people what they wanted. The brothers (the younger one was Jake) made their name through a series of gambling websites in America and then branched out into American newspapers and radio stations. In Britain, they owned about 80 local papers (mostly freesheets) and one national, plus a number of soft-porn websites and satellite TV stations although no-one in the newsroom was sure which ones. Jamie actually remembered the TV news item of the brothers acquiring the Daisies in 1984 after the Dunmores – the British family who owned it since its inception in 1881 – sold it for only £75,000. The paper was in the crowded mid-market, they felt, and had been losing readers to the *Mail*, *Express* and the *Mirror* for years. The Coby's came in and took it downmarket, some people said, but Jamie felt it was the right move because it appealed to the masses: the meat and drink of the country as he liked to call it. He may not have got a job here otherwise.

So the Coby's chickened out of a proper tour of the newsroom but one person who didn't chicken out was Louise who, surprisingly, had performed a u-turn and taken the job as Number 2 on newsdesk. The first thing that popped into Jamie's mind was that she would be in charge when Danny was off sick or on holiday. Jamie hoped she would let him continue to bring in stories the way he liked. It didn't take long to find out as Danny was away with his wife and family in Gran Canaria.

'Don't know about this mosque story,' said Louise, handing Jamie a Post-it note at his desk. 'Danny said there's some radicals in there, on a Friday. Just check it out but go easy if there's nothing doing.'

'If there's fundo's down there, I won't be going easy.'

'Did Danny teach you that?'

'No, we've just got to shine a light on these people if they exist.' Jamie turned his back and started typing on his computer. 'Amazed you took the job.'

'You'll be more amazed at how I operate. I want you to tone down a bit on the phone stuff you've been intercepting lately; I don't want anything to bite us in the bum later.'

'I know what I'm doing. Do you want good stories or not?'

Louise moved closer to Jamie and lowered her head above his shoulder.

'I want good stories but I want good practice too. I'm not taking the rap for lazy, shortcut reporting.'

Louise walked away back to newsdesk. Jamie looked at the number on the Post-it Note, a Mr Mohammed Qasim. Jamie didn't know him but felt hostile to him already.

The cars were parked haphazardly outside the mosque, some of them halfway up the pavement. Jamie left a message for Mohammed Qasim but he hadn't replied so Jamie decided to take his chances as a 'worshipper'. He took off his shoes and entered the spacious, incense-tinged mosque. He picked up a circular straw hat from a laundry basket and put it on his head. He sat down on the sparsely-populated back row, about 15 rows back facing the imam who was talking (in English) into a loudspeaker. He reached into his inside pocket and turned on his tape recorder. The imam waffled on a bit, thought Jamie, about Palestine, Iraq, Afghanistan and Bosnia and how it was a Muslim's duty to support their 'brothers' around the world. It was more of a humanitarian speech than a confrontational one and when it ended, Jamie was slightly disappointed with the material he had. Jamie stayed right at the back as prayers began. He tried to imitate what he could from the worshippers next to him: eyes down, hands clasped across the stomach, head down on the floor and so on. He felt a strange peace and air of serenity, although he was annoyed that he could still hear the sound of the tape recorder (which he hadn't stopped) ticking over. When prayers ended, Jamie desperately hoped there would be a few 'leafleting nutters' outside the mosque to help him get something, at least, because as it was he didn't have a story. But then, out of the blue, Mohammed Qasim turned up outside the mosque and pointed out to Jamie who he thought the suspected radical was. Qasim looked distant and preoccupied and disappeared as quickly as he came. He said his life was in danger. Jamie approached the suspected man as he got into his Nissan Micra, flicking his shawl over his sky-blue kameez in the process.

'What do you think of this WMD insanity, brother?' asked Jamie. 'Sounds a stitch-up to me.'

'Who are you?'

'Converted a few years ago. Come here regular now.'

'Saw you speaking to Qasim. How do you know him? I wouldn't believe anything he says.'

'He says you'd be willing to fight British forces in Iraq if they invaded.'

'I'm just against a war there like millions of others in this country. Now let me go and pick up my son from school.'

The man finally got into his car and shut the door.

'So you won't be supporting British troops?' asked Jamie, knocking on the window.

'Fuck off, will you. Who are you?'

He wound down the window and then started the car.

'Qasim has a grudge against me because I helped get this imam a job in our mosque. He wanted someone else. Now tell me who you are? You don't look like a Muslim to me. Are you from the dirty papers?'

'What did you think of 9/11?'

The man spat at Jamie but narrowly missed. Jamie got out his camera phone and quickly grabbed any sort of picture he could. The man drove off enraged. Jamie reached into his inside pocket to ensure his tape recorder was still working, which it was. He looked around and saw hundreds of worshippers still streaming out of the mosque. Jamie thought of Vicarage Road and the match he'd missed when Lenny was taken sick.

Louise asked a lot of questions about the mosque story – but it did make the paper. These kind of stories were 'IslamDunk' as far as Jamie (and Danny) were concerned because they were exactly what people wanted to read in the current climate. They were foolproof and had hundred per cent news value.

Danny came back into the newsroom a couple of days quicker than expected – just in time for the staff Christmas party at The Dorchester Hotel. Jamie agonised whether to turn up or not. He didn't really have any friends in the office now: Matt had been sacked; Louise had let power get to her head and night rider Angie was hardly in the office during the day – the rest were polite and accommodating enough but the thought of trying to make conversation with them in a formal setting wasn't appealing. The only hack he'd got close to had retired. But on the evening of the party at just gone seven, he was at home drinking brandy while eating a succulent Bengal Chicken from Santhi when Danny rang sounding as though he'd already knocked back a few.

'Jammy, where the fuck are you?'

'Home – and feeling very cosy, thank you… '

'I'll give you cosy. Didn't Louise tell you about Fitton's speech? He's starting a new campaigning charity. I assumed you knew.'

'Louise didn't tell me anything.'

'She might have been too busy. Anyway, all the other reporters are here so chop chop. Bring your bird if you want.'

'Can't you fill me in tomorrow?'

'I'll fill your teeth with the glass I've got in my hand. See you in an hour or two.'

Danny hung up and Jamie eventually got ready. He left the house and got to the Dorchester in an hour and a half. He went in but there was a massive scrum at the entrance. Jesus, who was that at the front with Warren Fitton? The Prime Minister? How did Jamie not know about this? The PM (or someone who looked like him) managed to get out of the building but Fitton stayed and bumped into Jamie. The editor put his arm round Jamie's shoulder as they walked down towards the Orchid Room where the party was being held.

'Where were you?' asked Fitton, with a smile. 'Doesn't power turn you on?'

'Didn't know about it? What's going on?'

'Not very clued up, are you? Unsung Britain is what's going on. Anyway, got to rush.'

'Wait, was that really the PM?'

Fitton looked over his shoulder and grinned. 'Make mine a double.' He then ran like a sprinter ahead of Jamie into the Orchid Room. Jamie eventually walked in and looked at the faces at the dinner tables. Gemma would have been good on his arm here. Jamie spotted Louise and Martin at one of the tables and walked towards them. Louise was sipping mineral water while Martin poured a glass of champagne.

'Can I have a word?' asked Jamie, whispering in Louise's ear.

'Who's this?' said Martin.

'Jamie; one of the reporters,' said Louise, smiling at Martin and getting up. She ushered Jamie away.

'Have you got something against me?'

'Don't embarrass yourself,' replied Louise. 'Fitton's going to be speaking any minute. Keep it civil.'

'Why didn't you tell me about this?'

'I did – every reporter got a memo.'

'I didn't.'

'It was in your in-tray.'

Jamie looked confused. 'Have I got one? All the press releases and Post-it's are always on my keyboard and monitor. There's a tray at the end but I thought that was the other bloke's. I never checked that.'

'Checking isn't your strong point,' said Louise. 'Just make sure you check out what Warren's about to say. If you get any of this Unsung Britain stuff wrong, he'll go ape.'

'Unsung Britain, what's that?'

Louise didn't answer and walked away towards Martin.

Jamie had wanted to meet him but he'd burnt his bridges for now. A few minutes later, Fitton stood up to the podium and prepared to make a speech. There were two celebrities either side of him, although Jamie didn't recognise any of them. After a mild roll of the eyes, Louise filled him in: one was a reality TV star and the other was a pop star who used to be a reality TV star.

'I knew most of you scoundrels wouldn't turn up at the official launch,' said Fitton, as his eyes darted around the dinner tables. 'That's why I chose to announce Unsung Britain here, tonight, in front of you, because I wanted all of you to have a stake in something special, something worthwhile and something you can take pride in.'

Fitton spoke for a few minutes about how Unsung Britain would work. There would be annual nominations, an awards ceremony and a substantial write-up in the paper. He wanted to find the 'real heroes' in the country: the ones who were underappreciated and overlooked, the ones who carried out noble deeds for the less fortunate. He spoke about a homeless couple (who were in the room) and their tireless work in getting food and shelter for those living even rougher than them. He called Laura and Pete Sharples to the podium.

'This couple are an example of Britain at its best: selfless, considerate and understated,' said Fitton. 'They will go to our inaugural awards ceremony as our nomination.'

There was light applause in the room and then Laura and Pete took it in turns to speak briefly about their time on the streets of St Leonards, where they were born and grew up. One of their stories was about how they helped a pregnant woman give birth in a takeaway. After more applause, Fitton wrapped up and a hum of chatter spread across the room. There was talk of a 'convoy' going down to the south coast for a special night out. Danny didn't waste any time in stumbling around the tables to get some idea of numbers. Fox-Tucker and Louise had other plans but before Jamie could finish his recently-poured glass of champagne, which he didn't like anyway, he was in a cab, as part of an eight-strong convoy of taxis hurtling down the A21 towards Hastings. Jamie didn't know but Laura and Pete Sharples were in the taxi in front. He could see the back of their heads but they were mostly kissing and giving v-signs from the window. Unsung Britain indeed. The taxis stopped in St Leonards, outside a huge, intimidating house. It was a white-brick Victorian building with 15 rooms, including nine bedrooms. It had a bar, snooker room and the biggest kitchen Jamie had ever seen – and there were plenty of cooks in there too (of the substance variety). The house was a 'special gesture' from Fitton to Laura and Pete for one night only so they could get a proper night's sleep, he said. Jamie never saw Laura and Pete again; perhaps they went to bed straight away to catch up on the hours of sleep they'd lost over the years. No-one else was interested in calling it a night: there were crates of beer, bottles of wine and generous blocks of cannabis to consume. There were also a few grams of white stuff knocking around, or so Jamie was told by sub-editor Gloria Wales, but he chose not to go into the snooker room where the lines were being drawn on the smooth green felt. After a couple of hours, the house was a hazy memory as Jamie was sprinting down the seafront, the icy wind and swishing tide ravishing his face. Danny was a few yards ahead of him with about six other people. Jamie was certain they were all doing the Conga but changing the words to 'Come on, We're Unsung Britain... ' The group stopped temporarily when they reached Fitton and his wife Grace. Jamie didn't even know she was here. The couple were leaning over the seafront railings, hand in hand, looking out into the English Channel. Danny continued on towards the Old Town swaying from side to side, leading his bleary gang while singing ever louder. Jamie couldn't go on: the exhilaration suddenly turned to deep fatigue; he knew the blend of beer, dope and spirits in that order was a risk. The dope first would have been better. He joined Fitton, looking out at the giant, threatening pool of water, wanting to soak his head in it immediately.

'My father was born a few yards from here,' said Fitton. 'The pier was a thriving place then: ballrooms, concert halls, theatres, even The Stones, The Who and Hendrix played here. Not much left now... '

Grace started playing an imaginary violin and laughed. Fitton smiled and put his head on her shoulder.

'Is he always like this in the office?' asked Grace, looking at Jamie.

'If you answer that you'll be sent to a mosque again,' said Fitton.

Jamie smiled and followed his editor's instructions. He felt he hadn't really known Fitton before tonight but there was something about him – and Grace – that made Jamie warm to them. Jamie was about to ask Fitton about Unsung Britain (it was the only territory he felt safe) but Danny shouted at him from about 200 yards away.

'Oi Jammy, we're going to an Old Town pub for a drink,' he screamed, with remarkable clarity. 'Get down here. You've got a two-minute deadline.'

Jamie smiled wearily at Fitton and Grace and ran towards his colleagues. His mobile phone rang but he ignored it. There was an office party pact or agreement that mobiles should be switched off for the duration of the evening but, like every other so-called rule in the journalistic world, it wasn't respected. The mobile eventually stopped ringing. Jamie caught up with Danny's group. He linked up and started doing the Conga, his hands locked tightly to Gloria Wales' hips. God, she had a behind to die for. Jamie's mobile rang again but, by now, he was deep into the Conga, his eyes fixed on the gorgeous Gloria bulge. He ignored it and the group were getting closer to the Old Town. His mobile rang for the third time – and that was always a signal for Jamie that it might be wise to answer it. He reluctantly broke off the group and got his mobile out. He answered it and continued to watch Danny who was trying to lead the Conga into the sea.

'WHAT THE FUCK DO YOU WANT?' shouted Jamie, down the phone. 'CAN'T YOU SEE I'M FUCKIN' BUSY?'

'Is that Jamie?'

'Who's this?'

'Eric Mathieson here. Lenny's dead.'

7.

EyeEye Captain, What A Lovely War

Lenny would have been in stitches. No-one from the paper had spoken to him since his retirement but now they turned up, in good numbers, to attend his funeral. Even Fitton and Grace were there, although Jamie had a slightly different view of them now since the office party shenanigans. There were also rumours that Callum Gordon would turn up but instead he persuaded the Reverend Mr Riley to allow a recorded message to be heard during the service. A distraught Eric cried as he paid tribute to the 'legend' and had already filled in Jamie about the circumstances leading up to Lenny's death. Lenny had been discharged from hospital three days after his initial admission. But the following morning, he woke up with breathing problems, shivering and hot flushes. This time, he managed to call emergency himself but spent two days in intensive care before he died. Cause of death was given as pneumonia. After the funeral, Eric approached Jamie in the car park. He put his hand on Jamie's shoulder and apologised immediately. Jamie could tell Eric hadn't been straight with him. Eric asked Jamie to come and sit in the back of his Transit van which he used for his gas and central heating business. Jamie agreed and the two men got into the back seats, although it was awkward because a radiator lay under both men's feet. Eric didn't want to sit in the front because Lenny had sat there so often. Eric handed Jamie a tape recorder and said it was one of the few items on Lenny's person, apart from clothes, that he brought home from hospital.

'I don't want you to play it here,' said Eric, dragging his feet rapidly across the radiator. 'You can get back to the paper and do what you want with it. Not my responsibility anymore.'

'You should have told the truth in the first place.'

'To ruin the funeral? Is that what you wanted?'

'Didn't mean that. Things could have been clearer, that's all.' Jamie looked at the battered tape recorder and turned it over in his hand. It had a small label on the back with Lenny's name on it. 'Don't tell me, it was the hospital's fault; always is...'

Eric stared at Jamie with a look of acknowledgement.

'There was a lot of confusion about the time of discharge from hospital,' said Eric. 'I was on a job in Rickmansworth dealing with a burst boiler when he first called at four-ish and said he'd be discharged at 7pm. I said I'd be there at about six but when I got there, he'd already been discharged. I went outside, to the cab stand, the bus stop and all the other places but couldn't find him. Eventually, I drove to his house and he wasn't there either. I was just about to call the police but he turned up at about half ten in his pyjamas, a bag of pills and his medical forms...'

Jamie felt sick. He put his hand up to say he didn't want to hear anymore – not from Eric anyway. He pressed 'play' on the tape recorder.

'You can stay here for a few minutes,' said Eric. 'I'm going for a fag.'

Eric opened the door and got out of the back of the van. Jamie watched the micro cassette rotating slowly like Lenny's tired and battered eyes.

'Jamie, old son, you made me feel so good in the last few days,' said Lenny's recorded voice. 'But now I'm out here in the cold in my pyjamas. It's dark and I don't know what time it is. Eric was supposed to come but he's done more than enough for me already. So, before I walk home, I'll give my tuppence on the state of the NHS. Isn't pleasant is it? You know I love a good story so I want to go out in style... '

Jamie turned the tape recorder off. A chilling thought entered his head as he looked out into the half-empty car park. Had he been partly responsible for Lenny's death because of the cannabis use? If not, then why was Lenny so confused and agitated about the time of discharge? How could a man who prided himself on his accuracy and fact-checking credentials give Eric the wrong time to pick him up? Of course, Eric could have checked the time with the hospital staff but he wasn't family and was probably fed up explaining that detail to stressed-out nurses. But it didn't matter now: the only thing that did was getting a story in the paper about Lenny's traumatic last hours; the hospital needed to be taken to task for that. It was in the blood.

A tribute to Lenny and the story of his final hours ran in a double-page spread near the centre of the paper. A spokesman for West Hertfordshire Hospitals NHS Trust passed on his condolences but gave a strong defence of the hospital and claimed the confusion over the time of discharge was nothing to do with them. Danny liked the story so much he bought Jamie lunch, although Jamie couldn't eat because of the sheer relief of getting the story out into the paper. Danny also had another surprise: he was nominating Jamie for Reporter of the Year at the Press Gazette Awards because of the solid stories he was bringing in week after week. Jamie was elated, if a little daunted, and he'd dedicate his win, if it happened, to Lenny. Danny had a scientific way of choosing who he'd put up for an award, it was called the Six-Hitting League Table for Reporters. The categories were: EyeEye (Islam and Immigration), SlebPlebs, NHSWets, DeadGood, ShagWag and NaughtySporty; any page leads that came under these banners were given Maximums (six) and the rest (say, a rape story) were given lower marks (four). Danny was really into this and relished the detail of these categories (he said the EyeEye category was amended after 9/11 to include Islam because the readers demanded it). There was also a Top of the Paps league table for photographers but this was disbanded when most of them became freelance.

Jamie finished lunch and got back to the newsroom feeling rejuvenated: the Lenny business had been well and truly purged. But there was another message from the annoying AB waiting for him. He thought about leaving it unopened but the vinegar-soaked scent of the envelope got the better of him.

**Meet me at 9am at Gerry's in Old Compton
Street if you want to end this.
If you don't turn up, I keep turning up.
Sunday's a good day for me.
AB**

Any day but a fucking Sunday: it was Jamie's day off and he wasn't going to waste it by trying to get into London on a lie-in morning. He threw it into the bin. If the weasel was that desperate, he'd send another one and sure enough, about a month later, another note came in the mail – this one wanting to meet on a Friday. Jamie was ready. He called Wallace to see if he was available but he would only come for a fee of £700. Jamie reluctantly agreed to pay out of his own pocket (getting it through expenses would be tricky with Wallace involved) but he wanted to put an end to this once and for all. He told Danny he was meeting a contact in Soho about George Michael's *Shoot The Dog* video and why most of the gay community were against the War on Terror. Danny wanted him back quickly so Jamie rushed down to Soho to meet Wallace. They got together and walked to Gerry's on the corner of Old Compton Street. A man with dark, floppy hair wearing a pinstripe shirt and black trousers was sat on the kerb outside Gerry's. He was wearing slippers and using them to make imaginary foot patterns on the double yellow lines. He smiled as Jamie and Wallace approached him. He suddenly offered his hand to Jamie.

'Alex Barnstable,' he said. 'Forget Meg Ryan, you and me could have starred in *You've Got Mail*. What do you think Nosey Parkes?'

'That was over the internet, you sent me post.'

'You're not clever, wordo.'

'Does your dad know about this?'

'Does he fuck. But I have to protect him from shafters like you. What did you have to stick you're oar in for?' Alex closed his eyes for extremely long periods when he spoke, only opening them when he delivered a long word. He carefully unbuttoned his sleeves. He rolled them up and Jamie could see the tattoos on his arms. One said 'Dads are never Dead' and the other 'Jack and Alex 4Ever'.

'Mum's have always been bitches,' he said. 'But my dad treated women fair and square. You're mum came onto him, that's how it was. But then you write your filth and our lives are ruined. We wanted to expand and open an offie here, in Soho, but now there's no chance. I could have had a job and a future.' He looked over his shoulder. 'We could have made it look like that.' He looked angrily at Jamie and got up off the kerb. 'But now we've had to close down 30 stores – and all because of some story you peddled.'

Wallace pulled out a comb, with a rather big handle, and brushed a few strands of hair. He examined Alex carefully and stepped forward. 'Where do you work, Barnstable?'

'In better jobs than any of you. The family business; know what that is? It has more honour than the jackanories you write. You lot ruin lives: I work for the family; notice the difference?'

'Sounds like you've got a mental illness there, Barnie,' said Wallace. 'Are you scitzo?'

'No, but I used to be.'

Alex launched at Wallace but he stepped away – and did something amazing. He took the top off his comb and it became a dagger. Was this really happening? Jamie was stunned, as though he'd walked onto a James Bond film set. Wallace pushed the dagger towards Alex's body but Alex grabbed his shoulder and the two men grappled on the ground. Jamie watched for a few seconds as passers-by watched the commotion. He took out his mobile and prepared to call the police – but that was a stupid move. He called Danny instead who was apoplectic he was taking so long.

'Stop fucking around in Bumland and get down to Heathrow,' said Danny. 'There's tanks down there and World War Three's kicking off.'

As Jamie watched the two men continue their struggle, he had an idea: he could be in business with Wallace's comb.

There were a few tanks and soldiers outside the airport but it was playground stuff. Jamie was about to get serious. He walked into Terminal 1 and saw a few more officers patrolling the shiny floors but their eyes were trained elsewhere: a young man with fair hair, a tie and a Puma bag wasn't enough to warrant their attention. His heart was thumping: not only did Wallace lend him the comb, the former copper also gave him a small cleaver disguised as a credit card and a knife disguised as a pen. Jamie's only concern was his complete lack of knowledge of how domestic flights worked and whether he could board one with standard ID with no need for a passport. It was worth the punt for another shot at glory.

After a trip to the Gents, he went to flight desk to check ticket availability for Manchester. There were a generous number of seats left in the day on a number of flights run by

British Airways and BMI. Some passengers, Jamie was told, hadn't turned up for their flights; the thought of martial law had obviously put them off. He booked a ticket, checked-in and prepared to get onto his flight about an hour and half later. During this time, a screaming protester had been lead away by officers saying it was all just 'propaganda for the war'. Jamie put the holdall over his shoulder and headed towards security. His put the bag down to be scanned and emptied all his pockets. He took off his ring, watch and tie pin. The sensors and scanners were kind to him but, as expected, the security officer asked him to open the bag. The security officer – a short, stocky man with a moustache – watched him with his arms folded.

'Not many dressed in a suit carrying a Puma,' he said. 'What have you got in there?'

'Food and domestics,' said Jamie. 'What's been going on, today? Bit of overkill, no?'

'You're telling me. World's going mad – still turning, I suppose.'

'Bet they're profiling people something rotten… '

'What do you mean?'

'Muslims, that kind of thing… '

'We don't do that. Come on, let's have a look at the bag.'

Jamie handed the security officer the bag and he started going through the items. He picked up the comb and the pen, examined them and put them back in the bag. The credit card was concealed in a wallet that remained unopened. He handed the bag back to Jamie.

'Where are you going?'

'Manchester… '

'Give my love to City… '

Jamie nodded and walked on. He grinned and loosened his tie. He felt as though he was flying already. He went into the departure lounge and sat next to an overweight man who was reading *FHM* magazine. Jamie peered over the man's shoulder and looked at some of the racy pictures. Noting better than a bird and an exclusive. Half an hour later, Jamie was walking onto the Boeing 737. As he stepped inside the plane and took his aisle seat, he could not contain his excitement; an inner glow of satisfaction took hold and he almost wanted to get off again and get the story written immediately. But he had to wait until he landed in Manchester – and then he could tell the world how he'd single-handedly embarrassed the state, the army and the police.

Jamie was sat in the departure lounge at Manchester Airport compiling his story in his notebook. There were a few details to add. He had been detained for more than an hour on arrival as he walked into the airport – but not for the reasons he expected. Two suited men, who were carrying out random checks mainly on groups of foreign-looking men, approached him and asked him a number of questions about his family, his background and his personal interests. They escorted Jamie to a small room and asked him if he knew a Mohammed Qasim? Jamie told them he worked for a tabloid newspaper and had recently run a story on this man. One of the men laughed at the 'tabloid' revelation – and said he preferred *The People* anyway. Qasim, it transpired, had been under surveillance because he was the alleged ringleader of a radical group which had connections in the north west. How did Jamie miss that story? Best not to let Danny know. The two men told Jamie he had been 'brought in' because they had CCTV of him talking to Qasim outside the mosque, as well as audio recordings. Jamie explained the mosque story and the men were satisfied he wasn't a 'white sleeper'. By this time, all three men had completely forgotten about Jamie's bag – and the weapons inside it. Jamie was eventually released and didn't see the two men again.

After Jamie had compiled the intro and first six pars of the story, he tried to give Danny a ring. Danny had been calling his mobile repeatedly but Jamie wanted to wait until he had the whole story clear in his head so he could mount a strong defence of his AWOL methods. Jamie was asked to hold (Danny was on his way), always a sign the news editor would give him both barrels.

'You're banned from the Press Gazette awards,' said Danny. 'Now give me a world exclusive or you're sacked.'

'Fuck the awards, I've got a belter,' replied Jamie. 'I took weapons onto a Boeing 737 on the day Heathrow was armed to the teeth with soldiers, police and tanks.'

There was pause on the end of the line.

'Pictures?'

'Not great but got a couple on my phone.'

'Where were you this morning? Wallace called and said you got into a dust-up with some mad-arse.'

'Does he tell you everything?'

'No, only the important things. Weapons came from him, I take it?'

'Er yeah, a dagger, knife and a cleaver... '

'... And no-one stopped you?'

'No. Army of Clouseau's. Bang to rights.'

There was another pause as Danny shouted across the newsroom to picture desk.

'Fitton's not in, so Fox-Tucker's in charge,' he said. 'He doesn't like 'security breach' stories but I'm in the ring with you on this one despite your fucking around. Get in here and bash it out.'

'Be a while yet... '

'Good. It'll give me time to get my gloves on – and deck your backside.'

Jamie got home on Friday evening knowing he had the front

page. Fox-Tucker did have an alternative splash – on a stabbing of a mother at a nursery – but Danny helped Jamie get over the line by persuading the deputy editor everyone was worried about the terrorist threat. Jamie was desperate for a can of Grolsch to celebrate but as he walked into his kitchen he nearly stumbled over a flimsy-looking placard resting by the door. Jamie picked up the placard and didn't realise his mother was behind him.

'Somebody's got to take a stand,' she said. 'Your rags won't do it so we've got to step in.'

Jamie shook his head in disbelief.

'For God's sake, mum, get a grip. There'll only be a few hippies there. Who's put you up to this?'

'I'm going with Gemma. She's very anti this war and she's right. It'll be a historic day – and I want to be there.'

'Since when have you cared about Iraq?'

'I got interested in it when that Blix character was talking on the TV. He looked genuine to me. I like him.' She walked towards the fridge and took out a fruit yoghurt. She grabbed a spoon, sat down at the kitchen table and started eating it. 'Our leaders aren't telling us the truth.'

'You don't say,' said Jamie, grabbing the placard tightly with both hands. He swotted it from side to side like a weapon. 'What's for dinner?'

'There's some pasta leftover from lunchtime,' she said. 'Haven't had time, I've been preparing for tomorrow.'

'Knew Gemma would put you up to this. Her heart always bleeds.'

'She hasn't put me up to anything. It's my choice. Lots of people are going to die over there.'

'People die everyday. Our paper's full of them.'

'Jamie, you don't believe in anything else but a story. I do.'

Jamie gave his mother a cold stare and placed the placard carefully on the kitchen table. He walked over to the cupboard and picked out a bottle of brandy. He poured a glass and looked out of the kitchen window, with his back to his mother.

'I got the front page again, if you're interested,' he said, finishing off his first glass in one go. He poured another glass. 'Worked really hard to get this one. Put my arse on the line. Might get an award for it.'

'That's good, love.'

'Got through Heathrow with some weapons. On the same day, soldiers with guns were roaming the place.'

'Jesus, you could have got killed. Weren't you scared?'

Jamie didn't answer immediately and took another drink. He smiled and then turned to face his mother.

'Course, I was scared... but it was fun though.'

Tina shook her head and got up. She finished her yoghurt and threw the carton in the bin. She poured a glass of water from the sink.

'That's the problem with you lot,' said Tina. 'Mischief and mucking about is all your papers are interested in.'

'Not true.' Jamie walked forward to the kitchen table. 'Still don't think you should go, mum.'

'I'm meeting Gemma in London at ten tomorrow morning. She came in here and showed me all the tabloids that are supporting this war. I couldn't believe it. Most people don't want it. Even the guys at the brewery who were pro-Afghanistan are against this one.'

Jamie sat down and finished off his second glass. He poured another. He took out Paul Markham's lighter from his inside pocket and eased the placard towards him. It was an extremely badly-made placard, a wobbly piece of card slotted into a wooden pole. Jamie ignited the Zippo lighter and pointed the flame under the card. Tina was horrified and threw the glass into the sink. She rushed over and tried to grab the placard from Jamie's grasp – but the piece of card had ignited.

76

'We only create mischief, yeah,' said Jamie. 'Well, here's a piece of it, with knobs on.'

Jamie let go of the placard and smiled. His mother managed to blow out the flame within seconds.

'What the hell are you doing? Have you gone mad? And why haven't you given that lighter back?'

Jamie got up and handed the lighter to his mother, which she reluctantly took.

'Don't come to me for another story when you get arrested,' he said.

Jamie ordered a late night-curry and browsed through Lenny's old contacts book and his old photos. He missed the old man's scathing humour and regretted not spending more time with him. As he went down the list of contacts, he came across Mike Trevena's number. Trevena had been in the news for the past few days, particularly the tabloid dailies, because he was against an invasion of Iraq – and claimed it would be a 'war crime' if it went ahead. As per standard, most of the pack went for him and digged into his daughter's private life as well gathering the dirt from acquaintances and friends. One of Jamie's colleagues had filed a similar story for Sunday. Jamie did consider why these stories were so vicious. Yes, it was part of the territory but some of these tales, particularly the one about Trevena's former teacher caning him on the buttocks and making him squeal, made even Jamie cringe. Jamie decided to give Trevena a call, on his mobile, to see if he could garner any fresh leads for next week. His phone was switched off and Jamie spent too much time listening in to voicemail messages from dreary charity workers, politicians and councillors. Jamie remembered that Trevena supposedly had a dossier on Warren Fitton's shady dealings, although he had to admit Don Leaver wasn't the most reliable of sources. Yet, Jamie still had a niggle with his editor for burying the

Lar-Lar story despite his good work with Unsung Britain. So he called Larna, under the umbrella of interrogation although it was companionship he really craved. But to Jamie's annoyance, the line had been disconnected. She had obviously changed her number. Jamie lay back in bed and picked up one of the photos from Lenny's leaving party. It showed Fitton handing Lenny a spoof newspaper with Lenny's life story being told from front page to back. There were pictures of Lenny as a child and cuttings of stories he'd covered. Jamie's mobile rang to startle him.

'Mike Trevena, here, can't you give it a rest?'

'Er yeah, Jamie Parkes, how did you know I was from a paper?'

'Have you got a question for me? It's late on Friday evening and I'm in a deep conversation with my daughter about the wonders of Tommy Steele and Dusty Springfield.'

'She's got my condolences.'

'Get on to your questions... '

Jamie's mind went blank. There was a journalistic term for this which Ben Fox-Tucker had shared with the newsroom on one heated, pre-deadline evening. The problem was, Jamie couldn't remember that either.

'Don Leaver said you have a dossier on my editor,' said Jamie. 'What are the allegations?'

There was a pause on the line. Trevena coughed and cleared his throat.

'Why should you care? You work for him.'

'Any wrongdoing is important.'

'I don't believe you're serious. Anyway, we can't do this over the phone – and definitely not now.'

'Where can we meet then?'

'You need to show me you're serious first. That's going to take a lot of persuading after the depraved intrusions of the last few weeks... '

'Your hospital stuff's proved to me you're not like the others. Tories, Labour, Lib Dems, they're all as bad as each other, at least people trust you.'

Trevena laughed down the phone. He shouted across to someone, who Jamie presumed was his daughter. 'Listen to this, Annabel, a tabloid reporter dealing in flattery. Wonders never cease.' He put the phone back to his ear. 'Let this war hysteria die down a bit – and then I'll give you both barrels. Be in no doubt, that I am coming after your so-called tabloid industry, not just Mr Fitton who I'm sure is not the only one bribing officials and intercepting phone calls. I have nothing left to hide because it's all appeared in the papers already. Make no mistake: I'm going to bring you down.'

Trevena hung up and Jamie paused to reflect on what he'd just heard. Then he laughed for at least two minutes, had a couple of cans of Grolsch and went to bed.

8.

The Joy Division Experience

Jamie was mildly disappointed he didn't win Reporter of the Year at the Press Gazette awards even though he was banned from attending. His stories were as good as any other journalist's in the industry – the 'Heathrow' story proved that: even CNN and Al-Jazeera picked up on it. When Danny told him the next morning who'd won, he didn't care; it was probably rigged anyway. There was no punch-up this year which was a shame (2002 was the last one); Jamie would have been willing to give the unworthy Reporter of the Year a bloody nose.

But the awards were quickly forgotten when the Iraq war began because EyeEye stories, soldier heroism tales and flag-waving fillers dominated. Jamie was relieved and delighted when George Bush announced Mission Accomplished because it got the paper back on stories the punters wanted to read – and it proved his mother wrong in going on a meaningless protest march.

One of the stories Jamie was asked to cover was on the Human Genome Project, more appropriately titled by the paper as the Human Gnome Project. Jamie's job was to find the tiniest celebrities which he did with plenty of belly laughs and sarcastic relish. The tiniest was a dwarf actor of 1ft 3inches who claimed he'd been an extra in *Time Bandits*.

Jamie also nailed his first story from Pub C. Serial mugger Liam Birtwhistle met him wearing a balaclava and claimed he'd nabbed a handbag from tennis star Anna Maicon while she was shopping in Bond Street with her fiancee. Jamie called the police afterwards to firm up the story and a mugging had been reported in that specific location. Jamie got a lengthy interview and picture with Birtwhistle who boasted he'd mugged hundreds of celebrities. He didn't name them all – and Jamie couldn't be bothered to check so many anyway.

One person who was obsessed with checking, however, was Callum Gordon who got back to Jamie with Larna's number after weeks of digging. Jamie gave the number a call.

'Larna, it's Jamie Parkes… '

'What do you want, Jamie? I'm just going in to watch *An Inspector Calls*.'

'Why did you change your number?'

'Because other papers got a whiff of the story, that's why. Is that what you wanted? Please, just get off my back. I was unlucky enough to be charmed by a Royal but that's history now. No-one will ever know about it.'

'You sure about that? I have more power than you think.'

'Not more than your editor. He holds all the cards.'

'Talking of which, is it over between you?'

Larna sighed and then sneezed. 'I'm looking forward to this show.'

'I'm gonna get your affair with the Prince out there if it kills me.'

'Fitton won't let that happen. It only lasted a few months anyway. Nobody cares about it. I'm not anyone important. Why am I news?'

'Trust me, you are news. Do the Prince and Fitton go riding together?'

'I don't know. Ask them.'

'Okay, do you think Fitton's a good man? Lots of people think he's corrupt.'

Larna hung up.

Jamie went home and was stunned to find one of his old school friends – and another man – in the living room drinking tea with his mother. Mark Hoy (who Jamie didn't know) and Larnell Bright had seen Jamie's 'Heathrow' story plastered all over the media and wanted to speak to him about getting their own piece in the paper. Mark's brother, James, had died suddenly a year ago after developing a blood cot on his brain while playing football. Mark had set up a fundraising charity in his name but felt the local paper wasn't covering his efforts well enough.

'This is a surprise, lads,' said Jamie. 'Larnell, how are you? About six years isn't it?'

'Safe. Can't complain too much. I'm still doing community work at the football club. Team up with Mark to do some deliveries too. He's got a request for you. I know you're sick busy but I thought it might be worth coming down.'

'Well, if my mother's put you up to it, then I better listen.'

Mark bit into a bourbon cream and wiped the crumbs from the side of his mouth. 'My brother James always carried your paper around with pride,' he said. 'He was one of your loyal readers.'

Jamie looked sceptically at his mother who continued to drink her tea through a straw.

'… We had a big delivery to the brewery and your mum spotted us,' said Mark. 'So we got talking and when she told us about Lenny's death, I thought I'd come down and tell you about Mark, maybe you'd be open to his story too.'

Jamie loosened his tie to the lowest it would go without untying it. He sat down on the sofa and looked up at the ceiling.

'I don't want to be insensitive,' said Jamie. 'But what's the story?'

'He was 19-years-old,' said Mark.

'Probably not enough.'

'He had trials for Leicester City, Nottingham Forest and Watford.'

'Watford?'

'Yeah… '

'No Premier League trials?'

'No.'

'Sorry, but it's probably still not enough to get in our paper. Terrible things happen every day and we only cover a fraction of them.'

'Oh come on, Jamie, this lad was going to be a pro footballer,' said Tina. 'This is the kind of story your paper runs all the time.'

'Might make a nib.'

'What's that?' asked Larnell.

'News in Brief.'

Larnell looked at Mark who nodded in resignation.

'He was a member of Fathers for Justice,' said Mark.

'At 19?'

Mark nodded.

'How many children?'

'Just a son, Theo.'

'Why did he join?'

'It was a mistake, the whole thing,' said Mark. 'They got married at 16 and divorced a year later. Got a bit messy and Tiffany, the wife, my niece I suppose, made sure James wouldn't see Theo. It killed him literally.'

'Yeah, but that's not what killed him… '

'No, but you know what I mean. Surely, you can run something from what we've given you.'

'There's a lot of stuff there, potential angles, but it's all a bit messy,' said Jamie, glancing at Larnell and wondering why he was letting Mark do all the talking. 'Look, I'm not promising anything but I'll try and make it more than a nib. I'd want to talk to Tiffany though.'

'She won't talk; no chance.'

'Well, that'll save me a job calling her.'

'There is another sort of angle, if that's what you call it. He had these ideas of protesting like breaking in to the House of

Commons or scaling Buckingham Palace in a superhero costume, that kind of thing.'

Jamie raised his hand. 'Let me stop you there. This is tragic, I know. Your family must have suffered untold grief but if we run a story like that he's unlikely to get any sympathy from our readers. Protests turn people off, ask my mum.'

Tina wiggled the straw in her tea. 'At least these lads care, hey Jamie?'

There was a long, awkward silence and then Larnell got up.

'Sorry to waste your time, Jamie, I knew this one was going to be difficult,' said Larnell. 'There's a five-a-side competition we've organised in James' memory. It's happening next month at Handy Cross Sports Centre, come along if you can. Tina's got my number.'

Mark got up and joined Larnell in walking to the door.

'Say hello to your brother and mum for me,' said Jamie. 'Sorry, I can't do more with this story.'

Larnell nodded and left the room with Mark.

'Nice one, son,' said Tina, sucking the last drops off the other end of the straw. 'I thought reporters always asked the right questions… '

'Meaning?'

'Poor lad, Larnell, watched James die on the pitch in front of him.'

Jamie had erased the Wallace/Barnstable episode from his mind. He didn't know what happened to either of them and didn't really care: they had inadvertently helped him land a memorable scoop. It was a story that led to two radio interview requests for Jamie but Danny felt he wasn't ready for that kind of exposure and vetoed his appearance. Jamie did go down to his local Blockbuster and hire *The Insider* on DVD just so that he could see how reporter Al Pacino carried himself but, in the end, the media training wasn't needed.

There was also another result Jamie became aware of – and it astonished him. Wallace had kissed and made up with Alex Barnstable and hired him (with Danny's blessing) as the paper's new 'BinMan' after Olly White AKA Aussie Bin Lardy had left to go back to his home country to work for another newspaper. Alex was given the not-so-memorable title of Barnaby Bin and it was good money (and regular work) so he 'jumped' at the opportunity, according to Wallace. Jamie got assurances from Wallace and Danny that Barnaby Bin would never pester him again and Danny, in particular, made it clear he'd be sacked if there was any wrongdoing. To test the water, Jamie asked Barnaby to rummage through the bins at the back of a pop star's house to see if a story about keeping the lights on 24/7 could be firmed up. Barnaby came back with a negative, but coherent, response – he even apologised to Jamie, claiming he had been desperate to hear from him so he could 'pour his soul out'. Barnaby went on for too long but Jamie felt he could rely on the paper's new BinMan for any sort of work, no matter how dirty.

The Don Leaver case was certainly that – and Jamie had one eye on it because it had finally reached the High Court. Fitton had been spending most of his time there defending the paper and Jamie desperately hoped he'd come back having won the case. Leaver was claiming the paper's 'Whipping Dictator' story was an invasion of his privacy while also being untrue but the paper claimed it was in the public interest. Fitton and Danny had supported Jamie all the way on this story so far and Jamie hoped they'd still be on his side if the ruling went against the paper.

Danny asked Jamie to prepare a small comment piece of about 800 words if the case went their way. Jamie was writing this story, which was surprisingly enjoyable, when Mike Trevena called to organise a time and place to meet. Jamie was surprised he'd got back to him so soon. He wanted to meet at Sparrow Hill, the hospital he'd worked so hard to save and Jamie agreed.

Trevena was sat on a wooden bench in the gloomy hospital

car park when Jamie arrived. He had a thick A4 document in his hand inside a see-through, plastic blue wallet. He was watching people go in and out of the front entrance of the hospital.

'Is that the famous dossier then?' asked Jamie, sitting down on the other side of the bench.

Trevena looked at Jamie and smiled.

'Typical tabloid man,' said Trevena. 'No time to waste, eh?'

'You know how it is: deadlines and dodgy sources.'

Trevena looked away towards the hospital again.

'Look at that man limping into hospital,' he said. 'Arms round two people, distressed; do you think he would have had a better service if he had to go 30 miles to another hospital? Would that improve his health?'

'Look, Mr Trevena, I'd love to do another piece on your hospital triumph but I thought I was here for something else.'

Trevena laughed and smacked the file on the bench.

'Hospital triumph? Is that what you call it? Can your mob not talk about anything other than triumph or disaster? There are shades of grey too – and I can enlighten you on these, one day. No, this was no hospital triumph: it was a concerted campaign to keep key hospital services in the town – and, in that, we succeeded.'

Jamie shook his head and keyed in some numbers on his mobile just to look busy.

'So why agree to meet if you don't want to talk about the so-called corruption allegations,' asked Jamie.

'I wanted to see if there's any substance in that tabloid heart of yours.'

'… And is there?'

Trevena looked doubtful. 'Everyone can change. There's always time.'

Jamie watched an ambulance pull up outside the A&E department. Paramedics pulled out an elderly woman on a stretcher. Jamie looked at his watch.

'I've got to drive down to McDonalds to cover a knife attack on a customer. Spill the beans if you've got anything. If not, we'll say our farewells.'

Trevena looked down at his file and opened it. He flicked through the first few pages and nodded to himself.

'What makes you think I'd give this to you first anyway?' he asked. 'The broadsheets had first refusal and most of them, as expected, aren't as courageous and crusading as they claim. None of them wanted to investigate their clubby, chummy world. There's a still a couple more to do, but I'm not holding my breath.'

'If the allegations are so bad why haven't you published them – and got them out into the open?'

'I'm still gathering evidence.'

Jamie got up and wiped the dust off the back of his trousers.

'Well, gather some more then. When you've got enough, get back to me.'

'Wait… '

'Go on… '

'Why are you doing this? He's your editor. What could you possibly gain from knowing about his misdeeds. Did he spike one of your stories or something?'

Jamie looked Trevena in the eye. He had underestimated him. He sat down again and spread his arm over the top of the bench.

'You've got an unhealthy knowledge of tabloid newspapers,' said Jamie.

'Well, I have experienced the sharp end. You have to keep your enemy close.'

'Trust me, I've got nothing against my editor. I'm just curious about him because from what I've seen he's a decent bloke.'

Trevena smirked and didn't answer. Jamie put his hand out, asking to look at the file.

'Not so fast,' said Trevena. 'I've been turned over once too often. I'm still sizing you up.'

'Just give me a couple of names to get going. Who's the cabinet minister involved?'

'What a surprise. Zoom in on the politician, why don't you? Like I said, I'm still sizing you up: I'm zooming in on you moral radar and whether it's worth exploring... '

'... And is it?'

'It might be. One day.'

Louise and Jamie were standing in silence watching the TV screens as Don Leaver stood outside court reading his statement. Jamie couldn't absorb the MP's words: he failed to get past the politician's gleeful face which was dripping with pride and vindication. Had Fitton left court? Jamie needed to hear from him because Leaver's satisfying demeanour was making him sick.

'This is a day to celebrate because the members of the press who drink from the gutter have been stripped of their power and given a lesson in truth, democracy and fair play. This so-called newspaper invaded my privacy and claimed it was in the public interest. Today's verdict demolished their argument. But, of course, they argued. I gave their reporter James Parkes an opportunity to save himself and the paper but he blew it and now they've had to pay the price – a heavy one, I may add.'

Jamie walked back to his desk to finish his story on the McDonalds knife attack. Louise continued to watch for a couple more minutes before walking towards Jamie.

'What was the name of the woman he slept with?' asked Louise.

'Hannah Rocheman.'

'Get a follow-up on her. See what she thinks of the verdict.'

'We should let it drop.'

'You made the bed so you've got to sleep in it,' said Louise, walking back to her desk.

Jamie cupped his hands over his mouth. 'You're not

funny,' he shouted. 'Hope Danny gets back from court soon.'

'You wish...'

Jamie was summoned to Fitton's office late in the afternoon. Danny was already there, sitting in a tub chair. Fitton was watching a Don Leaver interview on Sky News while tapping his blue-rimmed glasses on his hand. Jamie was forced to become a spectator too. Nothing was said for 10 minutes and Jamie was getting nervous.

'Why haven't you sat down yet?' asked Fitton.

'I wanted to stand.'

'You sound worried? It's only 60 grand, man. Now, empty your pockets.'

Danny and Fitton laughed and Jamie eventually joined in. Fitton put his glasses down and slipped two fingers underneath his brace strap, cutting them like a pair of scissors.

'I'm not joking,' said Fitton. 'Only about two year's wages now for you, isn't it?'

'More than that. Two and a half, probably.'

Fitton's phone rang. He didn't answer it.

'Leaver may have won the case but he's kept this story in the papers and TV,' said Fitton. 'That means there's only one winner. Our rivals may have given us, and me, in particular, a good kicking but if they saw our mailbag and emails they wouldn't crow as much. Our punters love this story: a Tory MP is a Whipping Dictator, full stop. They can't get enough of it. So well done on this story. Have you got the follow-ups ready? Any more stains on Leaver? What about the girl?'

'Hannah's not got back to me yet. As for Leaver's circle, no-one wants to talk about anything other then the court ruling.'

'Offer his wife 60 grand to speak.'

Danny interrupted. 'The Screws and *The People* have already done that?'

'And?'

'She said she'll take them to court if they don't stop harassing her,' said Danny.

Fitton laughed and walked over to the dartboard. He picked up the darts and started throwing them, haphazardly, at the board. One hit the board and landed on the floor.

'I would have loved his face on this dartboard,' said Fitton, picking the dart up off the floor. 'Everything in this game for two in a bed… '

Jamie had Hannah in his thoughts when he turned up for the five-a-side tournament at Handy Cross Sports Centre. He hadn't been able to get in touch with her for weeks and he hoped she hadn't done something silly or left the country: the media interest had been intense. But as his bright new trainers squeaked round the shiny gym – and his t-shirt and red Watford shorts became embarrassingly drenched with sweat – he had more pressing matters to deal with: namely, his gut. He knew he was out of shape: he hadn't done any physical exercise for at least five years and he hadn't wanted to do this now but he felt he had to do the honourable thing and turn up after giving Larnell and Mark such a frosty introduction. A big mistake. At the end of the hour-long kickabout with a spongey yellow ball, Jamie was on his knees, eyes watering, head thumping and suffering from severe cramps in the stomach. After the game, Larnell told Jamie in detail about James dying in front of him on the pitch. Jamie had to cut him short and go home – but he promised a substantial story would eventually go in the paper. Jamie had difficulty sleeping that night and called in sick next morning. He managed to get a same-day appointment with the GP (although the line had been engaged for 25 minutes). When he got the doctor's surgery, he was already feeling better and wondered if he should turn back. There was a nice-looking receptionist at the desk so he decided to go ahead. After a short wait, Dr Hobson called him in and Jamie told him about his symptoms. Dr Hobson carried out his standard checks and felt Jamie should have a blood test.

'Can't you just give me some pills?' asked Jamie.

'Yes, but the underlying problem will remain.'

Luckily for Jamie, he could get the required blood test done at the surgery and not have to trek up to the hospital. It did occur to him that Trevena's point about having local services close together, in one location, was more valid than Jamie had once assumed. So the blood test was carried out and Jamie headed straight back to work in the afternoon. He was feeling fine and felt guilty about taking the morning off. He remembered doing stories on patients not being able to get appointments with their GPs on the same day (or even in the same week) and expected more of a struggle when his own time came. It was smoother than he expected. Best not to file.

Trevena was quoted in some of the broadsheets saying the PCC wasn't fit for purpose and needed a radical overhaul. It got Jamie thinking about whether he'd ever get his hands on Trevena's dossier and, moreover, whether it was worth the trouble. He remembered the blue file in Trevena's hand and, all of a sudden, the image of Barnaby Bin lurking outside the MP's house came into his mind. It was a teasing, tantalising thought and Jamie felt it was worth a punt despite his generally cordial relationship with the Independent MP. Jamie called the man formerly known as Alex Barnstable and wondered if he'd be up for it. He took a while to answer as he was relieving himself in a restaurant toilet after having eaten pepperoni pizza and fries.

'Hold your horses, just pulling the zipper up, now,' said Barnaby Bin.

'I've got an address for you. It's an MP house.'

'What do you want doing?'

'Your normal stuff. Go through the bins, see if you can get some phone records… '

'Bills?'

'Not sure about them. Just get what you can.'

There was a pause as Barnaby Bin walked out into the eating area of the restaurant with the feint hum of jazz music being drowned out by a baby's cries.

'I have forgiven you, brother,' said Barnaby Bin. 'No hard feelings.'

'Stick to your job and you'll be fine.'

'Saw my dad the other day. Wrote to your mother to say sorry. He did wrong so he's fronted up like a man.'

'This is not the time or the place.'

'Mummy not shown you the letter? Women, eh?'

'Call me when you're done.'

'Wait on, I haven't finished yet. I just want to say sorry for sending you those silly letters… '

'Trust me, you have.'

'I know, I know. Journalist, too much to do, people to ring and all that jazz. You say, you talk to loads of people but you don't actually *talk* to them, you just use them and then discard them when you're done, yeah? I know your game. Lift em up, knock em down. Joy… Division… Joy Division.' He paused and screamed loudly down the phone. 'JOY… DIVISION.'

'You've got that wrong: Joy; yes, Division; no. Get back to me soon.'

Jamie hung up and mentally took note of how many Joy Division songs he knew. None. Not one. Blue Monday? Was that one? Think it was New Order. Were they the same band? *Love Will Tear Us Apart?* That was Paul Young, surely? Mum had one of his albums and played it way too much.

9.

Come On Love, Pull The Other Leaver!

This time there was no way back. Louise was leaving the paper and going to the Squires. Jamie had thought she had settled down in her newsdesk job but that obviously wasn't the case: she had just been biding her time from a position of greater power than before. But why go to the Squires? It was a stuffy broadsheet full of dreary stories about the UN, social workers and party politics. There was no fun in it. On the other hand, if Louise was serious about her book on Afghanistan then maybe it was the right place for her. She also wasn't having a leaving party which Jamie couldn't understand. Jamie waited until Danny was away from his desk and then walked towards Louise who, annoyingly for him, had just picked up the phone. She acknowledged him as she continued to talk while also looking down at a proof of a page lead, which had red marks all over it. Finally, the call ended.

'That was Hannah Rocheman's mother,' said Louise. 'Hannah tried to commit suicide. She's in hospital now. Why didn't you get any of this?'

'I called her but she didn't get back to me. She's changed address. Gordon's tracking her down.'

'Get down there, now. She's expected to be released today.'

Louise used her teeth to take the lid off her pen and made some marks on the page.

'Why aren't you at least having a leaving do?'

'Not now. You've got a story to get.'

'Come on, I've been waiting here five minutes. Give us a scrap, at least.'

Louise sighed and threw her pen down on the desk.

'I just don't believe in this paper, anymore. Satisfied?'

'That doesn't mean you shouldn't have a last drink with your friends.'

Louise smiled and looked up at Jamie. 'Good one that. You'll have me in stitches if you're not careful.'

'Well, I'm gonna miss you.'

'Look, I always miss people when I go. I worked in Timpsons for three years and still talk to Karl and Bethany. But here it isn't the same. Everyone's swallowed up by the paper and it affects their personality. I'm no better than anyone else but people here are forced to open up a side of their character they never knew they had.'

'Don't know what you mean… '

'You never will. Anyway, Danny's just come out of Fitton's office so you better hurry up down to the hospital.'

'The Squires is a shit paper. You'll be wasted there.'

'Maybe. But at least I'll be a human again.'

Jamie was on his way to the hospital when Barnaby Bin called his mobile. He had a stack of material in his possession – letters, bills, junk – and talked so fast Jamie couldn't keep up. Jamie had his mind on Hannah lying in a hospital bed and cut him short.

'Fax them to me,' said Jamie. 'You know how to use a fax machine, yeah?'

'I know more than you think. Want the junk too?'

'Sift out what's important.'

'Thought that was your job?'

'Get it done. I want them peeping out of the fax when I get home tonight.'

Jamie ended the call and drove into the hospital. He went to A&E first to see if they had any record of Hannah. He claimed he was her brother. After a bit of digging, Jamie found out that she had been admitted to the Dyson ward but had been discharged three hours ago. Jamie was annoyed and felt he should give Callum Gordon a ring to ask why he hadn't located Hannah's new address yet.

'18 Greatbatch Alley, it's the only one,' said Gordon. 'Anything else?'

'Why didn't you call me before? Could have been down there ages ago.'

'I tracked down the address a long time ago. I was waiting for your call. It didn't come.'

'YOU SHOULD HAVE CALLED ME! I'M THE FUCKIN' JOURNALIST.'

'Journalists don't wait: they're proactive. I could ring every client in my portfolio but it would end with a call to my psychiatrist. Regards, Callum Gordon.'

'WAIT… '

'Regards, CC.'

Gordon hung up and Jamie left the hospital. He felt Gordon had got a bit too big for his boots. Who was in charge here? Jamie drove down to Greatbatch Alley, which was only 20 minutes away, but was shocked to find it was an even bigger dump than the neighbourhood Hannah had left. What the hell had she done with that money? The paper had paid her well.

Jamie parked up and knocked on the door. After a long wait, an elderly man came to the door in brown cords and burgundy sweater. His shoulder shook jerkily and triggered the rest of his body into a mass frenzy of palpitations, shakes and involuntary movements. He stooped awkwardly and had a mask-like face with a pill-rolling tremor in his right hand. He said nothing and continued to shake, all the while gawping blankly at Jamie.

'Is Hannah in?'

Ted Rocheman slowly lifted his finger and pointed behind him.

'In there, is she? Can I come in?'

He didn't – or couldn't – reply. The head was now getting a full-on, no-no tremor. He tried to turn but found it hard to swing his head around at the same time as his body. His neck twisted and Jamie cringed.

'I'm coming in, okay?' said Jamie, neatly sidestepping Ted and walking into the house. 'Have you seen your daughter, today?'

No answer again. Jamie walked down the hall into the living room which was barely furnished with a settee, a TV, retro wallpaper and a sturdy-looking glass table. After going through the kitchen, he headed upstairs. He turned and looked over his shoulder, Ted was still staring. There were only two bedrooms and Jamie headed into the one which smelt better, a sort of fruity perfume scent which exorcised all that had gone before. He walked in but heard the sound of a car outside the front door, pulling up, stopping and the yank of an unhealthy handbrake. He peered out of the front window and could see Hannah getting out of a Citroen Saxo: a perfect paparazzi shot; legs to die for. Jamie ran downstairs quickly and got into the kitchen just in time before she walked in. She looked up at him but wasn't startled. She looked pale and tired. She put the carrier bag down and started taking out tins of asparagus soup.

'Bloody hell, got the Andy Warhol bug or something?' said Jamie.

'It's for my dad. The soup reduces his tremors.' She paused and looked up at him. 'Have you no shame? Prowling around in people's bedrooms?'

'I had to come round when I heard you were unwell.'

Hannah smiled and started putting the tins of soup carefully in the cupboard.

'Mum gave you that info did she?'

'Sort of. Shouldn't you be in bed or something? You've just been discharged. Swanning around in a supermarket isn't gonna help.'

'Do you have a father to look after?'

Jamie didn't answer and walked towards the sink. He jumped up and sat on the kitchen worktop.

'You look good for someone who's just attempted suicide.'

Hannah sighed and looked at the final two tins in the carrier bag. She took out a tin opener and started opening one of them.

'You lot are more gullible than I thought,' she said. 'My mother rarely tells the truth these days. I didn't try to commit suicide. I was depressed and the sleeping pills caused a terrible reaction. I turned blue and felt numb, I thought I was dying. That's what I went in to hospital for.'

'Why would she lie about that something like that?'

'She's ashamed of me. After the Don Leaver story broke she's hardly spoken to me. She's got her own life now, with a solicitor called Robert Norden. Me and dad aren't part of her life.'

'Did she leave before your dad started, you know... '

'What?'

Jamie couldn't help it but he gestured with a shaking motion to demonstrate his point.

'You can fuck off right now if you're going to be like that.'

Jamie held his hands up. 'Sorry, didn't mean that. Look, I just don't understand how your mother would want to stitch you up like that.'

'Because she's cut from the same cloth as you lot. She was already separated from dad when he got sick so the illness just gave her a further excuse.'

Hannah poured the contents of the tin into a bowl and put it into the microwave. After a couple of minutes, Ted walked into the kitchen with his hand over his ear. He walked over to Hannah who grabbed his shaking hand and soothed it with both her hands. She then raised her hand and softly put it over his ear.

'Sound of the microwave is too loud for him,' whispered Hannah.

The microwave beeped and the soup was ready. Hannah grabbed a spoon and fed her father carefully.

'So what am I gonna do now?' said Jamie. 'You're not going to talk so I haven't got a story.'

Hannah glanced at Jamie while she continued to concentrate on her father's erratic mouth movements. Jamie got off the kitchen worktop and walked round the kitchen.

'So is this what the council gave you?' asked Jamie. 'Where's all your money gone?'

'We're still on the waiting list with the council. I think Leaver's got something to do with that; most of the money's gone into this. We had to get somewhere to live quickly.'

Jamie pulled at the loose towel rack on the back door. 'Maybe you should have waited a bit longer.'

'We had to get out of my mum's house almost as soon as the story ran. People were talking and she wanted me out. She even locked me out once. I said I wasn't going anywhere without dad – and that suited her because she was seeing Robert anyway.'

Ted smiled as Hannah wiped the corners of his mouth with a tissue.

'So just to be clear,' said Jamie. 'You've thrown all the paper's money away to buy this place.'

'Do you want to be thrown out?'

'Thrown together maybe... '

Hannah walked over to the sink with the dirty bowl and started washing it with hot water.

'I don't have a job anymore so how would I afford a

mortgage?' she said. 'I had depression and lot of sick days so the store let me go. Everyone needs a home, you know.'

Jamie reached into his inside pocket and switched on his tape recorder. The old journalistic trick of asking the most difficult questions at the end had to be attempted, even if it was odds-on to fail.

'What did you think of the verdict?'

'I'm not going there.'

'But you were vindicated. Everything you said held up… well, apart from the Whipping Dictator stuff.'

'I told you Jamie. I'm not talking about it.'

'Was Leaver anything to do with your depression?'

Hannah didn't answer and dried off the bowl with a cloth. She replaced it in a cupboard and ushered her father away into the living room. Jamie followed them in.

'He's still been pestering you, hasn't he?' said Jamie. 'Have you met him since the story went in?'

Hannah helped her father sit down on the settee. She took three cushions and lined them up vertically behind his back. She took his shoes off and reached under the settee to get his slippers. Jamie helped her get one of them.

'Honestly Hannah,' said Jamie, kneeling down on the carpet. 'You need to tell me if Leaver's still up to any funny business because Fitton will go big on it. Yes, we lost the case and have to pay the arrogant git 60 grand but there's no injunction against us. We can still expose him some more if we want.'

Hannah eased her father's feet into his slippers. She leaned back against the settee and Jamie did likewise: both of them were either side of Ted's fragile, jerky legs.

'I made a mistake in coming to you in the first place,' said Hannah. 'The story shouldn't have run. I was naïve but I've learnt my lesson. I simply don't want to talk about this shit any more. For what it's worth, yes, he has been pestering me.

He asked me out to some rich man's club a while ago. He wrote a couple of fawning letters too – and an email. But I've told him that it's over and that's that. And now I'm telling you it's over too: I don't want anything to do with MPs or tabloid papers any more because I've been burnt big time. You won't get anything else from me.'

'You see, I was right: he has been pestering you. This could be a big story for you. What about other papers? Have they come to you for an interview since the court case?'

'What don't you understand, Jamie? Yes, other papers have, somehow, got my details, but I'm not doing any deals. My mum's already talking to other papers, as well as yours. I'm not interested.'

'Double what you got last time.'

Hannah got up and put her hands on her hips.

'I think you should leave now.'

'You'll have full copy approval.'

Hannah pointed at the door. Jamie reluctantly got up. He shook Ted's hand and walked towards the door.

'Hope you get better soon, Hannah,' said Jamie, opening the door. 'If you change your mind, you know where I am.'

'I'm already better,' she said, sitting down next to her father and holding his hand. 'I'm with my dad.'

Jamie told Louise that Hannah hadn't tried to commit suicide at all and that her mother had exaggerated her daughter's depression. Louise was slightly annoyed she had been sold a dummy by Hannah's mother but she had more than enough stories from other reporters anyway. Jamie, who also didn't tell her about the quotes he had from Hannah, couldn't resist a dig before going home for the evening.

'Who's the gullible one, now?' he said, taking a drink from his plastic up of coffee. 'You'll fit right in at the Squires. They never see the worst in people.'

'At least I'll fit in somewhere. You don't look like you fit in your shirt at the moment, are you all right?'

'Yeah, I just had to see the doctor for mild stomach cramps. No big deal. I'll get the results tomorrow.'

'Drink some peppermint tea,' she said, getting back to reading a story intensely on her computer.

'This *definitely* isn't the place for you,' he said, with a smile.

Jamie went home that evening and had completely forgotten about his request to Barnaby Bin to fish around in Trevena's rubbish. His bedroom was swarming with piles of faxed sheets strewn across the sturdy Brother fax machine and the carpet. He had asked the idiot to send him the salient documents but he had obviously chucked over everything. There were copies of a gas bill, a TV licence reminder, a birthday card, an out-of-date MOT certificate and a receipt for a garden fence repair. Jamie removed the paper from the mouth of the fax machine to unclog it. He glanced at the pages with little interest (there was too much material) but one near-blank sheet caught his eye. It was titled 'WarFit' and had about 25 or so names on it, with about half of these crossed out (but still visible) because they only had a line through them. Some of the names were familiar to Jamie already: Larry Anderton was the Assistant Commissioner at the Met; Vernon Wade was a cabinet minister; Tristan Boyce was a Royal aide; Giles Rixon was a Sergeant in the British Army and Libby Javine was PR chief for an airline firm. The other names were less familiar to Jamie but he recognised another two that were crossed out. Al Perez was a Hollywood publicist and Simone Saville, a pop star-turned-music mogul. Jamie analysed the lettering and spacing on the page: it looked a bit haphazard to him, like a draft that had been thrown away. He started ploughing through the other documents and found three letters that perked up his interest once more. One was from Larry Anderton's office, the other directly from Giles Rixon and a third from Vernon Wade. Anderton apologised that he had to cancel a meeting with Trevena and Rixon thanked Trevena for a 'nice meal' even though he couldn't 'disclose' the information Trevena wanted. The letter from cabinet minister Wade was more abrupt saying he was too busy to deal with such 'trivial' matters. There was nothing exceptionally revelatory about these letters but a pattern was developing. Jamie looked down at the messy pile again and started searching – and hoping – that he'd be able to find some of Trevena's phone bills. It took him a while but he managed to find and gather a whole year of quarterly bills and place them in front of him in chronological order. The calls to Luton were comfortably into three figures. Obviously they could have been for anything but it just happened to be Vernon Wade's constituency and no-one (at least no-one with all their marbles) called Luton so many times in a year. Jamie looked at the mobile number and called it direct. It kept ringing and he waited. It went to voicemail.

'This is Vernon Wade MP, keep it short and I'll be pleased… '

Jamie listened to some of the MPs messages but there was nothing there from Trevena. Jamie scanned the phone bills again: nothing really leaped out in terms of locations or numbers; there were two international calls to Germany and four to Durham. He looked at 'WarFit' again and stopped at the name of Tristan Boyce. Jamie recalled this royal aide being in the paper about six years ago after he was injured in a skiing accident involving the young Prince. Jamie looked at his watch and decided to call Palace press officer William Reeves on his mobile.

'Is Tristan Boyce around this evening, Will, it's Jamie Parkes… '

'I know who you are. What do you want at this time of night? You know Mr Boyce cannot speak to the press. That's my job. What's the damage this time?'

'Has Mike Trevena ever called you?'

'Why would you want to know that?'

'Has he?'

'Not to my knowledge.'

'... And has Tristan ever mentioned anything?'

'No. What are you getting it? I know of Mr Trevena – quite an honourable MP, I think, but he has no connection to the palace or the royals that I'm aware of.'

'Okay, thanks then... '

'Is that it?'

'Yes, bye... '

Jamie hung up. He looked around the room at the stray pieces of paper and wondered whether he was up for this. Why risk his job for the sake of a story that no media outlet would run anyway? Every paper did it so there was nothing to reveal. Yes, some more than others but so what? Trevena's heart was in the right place and Jamie would have helped him on any other story – but not this one.

Jamie was diagnosed with lactose intolerance and remained calm as Dr Hobson listed some of the foods he would have to eliminate from his diet. Milk and cheese were the main culprits so the toasted cheese sandwiches with brown sauce (that he liked so much) would have to be rationed or eliminated altogether. Milkshakes also caused some discomfort although cereals curiously didn't. Dr Hobson didn't offer any medication; the slight change of diet was deemed to be enough to improve his condition. After this surprisingly reassuring appointment, Jamie felt much better when he got into work that afternoon. He called Hannah and apologised for his behaviour at the house and said the paper wouldn't be running a story despite having some good quotes. This was a first for Jamie. It was an excellent follow-up story and he would always publish first and take the flak from the source later but this time there was something about Hannah that made him think again: a vulnerability, an inner strength to look after her father, her eyes, her presence, he couldn't turn her over; not this time.

'Look, I need a favour,' said Hannah. 'I've got to see the specialist for a follow-up appointment and I can't take my dad with me. Can you help us out?'

'Want me to call a nanny or something?'

'Can't you spare a couple of hours?'

'I do work, you know... '

'You take long lunches, don't you?'

'Not anymore.'

'I'll make you dinner that evening. How about that? Make it a date.'

'A date?'

'Come on, Jamie, stop getting all Britney about it. Can you or can't you? My appointment's at two so I'll be back quickly. You can do it in your lunch break.'

'When is it?'

'In two weeks. But I need to know now so I can make the arrangements.'

Jamie paused and looked over to newsdesk. Louise was watching him.

'A date, you say?'

'Yeah... '

'As long as you cut down on the cheese and milk chocolates.'

'What do you mean?'

'I'll tell you on the night.'

Jamie ended the call and Louise called him over. He walked over to her desk which was full of cards and gifts.

'So absolutely nothing on the Leaver story, then?' she asked.

'She wasn't playing ball.'

'Bit of a French farce; we've got enough good stories anyway.'

Jamie picked up one of the cards and started reading it.

'Sorry I forgot to get you one of these,' he said. 'You last day's next Saturday isn't it?'

'Next Wednesday. And I'm getting married on Saturday. Start the new job a week after that.'

'Don't think I'll ever get married. Not for me.'

'Are you seeing anyone?'

'No, er, well, maybe... '

Louise's swivelled round in her chair and put her arms across the rest.

'Come on, you brute, tell me, who's the lucky girl?'

'It's no-one. I haven't even had a date with her yet.'

'Who is it?'

Jamie put the card down and shook his head.

'I have to protect my sources,' he said, and walked away.

'Yes, sweet, sour and brown ones,' she shouted. 'But I detect a little white lie in there too. Get me 1200 words on this ban on mobiles while driving.'

Jamie walked back to his desk past a bemused Danny who was just coming into the office.

'What's up with her?' asked Danny. 'Didn't you get her a card or something?'

Jamie shook his head.

'Mother superior,' whispered Danny, winking at Jamie. 'Not long now.'

10.

Henry The Filth Returns With A Vengeance

Larnell had contacted Jamie to ask him if he wanted to join up for a few drinks at the Kings Arms in Amersham Old Town. Larnell had already sent one email for a previous night out but Jamie declined that offer because it was partly a celebration for England winning the Rugby World Cup. Jamie was happy with the victory, of course, but an evening spent discussing drop goals, lineouts and Jonny Wilkinson didn't appeal to him. On this occasion, however, Jamie felt he had to go, simply to exorcise the ghosts of the five-a-side tournament which had left him gasping and spluttering on the floor. Once he got there, however, he wanted to leave immediately. Larnell, Mark and two other friends – Stewart and Wyatt – all had girlfriends and spent most of the evening talking about films shot, or partially shot, in Amersham (like *Four Weddings and a Funeral*), the print media (probably because Jamie was there) and the popularity of MySpace. Wyatt said there was a new network called Facebook that could challenge in the future but he was shouted down. What struck Jamie throughout the evening was the ease in which the couples engaged with each other as well as the wisecracks, the flirtiness and genuine moments of intimacy. Wyatt got drunk quicker than the rest but apart from him the others had a maturity and confidence that made Jamie feel uncomfortable and slightly diminished. Had the death of James Hoy made them better people? Perhaps, but Jamie had a few nagging thoughts when he left the pub: why did that lot look so happy and secure when he had a better job than the lot of them? Why did it look so easy to hook up with the opposite sex? What did those girls see in Wyatt and Mark that they didn't see in the likes of him? Why not just try and settle down with a girl rather than chasing stories? After this slightly chastening experience, Jamie had made up his mind: Hannah was the one – and nothing would stop him.

Most of the people in the newsroom had their eyes up and arms folded as Fitton paid tribute to Louise who was standing by his side. He handed her a spoof front page which had a picture of Louise in her running shorts and vest but with a nun's white veil on her head. The headline screamed 'Nun on the Run' and the sub deck said 'Sex-starved Louise Dorrans sprints to the Squires for some posh totty'. Applause rang round the newsroom and Louise took it in good heart. She actually rolled the page up and tried to smack Fitton on the head with it but he neatly sidestepped the flimsy blow.

'Always been a hard-hitting hack, our Louise!' said Fitton. 'So hard, club owners won't let her have a leaving party.'

The applause died down and Louise looked round the newsroom. She put the spoof page down on the desk next to her, alongside other gifts from staff including a bottle of wine and a box of Belgian chocolate truffles. A greasy box of doughnuts also lay there but Louise detested the sight of them. She took a piece of chocolate from the assorted box and put it into her mouth.

'Thanks for the cards and gifts everyone,' she said, pausing to chew the chocolate. 'I really am grateful. I'm going to miss you more than words can say… '

Fitton picked up the box of chocolates truffles to offer her another one. She politely declined and swallowed the first one.

'But there's something I'm not going to miss… '

Fitton picked up three chocolate truffles and put all of them into his mouth in one go.

'… And that's the culture of spite and vindication, not only in this newsroom, but across all tabloid newspapers… '

Total silence in the newsroom.

'That's how it is, you say. Get off your high horse, you bitch. This is what I hear all the time. Well, I'm not going to get off anything even if I'm given a big shove.' She picked up another chocolate truffle and ate it. Most of the newsroom could almost hear her mouth moving. 'In my 12 years here, I've exploited victims of crime, lied to sources, humiliated vulnerable people, paid for information, lifted people's possessions, bullied prostitutes, flirted with dirty old men and dressed up as Wonder Woman… '

Fitton put his hand on Louise's shoulder.

'Don't you think that's enough now?' he whispered.

Loiuse shook her head and brushed his hand off her shoulder.

'So I regret the things I've done – but I'm going to change… '

'YEAH, BY FUCKING OFF TO THE SQUIRES,' shouted a celebrity reporter. 'WHY DON'T YOU FUCK OFF NOW? YOU CAN SAVE US FROM THE RED-TOP PERIL BY GETTING STARTED NOW. GO ON, LOVE, CHOP CHOP.'

'This is exactly what I mean,' said Louise. 'This is the kind of culture we've got to examine… '

A slow handclap started and gradually got louder.

'Come on, Louise,' said Fitton, holding her arm. 'We can talk in there.'

'NO!' Louise looked out at her colleagues again. 'The problem with you lot is you don't like anyone else's point of view but your own. You don't like to be challenged. You've got a mob mentality and shout down everything you find difficult. You're used to getting your own way – but that's going to change... '

'OH, YEAH, YOU AND WHOSE ARMY?' shouted one reporter.

'GO AND FIND A STORY, YOU BROADSHEET BINT,' said another.

'GET YOUR SANDALS ON,' said one of the sports staff.

Louise smiled and nodded but the jeers, heckles and insults continued. She was surprised to see a few of the female staff joining in, although most of them just sat there, bewildered by the unsavoury atmosphere around them. Fitton ushered her away again – and this time she moved off. Jamie couldn't believe what he'd just seen. He was hardly a close friend of Louise but was it worth most of the staff laying into her like that? She had given a lot to the paper and to be turfed out like that left a sour taste in the mouth. He wanted to make sure he had a drink with her – wherever, whenever – before she left the paper. She deserved that, at least.

Louise left the paper the next morning and Jamie never got a chance to say goodbye. He was annoyed because he didn't have her mobile number either. She had a new life and job on the Squires and it was better to leave it at that. Over the days, he gradually forgot about her but he was still haunted by the jeering and slow handclap; that image and noise stayed with him for weeks. The date with Hannah was the only thing that kept him going during this time.

On the day of this dinner date, however, he got a call that unnerved him. It took him almost a minute to absorb the character and profile of the voice at the other end of the line.

'Do you know any Mountbatten-Windsors?' said a deep, assured voice.

'No.'

'And you never will. What did you want with Mr Boyce?'

'Usual; information on a story.'

'He deals with royal business not showbusiness. He's finished anyway.'

'Fuckin' hell, why?'

'I don't get into reasons with foul-mouthed Fleet Street urchins. A higher standard of paper, perhaps, but you? No.'

'How long has it been since you saw Larna Wilson?'

There was a pause and an extended laugh.

'Do you want me to get my nob out for you?'

'Er no, course not.'

'Because that's the game you're in, is it not? You want me to do silly things. Drop my pants, that kind of thing. I'm still a young man so I can be drawn into these things.'

Jamie wrote 'NOB' out in full just to ensure there was no confusion in reading his shorthand back.

'So let's see,' said the Prince. 'An unmarried man sees an unmarried woman for friendship, companionship and a bit of boundary hitting. Doesn't sound very interesting to me. Is that a story in your dark, twisted universe?'

'Course it is, you're the Prince.'

'I'm a citizen of this land too – and I deserve to have the same rights. I came to warn you about Mr Boyce, not to talk about these private affairs.'

'What about Mr Fitton? Good mate of yours, is he?'

'Funny sort of reporter, aren't you?'

'He's not my master, I work for him.'

'You're more stupid and naïve than I thought. I wanted a bit of fun making this call – and now I've got it.'

'Don't use your age as an excuse. Are you 23 yet?'

'Thought you'd be better in the fact-checking department… '

'So what's your answer?'

'To what?'

'Mr Fitton… '

'I know of him – and I vaguely know of your royal

reporter, Mitcham something, but that's it. I really don't know what you're seedy mind is fishing for. Whatever it is, keep me out of it. You will not hear from me again.'

'Wait; why did you and Larna break up?'

'Oh sorry, you're breaking up… and my pants are falling again. Goodbye.'

The young Prince hung up. Jamie looked down at his shorthand notes and wondered if there was a story there. Yes, something could be stitched together but, curiously, Jamie didn't want to do it. Being rude or aggressive to journalists was not news, even though the Daisies had run lots of these stories before. Jamie looked round the newsroom and wanted to tell them Henry the Filth had just been on the line. But who would he tell? Louise was gone and the rest weren't really worth it. Dinner with Hannah never sounded so good.

Jamie had been coming in earlier and staying late to ensure he had moral cover for taking an extended lunch break. He also told Danny he was going back to Hannah Rocheman (which he was) to see if he could persuade her to open up on the Leaver story. When Jamie got there, Hannah was in a rush and only briefly told him about her father's habits and medication needs. She had done everything already – fed her father, given him pills and helped him to the toilet – so there was no need for Jamie to do anything; apart from watch over him. But about an hour after Hannah had left, the phone in the hallway rang. Jamie knew Ted couldn't answer it but he didn't want to either for the obvious reason that it wasn't his house. But it rang again ten minutes later. Could it be Hannah? Had they admitted her into hospital again? This time Jamie walked out into the hallway to pick it up. He sat down on a stool by the phone which was attached to the wall.

'Billy Legg, from *The Sun* newspaper. Is Ted Rocheman about?'

'What do you want with him?'

'I have some questions on a big story we're working on. Get him on, please.'

'Hannah's made it clear the family doesn't want to speak to your sort so that won't be possible.'

'Just who are you, mate? Lay your cards on the table.'

'I'm staying here, that's all. I'm Mr Rocheman's stepson.'

'What a surprise, the steptoe's are always the worst. Get old Teddy boy on, can you?'

'He can't talk. What are you gonna say to him?'

'Only be a quick one. We want to know what he thinks of the Don Leaver case.'

'He's obviously happy but he can't talk, end of story.'

'Hannah can though, can't she? She can do plenty of other things an' all. She's got form. When's she back home, anyway? We know she's out on an appointment right now.'

'Spying on her isn't going to get you very far,' said Jamie. 'She's said all she wants on the Leaver case so you can write your shite on someone else.'

'We write what people want to read, Steptoe. What do you read *The Telegraph*?'

'I only read good stuff. Now, go away and have some lunch.'

'Is Mr Rocheman there?'

'For God's sake, yeah, but he isn't speaking to you… '

Jamie looked over his shoulder and was startled to see Ted standing right by his side. Ted's arm was pulling down to the floor and the right side of his body was swaying to one side as though the wall acted like a magnet drawing him towards it.

'Don't call here, again,' said Jamie, and hung up.

'No worries, Steppenwolf, I've got what I need.'

Jamie looked perplexed and put the receiver back in its vertical position against the wall. Ted was swaying towards him now, shaking and losing his balance. Jamie held him to

112

try and keep him stable but Ted's wobbly legs weren't strong enough to hold him. There was a stool a few yards away so Jamie tried to usher him towards it but Ted had almost lost the ability to move: his body was frozen, his legs stiff and his face blank. He shuffled a few inches as Jamie tried to get right in front of him to direct him better but Ted seemed to get heavier by the second. His stooped shoulders were hard to get hold of as Jamie aimed for a big heave to get him towards the stool. It worked for a couple of feet and then Ted became completely stiff and frozen again: the tremor was completely gone, no shakes, nothing, just a blank silence which Jamie found troubling. The phone rang again. Jamie was furious and used his anger to pull Ted closer to the stool but as he did, Ted lost his balance and fell onto the floor. Jamie's heart jumped and his eyes watered like never before. He crouched down to grab hold of Ted and was relieved to find no sign of injury. He tried to help him up but as he did, Jamie could feel warmth and dampness on his hand. He looked down at Ted's grey trousers and a big, wet patch had developed just above his thighs. It was getting bigger and bigger. Ted started shaking again and Jamie was genuinely frightened. He gave up trying to get him on the stool, which would create an even bigger mess. He slumped to the floor and leaned against the wall. He watched Ted as he tried to catch his breath. Jamie looked down at his damp hands. He didn't feel like picking up a notebook ever again.

Now she tells him. Hannah's dad, apart from his well-documented condition, had a major anxiety about the sound of the phone ringing. It sent him into a tailspin and he hated it. Jamie could laugh about it now (sort of) because he was at a dinner table with a radiant Hannah listening to her favourite Tracy Chapman songs. At the time, however, it wasn't so pleasant. Jamie did look over his shoulder once or twice to see

113

if Ted was lurking but he was safely tucked up in bed too so there was no chance of a repeat; for now. But as so often happens in these things, the phone rang within five minutes of Hannah and Jamie sitting down to eat. It was Jamie's mobile but, thankfully, it was only his mum and not a story.

'Adam's coming round to dinner tomorrow night,' said Tina. 'I just thought I'd tell you because you're always a bit funny when you come home from work.'

'Did you get my soy milk?'

'Yes – and loads of cheese for me and Adam.'

'Cut it out, mum.'

'Are you staying at that girl's house, tonight?'

Jamie looked up at Hannah.

'No, course not.'

'See you later then.'

'How did you meet Adam?'

'Gemma introduced us at the march, then we had email contact for months… '

'Okay mum, I'll see you later.'

'I knew Gemma's name would get your back up. Anyway, be good for me tomorrow night – and be good to your host this evening. Bye.'

Jamie grunted and ended the call. He looked up at Hannah and only had four words in his head: Settle. Down. With. Her.

'Your mother?' asked Hannah, picking up the salad bowl and ensuring most of the pine nuts ended up on her plate.

'Nagging, as usual.'

'Should be grateful. She's working, got a good house and gets you soy milk from the supermarket.'

'I am. How did you make this lamb and spinach curry. Tastes good. Got a nice kick.'

'The Maliks three doors down made us really welcome when we moved in. Shabina invited us over after a few days and served us this dish. I nicked the recipe. Even dad liked it.'

'Sorry about your dad. He was a bit of a handful at lunchtime. I've learnt my lesson.'

'So that call?' said Hannah, nearly allowing a leaf of lettuce to escape from her mouth. 'Was it from *The Sun* or *The Star*?'

'*The Sun*. He knew all about your appointment.'

'They've been following me for ages. I told one of them to fuck off – and he made a pass at me! Even my doctor said they contacted him. Worse thing is, they even contacted the Maliks and said their son would be accused of terrorism if they didn't spill the beans on me.'

Jamie ate slower and slower as he listened to Hannah talking. What was coming out of her mouth was genuinely beginning to sicken him – and that was a fresh phenomenon he'd not experienced before. But instead of lingering over this unsettling stuff, Jamie was diverted by the shape of Hannah's mouth, her shoulder-length hair, a rainbow hair clip and her immaculate figure-hugging black dress. She looked so lovely that Jamie couldn't eat his food fast enough so he could keep his eyes fixed on her.

'Been thinking about getting a mortgage for a while,' said Jamie, dipping a rubbery naan bread into the curry. 'They're piss to get at the moment – and mum's got her own thing going on.'

'Trying to hint something?'

'No, just that I can't stay with her all my life.'

'Getting more action than you is she?' said Hannah, sipping her glass of red wine. She took off her high heels and curled up on the chair. 'Maybe I should meet her one day.'

Jamie smiled and looked at Hannah. He hoped he was reading her signal's properly. He looked beyond her at a small framed picture on the wall. It showed a very young Hannah with her father standing in front of a black cab in Oxford Street. Ted had driven taxis for 45 years but he hardly looked any different now. As Jamie examined the picture, a series of thoughts tumbled out of his head: Lenny's death, Larnell's night out, Ted's shakes and Louise's handclap. He couldn't shake them off. There was a haunting quality to them that made him reassess which way his life was heading.

'What are you looking at?' asked Hannah, looking over her shoulder.

'That picture of you and your dad. He looked so energetic there.'

'Had an affect on you, hasn't it? Hannah took another sip of wine. She smiled and looked at Jamie. 'Enough to stop you being a sneaky tabloid hack?'

Jamie stopped eating and took a long, lingering drink of his brandy.

'A more responsible one, maybe… '

Danny was furious when *The Sun* printed the Leaver/Rocheman story two days later. Jamie was called into Fitton's office to explain himself. Danny had a copy of *The Sun* open at the relevant page and stood right in front of Fitton's desk, leaning against it as Jamie sat down. He was a bit too close for comfort, thought Jamie, who genuinely feared one of his Southpaw specials if he didn't get the right answer. Fitton was calmly sat behind his desk, drinking a glass of Kia-Ora while reading *The Economist*.

'They've got a few quotes from the KAT girl here,' said Danny. 'Why didn't you get them?'

'They're a lie. She never spoke to them.'

'What about father Ted? Was that made up too?'

'I don't know how that happened. He can't talk, he's got Parkinson's and dementia. I wanted to be a bit sensitive.'

Danny hastily rolled up the copy of *The Sun* and smacked Jamie over the head with it.

'Have you got dementia?'

'No,' replied Jamie, rubbing his shoulder.

'Well, how come you're forgetting things then? Have you got something going with that KAT bird? You've been seeing her a lot lately.'

'She doesn't want to talk anymore. Simple as. Won't be the first time we haven't got a story we should have.'

'Explain?'

'Well, the Lar-Lar story,' said Jamie, looking up at Fitton.

'Heard old Henry called here,' said Fitton, closing the magazine and looking up at Jamie. 'Why didn't you tell me?'

'Didn't think it was important.'

'What did you want from him?'

'It was about Boyce, not him.'

'Which was?'

Jamie looked at Danny. His new-found moral code of trying to tell the truth was already under strain.

'I don't know yet, I'm still digging,' said Jamie.

'Turning into a bit of a smartarse, aren't you Jammy,' said Danny.

Fitton finished off his drink and wiped his mouth with a serviette. 'Looks like you've still got a bee in your bonnet about this Lar-Lar story,' said Fitton. 'Good journalists get over setbacks immediately. Henry's spoken to me about you.'

'What did he say?'

'Forget that. Today is the last I want to hear about Lar-Lar land, is that clear?'

Jamie nodded reluctantly.

'Have you lost your mouth? Clear?'

'Yes.'

Fitton sprung up immediately and took his suit jacket off his chair. He put it on and smiled at Jamie. 'Good, now that's settled, I've got to get down to this website conference. We've got to improve our online profile. Not good enough. Papers will be dead in 10 years at this rate.'

Fitton left the office and Jamie also got up to leave behind him.

'I haven't finished yet,' said Danny, 'Get back here.'

'Got stories to do… '

'Yeah, and now you've got this one too,' said Danny.

Danny waited until Fitton had closed the door behind him and then took out a small handwritten note and handed it to Jamie.

'Been a murder at a dairy near Reading,' said Danny. 'Farmer looks like he's done another Tony Martin: leathered an intruder. He's been taken in but his wife Patricia Calf should be there. Get an interview with her.'

'Can I be excused on this one?' said Jamie, tentatively handing back the note. 'That environment's not good for me.'

'Get out there,' said Danny, pointing to the door. 'Get to the dairy farm and get the story. If you come back with nothing, don't show your face unless you've got something better.'

Jamie sighed and folded up the note. He put it into his pocket and left the editor's office.

11.

A Big Broom To Sweep Sooty

Jamie had to forget about his health: this was a big story. He had been to Reading twice before – once to cover a GBH case at the Crown Court for his local paper and another for a football match at Elm Park in the early nineties – but this time he drove further down the M4 and got off at junction 12. He managed to find the dairy farm in Padworth quite quickly and parked up a safe distance away because he could see the cows grazing in the field. There was a dirt-track road leading up to a small red-brick building which had a wooden sign over the top of it. Jamie looked at his note and it matched up: SU Lawton & Sons. What was the name of that woman? Patricia something? He looked down at the note again but it didn't mention her. He got out of the car but, as soon as he did, a savage, overpowering waft of air entered his nostrils making him feel violently sick. He bent down by the front wheel but the burning rubber and exhaust fumes merely compounded his problems. Out came his breakfast of marmalade on toast, pineapple fritters and black coffee. He put his hand on the bonnet for leverage but it kept slipping off. The stomach cramps and vomiting continued for about ten minutes and Jamie's eyes watered so much he thought he was going blind. At one point, he thought he was going to choke on his own saliva. He could hear footsteps coming quickly towards him.

'You all right, young man,' said Eddie Lawton, taking off one of his green wellies and handing it to Jamie. 'Heave it all up in there. Don't leave any in.'

Jamie politely brushed Eddie's welly away.

'Have you got any tissues or towels?'

'Sure. Down in the parlour. Come on, we'll get you going in no time. What are you doing in these parts anyway?'

Jamie finally got up but stooped over to try and deflect attention away from his appearance.

'Have you had any problems round here,' asked Jamie.

'Like what?'

'A murder or something?'

Eddie laughed and put his welly back on. 'Be lucky to get a blister on your toe round here. Nothing happens. We just produce our stuff and it's taken out into the big, bad world. What's your trade, then?'

Jamie hesitated and looked out at the cows grazing in the field. The name of the woman suddenly came back to him: Patricia Fucking Calf. How could he have been so stupid to fall for that one? He knew Danny liked Steve Coogan but he still missed it. His head had been swirling with so much shit lately he couldn't think straight.

'There's no Patricia here, I take it?'

'No, wife's called Beatrice. What are you getting at?'

'Sorry, there's been a misunderstanding. I'll just get cleaned up and won't waste any more of your time.'

Eddie paused and examined Jamie closely.

'You from the city?'

'I'm from a newspaper in London. The story I was looking at hasn't worked out. I apologise for all this.'

'Okay, come down in the parlour – and I'll get you some fresh towels. I can get you the best cheese sandwich in the world too. We could grab an early lunch, what do you say?'

'Oh no, you're too kind. I've got to get back to the office.'

'No, I insist. You're a guest here. Beatrice will have a meal made up for you in no time; dripping with the best dairy known to man.'

Jamie felt a crushing anxiety and the knots in his stomach multiplied again. He looked at the faces of the cows once more and reluctantly followed Eddie deep into the dairy farm.

Jamie rang in sick for the next three days. He went to see Dr Hobson for a stomach ulcer and a rash. He also felt a shortness of breath and, at one point, thought his bladder was about to erupt. He was sure he had developed cancer down there because of the amount of milky mucus and other shit that was floating about. The doctor's medication helped but what helped more was his mother sacrificing two days off work to help him recover and bring him lunch and hot drinks when he needed them. She wasn't allowed a third day off. Jamie eventually got back to work on a Friday – the busiest day of the week – and discovered Madrid had suffered a major terrorist attack which he knew nothing about (his mother shielded him from all news). He wanted to go home immediately and stick his head under the pillow once more. But if he had, he may not have taken the call from an unexpected source on a rival newspaper.

'Jamie, it's Elliot Broomfield on the line from the Squires,' said Simon Megson, the new number two on newsdesk after Louise's departure. 'Don't know what the fucker wants. Do you want to speak to him?'

'Put him through.'

'What's your number?'

'1989.'

Jamie looked out of the window and thought about the Louise for the first time since she'd left.

'Hello, Elliot Broomfield from The... '

'Yeah, I know who you are. Slow news day at the Squires?'

'No, a good news day, as it always is. We run good stories... and truthful ones.'

'Okay, get on with it. What do you want? I'm not feeling too good.'

121

'Has there ever been any wrongdoing on your paper?'

'What do you mean?'

'Voicemail interception, paying sources, that kind of thing…'

Jamie paused as he watched Danny come back from the vending machine with a cup of coffee.

'How's Louise Dorrans doing?' asked Jamie. 'Has she settled in well on the paper?'

'Answer my question.'

'Have you done that kind of thing?'

'I'm asking you…'

Jamie watched Danny grimace as he took a drink of his coffee.

'All papers do it, you know the score – or are the Squires superior to everyone else?'

'We're not superior. We just don't like civil war. Anyway, do you know Mike Trevena?'

'Yes, the MP, I know of him…'

'You haven't met him?'

'Why if I have?'

'Well, he's given me some information about possible illegal payments to sources and voicemail interception.'

'Bloody hell, stop waffling. Ever wondered why your papers scrape a circulation? Yes, I've met Mike Trevena and he did mention something similar. But there was no evidence – and besides you'd have to bang up half of New Fleet Street. We all know that isn't going to happen.'

'Lots of things happen that are not expected: 9/11, David Kelly, Peter Andre having three number ones. The culture in newsrooms is ingrained but, one day, it will change too…'

'And you're going to be crusader-in-chief for that, yeah?'

'With knobs on, but also, with other people's help. I've been told that you're not happy with a few things, so let's talk.'

'Who told you that? Louise?'

'You know the spiel: I can't reveal, etcetera and so on... '

'I'm not ready for this... '

'You're not ready? But you will be one day?'

Jamie looked at Danny who was on the phone while also trying to text on his mobile.

'... Could be sooner than you think.'

Danny had bought his family into work. His wife was taller than him and his three young children ran around the newsroom as though it was a playground. It was one of the boy's birthdays and Danny brought a cake round the office to share with colleagues. The family seemed happy enough and Jamie wondered how: it didn't square with Jamie's day-to-day experience with Danny. The cake eventually came round to Jamie, with Danny's son, Josh, holding it tentatively while his father steadied the ship.

'I'm not going to offer you any in case you're off sick for another few days,' said Danny. 'Josh wants to give you a peace candle.'

Josh pushed the cake towards Jamie's face. Jamie looked at Danny who smiled. Jamie plucked one of the (unlit) six blue candles out of the cake and eased his hand over Josh's hair to congratulate him. He looked down at the candle in his hand and wanted to poke the little bastard's eye out with it.

Tina and Adam were sat on the sofa watching *Little Britain* when Jamie got home. It had been a late night due to Jamie meeting Melvin Moon in Pub E. He needed a light sixteenth to get him through the next couple of weeks. He had met Adam briefly at the house once before (when his mum invited him for dinner) and learnt he was a former soldier who fought in the first Gulf War but was now a human rights campaigner. He met mother at the Iraq War march in London, through

Gemma, and, after an awkward start, they were now seeing each other properly, going to pop concerts, restaurants and football matches (he was a Leyton Orient fan). Jamie wondered if this was the real thing: that he was *the one*, because his mother had been disappointed many times before. He hoped it was, although if he wanted to live here, Adam would have to tone down some of his liberal views. It was understandable in a way because his first wife, Eva, died suddenly of a stroke at the age of 33.

'Turn over any victims, today?' asked Adam, stroking Tina's head which was on his shoulder.

'Yeah, a little lad of six,' said Jamie, with a grin. 'Epic tale, you don't want to know.'

Jamie slumped on the sofa and untied the buttons on his waistcoat.

'Adam wants a word with you, tonight,' said Tina. 'Is that okay, Jamie?'

'I'm a bit knackered but, yeah... '

'Don't worry, I won't be turning into the Whipping Dictator,' said Adam.

'I wish somebody would. Put me out of my misery.'

Tina raised her head from Adam's shoulder and looked at Jamie.

'You all right, love? You sound depressed. You never told me how you got that sick. Was it work related?'

'Don't want to talk about work, now. Done 13 hours already.'

Adam looked at Tina. 'And they say the sweatshop workers in China, India and Bangladesh are flogged to death.'

Tina nodded and got up. She walked towards Jamie and kneeled down by his side. 'Come on, the milk-free souffle's in the fridge,' she said. 'Grab that and a hot drink. You'll feel much better. Adam just wants a quick word with you before you go to bed tonight.'

Jamie acknowledged his mother but then looked at Adam. 'Say it now. I'm a big boy.'

'Friendly fire's started quicker than I thought,' said Adam, with a smile.

Tina sighed and looked down at the floor.

'Your paper blurts out stuff so I'll do the same,' said Tina. 'Me and Adam are getting engaged. We're hoping to get married some time next year – around July. He'll be staying here some nights and I'll be staying at his place in Beaconsfield on other nights. We're not moving in together yet. I really hope you're okay with this; I need you on my side.'

Jamie squeezed his mother's hand and smiled at her. He looked up at Adam and sized him up as a future dad-in-law. Yes, his views were extremely dodgy but he looked a sturdy, generous sort; he'd probably spent too much of his early life in combat and had now overcompensated the other way. Jamie felt his trouser pocket and the small block of cannabis was like a second erection waiting to come out.

'Do you smoke, Adam?'

'Never have,' he replied. 'Not tobacco, anyway.'

Jamie paid the price the next morning. He had stayed up with Adam till nearly 5am, smoking weed in the garden while listening to Kraftwerk (Adam's favourite band). He had a serious attack of the munchies at about 11am which meant he devoured a hefty pasta dish from the staff canteen and, then another one, three hours later. During one of these binges, Trevena called and wanted to meet. Jamie had his story prepared: he would come clean about where the information on WarFit had come from – and hoped he would take it like the honourable MP he was.

This time, Trevena was in the tiny hospital canteen sipping tea while an elderly woman had her photo taken with him. Jamie sat down next him after the happy woman had got her picture.

'Nice picture,' said Jamie. 'Is that going in the local rag?'

Trevena smiled but didn't say anything. He continued to stare at Jamie who started to feel anxious and unsettled. Trevena reached into his inside jacket pocket and pulled out a white envelope.

'Talking of pictures,' said Trevena, pulling out a range of fuzzy black and white photographs from the envelope. 'Do you know who that is?'

Jamie peered at the low-quality photos and shook his head, more because he wanted the move the conversation on than deal with the MPs hang-ups.

'Take a closer look.'

Jamie could just about make out a couple of rubbish bins – and it hit him so hard he could almost smell the warm crap being recycled.

'Did you authorise that?' asked Trevena.

'No, I mean, yes... look before I came here, I had an apology prepared.'

'Do you think I'm stupid? This is the problem with tabloid newspapers; they think everyone is as dumb and wicked as they are. What's this man's name – if you can call him that? I was about to call the police after taking the pictures from bedroom but the more I looked at this pitiful individual the more I felt sorry for him. Is this what he does for a living? Go through the bins of MPs and celebrities to find nasty nuggets for the papers?'

Jamie nodded and played with the pepper pot on the table.

'How much of my stuff did he steal?' asked Trevena. 'I only saw him once but he must have been there before. Three months? Six months? How long?'

'I honestly don't know,' said Jamie, pouring some pepper out onto his thumb. 'But I'm really sorry. He faxed over what he had.'

'Why shouldn't I go to the police right now? You – and

126

your paper – are the ones who should be locked up, not Mr Bin Laddie... '

'Barnaby Bin.'

'What?'

'That's what he's called: Barnaby Bin.'

'Answer the question – and stop trivialising. That's another tabloid trait that needs liquidating.'

Jamie tasted the pepper on his thumb and put the pepper pot down.

'You shouldn't go to the police because I'm a different person to the one who authorised that stupid little operation. I've learnt some harsh lessons recently and there's no going back to the way I was. If you want to expose the way some of our media operates then you're going to need me on you're side. The other day I got a call from Elliot Broomfield from the Squires. Together, we can make things happen even though we're going to be pissing in the wind for a while.' Jamie paused and looked up as a nurse with an elegant shawl over her shoulders sat at the next table. '... And besides, I want to keep my job.'

'You're lucky to be sitting here at all... '

'Why?'

'This exact spot was destined to be rubble. A block of luxury flats that no-one wanted to live in would have sprung up.'

Jamie looked up at the ceiling of the canteen. He imagined a number of families living on top of each other, each not having a clue what the other was up to.

'Elliot did a good article on this hospital,' said Trevena.

'You've spoken to him?'

'We've been in regular contact. We've already compiled some evidence on tabloid ethics – but it's not enough.'

'Maybe the three of us can make a difference... '

'Hmm... what did this Mr Barnaby Bin send you? I'm sure

you were sadly disappointed by my lack of sexual activity. As far as I could tell there were only phone bills, gas bills and TV licence reminders. Of course, there was some research on Fitton's activities but that was about it. All very rough stuff. Hardly, any big revelations.'

'Do you think he paid all those people?'

'Yes, but I have to prove it – and that's difficult.'

'A lot of papers are doing the same... '

Trevena looked angry and interrupted Jamie. 'They won't be when I've finished with them.'

'One of those people named in your fund, Tristan Boyce, the Royal secretary, has already left.'

'Sacked?'

'Prince Henry called me at the office. I couldn't believe it. I was probably hasty in calling the palace when I heard about Fitton's fiddling but I got carried away. He warned me off digging further.'

'I know the Prince and Fitton fell out spectacularly recently... '

'Over what? I thought they were still friends... '

'Not any more. The word is it's something to do with that girl... '

'Larna Wilson?'

'Yes, but look I don't want to get into the titillating details of the Prince and Fitton's romantic entanglements. I want us to concentrate on the job in hand... '

'But this is the heart of the tale right here,' said Jamie. 'Perhaps Fitton was spying on the young Prince?'

'A tabloid boy till the end. Let's get back to the bigger picture. There are other sources, like the army sergeant, that I'm convinced were on Fitton's payroll but, as yet, he's not playing ball. You need to use your journalistic skill to get onto him – and the others.'

'I'm not sure I can get too deep yet. I'm up to my neck in

other stories and I don't want Danny to get suspicious. I'll make some calls out-of-hours and we'll take it from there.'

Trevena finally finished off his cup of tea. 'So you do want me to call the police?' he said, with a smile.

'Don't start that again. If I went down, I'd take half of the MPs down with me.'

'Be my guest! Bang up the Tories and then move onto Labour. How about that?'

'We can only dream... '

'Right, if we're going softly-softly on our slush fund colleagues to begin with then this is what I need from you. A comprehensive rundown of the immoral, unethical and illegal practices you've taken part in while you've been on the paper. I want to know what you've done, who've you've done it to and why? I want names, numbers and details. Absolutely, no one is listening at the moment: MPs, the Met, the quality media or even, my wife. Once you've told me all this I'll collate the evidence into a dossier. I'll then present the dossier to parliament and the police. They have to take action or we'll keep paying the consequences.'

'Gosh, is that all,' said Jamie folding his arms. 'Immoral and unethical? You'd need the whole of Ottakar's to cover that.'

'No, that's not all. If we don't clear out the stables now, we'll be paying the price for another hundred years.'

Jamie looked up at the ceiling once more. He imagined the whole block of flats crashing down like a house of cards. Survivors would emerge shaken, bruised or injured but at least they could walk away with their dignity intact.

12.

Peep Show On The Jubilee!

Tina stayed at Adam's house three nights a week after her engagement – and this had knock-on consequences for Jamie. Trevena had asked him to start collating some evidence but he was so drained having to iron his own shirts, make dinner and do the washing up that he didn't have the time or the energy. One night, when he did make the effort, he tried to work out which tabloid activities constituted immoral behaviour and which actions were strictly illegal. The list was extremely long. After successive nights, sleeping at 3 and 4am, he decided to abandon WarFit for now, at least until the summer, when the paper was generally quieter – and less pressurised.

It definitely felt like that when Fitton announced to the staff in a memo that he'd be installing a special bar and big screen for the staff in the training room for the European Championships. He called it EuroBar and wanted to create a unique, patriotic atmosphere in the newsroom to support 'our boys' in Portugal. The turnout was good (for an evening match) when England played Croatia for a crucial group game. About 40 people were packed into the training room with bottles of Stella in their hands, a nice spread of sandwiches, multiple bowls of Doritos and plenty of well-proportioned olives. Jamie was sat on one of the stools by the hastily-arranged mobile bar area but, during the second half when England were 3-2 in front, he noticed Fitton, who was sat on the leather sofa with his shoes off, looking at him. After a brief conversation with a female reporter who then moved away, Fitton called Jamie over to join him. Jamie was slightly nervous as the last time they had spoken – the dairy affair – wasn't exactly cordial. Jamie sat down on the sofa and Fitton sat up from his leaning position.

'No more cost-cutting then,' said Jamie, with a smile. 'Redundants'll be happy.'

'Six of those who left are here tonight,' said Fitton, eating another olive.

Jamie looked up and was shocked to see some old staff colleagues (although he'd never spoke to any of them) standing near the big screen.

'Maybe, I'm not the monstrous rogue, you imagine,' said Fitton.

Jamie didn't answer and looked down into his bottle of Stella.

'Look, you've got to take Danny with a pinch of salt,' said Fitton. 'I know he's been roughing you up but he does it to everyone. He once asked a female reporter to become a call girl and film the celebrities she took on as clients.'

'Did she do it?'

'Hell, yes, but she forgot to turn on the camera.'

Jamie laughed and looked up as a few people started singing *God Save The Queen* – someone also sang *No Surrender to the IRA*, although not very loud.

'So I'm apologising on Danny's behalf,' said Fitton. 'He boxed as a kid so saying sorry isn't for him. I've told him that he needs to be more sensitive about your health problems – we're in a different world now.'

Jamie was surprised, if a little flattered, by this display of humility. He wondered why Fitton chose this moment to bring it up again – it happened months ago.

'Are you seeing anyone?' asked Fitton.

'Not seriously,' replied Jamie. 'Had a couple of dates… '

'I genuinely feel sorry for our WAGS… '

'WAGS?'

'Wives and girlfriends, not heard the term yet? What kind of hack, are you?'

Jamie looked sheepish and emptied a few Skittles into his bottle.

'Anyway, the point being that I feel really sorry for partners because they wait around for us but our brains are wired for the next story. Grace says I never really engage with her.'

'… And what about the blokes?'

'The house husbands? Fuckin' hell, those pansies deserved to be ignored.'

Fitton laughed extremely loud and nearly spilled his drink all over Jamie. There was a freedom and carefree relish about Fitton tonight and Jamie was enjoying it.

'My mother just got engaged,' said Jamie.

Fitton offered his wet hand. 'Congrats, wiser buddie, put it there.'

Jamie reluctantly shook his hand. Fitton laughed again. England had another attack and scored to make it 4-2. Fitton and Jamie both got up and put their arms up in the air, cheering and whooping. Fitton gestured to the sports editor who was by the big screen to get back into the newsroom to work on the back page.

'Looks good for the boys,' said Fitton, putting his arm round Jamie. 'We're going all the way.'

'We'll never do '66 again,' said Jamie, with a smile. 'Not as long as I live.'

'Bloody hell, you're a right brother grim. Anyway, we're talking about the Euros not the World Cup. As it happens, I had one of those ex-World Cup winners in the office a couple of weeks ago. Shit, I can't even remember his name… '

'Martin Peters?'

'No, no… a defender.'

'Can't remember any of them. Bobby Moore's dead isn't he?'

'Yeah, he's a left-back, this guy... '

'Thought, you were a mad England fan?'

'I am, but liqueur's a lethal enemy. Wilson, got it, yeah Ray Wilson. Can't believe I forgot him? Ray Wilson, a legend.'

Jamie laughed and patted his editor on the back. 'He's a legend, all right, father of Larna, yeah?'

Suddenly, the colour drained from Fitton's face and he took his arm off Jamie's shoulder.

'I TOLD YOU NOT TO MENTION HER NAME AGAIN,' shouted Fitton.

'It was only a joke.'

'Well, you're not as funny as you think. Finish your drink and leave.'

'I have.'

'Well, just fuck off then.'

Jamie put his empty bottle down on the table and got up off the sofa.

'I'm not leaving yet. I'm gonna finish watching the game.'

Jamie walked back over to the mobile bar area and sat on the stool. He continued to watch the game and, sadistically, hoped that Croatia would grab two late goals to make it 4-4 and send England packing. WarFit had been revived quicker than he imagined.

Jamie called Larna immediately the next morning. She didn't answer. He checked her voicemail but there was nothing there of note. Why was Fitton so touchy about Larna? Jamie gave Callum Gordon another ring: he wanted some more background on Larna. Six days, after the call, Gordon got back to him and Jamie had one of those journalistic moments that reminded him why he was in the industry in the first place.

'She went to Helenswood School in Hastings,' said

Gordon. 'Then it goes blank for a couple of years, presumably because she left school at 16, and then emerges again when she takes an acting course in London.'

'Did you get a home address?'

'Marine Court, St Leonards... '

'Fuck me.'

'No, thanks. Regards Callum Gordon.'

'Wait, I wanted to ask you one more thing... it's a bit delicate.'

'You may need a prostate specialist for that... '

'For God's sake, it's not that.'

'What is it then? My time is precious.'

'Don't you ever get concerned about the things you do... '

'Like what?'

'Digging out personal details, blagging, bugging, hacking, that kind of thing?'

'Do you?'

'Sometimes... '

'That's good enough for me. Regards Callum Gordon.'

Gordon hung up. Jamie put the phone down and looked across to the editor's room. The door was wide open with Fitton and Fox-Tucker scurrying in and out, peering at the chief sub-editor's screen and then walking back in for further discussions. Jamie imagined Fitton as a schoolboy walking down the seafront with a copy of the *Hastings Observer* in his hand. He regularly mentioned William Parker School, a specialist sports college, and told lengthy tales of how bad he was at all sports. Fitton's was a boy's school; Larna's was a girl's but they shared a sixth form: Parkwood. Jamie's mind was racing so fast he couldn't keep up. He called Larna again. This time she answered but told Jamie to wait while she finished her champagne.

'Your birthday or something?'

'My brother Shaun's had a daughter. He's in tears.'

'That's great. Tell me about Fitton and you at that sixth form college. Round the bike sheds and all that?'

'Forget about that. I'm in a play at Windsor Arts Centre in a few weeks – I want to get a good write-up. Are you the man or shall I contact someone on arts desk?'

'Larna, we don't really do that arty-farty stuff on this paper. Films and music, yes, but plays aren't our scene.'

'Yes, your scene is bugging phones and exploiting women, I know. The Prince and Fitton were part of my life but they're not now and I don't want to dredge it all up again.'

'But you were the one who wanted it in the paper in the first place... '

'That was a mistake. I've made a lot of them.'

'How many years did you see Fitton? Did you live together?'

'Can you help me with the play or not? It's called *The Princess Who Never Was*... '

'Did you write it?'

'I co-wrote it... '

'Fitton might not want your name in the paper. He doesn't like you, remember... '

'We have to get as much publicity as we can.'

Jamie paused and watched Fitton from the corner of his eye. The editor asked the chief sub to get out of his seat so he could take over and sub the all-important front page.

'I suppose we could get a little news piece in,' said Jamie. 'What it's about, anyway?'

'A futuristic reality show about a maid who gets revenge on a Prince... '

'Sounds a bit heavy to me... '

'Your paper finds everything heavy.'

'Look Larna, I've changed a bit since we last spoke. I genuinely wish you well with your play – but just tell me about Fitton and I'll be off your back for good.'

Larna took a sip of her champagne and started talking to her nephew Shaun in a baby-like voice.

'You've got more brains than those idiots, haven't you Shaun,' said Larna. 'They'll bring the whole country into disrepute for a sleazy story, won't they Shaun? Yeahhh, that's the kind of people they are: they need nappies round their mouths. Yeahhh, come here, my gorgeous little darling... '

'Come on Larna, just this one time... '

'You said you've changed... '

'I have.'

'So why are you pestering me?'

'I'm not.'

'Do you want some details about *The Princess That Never Was*? One of our actors is a full-time accountant, another is a bus conductor... '

Jamie sighed and picked up his notebook. He flicked over the pages and looked out of the window at the dreary grey skies and light drizzle. Scratch my back, scratch your back – and the bleeding will follow.

'Go on then, fire away... '

'Smashing... '

Jamie's car had a problem with the drive shaft and had to be repaired. The drive into work was wearing him out anyway so it was a welcome break from the grinding M40, the pounding noise and the endless sight of a moving car boot. Jamie started taking the Tube for the next couple of months and even left his car at home when it was fixed. About a month in, however, Jamie was sure he spotted Peeper Wallace, a carriage down on the Bakerloo Line, standing against the double doors, hands in pockets, watching him intensely. Jamie continued to flick through his copy of the *Evening Standard* – and then looked up again. This time he couldn't see him because an overweight man with a suitcase had got in the way. Jamie got off at Baker Street and headed up towards the Metropolitan Line. He looked up at the monitors and ambled up the stairs for the connection to Amersham. He walked onto the platform, which was quite busy, and the train was waiting to depart in six minutes. He got on immediately but as he glanced to the left, about three carriages down, Wallace was there again. Jamie went in and sat down but, as the doors remained open for at least another five minutes, he thought of leaving the platform and heading for Marylebone where he could catch a train to Adam's house in Beaconsfield. The thought didn't last long because he needed a good night's sleep – and he could only do that in his own bed. He got off at Amersham and examined some of the faces going through the ticket barriers but they were unfamiliar. He walked down Hill Avenue feeling more relaxed but as he looked over his shoulder, he was convinced Wallace was lurking on the corner, hands in pockets again, coat collars up and a dark baseball cap on his head. Jamie started to run – and eventually sprinted home out of breath. He pulled out his keys and looked over his shoulder once more. Nothing. He got into the house and its eerie silence and emptiness didn't make things better. He should have gone to Adam's.

A couple of nights later, Jamie invited Larnell and Mark over to his house and they shared a wonderful night of anecdotes, banter and serious drinking. Jamie was so drunk that Larnell and Mark had to place him in his own bed after he had slipped into his mother's. The next morning Larnell called Jamie on his mobile and they revelled in the previous night's humiliation. After the call from Larnell, Jamie had four silent calls in succession on his mobile. He ignored them and continued to work on a story about a gardener who slept with his plants and spoke to them. But in the afternoon, two more silent calls infected Jamie's mobile. He looked up at newsdesk and Danny had his arms folded, feet on the desk and hands behind his head as he talked to a work experience student. His mobile rang again.

'Fuck off, twat. Trust me, I'll give you hell. Don't call here again.'

'Jamie, it's Elliot Broomfield… '

'Oh, how you doing? Sorry about that.'

'Are you okay?'

'Yeah, all in a day's work. How are we doing, breaking into these sources?'

'None of them are talking. I would say the copper and the airline PR are the best ones to target. They've been the least hostile so far.'

'I think I've spoken to that airline bod before… Libby Javine… it was about a story on an ageing rock star abusing a stewardess.'

'Yes, that's the one.'

'I'll take her and you take the copper. What about the cabinet minister?'

'Bit of a weasel, really. This is going to be a slog with a lot of dead ends. Did someone call you before me?'

'Some dickhead. Why have a thick skin if you don't use it?'

'Quite. Have you compiled the dossier for Trevena?'

'It's quite a long list… '

'You better start writing it, then. Tabloid crimes tend to affect other organs. If we don't start cutting out the cancer soon then the fear and loathing will continue. Do you want that?'

'There's enough fear already… '

Fucking hell, there was Wallace again, he was sure of it. This time, it was on the Jubilee Line and, because it was quite a few stops up to Baker Street, Jamie sweated nervously for what seemed like hours before he got off. He'd hastily bought an MP3 player online just to help him ignore most of the stuff around him but when one of the songs was *Take Me Out* by Franz Ferdinand, it didn't help as much as he expected. When he got home, he decided to revert to the car for his commute to work. He had to cut Wallace out of the picture. To settle down, Jamie gave Melvin Moon a call as well as Larnell and Mark and they came down for another night of partying, drink and marijuana meals. Melvin also introduced Jamie to hot knives and bongs topped up later with some brandy; it was a wild, barnstorming combination. The only downside of the night was when Larnell and Mark brought their girlfriends round and disappeared into the bedrooms. Jamie was left with Melvin to talk about grasshoppers, meditation and Chuck Norris. At about 3.30am, he got tired of this and gave Hannah a call.

'Do you know what time it is, Jamie?'

'... Deadline time. Tick-tock, tabloid cock... '

'Oh, you're drunk. Go to bed. I have to get up early to take dad to the doctors.'

'Sorry Hannah, I was having a go at the paper, not you. Is he okay, your dad?'

'It's just a normal check-up.'

'Can I come round now?'

'What? No, course not. You probably stink of booze as well.'

'Not booze... '

'So you've been doing drugs as well?'

'Can I come?'

'NO! I need to get some sleep. I've got insomnia anyway and you're just making it worse.'

'Please... '

'Haven't you got work tomorrow?'

'Yes, but fuck Peeper Wallace and fuck the rest... '

'Who's Peeper Wallace?'

'Fucker's been following me. Danny's put him up to it, I know he has. I don't care, I'm a tough boy. I've got a thick skin-up. Thicker than he'll ever have. Please let me come Hannah Solo... you're my... '

'What?'

'Heroine... '

'Sounds like you're on it... '

Hannah sighed and there was a long silence.

'If I could just snuggle in by your side, just for one time, it'd mean everything to me... '

Another long silence followed – and then Hannah took a drink of water.

'Come on, then,' said Hannah. 'No friends – and you're on the sofa.'

A warm hand soothed Jamie's thumping forehead as he woke up on a sofa. He didn't know how he'd got there – must have been a cab – but Hannah brought him a cup of viciously strong tea and was adamant he had to go into work. After Jamie's futile defence, she drove him there herself. She pecked him on the cheek before saying goodbye. All day, he thought about her, and called her again in the afternoon. She agreed to dinner that evening. They had fish and chips which Jamie had to hastily buy from the shop after Hannah's pasta bake turned black as coal. Hannah had been attending to Ted who nearly choked after being unable to swallow one of his many pills. She had to yank it out of his mouth and slap him on the back a few times, even though she wasn't sure it was the correct procedure. Ted was helped into bed just after nine and, when Hannah came down, she was in no mood for compromise: she wanted to know about Jamie's troubles. He told her about Wallace and Danny but she was sceptical. Was it actually Wallace he saw? Jamie didn't expect this level of scrutiny. Who was the fucking journalist here?

'The items you borrowed from Wallace; what were they?' asked Hannah.

'A knife, a cleaver, can't remember the others... '

'Maybe he wants them back.'

'He could just ask. He doesn't have to get all Smiley on me... '

Hannah asked Jamie to hand over his notebook, pen and tape recorder. Jamie was surprised but did what he was asked. She then went over to a set of drawers in the corner and pulled out a pair of glasses and a trilby hat. She came back and stood in front of Jamie. She put on the glasses and the trilby hat.

'These are my father's,' she said, flicking open the notebook and clicking the pen with her thumb. 'Now Mr Parkes, you've worked for tabloid newspapers for years but now you claim they're shit, yes? I put it to you that they've always been shit. How do you respond?'

Jamie smiled and looked Hannah up and down. She looked absolutely gorgeous in her tight jeans and black boots topped up with glasses and a trilby. He wanted to throw off her disguise and revert to his own version of kiss and tell.

'Come on then, answer,' she said. 'Or I'll turn into the Whipping Dictator and publish it anyway.'

'Okay, you can stop the act now. I really enjoyed it. Seriously, I don't want you involved in any of this at all. It's too messy.'

Hannah took off the trilby and put it on Jamie's head. 'Dad wore that for 53 years. A lot of thoughts are embedded in here. He did a lot of public good so I'm going to do a little. You said you've got this copper and airline girl that might be up to no good. They're not talking? Let me have a go... '

'Whoaa, sorry Hannah, no chance,' said Jamie, getting up and nearly losing the hat off his head. 'It'd be madness to let you do that. You've got your dad to look after – and your health problems.'

'What's the policeman called?'

'Larry Anderton; he's Assistant Commissioner of the Met. Forget about all this. It's not your scene.'

'... And what is my scene?'

Jamie walked towards Hannah and eased the notebook, tape recorder and pen out of her hand. He then took off her glasses in silence as she stared down at him.

'Forget about Anderton,' said Jamie. 'He's too high up and you'd never get to him anyway.'

Hannah took the trilby off Jamie's head and put it on her own.

'I know but it will be fun trying... '

13.

All Ants On Deck

Adam's mother and father came over for Christmas dinner and Jamie enjoyed their sedate company and occasional ribbing of their son's crushes on older women. Robert Solent was also a former soldier who served in Suez while his wife Rita ran a boutique clothes shop in Gerrards Cross. The only downside for Jamie was having to watch *The Vicar of Dibley* in the evening but luckily Tina saved him just before the end, asking him to come into the kitchen for a chat. Tina closed the door behind Jamie and gave him a hug.

'Thanks for being so good,' said Tina, wiping a tear from her eye.

'Come on, mum, get a grip. What did you expect? The Christmas from hell?'

'I just thought you might not get on, that's all. We've had too much experience of that.'

'Have you set a date for the wedding?'

'We're looking at July 7, a quiet weekday. Adam's sister Melissa is hoping to fly in from New York. She can't do weekends. She was a bit worried about getting on a plane again after 9/11 but she's desperate to make it. Seems like an age ago anyway.'

'What does Melissa do?'

'Advertising, I think – or publishing, I get confused.'

'Tell me you're not inviting Auntie Trisha from Aberdeen... '

'I have to. Whether she comes or not is a different matter.'

Sisters Trisha and Tina hadn't spoken in 12 years because

Trisha felt her younger sister had drove her own husband away due to her drinking and erratic behaviour. Jamie remembered it the other way round: he felt his father's infidelity led to his mother's problems. Add in, Tina's breast cancer ordeal and a tense relationship became even more complicated; particularly as Trisha claimed she wasn't told about her sister's health problems immediately.

'Hey, what about Hannah?' said Tina. 'Are you bringing her? Hope it's got a bit serious now.'

'It's getting serious all right, but not in the way I imagined.'

'What do you mean?'

The kitchen door opened and Adam walked in.

'What are you two plotting?' he asked. 'A tabloid sting?'

'Had enough of Dibley?'

'For a lifetime. Look, the folks are going into London tomorrow for the Boxing Day sales, see if they can pick up a bargain or two. Do you want to come? Make it a full house?'

Jamie looked at his mother and shook his head.

'Oh, go on,' said Tina. 'Are you just going to sit at home and fiddle with phones and faxes in your bedroom?'

Jamie gave his mother a cold look but then nodded.

'Okay, but not on the Tube,' said Jamie.

The Boxing Day tsunami put paid to the planned shopping trip. Jamie was called into work which annoyed him because it was Sunday morning and Adam's human rights charity CherishUs also began an immediate operation to send food parcels, clothing and water which Adam had to organise from the group's London base. Tina, Robert and Rita stayed at home to wade through the Christmas leftovers.

When Jamie got into the office, he realised about a quarter of the staff were already there. He didn't look at any of the plasma screens before sitting at his desk. He could hear the howling, crying and wailing followed by swishing movements of water before periods of deep silence took hold. Danny wanted Jamie to do a piece on the rescue effort so it wasn't too bad because he could start with CherishUs and take it from there. But he didn't get started at all – his mobile rang.

'Are you watching this?' asked Elliot.

'Yeah, sad isn't it?'

'Makes you wonder if our trade is worth it at times like this… '

'You'd be all right but our paper'd be out of business if one of these happened every week.'

'Apologies for the digression. Hannah Rocheman called. Did you have anything to do with it?'

'Trust me, if I'd had anything to do with it she wouldn't be phoning reporters. But as I couldn't talk her out of chasing coppers, I thought you might.'

'She wanted some background on Anderton. I cheekily asked her some questions on the Leaver ruling.'

'Did she play ball?'

'I gave her a bit of info – but she didn't reciprocate. Is she your girlfriend or something?'

'Why, did she say she was?'

'She said she was a good friend of yours.'

'… Suppose that's something.'

'Look, I don't think it's a good idea to get her involved. What's she going to do? Some sort of honeytrap? It could blow our chances of getting the information we need.'

'Don't fret. She won't get past the police press officer.'

'We're supposed to be eliminating this sort of behaviour not encouraging it.'

'It'll be fun to watch, though… '

'Once a rogue, always a rogue. Hope your coverage is sensitive. Speak to you soon.'

Jamie had been trying to get in touch with Libby Javine for

weeks but, finally, in early February, she got back to him while he was out covering a story on gang-related violence in Croydon. Most of the youths Jamie tried to approach told him to fuck off, some in racist language, so the call from Libby was welcome relief. He kept her talking while he got in his car.

'Why doesn't your paper cover the foxhunting ban?' asked Libby. 'My dad's apoplectic about that.'

'Our readers aren't interested in toffs. What's your relationship with Fitton?'

'Thought you worked for him?'

'I do... but so do you, yes?'

Libby laughed. The distant sound of a plane taking off could be heard although it could have been the sound of a kettle.

'Are you a mole or something?' she asked. 'At least I've learnt something new today.'

'Please answer, Libby. I know you've given me a lot of good stuff over the years: celebrity flight lists, pissed rock stars, nice pictures, but that's all ending now. I'm not that kind of reporter anymore.'

'Have you listened to yourself? You sound like a preacher or something. Let's get one thing clear: I've done nothing wrong. Publicity is a two-way operation. A lot of stars flying into London, New York or wherever want their details in the paper. You know that. I know that. Yes, I've co-operated with the paper – and your editor – but that doesn't mean I've done anything wrong.'

'Did you take any money from Fitton?'

'Do you? You get paid by him, don't you?'

'That's not what I asked.'

'Well, it's what I'm saying. He pays you a nice salary, no doubt, to peddle sewage-making shit in your newspaper. Isn't that what you do?'

'What was the fund called?'

Libby laughed and banged the phone on a wall or table.

'You paper won't be getting any more stories from me again. We've got enough clients anyway. Call me, if you ever want to run a foxhunting story.'

Libby hung up and Jamie wondered if he was becoming the kind of hack he promised he never would: a Squire.

Jamie woke up one morning and, after eating breakfast, prepared to use one of his CD covers to scrape ice off his car windscreen but, as he stepped outside, he got a shock. He looked down at the wheels and all the air had been taken out of them. It felt like a crushing, invasive act. He wasn't the only one looking forlorn and deflated. He walked forward and crouched down to take a closer look at the wheels. A daisy was sticking out of each one of the four wheel rims, blowing softly in the light breeze. Jamie got up and looked around him. He looked at the bushes, the houses, the road, the cars driving by but it was just like any other morning: a few early birds off to work but the rest, no doubt, still in there warm beds not having to deal with shit like this. Jamie leaned over the bonnet of his car and crossed his shivering hands. He closed his eyes for a few seconds and then opened the car door, throwing his CD cover onto the driver's seat. He zipped up his coat and headed towards Amersham Station. Fuck calling Danny to say he was going to be late: he was ready to confront Peeper Wallace.

Jamie knew Danny had been calling his mobile but he didn't care. He was sat in Pub B waiting for Wallace to turn up. Two Buds, a double brandy and a full packet of Skittles had gone down already when the languid, mean-looking bastard walked in. He stopped at Jamie's table slipping his coat collar up with his right thumb. Jamie reached into his coat pocket and pulled out four flimsy daisies.

'You've brought me flowers,' said Wallace. 'You shouldn't have. What's on your mind? I'm quite busy with this Charles and Camilla business so keep it brief.'

'What have you been hired for? Security?'

'Few levels above that. I don't ask the same question twice so blurt it out or I'm on the road.'

'You've been following me… '

'Being paranoid isn't gonna help you.'

'YOU HAVE BEEN FOLLOWING ME!' shouted Jamie, standing up from his chair. 'DON'T FUCKING DENY IT.'

Wallace eased the daisies out of Jamie's hand and smelt them. 'Hmm nice, where did you get these from? Near your house?'

'YOU FUCKIN' KNOW WHERE THEY CAME FROM. THEY WERE ON MY WHEELS. YOU PUT THEM THERE.'

'Calm down, Mr Scribe, you'll make yourself ill.'

'I'M NOT GOING TO CALM DOWN!' said Jamie, coming forward towards Wallace.

Wallace raised the palm of his hand towards Jamie like a PC directing traffic.

'You're seeing things, I understand,' he said. 'I gave you weapons for a good story and this is the thanks I get.'

'I'm going to give you one more chance: admit it was you… '

'Would I be here today if it was? Sit down and calm down. Give Dan Dare a call and get back to your news dungeon.'

'I'm fucking warning you… '

'Or what? You'll call the police. We own half of them.'

Jamie's eyes widened and he launched himself at Wallace who managed to brush him off easily. Jamie's knee smacked against a table causing excruciating pain. He tried to get at Wallace once more but the former copper merely kicked Jamie on the same knee with the sole of his boot. Jamie fell to the floor, clutching his knee in agony. The barman came rushing over to see what had happened. Wallace walked over to the table and put all four daisies into Jamie's empty glass. He pulled up his collars, which had sagged, and left Pub B.

Jamie was in a lot of pain but asked the barman to book a cab from Pub B to work. He hobbled into the newsroom and once he sat down the pain lessened. Danny was there but didn't approach him at all for the rest of the shift: an admission of guilt if there ever was one. The shift ended and Jamie got a cab from the newsroom all the way home – on expenses. He got in and raided his mum's cupboard (she was at Adam's) for a couple of Nurofen. He felt better for most of the evening and went to bed thinking he would be okay for work the next day. But when he woke up the next morning, the pain was unbearable and, this time, he had to ring Danny to tell him he wouldn't be in. It was a short call but Danny was much more sympathetic than Jamie expected. Jamie hired a cab to take him to A&E at Wycombe Hospital. He'd heard rumours that services at this hospital could be moved out of town. Was Trevena more in touch with common people than all the tabloid reporters put together? He sat in the waiting room for three hours before seeing a nurse. He wanted an x-ray but the nurse, after a thorough, laborious inspection of his knee, was adamant it was only severe bruising. He was sent home and advised to take painkillers and have plenty of rest.

The pain was vicious for the next couple of days. Tina came home and was annoyed he hadn't told her about his ordeal. He took two weeks off work, most of them in his bedroom watching Skinner and Baddiel DVDs, including *Unplanned* and *Fantasy Football 2004*. The throbbing and swelling lessened dramatically in the second week. He got back into the newsroom and Danny wanted to see him immediately. He got up and felt an uncomfortable twinge in his knee.

Danny asked Jamie to sit down on the swing in the car park of the newspaper offices. Jamie hesitated but then followed his news editor's instructions. With Jamie in position, Danny gave the swing a mild push. Danny looked around the car park and started whistling.

'You're turning into a sicknote; what's the problem?' said Danny.

'Wallace has been following me.'

Danny stopped the swing and genuinely looked surprised. He had it in his hands for a few seconds and then let go.

'You know Jammy, I had this swing placed here because young children are an inspiration,' said Danny. 'They're the best cub reporters in the world because they're never satisfied. My seven-year-old son has better journalistic and inquisitive skills than most reporters in this office. He likes to sit on his swing in the garden and give me tips – and most of the time he's right. So when I'm working on a challenging story, I like to sit out here and get into the true cub reporter spirit. It always works. I usually have 10 new stories after half an hour.' Danny gave the swing another push. 'I haven't been in contact with Wallace for at least six months. He's freelance so he's probably got other clients. Forget about him and concentrate on your own performance. You're falling apart and if you don't raise your game you'll be out on your ear. A man like me doesn't have time to deal with your paranoid theories.'

'I'm not paranoid. It's definitely him. How many clients has he got?'

'I don't fuckin' know. Find out. My son could do a better job than you.'

Jamie watched a female reporter sitting in her car furiously taking notes with a mobile phone perched on her shoulder.

'So it definitely wasn't you?'

'Man up, you wimp,' said Danny, looking at his watch. 'Some of us have got stories to do. I want a follow-up on those hoodies in south London.'

Danny pushed the swing hard and Jamie almost went horizontal. He held on as Danny walked away back to the office. After a couple of minutes of swaying to and fro, Jamie awkwardly jumped off the swing. He felt dizzy and disoriented for a few seconds. He fell to his knees and wanted to throw up but the ball of saliva in his mouth was gobbled up in the nick of time. He'd do anything to be a cub reporter again.

Hannah called Jamie round to her house. She was in an extremely good mood and cooked him lasagne for dinner topped off with carrot cake for dessert. Ted had been given some new medication which made him calmer and less erratic. As the evening wore on, Jamie's confidence grew. He felt this was his moment – and with Ted nicely tucked away, it was time to get serious.

'Do you want to go out tonight?' asked Jamie, helping to clear the dinner table.

'God, no,' replied Hannah. 'Why do you think I called you round? Because I've got something special for you.'

Jamie was convinced Hannah was about to pull out an engagement ring. He'd read a magazine article recently that claimed more and more women were buying their own engagement rings – something he was happy to be pragmatic about. Jamie placed the dishes into the sink and watched Hannah as she started washing up. He wiped his hands on her apron – and Hannah didn't stop him.

'Can you just check on Ted upstairs?' she said. 'The new pills are making him sleep for days.'

Jamie nodded and walked towards the door.

'Then you'll get what you've been looking for... '

Hannah settled down on the sofa with a mug of milk tea and three Bourbon cream biscuits. She slipped off her shoes and dipped one of the biscuits into the tea. Jamie sat down by her side after switching on the TV. She reached for the remote control and Jamie wondered what she was up to – he was beginning to get a sinking feeling that he'd misread her signals. She smiled at Jamie and then pressed play on the remote control.

Jamie was stunned to see a vivid image of a senior policeman, who he recognised as Assistant Commissioner Larry Anderton, calmly sitting at his desk, eating pomegranates with a plastic spoon while intermittently picking up a copy of *Police Review* magazine which was lying on the desk. After a few seconds, he put the magazine down and placed his hat over one of the pages as though he didn't want to see it anymore.

'I agree Miss Rocheman, MPs have a habit of not being able to keep their pants up,' said Anderton.

Hannah laughed and pressed pause on the remote. 'That's one of my favourite bits.' She pressed rewind. 'I love seeing it again.'

She watched it for a second time and then let the tape run on.

'We have all sorts of allegations against MPs,' said Anderton. 'But they're mainly immoral rather than illegal acts so there's not much we can do.'

'How the fuck did you get this?' asked Jamie, gawping at the screen.

'A bit of legwork and charm,' said Hannah. '... Amazed you can remember what they were.'

Jamie shook his head and looked perplexed.

'But how did you get access? We have to wait months to get interviews with these kind of people. Did the press officer organise it?'

'Proves that anyone can do your job, hey Jamie?'

Hannah laughed again and dipped another biscuit into her tea. She pressed pause on the remote.

'Don Leaver is still sending me messages,' she said. 'Got an email from him a couple of weeks ago. I was sick of it so I wrote directly to Mr Anderton saying this MP was harassing me. I didn't expect anything but he wrote back saying he was aware of the case and would we like to meet. So I took up his offer.'

'… And you took a secret camera in?'

'In my handbag, yeah,' she said, with a grin. 'I've learnt a lot with having to deal with your mob over the years.'

Hannah pressed play again.

'I really will look at this again for you, Miss Rocheman,' said Anderton. 'But unless it escalates, I'm afraid we might have our hands tied.'

'Which is what he wants me to do again,' said Hannah, with a smile.

'I apologise,' he said, with a chuckle. 'Not the best choice of words.'

'It's okay, at least you're doing something. Do you know Mr Leaver personally?'

Anderton's smile diminished. He finished his pomegranates and carefully placed the empty bowl under his hat. He pushed back the few strands of hair he had left on his head and then crossed his hands on the desk.

'I've met him a couple of times,' he said. 'He used to be on the Home Affairs Select committee. Lots of stuff on police reform and bureaucracy. A bit tiresome to be honest.'

'You didn't like him… '

'We got on fine. He was just a bit naïve on how all these changes would happen. These are giant, sacred institutions we're talking about. I suppose his behaviour after the court case against the tabloid was instructive. Instead of letting it all drop he's still stirring the pot by chasing after you.'

'… I do regret that story with the paper.'

Anderton raised his eyebrow. 'It made interesting reading

for the rest of us, I must say.' He tapped his hat. 'I really can relate to Mr Leaver's Napoleon complex but I'm afraid I don't deal in whips and waistcoats.'

'That Warren Fitton had a cheek going to town on it. Do you know him? I think he's the youngest editor in national papers.'

'Why do you ask?'

'Because he lost the case – and, strangely, I felt a bit sorry for him.'

'Yes, I do know him.'

'I suppose you work closely on some stories, help each other out, that kind of thing?'

'Many times – but it's the same with other papers. With Fitton, however, I do know him personally – and his wife Grace. She comes round to the house some nights to organise special Thai cookery evenings with my wife Denice.'

'Hope I can come round one night!'

'Be my guest. Grace and Denice have standards, though! A working class girl like you might have your work cut out! I know, because I'm a working class boy from Dagenham.'

They both laughed for at least a minute. Anderton picked his hat up and got out of his chair. He walked towards the window, put his hat on and looked outside.

'Do you think I should go back to Fitton?' asked Hannah. 'Make threats to get another story in. I've had lots of offers. Leaver doesn't understand anything else.'

'How much are they offering this time?' he asked, turning around to face Hannah.

'A lot. *The Sun* were offering close to a six-figure sum.'

'Hmm, tabloids are swimming in that stuff… '

'Has Fitton ever offered you any money?'

'If he did, I wouldn't be telling you would I, Miss Rocheman? You know this is a murky business. Money changes hands all the time. Just between you and me, there's quite a lot of traffic between the Met and the tabloids but that's just the way it is. We help each other out – and inevitably, at times, that brings its rewards.'

Anderton looked at his watch. He walked back towards the desk. 'My son's coming down to see me from Manchester. He's a barrister and the same age as you. He had all the opportunities in the world and seized them. I'll remind him that not everyone was born with a silver spoon in their mouth!'

Hannah paused the tape and finished off her drink.

'What are you doing?' said Jamie. 'Let it run?'

'Felt a bit sorry for him, here… '

'Don't waste your tears, he's fucking corrupt. Son is a barrister, whoopee doo, he's Fitton's chief fiddler.'

Hannah turned towards Jamie. 'Have we got enough, then? He's admitted there's a lot of traffic between tabloids and the Met… '

'How much more of the tape is there?'

'It ends in about 30 seconds… '

Jamie nodded and got up from the sofa. He walked closer to the TV and examined Anderton's face – which had been frozen on screen. He turned and faced Hannah.

'It's not enough evidence as it stands,' he said. 'Don't get me wrong, I'm well impressed with what you've done here – and he's made some startling admissions – but I don't think he's said or done anything illegal.'

'Yes, but he said money changes hands all the time… '

'It isn't enough.'

'I'll give it to Elliot… '

'He'll say the same thing. The Squires are even more wary of libel, contempt and all that stuff than we are. Tabloids can get away with more.'

'What about that MP you're working with?'

'Trevena? He'll be interested but you'll get similar reservations.'

The living room opened and Ted walked in, his sleeping suit slightly too big for him. He walked over to Hannah and sat down. She put her arm round his shoulder.

'I'll see what Elliot and Trevena have to say,' said Hannah. 'You've still got your tabloid head on so it's not cut and dried. If you're right though, it's bloody frustrating doing all that work and not having a story.'

'Join the club.'

14.

Major Currie Goes Down Nicely!

Jamie filed a small piece on Larna Wilson's play *The Princess Who Never Was* but it didn't get into the paper. In fact, he never saw the story again as it had been spiked somewhere along the laborious journey from reporter to chief sub. Jamie was thinking of calling Larna when he got home a few nights later but a more toxic issue was brewing. He was horrified to see his mother sat on the stairs in tears with a bottle of gin and a glass by her feet. He went over to sit by her side – and put his arm round her shoulder.

'Jesus Christ, what's up? We've only got weeks till the wedding. Come on, snap out of it.'

Tina picked up the bottle of gin and poured another glass. Just as she was about to take a drink, Jamie scooped it from her hands and took a drink himself.

'Hmm, got a good kick this one,' he said, licking his lips. 'I'll drink the whole fuckin' bottle if you don't tell me. It's about Adam isn't it?'

Tina gently put her hand over Jamie's and eased the glass towards her. She took a sip and leaned back.

'He wants to postpone the wedding,' she said. 'He's just come back from Aceh province and says it was so harrowing that he can hardly function, never mind prepare for a wedding. The relief effort took a lot out of him. I can tell he's lost weight.'

Jamie gently put his hands on top of his mother's. 'But you are still going to get married? It's only a delay. If he pulls out now, I'll swing for him.'

'Most of the preparation has been done for July 7. Gemma's already helped me with the dress and other things. He said he only needs a couple of months or so – but I'm scared he'll keep putting it off. He said he loves me but I'm not sure I believe that anymore.'

'Look mum, it's painful to see you like this. Get yourself together and I'll give him a call. We need to all pull together on the date that was agreed. If he was a journalist, he wouldn't last two seconds, with the amount of shit we have to put up with. We experience all sorts of horrors: murders, rapes, disasters, so why does he think he's any different? Thought he was a former soldier anyway? Come on, get yourself up.'

Tina got up awkwardly and Jamie ushered her to the kitchen where she sat at the table. Jamie called Adam but his phone was switched off. He made his mother a cup of black coffee and sat down by her side.

'I'm so desperate for this to happen, Jamie, I really am,' said Tina. 'I've been cursed for years... '

Jamie's mobile rang to interrupt Tina.

'CAN'T YOU FUCKING SWITCH THAT BLOODY THING OFF?' shouted Tina. 'I FUCKING HATE YOUR JOB SO FUCKING MUCH. RING! RING! RING! SOMETIMES IT DRIVES ME NUTS.'

Jamie calmly walked into the hallway and answered the call on the final ring.

'We may be able to run some of what Hannah Rocheman gave us,' said Elliot. 'I've seen the video and there's some interesting stuff there. Some of the quotes will go nicely into a story.'

'Anderton'll sue. I can't believe you're actually thinking of running something as flimsy as that.'

'Well, do you have anything better in terms of source material? It's the best we have so far. It's an admission by a senior copper that the tabloids and the Met have an understanding – and bundles of cash are part of this agreement.'

'When are you running the story?'

'Steady as she goes. However, you do understand we may have to use Hannah as a source. Did you say she was your girlfriend?'

'Do you ever remember anything?'

'I have a lot of stories to work on... '

'She is not my girlfriend.'

'All the easier to tell her about the consequences, then. This is a whole new ball game. If she is identified as the source then the Met's pigs won't just fly but they'll track her down by land, sea or cyberspace. Is she ready for that?'

'No – and I think she should abandon all this. But, as you know, I'm not her boyfriend so what can I say? She should tell you she wants nothing to do with your paper. Then we can just carry on our investigations. I'm sure we'll get big results soon.'

'You seem to be flip-flopping a lot. Got the John Kerry blues?'

'Who?'

'Doesn't matter. You sound more anxious than before.'

'Just got my hands full with my mother, that's all... '

'Give her my best. I want Hannah Rocheman's story to go in our paper. You need to come up with something strong to persuade me otherwise.'

'She's not credible after the Whipping Dictator story... '

'Most people don't even remember her name, they only remember Don Leaver and his ridiculous hat, waistcoat and whip. Those who do remember her name support her anyway.'

'She's a vulnerable woman, how about that?'

A shout could be heard from the kitchen. Jamie took the phone away from his ear.

Jamie placed the phone back towards his ear.

'Sounds like you're surrounded by vulnerable women,' said Elliot.

'Yeah, I'm about to become a bleeding heart too.'

Trevena had finally been handed Jamie's file of unethical tabloid behaviour which the MP labelled as the 'true dodgy dossier'. Jamie didn't even proof his copy – he would have felt sick having to read it more than once – and hoped Trevena would browse through it before presenting it to the Media, Culture and Select Committee in the House of Commons.

Trevena was in the middle of a general election campaign and Jamie nipped in to see him canvassing door-to-door. Jamie had already seen a few politicians out in the streets with their megaphones, brightly-coloured rosettes and leaflets but Trevena had none of that – he was a one-man band standing quietly at the door, hands in front of his lap, looking the householder in the eye. Jamie parked his car outside number 76 Milligan Street and walked up the path to greet Trevena as he spoke to an elderly woman holding a cat in her arms.

'Ah, Mrs Crawford, this is my assistant for today, Jamie, he's going to accompany me on my campaign rounds. I know you have an appointment at the vet's but I hope you can make it down to the polling station later…'

'Lovely to meet you, James.'

Jamie nodded and stood by Trevena's side.

'Keep fighting for us, Mr Trevena,' said Mrs Crawford. 'Please say something in parliament about that Royal Wedding. It was cruel.'

'I'll try. I'll also keep fighting to keep our services in the local hospital.'

'Never had to use it,' said Mrs Crawford, looking into the

cat's eyes and stroking it. 'Vet's more important isn't it, Mary?' She glanced up at the MP. 'Good luck, Mr Trevena. Hope the Independent party wins.'

'Thanks Mrs Crawford.'

She walked into her house and closed the door. Trevena and Jamie walked down the path and moved onto number 78. No-one was in so they moved onto number 80.

'You've done a good job on that dossier,' said Trevena. 'We've got plenty of material. A Miss Rocheman's been in touch – do you know her?'

'Afraid so… '

'I read about her in that seedy Whipping Dictator story so I was quite cynical but, I must say, she turned out to be pretty impressive once she laid out the reasons behind it. Anyone who looks after their sick father like that and can get the uptight Anderton to spill the beans deserves respect. We're meeting again. I understand she doesn't have a job so I have something in mind for her. Obviously, her father's situation permitting… '

'What kind of job?'

Trevena paused. 'Can you knock on this door? My knuckles are worn out.'

'Can't you post them a leaflet?'

'I don't have leaflets. For politics, they're useless. Only face-to-face contact works in local politics otherwise the chasm is unbridgeable.'

Jamie knocked on the door which had no doorbell, knocker or letterbox. A few seconds later, a dishevelled man appeared with spiky hair and a pierced nose.

'Fuck your WMD,' he said, and slammed the door shut.

Trevena and Jamie walked round to the next house at number 82.

'You didn't tell me what you've got in store for Hannah,' said Jamie.

'I've got a new campaigning charity in mind. Hospital services are moving out of town – or closing all together – round the country. Some heavyweight donors are already on our side. I think Miss Rocheman could bring a lot more – and she has first-hand experience of being a carer.'

'A kind of campaign or marketing manager?'

'Sort of… '

'She can't do it. She looks after her dad.'

'We'll see. As I said, it's still a proposal yet – and we haven't discussed it in detail.'

'So you have discussed it?'

'Yes. You seem to be quite obsessive about Miss Rocheman. Want to declare an interest?'

Jamie shook his head and pressed the doorbell on number 82. A couple came to the door together, middle-aged, with the woman wearing dark glasses and the man still in his shorts and white vest.

'Stop banging on about the fuckin' hospital, Trevena,' said the man. 'You got lucky by winning here because there's so many Type 2 diabetics needing treatment. This town's full of them. We want more police round here. Gangs have been causing havoc in this area for years. What are you going to do about that? We were burgled three years ago but where are the fuckin' culprits? You've got no solutions so I won't be voting for you. You're a one-issue, one-trick politician. In fact, I don't think I'll be voting for any of you cretins. Now fuck off, so we can enjoy our garden.'

The women smiled and waved before shutting the door. Trevena walked briskly down to number 84 with Jamie close behind.

'God, I thought we took some abuse,' said Jamie.

'We win on that score because you're locked in tabloid towers these days sitting in front of a screen, regurgitating PR piffle,' he said, with a smile.

Jamie didn't disagree and pushed the saw-like letterbox of number 84 a few times. A man appeared of about 50, well-dressed in dark blue jeans, pinstripe shirt and black v-neck sweater.

'Makes me laugh when I hear we need a debate on immigration,' he said, folding his arms and leaning against the door. 'We don't need one because we've already lost.'

'Who's lost?' asked Trevena.

'Me. Most of this street. The English-speaking majority. We've been abandoned and asked to hook our brains into clockwork capitalism. Immigrants are part of that – and now we're reaping the whirlwind with terrorist attacks and wars around the world. There'll be an attack on these shores, guaranteed.'

'But we're not like America, mate,' said Jamie.

The man laughed and looked at Jamie who felt extremely small. He shook his head and shut the door. Trevena looked at Jamie.

'You need some more training,' said the MP.

'Rather you than me,' said Jamie, with a smile. 'When are you publishing this dossier?'

They walked down the path and waited on the pavement.

'If I'm lucky enough to be re-elected, ASAP. If not then it might not have the weight and gravitas I'm hoping. But if I am, it's going to be presented to the CMS committee this summer, definitely before the recess. We've got some strong stuff – you've outlined all the phone interception, we've got Anderton and there's my findings too... ' Trevena put his hand on his head and then reached into his pocket for his mobile phone. '... Can't believe I nearly forgot this.'

'What?'

'We might have our Deep Throat... '

Adam was listening to music sitting in his front room when

Jamie arrived in his house in Beaconsfield. It sounded like a children's choir in a foreign language. Jamie sat down on the luxury green leather sofa and Adam acknowledged him but didn't say anything. Adam's hair was shorter, he had a cut near his chin and, as Jamie's mother had said, he definitely had lost a few pounds.

'A child of seven gave me this,' said Adam, finally breaking the awkward silence. 'He was in a group of 15 kids who sang together before the tsunami. He's the only one that made it. I went to the shack where he lived but even that had been destroyed: his mother and father were dead and his three sisters missing. But that wasn't the worst of it. When it was time for me to leave he pleaded with me not to go. He cried so much I haven't got over it. I left him there. I abandoned him.'

'Did he live in Aceh province?'

'It's a big place,' he said, turning to look at Jamie. 'It's like me saying does he live up North or down South.'

'What I mean is: that area was really badly hit unlike some other parts of Indonesia… '

Adam nodded and looked away out of the window again.

'There's a pointlessness about life when you see that kind of thing with your own eyes,' he said.

Jamie paused and absorbed the music for a few seconds. 'I've seen some bad things too.'

'Not on that scale.'

'Maybe… '

'There's no maybe about it.'

Jamie got up and walked towards the mantelpiece. He looked at an old framed photo of Robert and Rita outside The Chiltern Cinema in Beaconsfield.

'That cinema's closed now, hasn't it?' asked Jamie.

'What?'

'The old fleapit here in Beaconsfield. Shut down, hasn't it?'

'Ages go. Some time in the eighties. It's turned into a children's funhouse now.' Adam paused as the music stopped and another song started. 'Probably enough room for 1,000 kids from Banda Aceh.'

'You got plans to go out there again?'

Adam got up and walked towards the Pioneer stereo system in the corner of the room. He stopped the cassette and ejected it from the stereo.

'Do you want to take this tape home for a listen?' asked Adam.

'No Adam. Look, my mother thinks the wedding's off. You need to tell me, man to man, what the truth is.'

'Only been back a few days. I don't want to talk about this now.'

'But the wedding's in a few weeks. She's tearing herself apart.'

'Blokes only need a couple of day's preparation, you know that.'

'I haven't been that lucky yet.'

'Well, you're a hack, you believe in division not union.'

'Meaning?'

Adam walked back and sat on the sofa. He rubbed his finger over the Hitachi C60 cassette and looked up at Jamie.

'Your paper's coverage of the tsunami. It's just fuckin' evil, there's no other way of putting it. You went on about the lack of government response and slowness of the aid agencies like we were dealing with a plumbing leak in a kitchen. This was a horrific, apocalyptic scenario and we did everything we could – but all you could do was snipe from the sidelines and make wild accusations about people who are trying to help. It was sick, it nearly tipped me over the edge.'

'You read it all? Didn't think our paper got over there.'

'Read it when I came back. Tina gets your paper every week, as you know. The marriage plans only wobbled after I saw some of those stories. Not sure, I ever want to be associated with that.'

'I had no control over it.'

Jamie came back and sat next to Adam on the sofa, a bit closer than before.

'Only a few people know this but I'm working very hard to expose some of the darker goings-on in our industry,' said Jamie. 'If you're worried about what kind of family you're marrying into – and more precisely, what kind of stuff I'm engaged in – then those anxieties will be answered very soon. I'm not that man anymore. Please don't reject my mum. She wouldn't be able to take it.'

Jamie stretched out the palm of his hand. Adam looked surprised but pleased.

'It's the only way I'm going to learn about the things that matter,' said Jamie.

Adam placed the cassette in Jamie's hand.

'Your mother shouldn't worry,' said Adam. 'I don't break promises. July 7 it is. I love her and I always will.' Adam smiled and got up. 'But you better be right on your tabloid clean-up or else I'll take over and bash a few heads.'

'Won't be just bashed heads; they'll roll too.'

Larna called Jamie to say her play was a success but she had other news to break. She didn't care about the lack of media coverage because an American agent (in London for the Charles and Camilla wedding) had been in the audience and loved the play so much that he believed it could be developed in America, and, perhaps, even made into a film. Curiously, however, she almost sounded disappointed.

'I should have been born on the other side of the channel,' she said.

'So why are you going to America, then? Go to Paris.'

'What I mean is that growing up slap bang on the sea front

with that much water devouring your eyes, you always wonder what's on the other side. They take their arts a bit more seriously over there. I used to look out of the window, as a teenager, and hope a massive tide would swish me across.'

'At least you'd be clean. Heard they don't wash a lot over there...'

'Honestly, I don't know why I bothered calling. Look, I'm here to say goodbye because it's unlikely you'll ever hear from me again. I've got a brother-in-law in New York who I'm staying with for a while and then I'm going to look for my own place. I'm starting over.'

'So you don't care if your affair with the young Prince is never revealed?'

'You got it...'

'Bloody hell, you're already a Yank.'

Larna suddenly burst into laughter which surprised Jamie.

'Oh Jamie, Jamie, my poor little Jamie. Do you really think this is your story? That your journalistic digging got you a scoop?'

'What do you mean?'

'The number you originally called me on the first time we spoke, Lenny gave you that didn't he?'

'You know him?'

'Reply please...'

'Er, yeah, it was on a Post-it note, stuck on my computer. He said there might be a good story in it.'

'Lenny had been working on the story for a while. But when he was made redundant, he passed it off to you. He wanted to create the impression that it was all your own work. A bit like a parting gift.'

'Some gift. All I've had is aggro. But when he died, you weren't in the hospital or at the funeral.'

'Were you in hospital round-the-clock?'

'No.'

'Well then, how do you know I didn't visit?'

'... And the funeral?'

'I was there but when Fitton turned up, I disappeared. It was too difficult.'

'I want to know everything about Fitton, you and Lenny, right now. You can't vanish across the Atlantic and not tell me this. It's not fair on Lenny's memory.'

'There's nothing to reveal. I remember Lenny having to cover a book signing for *Harry Potter and The Goblet of Fire* very reluctantly. I was there with my 12-year-old niece Martha who was a bit of a Potter fanatic. It was before the phenomenon became really big – and I was a bit bored to be honest – but Lenny livened it up by asking people in the queue where they came from. Obviously, he was looking for far-flung places like Australia, Thailand and Venezuela. But when I got Martha's copy and we said St Leonard's, he laughed and said that's where my editor's from. I knew instantly who he was talking about. The last time I'd seen Fitton was when he was a showbiz reporter on the paper – and that's when things started going badly wrong... '

'What happened?'

Larna sighed and cleared her throat. 'I've talked too much already; I've got to start packing. Lenny has taken my secrets to the grave. He had his flaws but he was a good man. I'm sure you've learnt well from him. Make it up.'

'Wait, don't go. I'm going to do exactly as you asked. I'm making up a story. I'll tell you what happened and you'll confirm it yes?'

'Go on, but make it quick.'

'You and Fitton were childhood sweethearts and went to a school very close to each other.'

'Boring but true... '

'You were engaged to be married but something went wrong...'

'Too vague... '

'Through his contacts, you met the young Prince and he fell head over heels for you, causing Fitton to be jealous – and ending your relationship. Er, that's about it – although I've got to say you're coming out of this story as the two-timing sort.'

'I do like narrative detail – and this has none. Generally, you're in the right ballpark... '

'American shit again... '

'Get used to it. One detail is missing – and most women would like to keep that kind of thing private. You reporters couldn't find out about Edwina Currie's affair with Major so why do you think I'm easier meat?'

'Stop playing games – and just fucking tell me, will you?'

'I like stories, not games. See you in New York, one day.'

Larna hung up and Jamie felt like smashing the glass window with the phone. Jamie had to admit defeat in getting the Lar-Lar story out to the public once and for all. Yes, it was a great tabloid story but, having listened to Adam the other day, he had to keep things in perspective; he had overestimated its significance. Now it was time to forget about Larna and get back to the stuff that really mattered: the slush funds, the phone hacking and the fresh new name of Doctor Clifford Noonan, who was more Doc Hollywood than Deep Throat.

15.

Legless Legend Takes A Fall

Trevena had been re-elected with a smaller majority. Jamie was happy for him but the MP wanted to get to business straight away. A meeting with Noonan was set up but the doctor was initially reluctant to meet Jamie. Noonan couldn't understand why a tabloid reporter was interested in what he had to say. Finally, Trevena's persistence paid off and, after several weeks of phone calls and emails, Noonan agreed to meet Jamie only if he could choose the time, date and location. It was two days before Tina and Adam's wedding – in a pharmacy called *Median*. Noonan knew the pharmacist who ran the shop and he'd given permission for the doctor to sit in the small room at the back which had a small window and a table. Jamie came in through the back entrance and Noonan, who was drinking camomile and honey tea from a glass, didn't look up or say hello. The doctor, in a tweed hat, cardigan and brown bow tie, was looking out into the dispensing area as a pharmacist handed over another prescription to a patient. *Median* was like a mini-supermarket and Jamie's eyes hurt as he looked at the endless, gleaming rows of pills, bottles and health foods on display. He pulled up a chair and sat down.

'Did you see how obese that man was?' asked Dr Noonan, pushing his hat with his finger so it loosened a little. 'Over 270 pounds, at least. Slimming pills are not his problem.'

'… Thought you didn't want to see me.'

Noonan finally gave Jamie his full attention. He smiled and took another sip of tea.

'If my secretary was to turn on me and start briefing the media, that would be a better story than, if say, a reporter like you dug it up by conventional means,' he said. 'It's more fascinating when an internal division develops; it's more potent. I don't know what your gripes are but you've got some balls to take on your buddies... '

'Were you born in America?'

'What a personal question. No, Maidenhead, Berkshire, Great Britain, as it happens. Left at the age of 11 to go to America. Dad found work there in a healthcare company. Want to know about my wife, kids and pet llama too?'

Jamie shook his head and smiled. 'No. Not yet, anyway. But I hear you've got clinics here and in the States... '

'Two in LA, one in New York, one in London, Three in Rome... want me to go on?'

'Tell me some of your big-name clients... '

'What, so members of their entourage can lay me out? No, I'm here to shine a light on your business, not mine. I've done some terrible things – and temptation is the greatest addiction of all – but let's be clear who dangles the carrots here... '

'Okay, what procedures did you carry out? Plastic surgery? Botox?'

'I facilitated some of them, yes. I referred others. One Hollywood actor, who gobbled $15million for his latest blockbuster, came to me and wanted to do something about his double chin. Good looking chap, too. Another wanted valium on tap. A third just wanted to talk and talk and talk, a fourth wanted a nose job... '

'But what about here in Britain?' said Jamie, interrupting. 'We're not that precious, surely?'

'Don't bet on it. Susan, who runs the clinic for me in London, says the Brits are gloomier than anyone on the planet. They need bigger kicks.'

Noonan then surprised Jamie by pulling out a bottle of pills from his pocket. He slid them across the table towards Jamie.

'Not me,' said Jamie, raising his hand. 'I don't need that kind of kick.'

'It's not for you,' said Noonan, taking his hat off and placing it carefully by his glass of tea. 'It's the reason you're here today.'

'Is it someone's medication?'

'My son's. He was 23 when he committed suicide.'

Noonan paused and ran his fingers around the rim of his hat. He took another drink and looked away from Jamie.

'Jake went to a lot of Hollywood parties and got caught up in drugs and money troubles. He wanted to be an actor so much it hurt – but things didn't work out for him. He became addicted to Tryptizol, Valium and cocaine.'

Jamie was about to ask a question but thought better of it. There was a long silence and another little drink.

'I introduced him to all of that,' said Noonan. 'When I was helping patients with their medical needs, I felt very little emotion, it wasn't worth it. But when Jake died, the guilt came on like a freight train. It was overwhelming. I had to shut my clinics in LA for five months.'

Noonan looked up at the pharmacist dispensing medicine to another patient.

'Losing Jake has made me reassess my values. He wasn't a bad boy, he just got into the wrong environment. But I've been both. I've been bad, really bad and I'm also in a terrible environment. That is going to change from today, onwards.'

'How did you know Fitton?' asked Jamie.

'Look at that woman,' said Noonan, pointing at the mother-of-four by the counter. 'My guess is she's got arthritis. All that fish oil.'

'… I asked you about Fitton.'

172

'Never met him. I deal with Callum Gordon. He's the one who asks for all the medical records, their procedures and what they have for dinner.'

'… And you gave them to him?'

'For a price… '

'How much?'

'Never less than five figures. Four figure fees in dollars isn't much when you're in London.'

'Was it just medical records you passed on?'

'Isn't that enough? That would include medication details, home addresses, cell numbers, family details, occupation, the works. The angles are limitless.'

'Did you meet Gordon face to face?'

'Only once, here in London. Had dinner with his family.'

'He's got a family?'

'You didn't know?'

'Kids?'

'Three knockouts… '

Jamie shook his head and looked embarrassed. He picked up the bottle of pills and examined it.

'So I hope this is going to mean, how do you guys say it, full disclosure?'

Noonan nodded and eased the bottle of pills out of Jamie's hand. He put them in his pocket.

'Medication has never been the solution,' he said. 'I've always known that. But why did I have to suffer the bitterest pill of all to realise that?'

A couple of nights before his mother's wedding, Jamie got a strange email from Wallace, apologising for all the 'funny business' and offering him free tickets to the Ashes Test match at Lords. Jamie didn't like cricket and politely declined the offer. Jamie accepted Wallace's apology and the former copper replied with the greeting 'Yo' which Jamie found slightly unusual. Irrespective, Jamie was relieved because it was a huge weight off his shoulders.

Gemma had been helping Tina with all the preparations so Jamie stayed out of the way most of the time. In fact, Gemma's presence only heightened Jamie's feeling for someone else: Hannah. Adam wasn't having a stag night (for obvious reasons) so that meant Jamie was freed up to give his full attention to Hannah. She had been invited to the wedding and was due to come to Jamie's house and stay over (with Ted) the night before the wedding. But she didn't turn up. Jamie called but she didn't answer. It was too late for Jamie to drive to her house. On the morning of the wedding with Jamie feeling extremely uptight in his butterfly collar, red bow tie and new shoes, he got a call from Elliot. Jamie had pulled into the car park at the Bull Hotel in Gerrards Cross where the ceremony was being held – and had already been sat in his car, stewing for 15 minutes.

'Hannah Rocheman's been arrested,' said Elliot. 'She spent last night in a cell. As far as I know, she's still in there.'

'On what charge?'

'Not sure there is one yet, lots of suspicion of this, suspicion of that but nothing concrete. Obviously Mr Anderton didn't like being caught with his trousers down. Probably, a case of a dictator asking his secret police to extract some revenge.'

'Look, I'm at my mother's wedding. I don't want to fuck things up for her. I'm staying here all day, whatever happens. Did you actually run the Anderton story in the end? I don't read the Squires, as you know.'

'Which is a big deficit in your life. No, I was waiting to get a right of reply from Anderton but it hasn't been forthcoming. There's a bit of self-censorship going on in all papers. Even my editor's sceptical about these kind of stories.'

'He should have run it anyway… '

'We will. Look, I will make some more calls to see what's going on with Miss Rocheman.'

'Do you know what's happened to her father?'

'No.'

'Okay, listen, call me if there's an update. I'm afraid I'm going to be out of action all day. It's the least I can do for my mum.'

'Who's the lucky man?'

'Adam, a former solider. He's now a human rights campaigner. He's just come back after helping out in the tsunami in Indonesia.'

'Sounds impressive. Is he younger than your mother?'

'Six years, you nosey bastard.'

'Ah, middle age is a desert. No problems there.'

'God, I don't know what you're on about half the time... '

'I do – and it's this: If your girlfriend is released, I'll call you.'

'SHE'S NOT MY FUCKIN' GIRLFRIEND. How many times have I got to tell you? And why are you so interested in it anyway?'

'Because I've never had a girlfriend... '

'You sad man.'

'I like boys. I'm living with a rather grown-up one now. Hope your mother has a wonderful day – and years of bliss. Speak to you soon.'

Elliot hung up and Jamie didn't even think about the Squires' reporter's love life: he was more concerned about keeping Ted and Hannah's troubles away from his mother's special moment.

Tina and Adam had discussed having a church wedding rather than a civil ceremony but as Jamie sat in the packed Chalfont Suite inside the hotel he wondered why. Everything was here: the guests, the setting, the facilities, the food; so why bring religion into it? Once Adam returned from Aceh there really was no debate at all – he claimed he never wanted to set foot in a church ever again although Jamie didn't quite believe him.

Adam looked as though he'd put all that behind him as he gently held Tina's hand with the grace of a ballet dancer. She looked 15 years younger and Jamie would have been happy for *Hello* or *OK* magazine to be here snapping away getting their spreads under the headline '48 and great'. A boost in circulation was guaranteed.

A smooth Chiltern Hills registrar was ready to ease the marriage vows from Tina and Adam's lips. Jamie settled down. The atmosphere was electric. But five minutes later, as he watched his mother begin her nervy repetition, he got a call on his mobile (which he'd kept on for an update on Hannah).

'You need to come in,' said Danny. 'There's a big terrorist attack at Kings Cross, Edgware Road and fuck knows where. We need everyone in. You can take holidays later.'

'But it's my mum's wedding. Booked it off ages ago.'

'A power surge was blamed but it's more likely to be a suicide bombing. This isn't the pipsqueak IRA we're talking about. It could be the big one. I'll give you a couple of hours because the city's roasting.'

'… People dead?'

'At least 20, probably more.'

'I knew you'd do this to me. They've just started the marriage vows.'

'I'll just be clear with my own vows. I NEED YOU – I FUCKING DO. You've got two hours.'

Danny hung up and Jamie looked round the suite. The guests were transfixed by the ceremony, like a theatre audience watching a gripping play in silence. Jamie looked at the mannequin-like figures of Tina and Adam one last time and slipped out of The Bull Hotel.

Fucking carnage was the best way to describe what Jamie could see on the TV screens when he got into the office. Religion again, what a surprise. He'd already made his mind up on a civil ceremony if his day ever came. Christianity may have nothing to do with these horrors but they were all the same: poisonous and divisive. If it was up to Jamie they'd all be banned.

He got to his desk and there was still an emergency conference going on in Fitton's office. When Danny came out, he asked Jamie to spend the rest of the day compiling a round-up of all the emergency services and how they'd heroically reacted to this major event. The atmosphere in the office was gloomy. Many of the staff had family working in and around the affected areas. Jamie found it hard to concentrate and the lack of response to his calls – which was expected in the circumstances – didn't improve matters. When 9/11 happened, Jamie had felt exhilaration mixed in with a nervous anticipation – pretty standard, he felt, for a news reporter covering a major story. But this time, there was no exhilaration – just cold, hard anger. He felt angry at having to leave his mother's wedding – but it was nothing compared to what he felt now.

Hannah had been released the day after the attacks but Jamie could only call her, not visit, because he was too busy. He promised he would come round to see her soon but, in the meantime, he had to be content with Hannah's version of events that Anderton had called out his dogs to arrest her on trumped-up charges. He wanted to teach her a lesson, she said. He'd done that all right because Ted was back in hospital, on a drip for two days, because there was no-one to care for him. Hannah was seriously concerned that Ted would be taken away from her. Anderton's mob had already got the local council involved. Jamie didn't want to hear anymore – it was too depressing.

Trevena called to say there was a new political reality but Jamie was already well aware of it. Yes, phone hacking and illegal payments in the tabloid press were important but they had shifted to one side by 7/7 and, then later, 21/7. Trevena had presented his report to the CMS committee with little fanfare and it had been met with a shrug of shoulders from most of the MPs. It went on all the time, they said, what could they do? Jamie agreed with Trevena that they were facing a long, hard slog again: the spectre of suicide bombers crawling across the country, particularly homegrown ones was a huge escalation and would take precedence. Yet again, there had to be a reassessment, a delay, a pause; until the authorities decided it was time to turn their attention to the darker elements of the media. Until then, those same media organs were being relied on, in times of crisis, to show the way, unite the country and be a trusted source to an anxious public needing reassurance and guidance. Jamie was proud of the coverage in his own paper but knew some of the transcripts from victim's families, paramedics and the police came from hacked phones. He had drawn a line in the sand but Danny had a 'whatever it takes' policy and there were enough reporters in the newsroom to please him.

The terrorism stories came thick and fast and Don Leaver was one of the first public figures to cause a stir. He claimed he'd been misquoted after saying that Muslim sympathisers should be deported out of the country. Leaver said he meant 'terrorist' sympathisers not Muslim. As usual, he didn't like to talk to the reporter in question but liked to go up the chain of command, this time to Fox-Tucker, who agreed to a clarification.

In this kind of atmosphere, it was impossible not to absorb the low-level anxiety on public transport. Jamie had to admit he started looking at some of the faces on the Tube with more suspicion than before. Anyone of a Black or Asian background

– and he admonished himself for being so crude – was getting a second look, particularly if they were carrying a big bag or a rucksack. This feeling wasn't just confined to London. Back at home, Jamie even had strange thoughts about Larnell. Was he Muslim? He did come from the same background as one of the bombers so anything was possible. To try and banish these thoughts, Jamie went to see Guy Ritchie's new film *Revolver* at the cinema for some well-needed escapism. Larnell came too and but the film simply turned Jamie's head to mush – and that was the last thing he wanted.

Luckily, Tina and Adam's marriage was going well. They went to the south of France for their honeymoon and Tina was feeling so good she forgave Jamie for disappearing during the ceremony. But Adam still had his hands full with his work: Hurricane Katrina, the Bali Bombing and the Kashmir earthquake all happened within weeks of each other and he did admit to feeling utterly inadequate and wondered if he was making any difference at all.

Tina was spending all week in Beaconsfield with Adam – and only weekends back in Amersham. She had reduced her hours at the brewery and started helping Adam out with his work simply because he needed an extra pair of hands. This created a new problem for Jamie. She had transferred most of the bills and the mortgage to him. It was a shock to the system. Had he been naïve? There were no financial problems but the cost of everything was much more than he expected. Sitting in an empty house going metronomically through the gas bill in crushing silence wasn't his idea of being in the thick of the action. He was feeling lonelier than he'd ever felt. He missed his mother.

Two things shook him out of his despondency. The first was George Best, even though he had just died, and the second was the reawakening of WarFit. When the news broke that Best had died, Jamie felt no sadness at all but a kind of elation that made him want to celebrate the man's life despite his self-destructive tendencies. The paper went big on him – cleared out the first 12 pages and a supplement – and Jamie pored over every word. Jamie didn't think he was a hero and found his drinking exploits a bit silly but there was a reassurance about his story that restored a bit of faith after all the talk about religion, terrorism and 'our way of life'. As far as Jamie could see, Best encapsulated our way of life: play the game hard, earn success, don't settle, relish banter and accept the world of liqueur and tabloids is part of the island's DNA, like it or not. This was a world that had taken a knock because of the homegrown terrorist attacks but the Best story meant some light was beginning to emerge. Jamie had to admit, however, there was a huge gender split in the office about Best's life and legacy. Most of the blokes related to him – the women rarely did.

The second thing to reenergise Jamie was Ted being taken into care because the authorities felt Hannah wasn't providing adequate support for him. Hannah felt this order had come from the very top of the Met and was finally ready to go public – the first time she was willing to speak to the media since the Don Leaver case. Elliot had a big spread in mind – and had been given the go-ahead by his news editor. Jamie felt this was his opportunity too. Elliot had wanted him to become 'the tabloid source' for the Squires since they had first spoken – and now he felt the time was right because the Met's dirty tricks had to be answered. He calculated they had Noonan, Anderton, Hannah and himself as solid sources and that was only a start. The WarFit files were long and detailed – and Jamie was determined to break them. He had to start speaking to the Squires, anonymously, and give Elliot everything he wanted. It was a huge risk, as he now had responsibilities at home, but he had to dig deeper and start playing the game hard – in the spirit of good old Georgie Best.

16.

Gloves Off When Love Comes To Town

Elliot had promised a surprise in the Squires coverage of tabloid wrongdoing and Jamie wasn't disappointed. Elliot sent a copy of the broadsheet direct to Jamie's house just to ensure he saw it; he knew Jamie was a little slack in reading other papers apart from his own. But in a note attached to the paper, the Squires' reporter wanted Jamie to read another article first on a different page – about the death of Richard Pryor. Elliot said he was a hero of his but Jamie only knew of him through films like *Stir Crazy* and *Brewster's Millions*. Jamie read the piece and was drawn to the late passages on MS, which Pryor suffered from. It made him think about Ted – and how he was coping with a similar, cruel condition.

After this eye-opening detour, Jamie moved on to the business at hand. He expected Elliot to do a good job on the usual suspects (Noonan, Anderton, Hannah and himself) but he was impressed with the revelations in two other key areas. Jamie hadn't known anything about them. The first was under the heading 'The Three Omegas' and claimed that three people working for separate mobile phone firms were actually in the pay of Callum Gordon. He called them Mr Orange, O2Joy and VodaSkoda and paid them five-figure sums to hand over customer details, bills and celebrity numbers. The second was about a man using the alias Safe Hands who worked for the DVLA and, he too, had contacts with Gordon. It was alleged that Safe Hands passed on details about speeding fines, points, licences and car registrations. Elliot had tried to call Gordon for a response but he wasn't available. Throughout all these stories, Fitton's name weaved in and out like a smooth Formula One car nipping through the chicane – but there probably wasn't enough to pin him down; yet.

Jamie read his own story again. It was strange to see his words quoted anonymously. He used to get extremely annoyed when sources didn't want to be named – yet here he was conveying the dark arts of tabloid journalism doing precisely that. The words floated in the air and had a ghost-like quality. The story was only nine paragraphs long and there were no personal details at all about Jamie. Still, he knew the shit would hit the fan because, even though he didn't name names, the reputation of the paper (or at least the bosses who worked there) was being tarnished by one of its employees. As far as Jamie was concerned, he was doing his duty – a duty to speak out against a dizzying power that was spiralling out of control. He went back and reread the Richard Pryor story. He admired the bravery of anyone going up on stage trying to engage an audience. Pryor was brilliant at it – but that's what was missing in the current hacking tale: the punters weren't engaged. Most people didn't care if tabloids were up to no good as long it was the great and good who were getting in the neck: celebrities, politicians and pop stars. The tabloids needed to lay into someone sacred and ordinary. Jamie didn't want this to happen but believed it would be a game changer.

Jamie counted the number of staff in Fitton's office, including himself. There were 32 crammed in with reporters, feature writers and the odd sub joining most of the showbiz team. Thankfully Danny wasn't there but Fox-Tucker, tapping his pen on his chin, was stood in the corner watching like a hawk. Fitton was sat behind his desk and slowly pulled out a copy of the Squires from one of his drawers. Jamie felt his heart sink and was thankful the two rows in front of him could act as human shields.

'Whichever fucker did this... ' said Fitton, pausing and looking up. '... I'll hunt you down. I could sack the lot of you but we need to get a paper out. We've had moles before, Matt Armistead was the last one and we carted him out. I know you've all got gripes but I suspect each and every one of you. If you don't like tabloid newspapers then fuck off to the Squires like Louise Dorrans did. If she was here, she'd probably be in this office on her own right now.'

'You're libelling all of us, we could sue you,' said Jimmy Betson.

'How did you get that story on the TV presenter doing e's?' said Fitton.

'... The usual, got some quotes from a good source.'

'From his phone?'

Jimmy didn't answer.

'Precisely,' said Fitton. 'That's why I don't trust any of you fuckers. You're all up to your necks in it. Now, get the fuck out and find me some heroes for Unsung Britain. Better still, if they shopped a suspected terrorist.'

'But it's probably just one of the guys you made redundant having a pop,' said Jimmy. 'They're still not too happy about losing their jobs.'

'... Still got that contact on *The Express*, have you Jim?'

'Yes, he gives me good stories... '

'And what do you give him? Exclusives? I won't repeat myself. All of you, fuck off – or Fox-Tucker will become editor forever.'

There was a moment of silence and then most of the staff trooped out of the office. Jamie was astonished at what he'd just heard. The bitterness, suspicion and underhand dealings ran much deeper than he could have ever imagined. How come there were so many disillusioned staff on the paper?

Were they all feeding our rivals or was Fitton just paranoid? As Jamie left the office, he felt emboldened rather than intimidated. This was no time to relieve the pressure. He had seen a side of Fitton that he hadn't really seen before – and wanted to see more of it.

It didn't take long for Elliot's piece to be given the tabloid treatment. Most of the papers claimed Hannah was an unreliable source, which Jamie had expected, but Jamie's own paper had a more disturbing take on Dr Noonan. In a non-bylined piece, it claimed Noonan had helped section his wife – giving her heavy drugs and almost killing her on a couple of occasions. Jamie tried to shrug off the piece but it gnawed away at him for a couple of days before he called Trevena first and then Elliot to see if it was true. They knew nothing about it – so he called Noonan himself. He didn't want to speak over the phone and wanted to meet at the pharmacy again. Jamie eventually agreed to meet early in the morning. Noonan had all the papers which covered the story laid out on the table when Jamie arrived.

'They're very sensitive these tabloids,' said Noonan, with a smile. 'The pathological streak runs deep. I expected some criticism, of course, but this is wild.'

'Did you section your wife?'

'I gave a medical opinion, that's all. She never got over Jake's death. It sent her into a deep depression. One night, she locked herself into the bathroom and the fire service had to be called out. Another, she blamed me for introducing Jake to the wrong sort of people and attacked me with some garden shears. I tried to help with some medication but it just made her more angry.'

'Where is she now?'

'In a special unit. I know some of the staff there. They're very dedicated.'

184

'Why the fuck didn't you tell me this before?'

'Do you want to talk about your girlfriend – or mother?'

'It's none of your business.'

'Exactly – and that's why I didn't want to talk about it. There is a line of privacy that tabloids just don't understand. Even with my years of experience of damaged lives and patient traumas, seeing my family fall apart in a similar way was hard to take. So please save me your moral high ground trick.'

Noonan looked genuinely annoyed and one of his shoulders had a slight tremor. He turned to look at a man, with an awkward gait, who was carrying two bottles of calcium supplements pills towards the counter. He dropped one of the bottles and it rolled a few yards away towards a small child who was with his mother. The child picked up the bottle and ran off with it down the aisle.

'He's probably got osteoporosis,' said Noonan. 'The supplement's his lifeline. He wants to keep things serious: the kid wants fun. A Squire and a Daisy, right there... '

'He's too working class for a Squire. Look, I hope this isn't going to stop you speaking out. We've got some momentum going now. So we want to keep chipping away.'

'... I've only just started.'

'Good. Have you heard of any of these names: Mr Orange, 02Joy and VodaSkoda?'

'No, should I have? Sounds like they need a name change.'

'They're on Callum Gordon's list. He's got a few... '

'A few? You must be joking. He's got thousands of the bums working for him, feeding him information.'

'Thousands? I can't believe it.'

'If you don't believe, you'll never get to the bottom of it.'

Jamie felt extremely guilty when he finally met Hannah at the care home. He was stood with Hannah in a nicely-lit room watching Ted and seven other elderly people doing an extremely mild dance to BJ Thomas' *Raindrops Keep Falling on My Head*. Ted had settled in well which surprised Jamie because of his experience with him but perhaps Hannah had been too hasty in not considering this kind of environment for him in the first place. Hannah, who was eating a mint Aero and drinking hot chocolate from a plastic cup, smiled as she watched Ted put his hand on Ellie's shoulder.

'God, they get on well,' said Hannah, offering Jamie a piece of chocolate.

'No, not for me. Maybe there's still time for wedding bells?'

Hannah turned to look at Jamie. 'I would have loved to come to the Bull Hotel to see your mum in that gorgeous white dress. How's she doing now? Adam a good fella is he?'

'He cares – and that's what matters to mum. They live together most of the time, they've been abroad, you can't ask for more. Look, I'm sorry I couldn't help you get released earlier or come down to the house… '

'Yes, I know,' she said, finishing off her Aero and neatly folding the wrapper in her hand. 'Terrorism. It's the excuse for everything these days: wars, busy journalists and people getting arrested… '

'What are you on about? Didn't they arrest you because of the honeytrap sting that you did?'

Hannah looked at her father again. He raised his arms up in the air ever so slowly and turned around on the spot. Ellie watched him and did the same.

'I never put my arms in the air, like dad,' said Hannah, with a smile. 'The Maliks who lived three doors down from me, the ones who gave me some nice recipes, whose curry you enjoyed… '

'Yes… '

'Coppers thought their son might have something to do

with terrorism so that's why they arrested me. Just to ask a few questions, of course.'

'No, fuck that. Even they wouldn't go that far.'

Hannah gave Jamie a resigned look. It was as though he could see the night she spent in a cell for the first time. Jamie moved towards Hannah and put his arm on her shoulder.

'I'm really sorry about that. It's obscene what some of these fuckers are doing right now. We're going to town on them, don't worry about that. You should carry on doing those kind of stings. Fuck them, I'll help you out. I think you could be a good journalist. You, me, Trevena and Elliot, we're an unbeatable team.'

Hannah clapped as the song finished. Ted bent down and gave Ellie an awkward hug. Hannah wiped away a tear from her eye.

'Journalism isn't for me, nor is working in department stores. I've been working for Trevena's new charity as campaign director for a couple of weeks now. I'm enjoying it but I only agreed to do it because dad's in a better place now. I was totally against bringing him to a place like this – but Trevena recommended this one – so I agreed to have a look. He was right so it's freed me up to start full-time work again. We've already raised thousands of pounds because people want to keep health services local.'

A care supervisor ushered Ted, and the other residents, out of the room.

'When can we have dinner again?' asked Jamie. 'Both our houses are empty now. You can tell me more about your campaigns.'

Hannah looked over her shoulder. 'We'll see. I'm a bit busy. I've got some big ideas in mind.'

Jamie was certain his mobile phone was being hacked. Peeper Wallace, who Jamie wrongly thought had sent him previous emails about Ashes tickets, sent him two further emails (these looked genuine) which had exact transcripts of Jamie's phone conversations with Elliot. Jamie called Wallace to ask him what he was playing at – but he would only discuss the initial emails which he claimed must be a hoax.

'Aren't you up with the internet?' said Wallace. 'Accounts are hacked all the time. I sent you no emails about cricket.'

'You've made your point. What about these fresh emails?'

'... It won't go any further if you pay a one-off fee. Danny or Fitton won't be told you've been doing the dirty on them.'

'I've been doing no dirty. That's you. I won't be paying. We're closing in you.'

'Who? You and that MP's army? Give it a rest, journo.'

'Your greasy fucking arrangements are going to come crashing down.'

There was a pause on the line. Wallace cleared his throat and gathered himself.

'Okay, how much are you willing to cough up?'

'Changed your tune... '

'I don't change tunes, I make music by banging heads together. How much?'

'Fuck all... '

'Give me five grand – and I'll walk away forever.'

'Never.'

'Do you want me to get Stalky-Walky on your little botty again?'

'That was big and hard wasn't it? Putting flowers on the wheels?'

'Bit of improvement, I'd say. Don't you remember what happened to your kneecap last time?'

'Danny won't stand for me being off sick for that long again. He'll come down on my side rather than yours.'

'Oh yeah, he hasn't come down on his wife for years so what makes you think he'll turn soft all of a sudden?'

'We're part of the same trade, that's why. Go and trawl some rubbish like Barnaby Bin.'

Jamie hung up and breathed a sigh of relief. He immediately called Danny and set up a quick meeting with him in the morning.

Danny rushed into the training room, speaking into a mobile. He was unshaven and looked harassed. Jamie was sat at the table waiting patiently with a small tape recorder. Danny ended the call and sighed.

'What do you want, Jammy?' said Danny. 'Make it quick, we're snowed under.'

Jamie pressed play on the tape recorder. A small excerpt of the conversation between Wallace and Jamie was heard. Danny folded his arms and looked bored. Jamie raised his hand, asking Danny to be patient. Jamie had erased most of the conversation apart from the last few lines. As Wallace was about to say the killer line, Jamie felt a surge of excitement.

'... Danny hasn't come down on his wife in years... '

'Where's the rest of the tape?' asked Danny.

'It's all I've got.'

'Don't fuck with me... '

'Honestly, there's a little bit more but it's boring stuff.'

'Why's he after you?'

Jamie shrugged his shoulders. Danny tapped the mobile on his chin and walked towards the tape recorder. He rewound it and listened again.

'... Danny hasn't come down on his wife for years... '

Danny stopped the tape and calmly presented it to Jamie. But just before the handover, he flung it across the room and smashed it against the window. He pointed at Jamie to leave the room. Danny picked up the tape recorder – and followed him out.

Jamie bought a new mobile phone: a Sony Ericsson with a nifty, pocket-like camera. He put in a new security code – his mother's age added to his own. The first number he called was Elliot, who was amazed he'd kept his old phone for so long.

'I've changed mine six times in the last three years,' said Elliot. 'There is the argument that old contacts can't get hold of me in an emergency but that's better than being snooped upon. Who hacked it? Do you know?'

'Wallace, I think. He wanted cash to leave me alone.'

'Well, it is the silly season with these bird flu stories. How did you wriggle out of that one?'

'I haven't yet – but there is a plan. Got any more on Miss Orange or VodaSkoda? And what's the other one?'

'O2Joy… '

'What the fuck does that mean?'

'… Heard of Beethoven?'

'… Yes.'

'Ode to Joy.'

'What? Sorry, don't know that one. So have you got anything or not?'

'I'm meeting Miss Orange in a café in Uxbridge… '

'How did you track her down?'

'I didn't. She contacted me. She saw the stories we did in our paper where we named Callum Gordon. She initially wanted to be a friend on Facebook – and things went from there… '

'Facebook, yeah, heard about that round the office. Showbiz desk are always banging on about it.'

'How many friends have you got?'

'I'm not on it. You?'

'134. You should get on it immediately. Lots of leads. Anyway, how did Fitton respond to one of his charges being quoted anonymously in a broadsheet?'

'Not well. He took about 30 of us into the office.'

'30! All up to no good?'

'So he says. Maybe he's bluffing. I don't trust anyone anymore.'

'Even me?'

'You're a Squire – but I can make an exception.'

'Well, trust this: The Information Commissioner is releasing a report imminently called *What Price Privacy*. I've already seen a copy and the Daisies are near the top of the list for using PI's.'

'... And the Squires?'

'Near the bottom, of course.'

'Look, the PI stuff isn't really news to me. Is Trevena doing anything with it?'

'Well, yes, but the earmuffs are on around him. Not to worry, we've got some more material to publish with this privacy report – are you up for some more anon quotes?'

'Depends what you're asking?'

'More on this Peeper Wallace character. He seems to be everywhere.'

'I'd hold your horses on him – that story's got further to run.'

Jamie squinted a few times just to ensure he wasn't dreaming. He was astonished, as he stood in the paper's car park, along with eight colleagues, to see Danny and Peeper Wallace engaged in a brutal fist fight by the swing. Jamie hadn't moved since he locked his car, about five spaces from where the action was taking place. Colleagues inched forward tentatively, some aghast, some terrified and some simply gawping with the whites of their eyes bulging. Wallace was about two inches taller than Danny but was finding it hard to cope with the news editor's skilful ducking, rapid counter-punching and sly kick-boxing moves. Wallace landed a few blows but didn't want it as bad as Danny – and that gave the news editor the edge. Danny's eyes were as wild as when he wanted an exclusive in an hour – and he landed one blow which seemed to deaden Wallace's shoulder. Wallace collapsed in agony, clutching his left arm. Danny sensed his advantage and waded in with a few meaty punches and hefty kicks. He sat down behind Wallace and grabbed him in a headlock. Danny tightened his hold and squeezed Wallace's neck. Wallace's lip was bleeding and he checked if some of his teeth were still there.

'This is my arena,' said Danny. 'I can fight you in front of eight or 8,000, I'll still win. You cannot insult Suzanne and get away with it. Now lie the fuck down.'

Wallace awkwardly lay down on the harsh concrete. Danny got on top of him and put his knees on Wallace's arms.

'Aaarhgh… ' screamed Wallace. 'Get the fuck off my arm.'

Jamie flinched but couldn't take his eyes off the extraordinary spectacle.

'Now, am I coming down on you?' asked Danny.

'Yeees… '

'I CAN'T FUCKIN' HEAR YOU.'

'YES. I DIDN'T MEAN IT, FOR FUCK'S SAKE. I LOVE YOUR WIFE… '

'WHAT?'

Danny stuck his knees deeper into Wallace.

'The problem with corrupt ex-coppers is they get too greedy – eat too much, drink too much and their bodies pack up on them. Take a bit less money – and you might get back into shape. Now apologize to Suzanne… '

'… She's not here.'

Danny took his mobile out of his pocket and called Suzanne.

'Hello, honey, this fella's got something to say to you… '

'Okay love, put him on.'

Danny stuck his mobile firmly against Wallace's ear.

'Er, hello, Mrs Love. I'm sorry for what I said about Danny and you... '

'Don't do it again. When he told me, it genuinely hurt. Saying sorry is a good thing. It can be a healing process. Now put Danny on... '

Danny took the mobile away from Wallace and eased it back towards his ear.

'Can you pop into the chemist on the way back and pick up some cough syrup for Molly,' said Suzanne. 'She's had a flare-up again.'

'Course. I love you more than ever.'

Danny ended the call and finally looked around the small crowd. He allowed himself a mild smile and fixed his eyes on Jamie.

'Jammy, I'll be eternally grateful to you for this. A woman's honour has to be upheld. Stories come and go but family units are rock solid. You've done a great deed. All give Jamie a round of applause... '

Jamie's colleagues looked at him in a state of bewilderment. Jamie was equally bemused but the game-for-anything deputy sports editor Peter Belsham followed Danny's instructions and started clapping. The others eventually joined in. He wondered where this episode would fit into the neat 'tabloids are evil' narrative. Best not to file.

17.

Wristy Business For A Boss

Jamie had got used to living alone but had to deal with the alarming realisation it could become permanent. Tina and Adam had sponsored a young boy from Indonesia, an 11-year-old orphan, to come over and stay with them for six months. The boy, called Mohammed (Mo), had lost his parents and his sister in the tsunami and had been communicating with Adam since his initial trip to Aceh. Jamie knew they'd been planning something similar before the wedding (Adam wanted to invite him on the day but it wasn't possible) and if things went well, Adam wanted to think of adoption. Tina promised she'd sit down with Jamie and discuss it seriously if that was ever planned. For now, Mo, Tina and Adam were featured on BBC London in a short news item which covered the boy's journey from Aceh to Beaconsfield. There was also a small piece in *The Independent*. Mo spent most of his early days in England chained to the sofa supporting the Netherlands in the football World Cup. If Jamie met him; great, if not he wasn't going to make a big effort: he found it hard enough talking to kids from this country.

Eight days after the transmission, Jamie was in his bedroom doing light research for an obituary piece on Syd Barrett when the doorbell rang. He went downstairs to answer it – and was stunned to see Jack Barnstable standing in front of him with a bottle of Boodles gin in one hand and a wrist bracelet in the other.

'Stupid move, I know, but you must be Jamie… '

'Yes… '

'You don't know me but I used to be a friend of your mother's. Is she in?'

'No, she's not… mostly she's not here… a few days, yeah but… look, what do you want?'

The portly Jack hesitated and looked over his shoulder. He had a suit on but no tie and his Adam's apple stuck out horrendously. He handed the bottle and bracelet over to Jamie.

'Here, take these,' he said, stepping back after handing them over. 'Don't tell her I came. This is deeply embarrassing.'

Jamie took the bottle of Boodles but the engraved bracelet caught his eye. He held it up and had to look closely to read the tiny writing: 'My Jamie' it said in classic, cursive text. He wondered why Barnstable was sloping off. Wasn't he angry with him for writing that story about his groping? And why come back after all these years? Why didn't he sue?

'Jack, come back. I'll make you a coffee or we can share a tipple.'

Jack stopped and put his hands in his trouser pockets. He took out a handkerchief and wiped his brow – and then his nose. He put his handkerchief away and walked forward. As he got onto the doorstep, he looked at Jamie.

'I saw her on TV the other day – and it brought it all back.'

'Brought what back?'

Jack stepped in and touched the bottle of gin with his hand. 'Pop it open – and watch it gush out.'

Jamie and Jack sat at the kitchen table opposite each other sharing the bottle of gin and a bowl of walnuts. As Jack spoke, Jamie realised the liqueur boss knew absolutely nothing about his work as a journalist – but why not? Surely, Tina must have told him about her son? After all, she wore an engraved bracelet with Jamie's name on it.

'Do you still work for a local paper, then?' asked Jack, cracking open a walnut with his teeth.

'Er no, I left a few years ago… '

'My, my, she was so proud of you, getting a job for a paper. It's great you don't work for one of those scummy rags in the city. I could kill that man who wrote that filth about me… '

'So why didn't you sue?'

Jack smiled and ate all the walnuts he'd laid on the table in one go. 'I didn't want a queue of lasses at my door. I'm sure you follow… '

'There were other women?'

'Look, you're a man, you understand. I've made a few female enemies: ex-employees, those kind of people. I had a bit of fun – so did they – but they wanted more, a bit of advancement or commitment, that kind of thing… '

'What did you do to Mum?'

Jack looked at Jamie and chewed his walnuts a bit slower. 'Do you have to be so brutal?'

'Even local reporters can bite.'

Jack sighed and washed down the walnuts with a hefty glass of gin.

'I'm not going to get graphic, you're her son,' he said, finally clearing his throat and pouring another glass. 'All I'd say is she had been taking an audit – and she was bending down counting the bottles in the crate – when I approached her… '

'Go on… '

'… I'd been drinking all afternoon, our suppliers had been raided so I wasn't in the best of states… '

'I won't ask you again… '

'I went in behind her and grabbed her breast. Then I kissed her as close to the lips as I could get. She stumbled and fell over, banging her wrist on one of the crates. I somehow landed on top of her and tried to kiss her again – I got the bony part of her chin. She then grabbed one of the bottles and threatened to smash my head open. I got off and the whole thing lasted about 20 seconds. I realised what I'd done and apologised but she was quite angry.'

'Threatened to sack her, didn't you?'

Jack took another drink. 'Yes, I'm not proud of it.' Jack put the glass down and got up from his chair. He pulled up his trousers slightly which had sagged. 'I'm sorry for everything, I really am. My business is ruined because of my daily drinking and questionable activities… '

'I thought the tabloid paper had something to do with that? The story they put in?'

Jack walked towards the sink and turned to face Jamie. 'Oh, yes, I got a bit of flak for that but the business was already rocking – and I already had a few enemies, particularly of the female variety. I took big loans out to try and expand the number of off-licences we had but it was difficult to find the premises or get planning permission. The debts got bigger – and so did the bottles of liqueur. My wife had left me a blue moon ago. Subsequently, the business went under last year and I was declared bankrupt.' Jack took another drink but there was only a drop of gin left in his glass. 'But mark my words, I won't be the only one suffering this fate. A storm is gathering in the business world. Banks have been crippling us for years – and they'll be crippling everyone else soon… '

'You've got a son, haven't you?'

'How do you know that?'

'Have you or not?'

'Yes, Alexander – but I haven't seen him for donkey's years. He's had mental health problems all his life. He stole from us regularly. He left home in 96, I think, and last time I saw him was during the Cheltenham Festival in 2000. I remember that vividly because he said he didn't want to be there.'

Jamie paused and ran his fingers over his mother's bracelet.

'So you bought the bracelet back to say sorry... ' said Jamie. '... Or do you need money?'

Jack sighed and walked back towards the table. He sat down and stroked the bottle of Boodles with his thumb.

'I don't need money. A racehorse owner wants me to help train a couple of horses. I'm happy doing that.' He picked up the bottle of gin and took a swig direct from the bottle. He leaned forward. 'Tina talked about you all the time. She was proud of you. I don't have a son I can say that about – and that's the most painful thing of all.'

Jack Barnstable left Jamie's house and said the Parkes family would never see him again. He asked Jamie not to tell his mother about his visit and Jamie agreed. The revulsion Jamie had felt about what he'd done to his mother was alleviated slightly by his belated decision to come to the house and apologise. But as Jamie watched him getting into his battered old Rover, he only took one thing away from his conversation with Jack Barnstable: the engraved bracelet with 'My Jamie' written on it. He felt it between his fingers and smiled. It had fallen off his mother's wrist in horrifying circumstances all those years ago – but now it was in his hands, safe and sacred: an unbreakable bond than ran deeper than expected.

Danny gave the paper's royal reporter. Mitcham Miles, a gift of a crown, a robe and a wand. He christened him the new king to celebrate the Screws royal correspondent being arrested on phone hacking allegations. There were no such gifts for Peeper Wallace, however. After a trip to A&E at the local hospital, Danny told him not to come anywhere near the paper or its employees again. The paper's lawyer also ensured Wallace got the message.

Fitton was in a good mood because of the arrests but still sent a memo to seven staff, including Jamie, asking them to come into his office in 15 minutes. Before that, Jamie checked his emails and there was one from Elliot giving him details about Miss Orange who had given private numbers and details of celebrities to Callum Gordon. Elliot wrote that Miss Orange would rather speak to the Daisies because she liked the women's page and the health tips in the paper. Jamie smiled as he read that. If there was one thing the Squires didn't have it was the common touch. Jamie noted the number and gave Miss Orange a ring. There was no answer. He rang the number again – with the same result. Then his own mobile rang.

'Just like to keep you honest,' said Miss Orange. 'Are you taping this?'

'No. I didn't get your name.'

Miss Orange laughed. 'You reporters crease me up. Do you think I'm that stupid? I need to know why you're biting the greasy hand that feeds you. Only then, can we proceed.'

'I'm not biting anything. I'm just interested in clearing a few things up.'

'You sound like an Ombudsman. Extremely boring. Good luck with the tits and arse clean-up.'

'Sorry to repeat myself but you contacted Elliot on Facebook so you must have used a real name?'

'Is that so? Hmm, let me tell you what I did do. I read the stories in that heavy paper about Callum Gordon and the rest. Gordon referred to me as Miss Orange once and I had no idea about it. Now, I'd like to dress up as this mysterious Miss Orange figure every day of the week. Does she have a mask? A cape? Thigh high boots? I'd like to make tea for my boyfriend like that one day.'

'Save your sarcasm for your boyfriend. Did Gordon pay you any money?'

'Never – and you have no evidence to say I've done anything wrong.'

'But you gave him private information… '

'Has your paper ever published any of this private information you keep going on about?'

'Probably, but that's not my point.'

'But it is mine. Just like pressing 1 for yes, 2 for no and three to go back to the previous options, you are up to your neck in the madness. You are as culpable, if not more, than me. Take Melissa Evelyn, do you know her?'

'… She was on *Big Brother*, I think, then she released a record.'

'How many times would you say she has appeared in your paper?'

'God knows, hundreds, maybe thousands of times… '

'And that's just your paper. She is a client of ours and in normal circumstances, I would respect her privacy – but does she have any privacy to respect? There is zero talent, maximum publicity, boobs out every week, parties every day. She invades my privacy every day, even though I do everything to avoid her.'

'… So you handed over private information?'

'Four stories were published on the back of my helping hand. After the third, Evelyn sent a letter to our company saying she would only sue if they were unflattering stories. I wanted them all to be unflattering, obviously, but your editors were a little more balanced. "Keep up the good work" she said, as long as she was getting into the paper.'

'Come on, she didn't say that. You've made that up.'

'That's your job. She did say that – and I'd do the same again. Fame for fame's sake is very hard for me to take. If I'd done something immoral, fair enough, but I've lost zero sleep over it. Matty Yeoman was the same… '

'The talent show guy?'

'Don't use that fucking word in the same sentence as him. Aww!' She paused and took a deep breath. Jamie genuinely thought she was going to throw up at one point – and that he'd taste the sick on his own mobile. 'Okay, we know he can't sing, dance or play an instrument so why is he allowed to present a children's music show? My sister has been writing letters and auditioning for years to get on TV but suddenly these no-marks turn up and poison the landscape.'

'... So you sold him down the river too?'

'I didn't sell anything. I gave – like charity. I did something good, something to benefit the 120 million eyes around the country. So they could see the trash that passes for talent every day. One day, somebody will thank me for it but, obviously, right now, I don't expect people to understand because they're drowning in the stuff.'

'Even though no money changed hands, what you probably did was still illegal... '

'You can talk. If I've done 3 of those things, you've done 3,000. I like your paper but I don't like some of the people in it: Evelyn, Yeoman and a few others. I usually get told to stop reading it or switch off the TV, but when one of the fuckers is on your cereal packet, what then?'

'Eat porridge.'

'Fuck off. Your call has not been recognised.'

Miss Orange hung up and although Jamie tried to call her again she didn't answer. He was annoyed because he wanted to ask her about the other two mobile moles: O2Joy and VodaSkoda; Elliot said she knew about them too. Did they share information? Were any of them paid by Gordon? If not, then were these leads worth pursuing? There were a lot of questions but only one answer: Jamie wanted to eat from that cereal packet with Yeoman or Evelyn's face on it. With soy milk, of course.

*

Six of Jamie's colleagues were in Fitton's office waiting for him to get off the phone. Jamie stood right at the front, feeling quite exposed. Jimmy Betson was there again, along with two showbiz reporters, a sub, a proofreader and a feature writer. He was the only one smiling and joking but that stopped when Fitton got off the phone. He picked up a dart and hurled it into the dartboard. He pulled it out and feigned to throw the dart at the group huddled together. Everyone ducked apart from Jimmy. Fitton laughed with his face up to the ceiling and walked back to his desk. He sat down, leaned back on his chair and put his hands on his head.

'Jimmy, who do you think the mole is?' asked Fitton.

Jimmy shook his head.

'There's been three stories in the Squires so far,' said Fitton. 'Generally, in the past, our moles have been lured by money, a better job or a so-called better paper with more resources but this fucker seems to be a crusading prince or princess of infinite bullshit and extraordinary narcissism. I mean, who does he – and I'm sure it's a he – think he is?'

'So why am I here?' said Sally Cockerill, one of the subs.

'How many subs have expenses the size of yours?'

'But I've covered for features when they've been a bit short. Wrote a few pieces for them, went to a few events… '

'Your sums don't add up. A year of your expenses would close us down.'

'But I know nothing about this hacking stuff. Surely, it's got to be a reporter?'

'… But you were one.'

'Yes… '

'And your friend was too: the one who was made redundant. I used to see you together all the time – you were inseparable.'

'Yes, Marcie was let go – but you're still barking up the wrong tree.'

'Too right, I'm barking. Now please, button it – or you'll go the same way as Marcie. Now Parkesy, I reckon you're still incredibly pissed at your Larna Wilson epic not making the paper all those years ago. That's an age in tabloid papers. Why haven't you got over it yet?'

'I have.'

'So why are you in here?'

'Beats me... '

'Own up and save everyone some time.'

'I've got nothing to own up to. I'm doing proper journalism, right now, so there's nothing to add. I'm working on a huge story.'

'Which is?'

Jamie looked around at his colleagues and smiled. '... All will be revealed.'

They all laughed but Fitton wasn't amused.

'Okay smartarse, save us the Bernstein and Woodward number. I don't like spending time on this; I've got more important matters to deal with... '

'What, like your TV chat show?' said Jimmy. 'The one you've been asked to front by a satellite channel.'

'Where did you hear that?'

'On the internet.'

'Didn't know legends like you understood that world, Jimmy. Save that tittle-tattle for another day. This is about clearing the stables of a weasly traitor – because that's what he is... '

'There you go again,' said Sally.

'Shut up. He's saying one thing to one paper and creaming a salary of another. That can't go on. Anybody got anything to say? Admit it now, or things will get messy. I'm talking guillotines, electric chairs and Al-Qaida-style beheadings... '

Jimmy laughed and checked his phone as a message bleeped.

'... He thinks I'm joking,' said Fitton. 'I'm a fair man, just ask Grace. I do my share of the cooking, cleaning and washing-up. But in our cut-throat industry there's no place for little moles feeding their rivals a pack of lies and infecting their own great newspaper in the process. I will not let that happen.'

'How long is this going to go on?' asked Jimmy. 'I want my NUJ representative in here next time.'

'You know my views on those NUtJobs. If you want to bring so-called representation in with you next time, be my guest, but make you've got your P45 in your other hand. Now fuck off and get some stories.'

Everyone left the room. As Jamie stepped back out into the newsroom, he wondered whether, he too, should finally get some representation: the NUJ or the BAJ. They didn't have a great image round these parts and there were only a few members dotted in and around the newsroom. It could wait – but he didn't want to wait until it was too late.

18.

Little Mo Plays The Longest Rally

Trevena was sat in the ICU waiting room flicking through the pages of *Pulse* magazine when Jamie walked in. His father Edward, who was 87-years-old, had been in intensive care for four days after being initially admitted to hospital with a chest infection. Jamie felt awkward as he sat down by Trevena's side. He picked up a magazine too – *Autocar* – and breezed through it without absorbing a single word or image.

'My wife and daughter have just gone home now,' said Trevena. 'They've been here all morning. My son's coming in this afternoon.' He looked down at the magazine and folded it over at a relevant page. 'The old fighter's very sick – he's not going to make it.'

'Sorry to hear that… '

Trevena sighed and handed his magazine over to Jamie.

'See someone you recognise, there?' asked Trevena.

Jamie looked down at the only photo on the page. It was Hannah; smart, well-dressed, hair tied up – standing with two suited men who were identified as GPs. The story was about the doctors supporting Trevena's campaign to keep health services local. Hannah didn't look out of place at all. In fact, her presence enhanced the message.

'No wonder I haven't seen her for a while,' said Jamie, with a light smile. 'She'll be in *ER* next.'

'I'm proud of her,' said Trevena. 'She deserved a chance and she works damn hard.'

Jamie put the two magazines on the seat next to him. 'Why

did you want meet here?' he asked. 'I feel like I'm invading a family's privacy.'

'Won't be the first time,' said Trevena, playfully tapping Jamie's thigh with his hand. 'My father had a short stint as a bus driver, about six years, maybe seven. I told him about the plans for a bus shelter for this exact spot.'

'Here…

'Roughly yes, along with all the other flats, car parks and playground. He said he would never go to another hospital even he if had to die in the garden shed.' Trevena paused and crossed his hands on his lap. 'I'm going to miss him dearly but it's also making me see things a little clearer. This tabloid game is too much for me. No-one is listening so I can do no more. I've wasted years, if not decades, on it already. You should carry on fighting the good fight but I'm utterly drained and dispirited by it.'

'Don't be silly, you've still got loads to offer.'

'I'm not being silly, I'm being realistic. Being an Independent MP is incredibly isolating. No-one listens. I've done my best to put pressure on the police and the MPs but the bastards won't listen, what can I do?'

'… You are still going to run as an MP next time?'

'Unlikely.'

'What would you do?'

'Carry on with my campaigns, go on a long break with my wife, see more of my grandchildren. Failing that, I could always play the organ at the local church like my father when he retired.'

Jamie got up from his chair and walked towards the window. He looked outside at the wooden bench in the car park where he first met Trevena face-to-face.

'Me and Elliot won't allow you to do that.' said Jamie. 'You've got too many contacts, insight and wisdom for us to let you go that easily.'

'Tell me, have we made any progress on WarFit in the last few years?'

'Tons. Fitton's under pressure. The Squires are running our stories. There's multiple contacts like Miss Orange, Noonan and Melvin Moon... '

'Who's Melvin Moon. You never told me about him.'

'... He's not really related to this investigation. He's a contact in the drugs world.'

'Have you been using?'

'Fuck no. Look two Screws are about to go down because of phone hacking: their royal reporter and their PI. I'm convinced they'll be the fall guys for the rest.'

'But that was a royal story – that's why they're in trouble. If it had been about my father there would have been no outcry. Even if they go to jail, it won't change anything. Tabloid culture will stay the same.'

'There's loads more to come out on Fitton and Gordon... '

'... I've heard it all before.'

Jamie paused and walked back towards his extremely comfortable, sturdy chair. He sat down and leaned forward.

'Fitton thinks I might be the mole,' said Jamie. 'I could be sacked at any time. My mother's married so I live alone most of the time now. I've also got this health problem which means I can't eat certain foods. If you're finding it a slog, then I am too. You are my friend and I don't want you to pack it in now. Not now, that we've come so far.'

Trevena was about to respond but the door opened. A well-dressed man wearing a stylish flat cap walked in. He looked at Trevena and burst into tears. He walked towards Trevena and the two men embraced.

'Don't worry, son,' said Trevena, glancing at Jamie and stroking his son's back. 'We'll fight on, won't we Jamie?'

Jamie nodded and patted Trevena on the back before leaving the room.

*

207

Tina had brought Mo round the house for lunch while Jamie had been at work. When Jamie returned home that evening, they had long gone and Jamie had to admit some ambivalence in wanting to see his mother in tow with a young boy from Indonesia. Tina told Jamie that Mo would like to come to Amersham again but it was unlikely because he was leaving soon. Jamie wasn't happy or disappointed about this news, just apathetic: he was consumed by the next showdown in Fitton's office which was set for early next year. The delay was Jimmy Betson's insistence on having a NUJ representative with him in the room. On one level, however, he did want to ask Mo about his support for the Dutch football team. How did that come about? After that, however, he would be stumped to make any decent conversation. An embarrassment averted.

A couple of nights later, Jamie was sitting in his bedroom trying to work out why his Joytel tape recorder had no cassette in it. He was sure he had replaced the old one and put a new one in. Had it been removed by someone? He looked around the room and saw that one of the framed front pages on the wall was wonky. The shorthand notes on the wall also looked smudgy and had surely been tampered with. Some fucker had been in here. His mum wouldn't do that – so who? It didn't take him long to work out that Mo must have had his dirty mitts all over his bedroom. He was fuming and called his mother immediately. She didn't answer and he left a terse message. He went downstairs and poured himself a glass of brandy and then came upstairs again with the bottle. The anger hadn't subsided; he felt invaded. He sat down on the bed – and then stretched out and lay down. His pillow felt softer than usual so he looked underneath it. There was something there which surprised him. It looked like a messy, A5-sized pamphlet with its lined paper stuck together – about 16 sheets – with sellotape in one corner. There were pictures and scrawny handwriting in colourful crayons. Across the top it said 'THE SOONAMI TIMES' in big black crayon. It looked like the front page of a newspaper. The first drawing showed a big wave of water coming towards a man and a woman; the words above said 'Watch Out, Mother And Father'. Jamie ran his fingers across his forehead and looked through the rest of the 'newspaper'. On page 3, there was a picture of a little girl with the words: 'Sister Is Not Scared, She Is Brave'. On page 6, a big house stood on its own while everything else was in flames: 'A Home That Lasts Forever' it said. On page 13, there was nothing but a bird, the sun and a blue sky: 'Everyone Is Sleeping' was written in orange crayon. Jamie could look and read no more. He held The Soonami Times tightly in his hand and could nothing to reduce the speed of the tears in his eyes. He felt weak and dizzy. He fell to the floor on his knees, clutching the mini-newspaper. The tears ran down his chin and he used his tie to wipe them away. But he couldn't stop them trickling into The Soonami Times.

Jamie was thankful he didn't have a byline on a story about Saddam Hussein's execution. Where once he might have found it funny and irreverent it now smacked of flippancy and desperation. One of the shift reporters, Zane Williams dressed up as Saddam Hussein to illustrate a story on lookalikes. The story stated that there were plenty of lookalikes roaming the world, perhaps, with even one in the office and Zane happily played along comparing his wife to Saddam's as well as his salary, house and car. Somehow, it didn't chime with the chilling images Jamie saw on the nighttime news of the dictator's demise. A few days later, he knew which item he remembered – and it wasn't the story in his newspaper.

In the days leading up to Christmas, Tina was phoning Jamie up even more than usual. Mo had gone back home – and it was unlikely that he would return as he'd found a family to stay with in Indonesia. Tina told Jamie that Adam had been disappointed by the news but that he'd got over it – and wanted to invite most of the family around for Christmas. Jamie agreed but wanted to find out what Hannah was doing first. He called Hannah and it was all set up: Christmas at Adam's, New Year's at Hannah's and lots of shitty long hours inbetween.

Trevena's father had died and he rang on the day of the funeral to say he was raring to go again. He wanted more on the 'sly owls' like Anderton, Vernon Wade and Tristan Boyce because they were close to the 'big beasts' in power. He reiterated he only had a couple of years left, perhaps three, to make his case because once he stopped being an MP he might as well be a leper because no-one would be listening. He did have a habit of saying this over and over again but, for some reason, Jamie never got tired of hearing it.

But Jamie was very tired when Miss Orange called immediately after Trevena. He had been speaking on his mobile for three-quarters of the day and it was making his brain fry. But the fatigue didn't last long because Miss Orange had some stunning news to offer.

'Melissa Evelyn's going to be one of the guests on Fitton's TV show early next year, did you know about it?'

'One of the reporters mentioned it, yes – but it's still a bit of a shocker. How did you find out?'

'Melissa was boasting about it to one of our bosses and he told me. I felt utterly sick. We know your chap fancies himself as a sort of celebrity editor with his finger in all the pies but, for crying out loud, can't he find a better guest than that?'

Jamie rested the phone on his shoulder and typed 'Warren Fitton TV show' into Google; absolutely nothing came up, apart from Fitton's connection to the Daisies.

'It's obviously not been announced yet... '

'Course it hasn't; that's why Melissa blubbed. She can't help it. How's he going to do two jobs anyway? Yours is full time isn't it or do you just faff around in the week and write the odd story at the weekend?'

'Sunday papers are a bit less heated than a daily but we've still got to find exclusives. Fitton's hardly around, though, he's always at a lunch or a party. He's always there for morning conference but then we never see him again.'

'It's probably why he's got an army of footsoldiers to service his lifestyle. I've heard Melissa fancies him too.'

'Well, that'd make sense. He's married though... '

Miss Orange laughed. 'You blokes: you do make me chuckle sometimes. Are you saying Warren Fitton is a happily-married man who has never had an affair?'

'Not quite... '

'Go on then, who was it?'

'I'm not saying. You're loving this way too much.'

'No, what I'm loving is trying to stop zero-talents from soiling our TV screens. The pubic are on my side not yours. You would like this to go ahead so you can write stories. You want your free minutes and no restrictions but there have to be some restrictions otherwise we all go mad.'

'Do you know when it's first airing?'

'Late winter, early spring, I think. Not sure which channel; maybe one of the terrestrial spin-offs.'

'What's it called?'

'No idea. Fitton as Fuck sounds good. Have a good Christmas. Hit the host hard next year.'

Miss Orange hung up and Jamie tried a different search engine but the results were the same. His editor was either a master of concealment or an exceptionally poor publicist. Jamie concluded the Squires stories weren't landing any killer blows – but another little story about his TV show might turn up the heat on him.

One thing that annoyed Jamie about Christmas Day was the

lack of timekeeping and deadlines. First, Christmas dinner was delayed because Robert and Rita were enjoying *Genevieve* on BBC2 while supping a generous amount of red wine. Then, Adam dropped a piping hot plate of sprouts in the kitchen while helping Tina cook so more of the precious green things had to be prepared. Eventually, dinner was served at about 4.30pm by which time Jamie could have eaten almost everything that was served – and nearly did, paying the price to feel bloated for the rest of the evening. Jamie tried to ease his stomach by playing football in the garden with Adam (playing keepy uppies with sprouts) but this merely made him feel worse. But the day wasn't a complete write-off. He had a good, relaxing time with Adam who cunningly nipped in the revelation that Tina would now be staying full-time with him in Beaconsfield. The first time he got a chance to speak to his mother was just after midnight when she was slumped on the sofa eating raspberry cheesecake and sipping a glass of water. The film *Entrapment* was on the TV, Robert and Rita had gone to bed and Adam was cleaning up in the kitchen. Jamie sat down next to his mother and examined the glass of water.

'Bit of Vodka in there?'

'Don't drink anymore. Been about eight months now.'

'No way... '

'On your and Adam's souls. Wasn't doing me any good. Maybe you should do the same.'

'I will – in the next life. Look, Adam says you're going to stay here permanently from now on.'

'I'm his wife. This is my home now. I've got used to the bigger kitchen and the tidier bedroom.' Tina looked at Jamie and dropped the spoon into her bowl. 'Why don't you ask Hannah to start taking you seriously? I mean, do you want her or not?'

'... Seeing her in a few days.'

'Good, because I want progress.'

Jamie glanced at the TV and stared at Catherine Zeta Jones for longer than necessary. 'Saw you on telly a while back,' he said. 'Looked good. This adoption thing history then?'

'Probably, Adam's so busy with CherishUs, I can't keep up. It's not for me, anyway. Handling 300 punters when they're touring the Rebellion Beer Company is more my scene, I'm more comfortable there... '

'Mo a bit too hot to handle, was he?' said Jamie, with a smile. He picked up the bowl of cheesecake. 'Can I eat this?'

'Don't be stupid. It's dripping with lactose. You've had yours earlier on. No, as you're interested, he was a charming little boy: well-mannered, respectful and tidy... '

'Oh fuck, not tidiness again. He wasn't too tidy when he came into my room... '

Tina turned to Jamie and took the bowl off him. 'You made your point by sending that silly message. I must have been in the back garden watering the plants at the time. He didn't move anything did he? He was just curious.'

Jamie's mind went blank. He looked at the TV and wondered if there was a newspaper anywhere in the world that had ever produced the truth like The Soonami Times did.

'Lost your voice, have you?' asked Tina, finishing off the raspberry cheesecake. 'Or are you fantasising about Catherine Zeta Jones? Your paper's obsessed with her.'

'... And that obsession's going to bring it down.'

The plan had been to go to the New Year's Eve fireworks display in one of the less busy spots in London but Jamie's lights went out in the afternoon. After a lengthy shower, he was spraying Lynx deodorant across his body and applying a wet razor to get rid of his stubble when Hannah shouted up to him to say she didn't want to go. Jamie immediately came downstairs and asked her why. There were files and folders strewn across the table, piles of paper stacked on the floor and two mugs of stale tea that looked like they'd been there for days. There was also an ashtray with a couple of cigarette stubs in it.

'Look, I thought I could make it, Jamie, but I can't,' said Hannah. 'I've got so much work to do. I got behind because I've been with dad most of the time during Christmas.'

'Jesus, I'm away for half an hour and it's like a bomb site down here. What's Trevena got you doing? A legislation bill or something? And you're smoking too… '

'I only have a couple at this time of year. Might have a couple more before the smoking ban swallows us all.'

'You didn't answer: what's Trevena got you doing? I came here to go out, that's what we agreed.'

'Yes, but I can't. I've got these campaigns to run, press releases to write and meetings to organise… '

'Can't be just that. You've been doing that for months. It's New Year's Eve for fuck's sake. Loosen up.'

Hannah stepped forward and looked at the stale tea in the mug. She picked it up, examined it and then walked towards the kitchen.

'Oi, you didn't answer. I came a long way to make sure we had some fireworks tonight so at least give us an explanation.' Jamie stepped forward and started looking at some of the files and folders on the table. 'I don't mind staying in but you've got to tell me what you're up to. You know I'm on your side.'

Hannah glanced over her shoulder before opening the kitchen door.

'I want to be an MP,' she said, going through the door. 'Still on my side?'

Hannah sat in her father's favourite wicker chair and watched the arch-shaped clock tick on the mantelpiece. A piping hot lamb jalfrezi dish, a silver-foiled tray of brown rice and tiny triangular samosas lay on the small table next to her. Jamie was lying on the bed, hands under his head, legs stretched out, also watching the clock. There were only five minutes left.

'I know you think women like me can't be candidates,' said Hannah, scooping the plastic fork into the rice. 'But there's no-one to represent me, or my kind of views, in parliament so I've got to take the lead myself.'

'You've got a chance but it's a business that deals in bullshit; promises are never kept and their policies are all the same.'

'I think I could make a difference.'

Jamie laughed and sat up on the bed. 'They'll tear you to shreds. You're too gentle and caring. It's a roughhouse for posh boys.'

'Didn't do too bad with the roughians at the Met, did we? Anyway, thanks for the vote of confidence... '

'You'll need a few of those,' he said, picking up a pillow and easing it behind his back. 'But why now? Just when you're getting things together: job, house and a bit of stability. Why waste time knocking on doors, getting abuse and trying to win round the great unwashed? And I haven't even mentioned the dogs biting your skirt.'

'Because I care – and that's your problem: you don't.'

'I do – a lot. But politics is so dirty. I just don't want you to be scarred forever.'

'I'm tougher than that – you don't really know me at all.'

'Whose fault is that? I'm here like a puppy dog when you ask. I'd really like to know you better but you keep brushing me off.'

Hannah tilted the tray towards her mouth and scooped up the last bits of rice with her fingers.

'Hmm, that was nice,' she said. 'Better get used to it, I suppose. Won't be able to cook as much.'

'They get nannies and maids to do that kind of thing for them.'

'I think you feel threatened.'

'I'm not threatened – just concerned. I hope you know what you're doing. Are you packing in Trevena's job?'

'Not yet. But obviously, if things start happening, for me, then probably yes.'

'… And if things don't happen for you?'

'I've got dad… and you.'

'Now we're talking.' Jamie crawled across the bed and sat on the edge. 'Well, at least I know you don't hate me. But let me tell you a secret – everyone hates MP's.'

'Not as much as they hate you lot… '

'More. They've got worse rep by far.'

'I respectfully disagree… '

'At least you're learning the lingo; that's something. But you're going to need much more than that. One-issue politics is not going to work like it did for Trevena. Are you joining a party?'

'No, Independent again… '

'You've got no fuckin' chance. Not even UKIP or Green?'

'No, I've got my own agenda. If you've got advice, great, but I'm going my own way.'

'The only advice I can give you is how to fill in an expenses form. Journo's and MP's have that in common. Bit of a fiddle here and there.'

'How you lot get away with fiddling your expenses is beyond me,' she said. 'If it was up to me I'd jail any politician who did that.'

19.

Three Dumb Egos And A NutJob

Jamie, Sally Cockerill, Jimmy Betson and his NUJ representative Bill Marsden were standing outside Fitton's office like naughty schoolchildren waiting to go in. Christopher Wilmotts was still in there with Fitton discussing, no doubt, the news that the Screws royal reporter had been jailed along with the PI. The meeting finally finished and the group of four walked in. There were chairs for everyone: Sally and Jamie to the left and the NUJ team on the right. Fitton stood up behind his desk, sleeves rolled up, top two buttons undone, tie still too short. He looked at Bill Marsden.

'I don't want you here, I didn't ask for you and you're uglier than I thought but I've got no option,' said Fitton. 'Just don't get funny with your sly union bullshit. You're so-called member's got some serious questions to answer so don't butt in, okay?'

Bill looked at his watch and raised his hand to ask Fitton to move on quickly.

'Bloody hell, a union man who's lost his voice,' said Fitton. 'Right, Parkesy, how do you feel about the Screws' hacks going to jail?'

'Fuckin' delighted,' said Jamie.

Fitton paused and looked slightly taken aback by Jamie's answer.

'... Right, of course, everyone in the newsroom's delighted our rivals have got a bloody nose. Sally, you?'

'I'm embarrassed to be associated with journalism,' she

said. 'We're not all the same but people out there think we are.'

Fitton nodded but looked doubtful. 'Steady on, there's a lot of good reporters out there.' Fitton looked at Jimmy. 'I'm not asking you Betsy, because you've got your spokesman, here, to rant for you.'

'Will you stop being so rude?' said Bill. 'You call us in here half an hour late... ' He looked at his watch again. '... I had to be at the *Bucks Free Press* in an hour: reporters there are fed up with Gannett... '

'Get on with it, man,' said Fitton.

'You're not editing right now. We're equal in this room. Well, apart from the two who haven't got representation but, anyway, as I was saying, you were half an hour late and then you rattle on about something totally unrelated to the matter in hand. Deal with the matter in hand, I've got a train to catch.'

'Don't the NUJ give you cars anymore? Bloody skinflints. On second thoughts, don't answer that. I want to hear from Jimmy.'

'Jimmy's chosen me to speak for him,' said Bill. 'He's asked me help him out so here I am. Bosses need to respect workers.'

'... And what if workers don't respect bosses?'

'Few and far between in my experience.'

'One of these three dumb egos has done more than disrespect me: they've shat, kicked and spat on me. And no NutJob's going to stop me from finding them.'

'Don't call me a NutJob,' said Bill. 'Show me some respect. You were a member once.'

'Long time ago when the dinosaurs roamed. Look, you're giving me a headache so let's keep this brief.' Fitton paused and picked up a piece of chocolate from the bowl on the table. He eased it towards his mouth but then threw it across to Jimmy who caught it.

'That's my leaving present,' said Fitton. 'You're sacked. You've been chipping away for years but, with those Squires' stories, you went too far. You were a good journalist once but you've been past your best for at least six years.'

Bill stood up. 'You can't do this. He hasn't done anything wrong. He didn't do any of those stories in the Squires.' Bill tapped Jimmy on the shoulder. 'You tell him, Jim, you can't let him get away with this outrageous behaviour. Go on, put him straight.'

Jimmy said nothing and got up from his chair. He shook Bill's hand and then shook Sally's. He came to Jamie last and bent down towards his ear.

'I know what you did,' he whispered.

Jamie wasn't sure he'd heard him correctly but the relief he felt was all that mattered.

'You're a disgrace to the editing profession,' said Bill. 'You'll be hearing from me again. Clear your diary for a tribunal.'

'Oh Jimmy, clear you desk properly before you go,' said Fitton. 'The last idiot left his contacts book on the desk.'

Jimmy walked out of the office but the left the door open.

'You must be about half my age but you're double the scoundrel,' said Bill.

'More than half, get it right.'

'Forever young, eh? We'll see about that when the probes and investigations turn on you. You haven't heard the last of Jimmy.'

Bill walked out of the room and closed the door.

'Phew, thank God for that,' said Fitton. 'Thought we might be in for one of his sermons. Now, Jamie and Sally, have you got anything to say. We have our mole. You must be mightily relieved.'

'I'm not relieved,' said Sally. 'I'm annoyed you put me through this. I think you should apologise.'

Fitton gave Sally a paternal look and then walked round the desk towards her. He bent down and pecked her on the cheek.

'Sincerely sorry,' he said. 'Want another?'

'I'd rather have the chocolate.'

Fitton pecked the other cheek anyway. He walked back round his desk and handed the bowl to Sally.

'Sorry again – now get out there and write some decent headlines.'

Sally took the bowl, gave Fitton two fingers and left the room.

'That's my girl,' said Fitton, with a smile. 'Now Parkesy, you're the last man standing. You're not as pissed off as Sally are you?'

'No, but I've heard you've got a new TV show lined up – and that's going to piss off a lot of the staff in here.'

Fitton smiled and slowly nodded his head. 'Impressive journalistic digging, not bad at all. How did you find that out? It's supposed to be completely under wraps.'

'It's what you get not how you get it; that's what you've always preached.'

Fitton sat down on his chair and spread his arms across the rests on either side.

'What do you think though? Could I pull it off?'

'Be the next Parky or Jonathan Ross, you mean?'

'Pipsqueaks. Carson, Letterman or Leno are more my scene. Do you think the camera's going to be kind to me?'

'Yeah, but it might show you up to?'

'As what?'

'Someone who can't be trusted.'

'WHAT THE FUCK ARE YOU ON ABOUT? GET OUT BEFORE I GET A CAMERA UP YOUR ARSE AND SEND YOU TO THE MOON FOR AN EXCLUSIVE.'

'Okay, but when's the first transmission?'

'FUCK OFF!'

Jamie got up and left the room. He walked a few feet down the newsroom and eventually got to Jimmy's desk. Jimmy was arranging his notebooks into one pile and Jamie stopped by his desk.

'I've already got a job at the *Mail*,' he said, with a wink. 'I have fed them stories in the past but nothing in the last eight months. My stories were getting spiked so much I got fed up with it. Don't want to work in a phantom trade.'

'Same at the *Mail*; they'll spike them too.'

'I don't care. They've ran more stories of mine than this paper in the last two years.'

'What about your NUJ man? He wants to take it all the way.'

'Bill's just blowing hot air with the tribunal stuff. I don't want it. Too much other stuff would come out. Just promise me one thing.'

'What?'

'Nail Fitton for me. He hates older reporters.'

Jamie nodded and walked away. But as he got back to his desk – glancing at three elderly faces in the process – he became doubtful whether Fitton had an ageist issue. Yes, Jimmy and Lenny Calvin could be termed 'old' in journalistic terms but Pat Loakes, a sub-editor, and Bryan Livesey, on sports desk, were in the same age bracket and got on extremely well with Fitton. There were others but perhaps not enough in senior roles. But Jamie was certain of one thing: elderly guests on his TV chat show were a definite no-no.

After the draining uncertainty of not knowing whether he would keep his job, Jamie got home and looked forward to a few cans of Grolsch and a couple of DVDs. He started preparing dinner immediately: a slightly rubbery pasta dish with onions, tuna and red pepper was cooked up in 20 minutes. As he poured the sauce over the steaming pasta, however, he heard a sound from upstairs. Was Tina here? He put the pan down and headed upstairs. He opened his bedroom door and walked in.

'Regards Callum Gordon, how are you this fine day?'

'Jesus, you're taller than I thought,' said Jamie 'What the fuck are you doing in my bedroom? Get out now.'

'I was looking at some of your 'best of' on these walls. I got you some of these stories. I don't mind not being mentioned.'

'Answer me or I'll call the police. How the fuck did you get in?'

Gordon put his umbrella on the bed and reached into his trouser pocket. He pulled out a single key. He threw it over to Jamie who failed to catch it. Jamie picked it up and instantly recognised the digits on the key.

'How did you get this? It's the house key. Where did you get it from?'

Gordon pulled out a packet of Don Diego cigars from his inside jacket pocket. He took one out and prepared to light it with a match from a box of Swan Vestas.

'Don't you dare do that here,' said Jamie. 'I'll call the coppers if you don't tell me how you got this key.'

Gordon glanced at Jamie and then lit up his cigar. He took a long puff and then blew out the smoke on one of Jamie's front pages on the wall.

'There's been no break-in so what can our tooled-up friends do?' said Gordon. 'I came in safe and sound through the front door. Pleasant garden too.'

'Right,' said Jamie, walking a couple of yards to the side of his bed. He crouched down and looked underneath. He picked out a size 7 Gray Nicholls cricket bat and held it tightly in his hands. He drew the bat back about 90 degrees and took a deep breath.

'I'm no Tony Martin,' said Jamie. 'But this is my house and

I'll defend it for my life. I'm giving you a last chance to come clean.'

Gordon took another puff of his cigar and walked towards Jamie. He calmly raised his hand and lowered the bat from its elevated position. It was now down by Jamie's side.

'It's the gentleman's game,' said Gordon. 'Let's not spoil it over a petty dispute.'

Jamie raised his bat again.

'There's nothing gentlemanly about breaking in to someone's house.'

Gordon sighed and walked towards Jamie's bed. He sat down and put the umbrella on his lap.

'Your mother was in *The Independent* a while ago, confirmed?' said Gordon.

'So what?'

'One of the mid-markets saw the story and wanted to put their own spin on it. They wanted names and addresses. I got them what they wanted... '

'My mum's details?'

'Her mobile too. I heard some interesting details in her conversations.'

'You hacked her phone?'

'Spoken like a true veteran. In one of them, she told her husband the spare key for 'Amersham' was taped to the ledge of a bedroom window. It could only be retrieved with a ladder. Was that your idea?'

'I know where I can get ladders quickly. Doesn't matter if it was my idea or not. You nicked our spare key and got in, yes?'

'Holograms would be nice but, I'm afraid, I still needed the key. As I was saying, a mid-market title wanted to run a story on your mother's work with that charity... '

'CherishUs.'

'Yes, CherishUs. Seems like some of their funding has come from dubious sources, maybe of the terrorist variety.'

'Stop lying.'

'The story hasn't run yet. It's still being worked on. Messy business though. A human rights charity with links to Gaza, Kashmir and Iraq doesn't look good. Who runs it?'

'GET OUT!'

'Adam Solent? Married to your mother, yes?'

'GET THE FUCK OUT! NOW!'

Gordon sighed and took another puff on his cigar. He was looking around for an ashtray.

'Bring the bat over here. These are the only ashes that matter.'

Jamie walked towards Gordon while drawing back the bat over his head 180 degrees. He got to a couple of feet away and Gordon raised his arms.

'Wait a moment,' he said. 'I have something else for you.' He reached into his jacket pocket and pulled out a photograph. He handed it to Jamie who didn't recognise the young man with the quiffed hair and leather jacket standing in front of the bicycle.

'That man is dead,' said Gordon. 'Elliot Broomfield is responsible for it.'

Jamie put his hand on his head. 'What are you on about?'

'He's Broomfield's ex-lover. He drove that bike over a cliff. He killed himself because Broomfield played around with another man.'

'Fuck off, stop this,' said Jamie, throwing the bat on the floor and putting both hands on his head. 'Just leave.'

'This is the man you've been trusting as a comrade-in-arms, an ally. You've been duped. He's only chasing the hacking story so he can purge his own demons.'

'I don't believe you.'

'Well, believe this little tale… ' said Gordon, picking up the bat from the floor. He tapped the cigar ash onto the bat. 'Fitton sacks Betson and you get away with it. Fitton doesn't know how mucky your fingerprints are because he spends an unhealthy amount of time with celebrities, politicians and films stars. Editors, particularly thirty somethings, make mistakes all the time; this was merely another one.' Gordon took another puff and neatly arranged the ash in the pile on the cricket bat. 'Retreat or Fitton finds out. Losing your job might not be the wisest move. How much is the mortgage here?'

Jamie looked at the photo in his hand again. 'What's this lad's name?'

'He's older than you think. Details are on the back.' Gordon stubbed his cigar out on the cricket bat and got up. He picked up his umbrella and walked towards the door. 'There are worse things in life than paying for stories and listening in to conversations. Look after the things that matter – or I may have to look after them for you.'

Jamie sent an email to Elliott and he took 12 days to reply – 11 and a half longer than usual. He was reluctant to meet face to face but, after much persuasion, agreed to turn up at Vicarage Road to see Watford take on Chelsea in a Premier League game. He loathed football but said that there was an elegance about the teams as they ran out of the tunnel in their strips. He was stood in the Rookery Stand with Jamie, who continually buried his chin in his red and yellow scarf. At half-time, as Elliot ate his homemade sandwiches filled with salmon and sliced black olives, Jamie could hold back no longer.

'Look, I've got something I want to talk to you about.' Jamie pulled out a photo of Stuart Yates and handed it to Elliot.

'What's this? Another mole?'

Elliot looked at the photo and handed it straight back to Jamie.

'This some sort of ambush?'

'Just tell us what happened and we'll move on.'

'Where in fuck's name did you get that from? Are you going to run a story on me or something? Obsessing over Shilpa Shetty for three months not enough for your paper? Thought we were here for the football.'

'Did that lad commit suicide?'

Elliot pulled out his mobile, pressed a couple of keys and handed it Jamie. The image on the phone was of Stuart Yates, arm in arm with Elliot on a park bench.

'So what Gordon says is true?' said Jamie.

'You believe him over me?'

'I'm not sure what to believe. Did he ride his bike over a cliff?'

'Yes.'

'… Because you had an affair with another man?'

'We had broken up already. It was messy but I made it clear to him that we couldn't carry on. He was quite angry and obsessive but that's because he was lonely. He didn't take the news of my new relationship too well. He was sparky and I miss him.'

'It'll be in the papers soon. Gordon called me a couple of days ago to say at least three tabloids were interested. They're using Yates' diary, I'm told.'

Elliot looked as though an invisible football had smacked him in the face. The colour drained from his cheeks.

'How the hell did he get that?' asked Elliot.

'I don't know. It's his job. Is there anything damaging in there?'

'Damaging? There's probably nothing else if Stuey's got anything to do with it. He wrote everything down. He thought he was the better writer.'

A mild roar went round the stadium as the players came out for the second half. Jamie clapped but Elliot grabbed his drawstring bag and put it over his shoulder.

'This is a very emotional subject for me,' said Elliot. 'So I don't want to discuss it in a cold place like this.'

'Wait, don't go,' said Jamie, holding Elliot's arm. 'Gordon was making out you were responsible for his death but you weren't so what's there to worry about? You haven't done anything illegal.'

'Maybe I haven't, but the immoral charge sheet could be too much to bear.'

'Let them rake the muck; we'll have the big prize in the end.'

Elliot looked doubtful. 'Once they get their teeth into me, they won't let go. There's too many variables.' Elliot added a derisory clap for the players just as everyone else's applause had died down. He glanced at the exit from the stand. 'I'm going home. Watching football and discussing a messy private life are not my idea of a relaxing Saturday afternoon. I made a mistake in doing that thing that everyone's pressured me to do, that I also wanted to do but was too cowardly to face... '

'What was that?'

'It's something you should do right now.'

'What?'

'Come out.'

20.

Would You Adam And Eve It?

Hannah had packed in her job – and was already knee-deep into her new 'cause'. Jamie joined her at a residents' meeting in a community centre in her targeted North London constituency but found the mild, low-key gathering in front of him uninspiring. The 24 people (Jamie counted them, including Hannah) were protesting against Wishaw Investments wanting to build a shopping complex on the outskirts of town where Friar Street Chapel was located. Jamie was sat on the back row of three with Hannah but had his mind on other things, particularly the three newspapers on his lap: *The Daily Star, The Daily Mail* and *The Sun.* He knew the Daisies had had a similar story but couldn't face reading about it in his own paper. Earlier in the day, news had broken online that Fitton's TV show, although slightly delayed, would definitely go ahead in the summer. It would be called *The Fitton Well* and transmitted on Sky One – not one of the terrestrial spin-offs as Miss Orange had claimed. Producers gave the thumbs-up after being satisfied that Fitton's links to phone-hacking and other wrongdoing were not proven. Jamie didn't find it strange that these two pieces of news – Fitton's TV show announcement and the grubby stories on Elliot – were published or revealed on the same day. It was a simple calculation: go to town if you're threatened – and God did they got to town on Elliot Broomfield.

An elderly woman with glasses was speaking as Jamie flicked to a relevant page in *The Daily Star.* The headline was depressing, the story almost unreadable.

GAY HACK'S SEEDY GAMES LED TO LOVER'S CLIFFHANGING DEATH

SLEAZY reporter Elliot Broomfield hired male prostitutes to share with lover Stuart Yates – but it led to a tragedy as the young cyclist threw himself off a cliff.

According to Yates' diary, the crusading hack, 38, who has been investigating tabloid newspapers for illegal payments and phone hacking, was accused of 'running off' with one of the male prostitutes who was hired at £200 an hour.

Yates, 24 at the time of his death, felt betrayed by Broomfield's sick games and confronted him with his errant behaviour at a rock concert they were both attending.

Broomfield claimed he had done nothing wrong – as it was Yates'idea to hire the prostitute in the first place (the reporter merely paid the money) – and the two men had a bitter fall-out which resulted in Yates taking his own life by going on a drink and drugs bender and, days later, plunging off a cliff in the Chiltern Hills.

Jamie didn't want to read any more. He scanned through the other two papers but his feelings were the same: sadness and sympathy for Elliot but also a slight betrayal that he hadn't told Jamie, or even hinted, there could have been any so-called dirt on him that the ruthless New Fleet Street could exploit.

Hannah tapped Jamie on the knee and pointed to a new speaker getting up to address the small crowd. The elderly woman with immaculate silver hair had a batch of leaflets in her hand and started to speak in a rushed, nervous manner. Jamie eased one of his newspapers onto Hannah's lap, open at the relevant page. Hannah picked it up and read it, while also

229

glancing up and trying to listen to the speaker at the front. She handed it back to Jamie within a minute.

'So bloody what?' she said, in a low voice. 'I've done 50 times worse.'

'… And you want to be an MP? God, stop being so naïve. This demolishes Elliot's reputation. They'll do the same to you if you're not careful.'

'I knew about it already. He told me on a late night over a beer when we discussed Anderton.'

'What? Why didn't you tell me?'

'Privacy. Everyone deserves a little.'

'I hear an MP talking… '

'Better than the filth in there, moralising all the time. I'm sick of their witch-hunts. I hope it hasn't hurt Elliot too badly. I haven't spoken to him but he's a tough boy.'

'He's tough all right, but there's a limit. Hope he stays in his job or all the work we've down goes down the pan. Speaking of which, why did you leave your job? It's madness.'

'Needed to get my feet under the table early… '

'Well, you've certainly done that with this shithole.'

Hannah picked up one of the papers and smacked Jamie on the arm with it.

'If you went to few more places like this you wouldn't talk like that. Listen to Mrs Langdon. She speaks a lot of sense.'

Jamie did what he was told – and after a nervous start, Mrs Langdon did speak a lot of sense. She talked about the constant battle between tradition and progress and how the town was unrecognisable from the days she went to the most popular primary school and began worshipping in Friar Street Chapel. Mrs Langdon received light applause for her rousing speech. There was something reassuring about her – and the community centre Jamie was in: the bare, humble surroundings; the dignified unity on show; the age of the participants. It was a marked contrast to the hysterical, overheated media world he inhabited with its nasty, spiteful edge. He glanced down at Elliot's story again and, for the first time since he'd joined the journalistic arena, a local story meant more than the hatchet job in front of him.

Danny had asked Jamie to file a story comparing the US and Britain when it came to shooting massacres after the Virginia Tech murders which left 33 people dead. During his research, Jamie found it hard to concentrate as he went through the likes of Hungerford and Dunblane wondering what possessed these madmen to carry out their horrific crimes. Combined with the US massacre, most of the news channels were also running a taped interview with Anderton, the first time Jamie had seen the Assistant Commissioner talk in detail about phone hacking, privacy and possible corruption in the Met. Jamie took a break from his 'shooting' research and sat back to watch Anderton's interview on the plasma screen. Anderton was asked by the interviewer if hacking was rife in the industry – following on from the Screws' royal reporter's being jailed – but he claimed there was no evidence that other papers were involved. He was also pressed on his links to Fitton, which he'd admitted in the undercover tape with Hannah. He claimed that all senior figures in the Met (and other institutions) had to keep good relations with the media, politicians and the public. Anderton then went on to talk about terrorism and, in particular, the liquid bomb plot, when Jamie's mobile rang.

'Doesn't matter if anyone's listening in now,' said Elliot. 'I'm stepping down from this investigation. Anyone who's on a moral crusade against tabloid newspapers has to ensure their cupboard's clean but mine had a big Stuey skeleton in it. Stuey's sister kept the diary hidden for years to protect her brother but Gordon got to her in the end. I've been outed as a hypocrite – and there's no coming back from that.'

'What about your job?'

'My editor's backing me – but I don't know how long that will last. Even some of the staff are looking at me now.'

'You should have told me about all this earlier. I might have been able to do something, bury some stuff, make some calls... '

'It was private.'

'Nothing's private, you know that. What about WarFit?'

'Not my problem now. I have no moral authority whatsoever to pursue it. If everyone who asks questions is humiliated like me then why bother?'

'Can't you just do a bit of investigative work on the side? We had a bit of momentum after the Screws' reporter was jailed; that's all being destroyed now.'

'Destroyed is the right word: that's how I feel. There's nothing I can say about the tabloids that they can't say about me 100 times over. I'm a busted flush.'

'I feel so sick about this. Anderton's on TV talking about a lot of this right now. The smarmy git's getting an easy ride.'

'He probably enjoyed the coverage about me. But if you're feeling sick about this now, make sure you have plenty of sick bags ready in a few weeks.'

'Why?'

'I've heard that charity your family's linked with, CherishOurs... '

'CherishUs.'

'Pardon me, CherishUs. It's going to be featured heavily in *The Telegraph* definitely and, maybe, *The Mail* and *The Express* too as a prime receiver of terrorist funds from Gaza and Indonesia in particular.'

'They're fucking liars.'

'Note it isn't just the tabloids on this occasion. Broadsheets have been shifting into that dark territory for years. In a way,

I'm relieved I won't be consumed by this tabloid hunt anymore. Doesn't mean you shouldn't keep the flag flying... '

'Might raise the white one soon, if this goes on.'

Who the hell did Gordon work for now – or did he just give stories to everyone? *The Mail* and *The Telegraph* ran the CherishUs stories and they didn't make pleasant reading. Two suspected terrorist groups were mentioned – KhalifaMartyrs Brigade and 786 – and they were accused of having contacts with Adam, giving him donations, access to remote communities and even gifts. Adam wasn't quoted in the story and refused to comment. It wasn't a very balanced story but, after 9/11 and 7/7, anything with a whiff of terrorism, went in no matter how skewed, one-sided or unsourced. Jamie waited a week and hoped Adam and Tina would get in touch with him to discuss the story but they didn't. So he rang his mother to say he was coming down to Beaconsfield. Tina was stood near the ironing board in the back room staring into space while Feist's *My Moon My Man* played on the stereo.

'We're ruined. I hope you're satisfied.'

'Is he here?'

'Yes, but he doesn't want to see you. Let him have some peace. He's had donors and all sorts of people phoning him all week. People backing out, abuse, the lot. He's picked up a bit of flu now too so let him have a rest.'

Jamie walked out of the room and headed for the stairs.

'Don't go up there,' said Tina.

'I'll be gentle. Listen to the song, mum.'

Jamie walked up the stairs and stood outside Adam's room. He knocked on the door but there was no answer. He knocked a couple of times more with the same result so he walked into the room. Adam was in bed but he was sitting up, resting his back against at least three pillows while flicking through a small photo album. There was a colourful bowl of carambola on the bedside table along with strip of paracetamol tablets and a glass of water. Jamie walked forward tentatively and sat down on the side of the bed.

'You think I'm being stupid, don't you?' said Adam, finally looking up at Jamie.

'Well, no not really, I can understand it's been difficult... '

'And how fucking difficult would you say it's been for me? Not being able to feed a starving village? Not having the vaccines to save a child? One child, ten children, a hundred, how many? A few lines in the paper is always enough for you twats but for us, it's our lives. Do you know how many calls and emails I've had in the last week?'

'A few, I expect.'

'I've switched my phone off and I'm not turning my computer on. I know there's thousands from around the world.' Adam picked up the bowl and started eating the star-shaped carambola, a fruit Jamie had never seen before. 'Terrorism, fucking terrorism... ' Adam shook his head and wiped the side of his mouth. 'Honestly, it never crossed my mind when I was working across the world. Here, yes, it's in the papers all the time but in Indonesia, I never came across a single person who even mentioned it. It's a western obsession.'

'Had you heard of these suspected groups?'

'No, but do you know how your owners make money?'

'The Coby brothers? Sort of, through betting websites and stuff.'

'List them.'

'I don't fuckin' know.'

'Well, I don't either. Stop living in the black and white world of the press pack. Thousands of people have donated cash to charities big and small. I have to work with people in a community or village and sometimes they might also be responsible for security, that's how it is, that's the way of the world over there. Some of these people may have given money, I don't know. I can't vouch for every single penny.'

'But there was a group called Martyrs Brigade or something. Not easy to explain away.'

'I read that name in *The Telegraph* for the first time, like you. I called them to complain but they said they stood by the story. I've written to the Press Complaints Commission but I'm not holding my breath.'

'What about Gaza? You've never been there so how come some of your money ended up funding weapons?'

'Can you please stop lying? Must be a virus that runs through newsrooms. Again, I don't know. A lot of people who've helped our charity support the Palestinian cause too. There must have been some crossover, that's all I can think of.'

Adam abruptly got out of bed which surprised Jamie as he was still in a t-shirt and boxer shorts. He pushed two paracetamol tablets out from the silver strip and swallowed them with a glass of water. He walked over to the laptop computer in the corner of the room and switched it on.

'Thought you weren't going to do that now,' said Jamie.

'I prefer this company.'

'It wasn't my fault. How many times do I have to tell you? And why are you looking at pictures of Eva while mum's downstairs.'

Adam blinked a couple of times as though the tablets were harder to absorb than expected.

'Have some carambola to calm down or do you want me to revert to my Desert Rat days?'

'I have media training, not military. I don't want things to get ugly but I also don't want you to hurt mum.'

'Am I not allowed to look at pictures of my wife who only had 33 years on this earth? For God's sake man, it was nearly 15 years ago. Do you think I'm gonna get my dick out and wank all over her?'

Jamie got up from the bed and raised his hands. 'All right look, I'm sorry. It was probably a mistake to come here.'

'Too right, it fuckin' was. You're not welcome here anymore. Don't show your face here again.'

'I think you're overreacting.'

'No, I'm perfectly rational – like newspapers are. They're in charge of what they do; I'm in charge here. Get the fuck out – and don't show your mug in here again.'

'You can do it to me but don't treat my mum like this.'

'What do you take me for? One of your sneaky sources: a pal said this, an insider said that. I don't operate like that. I'm upfront. My relationship with your mother has nothing to do with you. Save your nosiness for your dirty rag.'

'Oh fuck off, Adam,' said Jamie, walking away towards the door.

'Don't tell me to fuck off,' said Adam, inching towards Jamie and then pushing him on the shoulder.

Jamie pushed him back but before he knew it, he was grappling on the bed with Adam. The photo album was kicked onto the floor. Adam was hurting him, twisting his arm and pulling his tie so tight it was crushing his neck. Jamie's eyes were watering, the carambola looked more like an octopus than a star shape and there was no way he could break free. He was sure Adam was about to break his arm and the pressure on his windpipe was unbearable. He tried to breathe but only managed to choke and came to a terrifying realisation that Adam might not let go. The door flung open and Jamie, from the corner of his eye, could see Tina walk in with a tray of tea and biscuits. The tray slipped between her fingers and the biscuits, tea and tray crashed onto the floor. The sound startled Adam who looked over his shoulder and then, gradually, reluctantly and mercifully, eased off. He eventually let go of Jamie's tie but flung it across his face as a parting shot.

'Have you gone mad?' said Tina, looking at her fingers wondering how the tray had slipped from her grasp. 'Well, answer me, macho men? You can fight me, if you want. Come on, I've fought more men than you've had headlines. Jamie?'

'Not my fault, mum,' said Jamie, rubbing his neck and straightening his tie. 'If you want to talk you know where I am.' Jamie got off the bed and walked towards the door.

'Hang around Jamie, we can sort this out,' said Tina.

'Sort him out first.'

Jamie left the room and ran down the stairs. He vowed never to step foot in the house again.

21.

A Pocketful Of Regime Change

Elliot had been sacked but wasn't returning his calls. Jamie hoped he hadn't done anything silly. Trevena felt it was the right time to give WarFit the nudge and questioned whether it was ever possible to lay a finger on the tabloids. In a lengthy call, he also said Hannah had disappointed him by packing in the job he'd worked so hard to establish, although he still supported her drive to be an MP. The only good news for Trevena was that 'the war criminal' Prime Minister had left the Commons before him, something Jamie thought, he was a little too obsessed about. A few weeks after this call, Jamie really did think it was pointless to continue the campaign. He was sat in his living room with a brandy and coke watching *The Fitton Well* on Sky One. Fitton appeared and cracked a couple of risky jokes, one on Bernard Manning's death which actually went down well. After these gags, Fitton invited his three guests onto the sofa at the same time. Melissa Evelyn, as expected, TV chef Marty Simms and ageing footballer-turned-pundit Ally Marsh were the guests. There was music from Mutya Buena and Jamie got a sinking feeling throughout the programme that, actually, it wasn't that bad at all. Fitton had a way with people; a kind of relaxed charm that put others at ease. He understood his audience too, ripping into Evelyn about her lack of talent and she was happy to oblige too, giggling her way through the interview. After Evelyn's interview, Jamie's mobile rang.

'If this depresses you as much as it does me, say yes after the tone… beep,' said Miss Orange.

'No, I win because I work with the bastard every day.'

'Do you want a story about Evelyn anyway? I heard she's seeing someone from a boy band now? Miss Orange broke off and paused. 'Wait on, what the fuck's that?'

Jamie couldn't believe what he was seeing on the TV screen. He had turned the volume down to take Miss Orange's call but now, frantically, turned it up again with the remote control. In a segment called Guest Wish in which Fitton tried to show all the guests something they approved of, up popped a grainy image of the editor's office with, unbelievably, the 30 or so hacks Fitton had called in as suspected moles. Jamie could clearly see his face and the worried expressions of all the other staff. The back of Fitton's head was clearly in view so the hidden camera must have been placed somewhere at the back of the room. Fitton was loving every minute of it.

'Look at their faces,' said Fitton. 'I called 32 of them in for a disciplinary matter and they all believed me. I only needed three of the blighters. There's nothing like a room of terrified tabloid hacks. Melissa, the ultimate Guest Wish for you?'

Evelyn clapped and laughed uncontrollably but didn't say anything.

'Marty?' said Fitton.

'Love it. One of your mob was in the bushes when I went out for a gluten free loaf. 2-0 from me.'

'Ally Marsh, legend, football god,' said Fitton. 'Top fantasy and Guest Wish for you?'

'Have to be careful, coz I'm a pundit now but they look shit scared to me. They don't like it when the boot's on the other foot. A full house from me.'

Fitton clapped and then raised his arms towards the guests. 'Ladies and gentleman, our wonderful guests. Join me again next week for more treats from *The Fitton Well*. The only story in town.'

Jamie switched the TV off from his remote and put his mobile down on the armrest.

'Jamie, are you still there?' said Miss Orange.

Jamie didn't answer and felt his stomach rumbling. He rushed into the kitchen and threw up onto the dirty dishes in the sink. After 10 minutes or so of painful cramps and brain-bursting heaves, he slumped onto the kitchen tiles and sat with his back against the cooker. Fitton was too skilful for a novice like him. There was no point in continuing this charade. He'd won, they'd lost and no-one would live happily ever after.

Trevena hadn't seen *The Fitton Well* – and said he wouldn't watch that rubbish anyway – but Jamie told him he was backing out and couldn't go on. Trevena agreed that the investigation had come to a dead end and wanted to meet at Sparrow Hill again, one final time, to tidy up all the information they had. Jamie felt this wasn't necessary. He was drained and frustrated by the whole process and wanted to get his head down, keep his job, keep the house running and, perhaps, even get an exclusive or two. Trevena said he'd keep the WarFit files in his 'chaotic' study underneath his collection of Dusty Springfield records and public information films. Jamie felt slightly guilty that Trevena's painstaking work would just rot away without anyone taking any notice but it wasn't as if his own stories had never been spiked. WarFit was history – and there was no point moping or mourning its loss. It wasn't the one that got away, more the one that couldn't be filed.

Jamie needed an escape and met Melvin Moon in Pub E. Jamie had a few drinks but, as Melvin didn't touch the stuff, they quickly moved onto a few well-endowed spliffs and a couple of ecstasy pills. Jamie didn't get the buzz expected from the ecstasy pill apart from most of the outlines in the pub looking more vivid and sharp. It was as though an artist had come along and traced black lines over the edge of every object or being: the bar, the tables, the pictures, the people. A couple of hours later – after an oily kebab, three trips to the toilet and a vomiting threat that didn't transpire – Jamie got home and slumped on the sofa. It must have been nearly midnight when he staggered into the kitchen, desperate for a violent aspirin to tackle his ripping headache. The doorbell rang – and Jamie didn't think twice about running upstairs and picking up his cricket bat from under his bed. He came downstairs and laid it carefully by the door. He opened the door and had to squint to recognise the face under the tweed hat.

'I saw a lot of patients at this time of night,' said Noonan, carrying a black doctor's bag in his right hand. 'I'd like to see if I could help one more.'

'I'm no patient, I'm in good nick. What time is it?'

'Late. Mr Trevena thought I could help out a little. When he told me you'd surrendered… '

'Nobody's fucking surrendered. This isn't a war. We've come to a dead end. What the hell are you doing here, anyway? I thought you only liked the bright lights and shiny aisles of pharmacies. And who gave you my address?'

'Can I come in?'

'Fuck no, I'm going to bed.'

'Have you been taking drugs? I can help with that. Depression is a dangerous illness.'

'I'm not depressed. Did Trevena tell you that?'

'No, I can see it in your eyes.'

Noonan opened his doctor's bag and showed it to Jamie. It was completely empty. Jamie nodded but looked bewildered.

'You've got no kit or medicine? I don't understand.'

'Pills don't make you feel better. People do. I don't want you to go the same way as Jake. That's why I am here.'

'I've told you, I'm not like your son. He was a junkie, I'm not.'

'You consumed drugs, tonight, yes? The bloodshot eyes kind of give it away.'

'I'm not answering that. I have to go to bed now. Thanks for coming round. You mean well but I'm not in the mood for consultation.'

Jamie started to close the door. Noonan stepped forward and put his hand on it.

'Here, take this,' he said, handing the doctor's bag to Jamie.

'But it's empty.'

'Yes, but it's reassuring. Take it – and keep it visible.'

'No, you'll probably have me for theft.'

'Take it, then I'll go. You can then get a good night's sleep and get rid of some of the toxins you've built up tonight.'

Jamie reluctantly took the bag, the leather handle feeling warm in his hands. Noonan smiled and began to walk away. He looked over his shoulder.

'Don't let yourself drown in the Fitton well.'

Fitton called in all the staff who were filmed apart from Sally, Jamie and, of course, Jimmy Betson, who had now left the paper. He promised all 29 a bonus payment in next month's wages and thanked them for being such good sports. Sally had gleaned this information from a fellow sub and then told Jamie about it. A few of the staff were still unhappy with Fitton's subterfuge but the sweetener in their pay packets was enough to keep the criticism mild and unthreatening. Jamie didn't care as long as he wasn't being docked – and it seemed Danny wasn't quite enamoured with the editor either. For the first time ever, Danny came to Jamie's desk armed with an opinion rather than a story for Jamie to dig out.

'Been watching your editor on TV, Jammy?' he said, sitting down and wheeling his chair closer to Jamie.

'Yeah, I saw the first two programmes, not caught the recent ones.'

'Be out on his ear soon; can't do two high-profile jobs at once. Who do you think could take over?'

'Why? Do you want the job?'

'Me? Nah. I'd miss my family. Couldn't do all the greasing and bullshitting with slimy politicians and fake pop stars.'

'I think you could do it.'

'I like to be heard not seen. If you run the show these days you've got to have a Facebook profile or Twitter account and show your face to people you'd rather deck, so it's not the world for me.' He held the back of his neck and twisted it slightly until it cracked. 'Although my wife does agree with you. It's not often that happens so take that as a compliment.'

'I will. I can see the headline in *Press Gazette*: Eternal Love at the Daisies.'

'Oi, watch it. Talking of headlines, how come you were one of the last three left in Fitton's office? Jimmy was always the mole so why the fuck were you in there? Still not got over Larna Wilson?'

'You knew all along that Jimmy was the mole?'

'Tons of his stories appeared in our rivals' papers, some were even in the Squires. He was as bitter as they come. A seasoned, deceitful bastard. A bit like you.'

'What?'

'Do you think I'm stupid? Fitton's up to his neck in plastic tits, coke and celebrity interviews but you won't pull the wool over my eyes. Why were you speaking to Elliot Broomfield?'

Jamie felt a shudder at the back of his neck and found it hard to swallow. It was as though the dizzy nights spent with Melvin Moon were catching up with him.

'Lost your voice? Or has it been saved for the Squires?'

Jamie still couldn't respond.

'Going against your own paper is a major crime. No defence.'

'Did Elliot get a defence?'

'Save me the wishy-washy stuff. I'm going to give you a chance to come clean right now.'

'And if I don't... '

'You know where the door is.'

'If I do... '

Danny put his feet on the desk and crossed his hands on his lap.

'The editor's chair on a national rag doesn't come round often so anybody with an unhealthy interest in Fitton – and fuck me, you really have one – could be useful. Obviously, you're a traitor but we're all mature, big boys here. Burying stuff is part of our business.'

'But maybe I'm looking a bit wider than Fitton... '

'Then you'll be looking at my fist. Haven't you learnt anything from Wallace?'

'I'm not going to be bullied... '

'Is that what you think I am?'

'More than that.'

'On the take too? Bit of hacking when I was a reporter?'

Jamie felt defensive as he absorbed Danny's intimidating look.

'No doubt about it.'

Danny laughed and felt his stubble. 'Show me a tabloid man who's never paid for a big exclusive and I'll show you my dangler. You're well in the game too – you've hacked phones, paid for stories... '

'I've changed – and I never paid for a story.'

'Whipping Dictator?'

'You authorised that.'

'Did I? I remember a J Parkes going on the invoice to a certain Miss Rocheman.'

'You fucking bastard.'

Danny sprung out of his chair and put his face inches

away from Jamie's, his doughnut-cream breath going right up Jamie's nose.

'This tabloid crusade ends today, mother fuckin' superior,' said Danny. 'You've insulted our paper enough. Fitton will eat himself soon enough, with or without your probing. Come with me – and run for a bit longer or go into Fitton's office now and be sacked, the choice is yours.'

Jamie looked away but Danny merely pushed Jamie's head back towards him.

'I don't want to be sacked,' said Jamie.

'Good,' said Danny, finally easing back and tapping Jamie on the thigh. 'Now, have you got any good stories?'

'Er, I don't know,' said Jamie, feeling incredibly relieved. 'There was a follow-up on Madeline McCann... '

'Get something else, you lazy bastard. We've had months of that shit.'

Danny walked away from Jamie's desk and headed off to the toilets. Jamie didn't have a Madeline McCann story at all, he would have said anything to make Danny go away. If there was a flicker of hope for Trevena's WarFit campaign before, now it was well and truly extinguished. Danny had hammered the final nail into its coffin.

Jamie joined the civilised queue outside the Golders Green branch of Northern Rock. He estimated there were about 60 or 70 people there, mostly elderly, and some of them were sharing sweets from a box of Quality Street. A bank official was also handing a letter to some of them and Jamie waited patiently until it was his turn. He turned his tape recorder on and moved closer to one of the customers at the back of queue. The customer was wearing a green cagoule and had a flask in his hand.

'They're not betting with my money anymore,' said Mr Cronshaw. 'My wife always thought the mattress was the safest place, she was probably right.'

'How long have you been queuing here?'

'Since three in the morning. I work shifts so I finished at two and walked the half mile down here. My two sons have got accounts here too.'

The bank official handed Jamie and Mr Cronshaw the letter. Mr Cronshaw glanced at it and then scrunched it up in a ball and put it in his cagoule.

'A message from Northern Rock... ' he said. 'Pah! Give us a break, you robbers.'

'Don't you want to read it?' said Jamie, examining the letter's contents in detail.

'Why? It'll be the same old story: "We take our customers extremely seriously blah, blah, blah... " It should say "We're on the take from our customers," that'd be more accurate.'

Jamie's mobile rang.

'Your paper says the Charity Commission are investigating CherishUs,' said Tina. 'Did you write it?'

'Course not, mum. Jesus, I haven't spoken to you for weeks and this is the first thing you come up with?'

'It's important to us, Jamie. Why don't you just leave the paper? It's full of cruelty.'

'Well, I'm working on a story right now that isn't. Can you call me back later? I'm outside a Northern Rock branch. There's a long queue.'

'Don't think your industry is any better than the banks. Pockets can be filled again but hearts and minds can be poisoned forever. I haven't been able to sleep since that first story.'

'But you slept okay when Adam was beating me up in the bedroom?'

'No, course not – and he's very apologetic about it.'

'Not to me.'

'Well, you have to understand he loathes journalists. One of them was adamant he had Gulf War syndrome... '

'Why?'

'Because he didn't give him any quotes when he came back from Iraq. And swore at him when he became persistent.'

'Not sure about that. Adam's probably made it up to get back in our good books.'

'Believe what you want. It happened. He really hates them. Something, I now agree with.'

'Enough to see your son being thrashed about?'

'No, don't put words into my mouth. He's under a lot of pressure. He's just had to lay off about 25 staff, it's not a big operation anyway. Now, the donations have dried up and our image has been tarnished, we might not be able to keep going for too much longer.'

'How do you know those allegations weren't true? Have you really asked him? His behaviour's been a bit funny lately.'

'Where do you get off asking me such a thing? All the stories are lies; total and utter lies. The media world has rotted your brain.'

'At least I haven't used my fists. Adam's learnt a lot from Al Qaida; he used his training against me quite effectively. Look, I've got to go mum… '

'Don't you dare say that kind of thing in my presence again; Al Qaida are evil, Adam is not.'

'Yeah, yeah, whatever mum, I'm in the middle of this big story, so I'll see you when I see you… '

'Don't hold your breath… '

Jamie hung up and put the mobile in his pocket. He kept his fingers in there and rummaged around until he picked out his mother's wrist bracelet. He looked at it and eased his fingers across the engraved words.

'That from your girlfriend?' asked Mr Cronshaw.

'Er no, my mother.'

'Solid as a rock. My mother Jean's still going strong at 83.

We've had our ups and downs but I swear to you when I go to see her twice a week at her flat, I feel a happiness I can't describe. She's the reason I'm still in one piece. Does your mother like your line of work?'

Jamie smiled and put the wrist bracelet back in his pocket.

'You could say she's not terribly impressed. Look, can we get back to money matters?'

'Why have you got any?'

Jamie checked his pockets again. He only had loose change.

'I need to go down the bank,' said Jamie.

Mr Cronshaw laughed and dipped into the Quality Street box as it finally reached the end of the queue. 'Join the club,' he said. 'I've got five grand in there and it's all coming out, today, or I'll get my balaclava on.'

Hannah was sat at the kitchen table with a dusty Compaq laptop open while eating a bowl of peaches and cream. Jamie was sat next to her, waiting to see a mock-up of her campaign leaflet on screen when she handed him a crude-looking flyer from her handbag. It was a touched-up picture of Hannah, scantily-dressed and carrying a whip, with the speech bubble 'I'm a tart with no heart'.

'It's started earlier than I expected,' said Hannah. 'I've only just sent my application to the electoral commission.'

'But there's a still a couple of years before the election, maybe more. Who do you think it is?'

'Most people have read the story so it could be anyone. But it doesn't take a genius to work out who is pulling the strings.'

'Leaver?'

'No-one's said as much but he's one stubborn bastard. The guy who's been selected for the Tories to fight this seat was really apologetic about it and he even came to my house to ask about my father. He thinks it might have been anyone from unruly kids to Wishaw Investments because they're not happy about people objecting to their plans for the town.'

Jamie looked down at the cheap, blue-coloured flyer again.

'Got to say, does get me going, though. Only the suspenders are missing.'

'Dream on, Jamie, I've got more important things on my mind. How is Elliot anyway? Been so busy, haven't been able to call him. It's sick what they can do to you.'

'Haven't spoken to him. Don't know where he is. Think he might have left journalism all together.'

'The things I did for you boys – and now it all falls apart,' said Hannah, with a smile. 'Got you an undercover confession with a top copper and still you can't make anything stick. Call yourself journalists?'

'They'll always be more important than MPs whatever happens.'

'Don't bet on it,' she said, concentrating hard on the laptop screen. She typed ferociously on the keyboard. 'What do you think of this? It's going to be my campaign leaflet. It'll probably be posted everywhere in the town. Trevena's seen it already.'

'Nice picture. That helps.'

'What about the policy?'

'Image matters; the fact you've got a nice face will get you more votes.'

Hannah shook her head and swung the laptop back in her direction. 'Don't know why I bothered.'

'Sorry, didn't mean that. Been under a bit of strain, lately… '

'Your mum's under strain too… '

'She called you?'

'Four times, at least. You need to get back in her good books.'

'Do you want me to look at this or not?'

'Of course, expert media advice is always welcome.'

Hannah smiled and got up. She picked up the bowl and started going through some of her post which was piled high on the mantelpiece.

'Hannah and her System,' said Jamie, reading off the screen. 'Jesus, you've been on the computer for too long. The rest of it's not too bad: the 'no promises' thing and the hospital stuff but that slogan at the top needs to change. It's almost militant.'

'I think it sounds right. People don't want bullshit. This tells them exactly what I'm going to do. There's nothing vague in it. I like it.'

'You should change it.'

Hannah put down the envelopes and walked back to the laptop. She sat down and eased the screen back towards her.

'You don't have a veto,' she said.

'You know what one is?'

Hannah smiled. 'I looked it up a couple of days of ago.'

22.

Tawdry And Dean

Jamie regretted spending another night with Melvin Moon as he could hardly get his head off the pillow. Melvin had noted Jamie's disappointment with his last 'e' so this time he gave him one of his 'specials', a sky-blue circular pill with an emu on it. This might have not been so bad had Jamie just taken it on its own and come back home. The problem was he felt so good and indestructible (in part because he had just filed a good story on the Government's loss of two computer disks containing personal details of 25m people) that he came back to Amersham and joined up with Larnell and Mark for a few drinks at The Kings Arms. After 10.15pm, his brain began to tilt so much to one side that he thought he was permanently on all fours while walking. The colours were also extremely bright and the ringing and popping in his ears became unbearable. His final image of the evening was one of Larnell and Mark laughing at him while he tried and failed to urinate in a resident's recycling bin. Jamie hoped nobody had their phones out to take a picture. He got out of bed groggily and walked towards the window. He nearly tripped over Dr Noonan's bag which was lying on the carpet next to the bed. He sat on the bed and looked through it again, examining it more carefully than he'd done last time which, after all, was around midnight after another rough evening with Melvin Moon. He put his hands deep into the leather and undid the only zip inside the bag: nothing. Then he looked underneath the bag and, for the first time, noticed a small pouch on the base. He wriggled his finger around and instantly recognised the familiar smell of a folded newspaper cutting. He pulled it out and looked at the page which was from the *San Francisco Chronicle*. He looked at the headline and then read the story.

MIRACLE TEEN WITH HEART DEFECT SURVIVES AMBULANCE CRASH

TEENAGER Paul James Noonan miraculously survived a five-vehicle accident which flung him 40 feet from an ambulance.

Noonan, who had a heart defect and was being rushed to hospital, ended up lying on the sidewalk with tubes and wires stuck on his body and face after the crash which was caused by a rushing police car involved in a chase with drug dealers.

The 14-year-old is out of danger despite his heart still needing a major operation. His injuries included a broken pelvis, bruising to the ribs, a broken tibia and a dislocation of the shoulder plus 35 stitches to the face and chin.

Speaking exclusively to the Chronicle from hospital, with his parents by his side, Noonan said: "When I was lying on the sidewalk, I thought I might die but I never gave up hope. I counted the number of years I'd been here and wanted to double them, at least. A kind mother and son came to my aid. They looked after me until the medics got to me. I'm only here because of them.'

But now Noonan faces another fight – an essential operation to repair his heart which, doctors believe, won't last much past his 20th birthday without intervention. If he's worried, he isn't showing it.

'I have life again,' he said. 'I can see my parents'

faces again so what do I have to worry about? The wheels were spinning out of control but I had faith. This setback has given me even greater strength. I want to get back to school, get my grades and help some people out. I'll never give up.'

Jamie had read enough even though there was another eight paragraphs. He felt guilty about sending Noonan on his way that night. How come there was no signal or indication of Noonan going through these horrors when they met in the pharmacy? The tabloid crusade felt insignificant and inadequate compared to Noonan's ordeal. Noonan's was an inspirational tale; Jamie needed one. He got up off the bed and walked over to his bedside table for some Blu-Tack. He walked towards the wall by the window and hung up the *Chronicle's* cutting near his front page exclusive on Lisa T's pregnancy. He stood back and looked at the wall for a few minutes. The Noonan story was a giant amongst meaningless midgets.

Jamie was annoyed the Maliks, Hannah's neighbours, wouldn't talk to him about the Gillian Gibbons' story. He wanted a simple quote about what they thought of a schoolteacher being arrested for naming a teddy bear Muhammad but they wouldn't play ball, although they did invite him in for sweet rice and milk tea. Jamie knew if he didn't get the family onside he would have to go out onto the streets of Southall and Luton, on Danny's instructions, and take out a teddy bear with a turban and beard and see the response. In the event, Jamie left the teddy bear in his car when he stopped outside a mosque because he felt it would be too provocative. He still asked some awkward questions and, in the main, people were respectful if a little niggled.

Danny didn't like what Jamie had brought in, however,

and smacked him over the head with the teddy bear in front of the whole newsroom. 'I might as well use Muhammad Oily for something because he's not involved in this story,' said Danny. He had another swing with the teddy but Jamie stopped it with his hand. 'At last, some balls.' Danny looked round the newsroom and ushered Jamie away from newsdesk. They sat down at an empty desk near the subs. 'Heard about *The Fitton Well*?'

'No.'

'Could be running in America soon. Been very successful over here. Don't know how.'

'I didn't take you for an eagle-eyed TV watcher.'

'Wife's the addict, I have to make do. I've got the paper's welfare at heart. Him pissing off on his chat show expeditions means my workload increases tenfold. He just doesn't get it – there's some redundancies on the horizon too.'

'Fucking hell, do they never stop?'

'Financial crisis… '

'It's only Northern Rock for God's sake.'

'Internet troubles too. Our website's shit and we're not attracting enough advertising. We've hired some techies to improve the site. They couldn't find a story if your paid them.'

'Am I safe?' asked Jamie.

'No-one is. This industry's going down the pan without serious action in the next 10 years.'

'… And you're the man to do it?'

Danny stroked the head of the teddy bear as it lay on his lap.

'My father worked at a car plant in the late 60s and early 70s. He never went on strike in his life but told me about this army general who was so sick of the state of the country that he wanted to overthrow the Government… '

Jamie smiled. 'What have you got in mind – a coup to unseat the editor?'

Danny stared at him and said nothing.

'Jesus, you're serious.' Jamie looked up at the editor's office and saw Fitton come out with two nice-looking women. 'But you're misguided. Work with me to clean up this industry and you'll get more respect.'

Danny picked up the teddy bear and pushed it firmly against Jamie's chest.

'You're part of the enemy within,' said Danny. 'But you could still be a useful idiot. Soon, when the shit and the fan collide, you'll have to make a decision: are you with me or against? For the time being, fuck off and have a pray with Muhammad here...'

Jamie took the teddy and straightened his turban. He got up and walked back to his desk.

Jamie didn't go out at all during Christmas and New Year. He stayed at home and gradually the dishes piled up, the empty cans of Grolsch lay on the kitchen tiles, the pizza takeaway boxes stacked up and the coffee mugs got darker. But on New Year's Eve at 10pm, the doorbell rang and his jaw nearly dropped when he saw Louise Dorrans standing in front of him with a bottle of wine in her hand.

'Evening stranger,' she said. 'Nice night for a talk.'

Jamie rubbed his eyes. 'Thought you hated Arnie?'

'I do. He didn't write that line anyway. Can I come in?'

'Er yeah, I'm just making dinner...'

'It's gone 10!'

'I've been sleeping late for weeks.'

'Lazy bastard...'

'Don't start, I'm not in the mood.'

'Okay pop off and have your dinner then. I'll make myself comfy in the living room.'

Louise walked in and took her coat, scarf and gloves off. She hung them on the hook and walked towards the living room.

'Didn't you have any new year parties to attend?' asked Jamie.

'Loads, but they'll come again. I only get one chance to take over from Elliot as tabloid tormentor-in-chief so I've got to ensure I don't mess it up.'

At two minutes to midnight, Louise was barefoot on the carpet sipping a glass of red wine while dancing to Robert Plant and Alison Krauss's album *Raising Sand*. She asked Jamie to join her and he awkwardly got up and did his best. He found the music impossible to dance to, although Louise had it sussed with a rhythmic range of loose, easygoing moves. She started counting down the seconds to midnight. As the last ten came, her voice got louder.

'EIGHT, SEVEN, SIX… '

Jamie was nervous about whether to hug her when the time came. Would he get a kiss? She did have a husband.

'THREE, TWO, ONE… HAPPY NEW YEAR! Oh come here, Mr Exclusive… '

Louise hugged Jamie and gave him a kiss on the cheek. She smiled, took another drink and then sat down on the carpet with her back against the sofa.

'Right, that's the fun out of the way. We've got work to do to improve the image of our industry.'

'Oh for fuck's sake, do we have to do this now?'

'I've been hollering at my editor for months to give me this gig. The way Elliot was treated made me so sick that I promised him I'd carry on his work. So here I am.'

'Do you know where he is?'

'He sent me an email a few months ago, said he was fine. He was thinking of a career change.'

'Look Louise, I've suffered a lot over the last couple of years. I don't want to open up this shit anymore, because there's nothing left to pull out. It's dead; give it a rest.

And anyway, I thought you came here to celebrate New Year?'

'I did – and I have. I also wanted to cheer you up a bit because I know you've been going through a hard time. Hope I've done that too. But now we have to revive some of the good work you, Trevena and Elliot have done… '

'No, my head will explode if I kick this off again.'

'… And I'll explode if you don't.'

'Like to see you try. You pop up after all these years with a nice bottle of wine and expect me to be an obedient puppy dog to fetch and carry up the mountain again when I've already said there's nothing there. I'm not going through that hell again.'

Louise looked at Jamie for a few seconds without saying anything. She then got up, put on her shoes and walked over to the stereo to take her CD out and put it in its case. She slipped it into her handbag and walked towards the door.

'Thanks for sharing the drinks,' she said. 'It was a nice New Year. I enjoyed it. If you change your mind, you know where I am.'

'I won't. The Squires should concentrate on its own readers; we'll concentrate on our own.'

Louise left the living room and Jamie listened as the front door opened and closed. Happy New Year indeed.

A 13-year-old girl called Mandy Dean rang the newsroom and eventually ended up talking to Jamie about her horrifying story. She claimed she had been raped by at least eight men (she had consumed so much alcohol she couldn't count) and to compound matters, the police had dismissed her story. That is why she was now calling the newspaper (her nan read the Daisies). Was this a story at all? They were only allegations and Jamie was doubtful a paper could get away with running this kind of material. But the other aspects of her story were too valuable to ignore: her escape from the children's home, being registered missing by a homeless man not the authorities, an alcoholic foster father and, finally, police laughing and ridiculing her story. It was the latter detail that Mandy felt was a humiliation too far.

'They're just not listening to us,' said Mandy. 'I want their names in the paper. I wrote them down, here y'are: Sergeant Rick Butterworth, PC Wayne Stubbs... '

'Mandy listen, stop, we can't run that.'

'Why not? I've got more; Detective Super-summat Pete Roberts. I want them to suffer.'

'They're just allegations so there's not much we can do. They've dropped the case and, unless they open it again, I might not be able to help you.'

'You can't help a lass who's been thrown around like a rag doll by packs of animals? Are you lot all the same? Dirty cowards who like a wink and a joke? Don't care, any road, one day, people will be on my side. You just wait and see.'

'We can't take sides, Mandy, we have to run what's true, backed up by the police.'

'Oh fuck ya', I'll go to another paper.'

'Don't do that. Look, tell me about other aspects of your story: your background, your foster family, the care home – and then we'll get to the other stuff later. I'll have a word with newsdesk to see what we can come up with.'

'Do you believe us?'

'What?'

'You? Do you believe those lads did these things to us?'

'It's not important what I believe. It's what we can run.'

'Is that all that matters? What you can print in your big-arse paper? They gave me so much to drink I couldn't stand up. The lights in the takeaway were so bright they were burning my eyes. I smelt their dirty fags and curry breath; their BO and deodorant. Why would I lie about all that? You have to believe us. Don't know where I'll turn if you don't. Got no friends left in town now.'

'Where are you living right now?'

'Pigs put us back in the children's home but I'm not staying there. Smelly Jeff, the ape who runs it, also took a liking to me. Not my fault I've got a decent pair, or so they say...'

'Who says?'

'Smelly Jeff and the Asian lads at the takeaway.'

'Have you got a mobile?'

'No, it was confiscated at the station. They're not giving it us back.'

'Here's my mobile number, you can call me anytime.'

'I don't want to call you all hours. Just believe what I say, that's all I ask for. Believe us.'

Danny wasn't interested in Mandy Dean's story – but Fitton was. Jamie didn't expect Fitton to seize on the tale of a 13-year-old girl from Lancashire who had suffered so much, first from the alleged rapists and, then, from the authorities. Fitton had an ambitious plan for Mandy to run a series of blogs in the paper (possibly under a pseudonym) covering her early days through to the rape allegations and the police interrogation. As the police had chosen not to investigate further, Fitton was in expansive mood. Even though it was a risk to let her tell her tale, he felt no proceedings were active so he wouldn't be doing anything illegal. The permission needed from parent or guardian could also be worked around because she had been treated so shabbily by the same people who were supposed to have her best interests at heart. Fitton felt the moral case was on his side so he asked Jamie to get in touch with Mandy and start working with her to present a weekly column in the Sunday magazine which may have to be ghostwritten if it wasn't up to standard. He also wanted Jamie to ring up 'boring lifestyle columnist' Sonia Moxon to tell her that her column in the magazine was being axed for some fresh material. Fitton knew he was taking a chance by planting this kind of column in the middle of a magazine full of celebrities, fashion tips, recipes and puzzles but he felt strongly that Mandy should tell her 'compelling' story of how the authorities across the country were failing our children. Fitton also believed no fee should be paid for the column but a small donation would be made to charity. Despite all the differences, Jamie was heartened by Fitton's stance. This was him at his best: bold, cavalier and innovative. He'd shown those characteristics before (in Unsung Britain) but he was now using them to pursue a proper story, not some stupid TV show.

23.

The Sack Race On A Hard Shoulder

Mandy's first column in the paper – a bylined effort with a silhouette for a picture – was dramatic. She dived straight in with the rape allegations (although nothing graphic), saving most of her criticism for the police and the care system. After three columns, *Press Gazette* claimed the Daisies had put on 35,000 copies and the postbag at the paper along with the emails and phone calls had been overwhelmed. But there was also plenty of criticism (including horrific abuse from readers) for allowing a 13-year-old girl to speak so freely. Grayson Black, as well as Don Leaver and 64 others signatories, wrote a letter to *The Times* claiming Fitton had 'lost his mind' while urging the PCC to investigate. Some, particularly those with young daughters, threatened legal action, but others were supportive and felt Mandy should be allowed to say what she wanted if the police and courts weren't doing anything to help her. Jamie watched this peculiar story develop from a distance, only communicating with Mandy by email to ensure the copy she sent over (from Smelly Jeff's computer in the care home) was readable and reasonable. Most of the time, it was riddled with spelling errors but the content was never short of spellbinding. She admitted she got too pally with the takeaway staff but there was no-one else to talk to. She could have deep conversations with these people late into the night because they listened. They were her only friends. Outside was dark, dangerous and hostile; inside was bright, warm and full of food. There was no comparison.

In one of her columns, she compared herself to Heath Ledger because she'd fancied him 'rotten'. They could have talked about Hollywood, drugs and role models, she said. They could have made such a difference. She sounded so sincere, Jamie felt guilty he'd never seen a film with Heath Ledger in it.

After three months of Mandy's columns, Jamie was ready to ask her to meet face to face for the first time. He didn't want to travel up to Lancashire so he wanted to know whether she was up for a trip to South Bucks, London or both. He wanted her to know she had a friend.

Jamie called her and she was up for a trip to London to see the 'weird' Palace, a 'proper chippie' and an Avril Lavigne concert at the 02 Arena. Jamie tried to talk her out of the concert but the whole trip was off if he cancelled so Jamie had to go along with it. First, Mandy was all set to come down to Jamie's house, by getting the train from Manchester Piccadilly down to Banbury and then onto Amersham station where Jamie would be waiting. But on the morning of the visit, a tearful Mandy called Jamie's mobile.

'Someone's blackmailing us,' she said, sobbing and sniffing down the phone. 'Knew I shouldn't have come to you lot. You're all the fuckin' same.'

'Hold on, calm down… '

'I'M NOT GONNA CALM DOWN!'

'Just tell me what happened. Are you still intending to get on the train and come down?'

'No, Smelly Jeff found the train ticket you sent for us. Can't come now.'

'Okay, what happened?'

'Someone were in the bins, here at the care home. They got summat of mine.'

'What?'

'A preggers test. I mean there's some dirty bastards in this town but that takes the biscuit.'

Jamie paused and contemplated his next question carefully.

'Are you pregnant?'

'Who the fuck was it? He were talking to Smelly Jeff. They were in it together.'

'I'm not sure who it was but I've got my ideas. I'll put that last question another way: was that pregnancy test related to the allegations you made before.'

'Where do you get off asking me that? And they weren't allegations. I've given the paper everything – and you still want more. I'm keeping my gob shut now. It were a mistake to print all the stuff in the first place. Knew I'd get done over – always have.'

'Was the test positive?'

The line went dead and Jamie was so angry he smacked his mobile against the wall. He called Barnaby Bin immediately and demanded a meeting. Barnaby was busy and said he'd already handed the pregnancy test kit to newsdesk. When Jamie got into the office, a provisional decision had already been made (to be rubber-stamped at conference) to pursue the story of Mandy's pregnancy further. Danny came out of conference in a rage and walked briskly towards Jamie's desk.

'Did you know she was pregnant?'

'No, she doesn't tell me anything.'

'Why the fuck not? Isn't asking questions part of your job?'

'Did you ask Barnaby Bin to look through the rubbish at the care home?'

'Don't be stupid. He does what he wants – then comes to us. Fuck him, Fitton wants to run this story but I think it'll be a disaster; 13-year-old, alleges rape, Muslim baby. It's a killer… '

'Even you've got limits then?'

Danny rushed towards Jamie and grabbed his neck with both hands. He squeezed tight and Jamie found it difficult to breathe.

'The only limit I have is not strangling you here and now,' said Danny. 'The rest is up for grabs. I want you to call your teenage missus and confirm the story is true. We've got a positive preggy test here but we need to hear it from the horse's mouth.'

'I can't ask questions if you don't let go… '

Danny eased off and took his hands off Jamie's neck. Jamie rubbed his sore throat and looked around the office in the vain hope that no-one was watching; plenty were.

'If you run this story, all the goodwill stored up for Mandy will turn to dust,' said Jamie.

'Fitton's choice, not mine. The time for regime change isn't far off. I'm gonna kick his arse all the way to America.'

Mandy said she would only speak to Jamie if he 'battered' Barnaby Bin so he 'bled like a bastard'. Jamie calmed her down by telling her the story of when he first came across Barnaby – as Alex Barnstable – and the death threats he sent to the newsroom. Mandy softened a little and Jamie was relieved. He didn't want to pour petrol on a fire already burning well out of control.

'Are you going to have an abortion?'

'Yeah, but I'm embarrassed to go for help. I feel like there's this evil thing inside us but it's still part of us. It's still life so who am I to take it?'

'Can't you go to your nan's? You said she still talks to you.'

'She's busy taking care of grandad, with his lung cancer, asbestos and all that stuff. I love 'em but they haven't got time for me. I don't listen to them any road.'

'I might be able to help… '

'Ta, but no. Papers give a little but take a lot; I don't need that kind of help anymore. I bled my wrist on one of the dirty rags the other day.'

'What? You're self harming?'

'Never heard of it. My body's doing better now. Made us feel good.'

'Mandy, you need to stop that.'

'Why? What else is there? Wherever I turn, there's people out to get us. Now, I've got this wiggly thing inside us it feels like I'm being punished again. My wrists feel better now, anyhow, there's a couple of plasters on them. Blade weren't that sharp.'

'Do you want me to come up and visit? Might have this present for you.'

Jamie reached into his pocket and felt the wrist bracelet with 'My Jamie' engraved on it. He imagined how it would look on Mandy's wrist.

'What is it?'

'A wrist bracelet. A special one.'

'I don't wear girly things like that. Look, I don't want you to come up; you'll just start asking more questions. Just promise us, this story's not going to get in the papers. I'm not sure I could take it.'

'I'll try but reporters can never make promises… '

Fitton was annoyed that Jamie had demanded to see him in the editor's office because he had a meeting with the deputy PM to attend. He had glanced at the clock above the door already when Jamie sat down.

'Make it quick, Parkesy,' said Fitton, flicking through a stack of rival tabloids. 'I've got hustling to do.'

'Don't run the Mandy Dean pregnancy story.'

'Why?'

'She's not in a good way.'

Fitton laughed and closed the newspaper. 'When has she ever been in a good way? We've been good to her, giving her a column and a focus for her grievances. We've taken a lot of flak for it, although we have flogged a few more papers too.

Other papers are sniffing around this story so we need to act fast. Bin's done a good job in getting some proper evidence. I think the risk is worth it.'

'So you ordered Barnaby up there?'

'Did I fuck. He's free to do what he wants. If it's something of news value, then he comes to us first. Anything else?'

'She might have an abortion… '

'So? Doesn't change anything. It's horrifying enough as it is. Readers will want to know what happened to her. She's well known now. People are interested in her.'

'… Be on your show soon.'

'What was that?'

'Nothing.'

'Look Parkesy, I know you're quite close to her but that's always been your weakness, getting too close to sources. We've taken good care of Mandy so far – and shielded her from some terrible abuse, the internet forums have been full of it so have the Muslim community – but this is too good a story to ignore. A young girl in care, raped, pregnant, probably a Muslim baby… if we don't act, the Screws or someone else will step in. We can't afford that right now.'

'But we can afford redundancies… '

'What are you on about, man? Stick to the subject. Now, go out there and see if Mandy'll play ball with some quotes. If not, we run the story anyway.' He peered at the clock. 'Anything else?'

Jamie shook his head. Fitton got up, grabbed his jacket and left the room with the door wide open. Jamie sat alone in the office for as long as he could until Danny barked at him to get back to his desk and get some work done.

Mandy didn't play ball and the story ran in the paper a few days later. It was a non-bylined, front page exclusive with the headline Teen Columnist Pregnant After Rape. The word

'Muslim' was used five times in the 18-paragraph piece. Jamie went back to bed on Sunday morning after reading it. He wanted to call Mandy to apologise but felt too cowardly to do so. He put his head under the covers and didn't emerge till 4pm. He didn't have work again until Tuesday and agonised over whether to at least send her a text message. The fingers did key in a couple of letters but they were erased. It was academic. On Wednesday night, Louise Dorrans rang up Jamie and said she had some shocking news, which the Squires was going to publish in tomorrow's paper: Mandy was dead. She had committed suicide by jumping into a canal in the early hours of Tuesday morning. Louise said she had drowned. Jamie couldn't speak to Louise for long even though he wanted to ask how she knew all this before the other news outlets. He was numb with shock and felt a profound guilt that he couldn't help such a damaged, vulnerable girl. How could the paper do this to her? Throw her to the dogs like that after everything she had done to improve people's understanding of the care system and all the misery it brought? Fitton had blood on his hands. On Thursday morning, as expected, the Squires went big on the story and the following day it went global. The BBC, Sky News, Al Jazeera and CNN all covered it and the Daisies suffered the kind of virulent criticism it had never experienced in its 129-year history. The media pack had turned on one of its own and was relishing tearing strips out of its coverage, judgement and, most of all its celebrity editor Mr Warren Fitton. Jamie got into the paper on Thursday and was called in to see Fitton and Danny immediately. He went in and saw Danny sitting on the couch to his right and Fitton stood behind his desk.

'Did you talk to the Squires?' asked Fitton.

What? No... '

'So how did they get this Mandy Dean story?'

'I don't know. She died, everyone would have got it.'

'Not necessarily. The Squires got it first, they spoke to someone here, saying that we were to blame for her death. That gave the story booster rockets, hence every man and his dog baying for our blood. Danny says you're the mole.'

'I'm not the fucking mole,' said Jamie, angrily looking across at Danny. 'You should be thinking about Mandy, not some internal fuckin' witch-hunt.'

'I'll ask you again; did you speak to Louise Dorrans about this story?' asked Fitton.

'No, it's not me. Someone else must have spoken to her.'

'So why was she at your house over Christmas?'

'How did you know that?'

'Answer the fucking question.'

'She just came round for New Year that's all. I hadn't seen her for ages; it was a complete surprise.'

'Got on well though, didn't you?'

'What the fuck is this? Stop playing your games because you can't hurt me. You've left a body in a canal so there's nowhere left to go.'

'I'll tell you what's left.'

'What?'

'The door. There it is. You've been sacked. Clear your desk by close of play tonight.'

'BUT IT WASN'T ME!' Jamie got out of his seat. 'I'M TELLING YOU, I'M NOT THE MOLE. I'M NOT THE FUCKING MOLE.' Jamie walked over to Danny on the couch. 'Tell him, Danny, I had nothing to do with this. You knew what the score was. Why would I do something like this now? I wanted to keep my job.' Jamie put his arm on Danny. 'Please, Danny, tell him the truth.'

Danny looked at Jamie's arm on his shoulder and got out his mobile. He keyed in a number and raised his index finger to Jamie.

'Yeah, can I have two up here,' said Danny. 'Getting a bit messy. Make it quick.'

Danny ended the call, put his mobile away and stood up. He put both hands on Jamie's shoulders and bent down to look directly into his eyes.

'You're quite emotional right now. Best to go out there and pack up in an orderly fashion... '

'No, I'm not going to be your scapegoat. I haven't done anything wrong.'

'Okay Parkesy,' said Fitton. 'Let's assume you haven't done anything wrong, who's been talking to Louise then? Her piece had some intimate knowledge of this place, Mandy Dean and the deal we struck for her columns. It all points in your direction.'

Jamie took Danny's hand off his shoulders. 'There's a lot pointing in your direction too,' said Jamie, looking at Fitton. 'Illegal payments, corruption, hacking – and that's just for starters – we haven't even got to murder. Mandy would have something to say about that.'

'All right, have it your way: fucking get out,' said Fitton. 'I've got enough on my plate without an idiot like you. Get a job at Northern Rock or something. See you behind a counter... '

'I'm not going until I get a better explanation.'

Danny stepped in front of Jamie. 'Listen Jammy, don't embarrass yourself. I could get my gloves on but my hands are full right now. I reckon you've got about 10 seconds left because, as you know, the security lads are very fast. They're not overworked to say the least. I'd walk out of here right now.'

Jamie shook his head and folded his arms. About a minute later, there was a knock at the door and two chunky, tooled-up security guards came into the office. Danny simply nodded and the two guards grabbed hold of Jamie's shoulders.

'GET OFF ME, YOU FUCKING GORILLAS,' shouted Jamie, as he was being dragged away.

They were too strong for Jamie as they pulled him out of the office with Danny and Fitton looking on. Jamie stopped struggling because he knew it was futile but the men still held him with a ferocity and nasty intent that Jamie thought was excessive. They lead him straight towards the exit.

'Hey, hold on, I need to clear my desk.'

'No time for that, Squire, we'll box it up for you.'

'Come on, I've got some important things there. Only I can sort it out properly.'

'WE SAID NO!'

The eyes of the newsroom were on Jamie. There had been plenty of humiliations in Jamie's life but after this, there was surely no contest. He felt utterly degraded and embarrassed. He had been carted out of the office he'd inhabited for nearly a decade like an animal. The two guards took him out of the exit and into the lift. They got into reception and Jamie's aching shoulders were still being held. He could see the receptionist watching a tiny, portable TV perched precariously on a shelf and Jamie just caught Mandy's name being mentioned on the news. The receptionist, who Jamie had never spoken to before, looked at Jamie with disdain. Jamie was ushered out into the car park and finally the two guards let go of him. The beefier one pushed him in the back which caused him to fall onto his knees and scrape his hands on the concrete. He looked up at the swing under the tree and imagined a 13-year-old girl sitting on it without a care in the world.

Jamie got home and sat in silence in the hallway for half an hour. He regretted not being a NUJ or BAJ member. At least they would have stood up for him. He remembered Louise saying the help was most valuable when you were at your most vulnerable. She wasn't wrong there. She was always smarter than him: she carried spare batteries for her dictaphone and a mobile phone charger in her handbag. Jamie was lucky if he had a spare pen. He called her mobile. The line was engaged. He tried again 17 times – and on the 18th she was available.

'Sorry Jamie, I'm up to my neck in it,' said Louise. 'They're all crawling out of the woodwork now: Tristan Boyce and that cabinet minister whatisname Wade or something... '

'Vernon Wade.'

'Yeah him. They've all called the paper saying that they've been the victims of phone hacking for years and that Fitton and the Daisies are the devil incarnate. Loads of celebrities and film stars are ringing us too. You couldn't get a peep from the cowards before but now they're ready to follow the crowd and lob a few grenades. An army sergeant and a prison officer called us too. It's been insane really. I've lost count.'

'Sounds like most of Trevena's WarFit list. Doesn't matter now anyway.'

'Why?'

'I've been sacked.'

There was a pause on the line and then a sigh.

'You should have listened to me when I came over for New Year. We could have put some pressure on immediately. Now the collateral damage is huge. A pregnant 13-year-old is dead and Fitton's fogeys are turning on him. What reason did he give?'

'He said I was the mole for the Squires.'

'If only. I still know lots of people on your paper. Lame excuse from Fitton. I think that TV show's inflated his ego to another level. He's taken some ridiculous risks lately, with that Mandy stuff. I actually thought his decision to give her a column was quite visionary but to run that story on her pregnancy was obscene. Did you ever meet her?'

'No, although it was planned. You're with the NUJ, yeah? Have you got a direct contact for them?'

'Oh Jamie, Jamie, not got round to being a member? It's no good trying to retrieve the situation now – the horse has bolted.'

'I did call them a couple of time in the early days but never filled in the forms. Danny said it wasn't worth it – and we were too busy anyway.'

'What a surprise. Our industry's going to need more protection not less. Journalists are losing their jobs all the time – and the graveyard of the web is still waiting for us. I'm not sure what he could do for you now. Hold on... '

Jamie waited as Louise flicked through the pages of her contacts book.

'Bill Marsden is one of the guys who covers the nationals. His number is... '

'He was the one at Jimmy Betson's side when he got kicked out. Does he deal with wrongful dismissal?'

'Don't know. Is that what you're going for? Because if you are, make sure none of your sticky prints are over anything, particularly those early days at the Daisies where showbiz and you were having a contest about who could hack the biggest name.'

Jamie sighed and lifted his head to the ceiling. 'But everyone did that. In this case, I haven't done anything wrong. They just made me the fall guy.'

'Are you sure they've got the evidence?'

'No, I'm not sure but this was a nasty way to go. I was thrown out of the building by a couple of heavies.'

'You didn't deserve that. Cruelty is part of their DNA. What you need to do is calculate whether it's worth pursuing a case of unfair dismissal and all the shit that will bring. You have to be certain there's no evidence against you. If you're happy with all that then the fight might be worth it. Look, I've got to go now, newsdesk are shouting, well, calling at me, and there's other people on the line.'

'Wait, I just wanted to ask you about freelance opportunities... '

'Jamie, I haven't got time. This is a huge story I'm covering here... '

'Come on, just a couple more minutes. Who's the features editor at your place?'

'Sorry Jamie, I've got to go... '

Louise hung up and Jamie didn't enjoy it. He remembered his own days cutting people off, speaking to multiple contacts, making excuses and saying he was busy when he only needed a coffee. He finally got up and headed to the kitchen to pour himself a glass of brandy. He went to the cupboard and poured half a packet of Skittles into the glass. He headed upstairs with the glass and walked into the bedroom. He glanced up at the exclusive stories on the wall and came up with one conclusion – the only power he had was to unleash the Larna Wilson story to the public. It had been sitting dormant for too long. The unfair dismissal claim was morally right but legally ropey – this was more the kind of language tabloids understood: if they get you, come back with something bigger. Jamie drank the whole glass and relished the sweet kick of Skittles swimming in his mouth. He slipped into bed with his clothes on and wanted to sleep for a very long time.

24.

The New FAAGs, The New Addiction

Jamie wrote a letter of condolence to Mandy's grandparents. It took him a couple of weeks. After posting the letter, Jamie went for a stroll in The Broadway in the Old Town. He remembered Adam saying he liked walking down the soothing, character-filled streets of Beaconsfield Old Town when he returned from active duty in Iraq and Kuwait. Jamie had to admit Amersham Old Town had a similar feel: the wide streets, the shape of the buildings and the way the cars were parked, in neat rows mostly facing the shop fronts, gave him the kind of unexpected lift he thought was only reserved for old people, his mother and broadsheet readers. A reassessment of the place he lived, which had always felt sleepy and mundane, was in order.

He came down with a bump almost immediately as he had no option but to head to Tesco in Whielden Street to do his weekly shop. He examined his receipt for the first time in years. He calculated the £60-plus shopping bill could probably go on for a few months yet but, if he wasn't back in regular work, he'd have to cut back by winter. The problem was some of the lactose-free goods were always more expensive – and they tasted shit too.

He went home and planned to tackle the Lar-Lar story – but after ringing Bill Marsden at the NUJ (who wasn't available) a troubling thought occurred. Yes, he had an amazing story about Larna's affair with the young Prince but there was a crushing realisation that it was all from hacked material. He had no direct quotes from Larna or anyone else confirming the story, just the intercepted voicemail messages which, granted, were explosive but would leave him exposed to the charge of being no better than Fitton or anyone else; he'd just be another tabloid rogue dabbling in the dark arts of phone hacking. Things were bad enough as they were: he'd be completely compromised.

Trevena called in the evening and was in chipper mood because the Commons select committee for Culture, Media and Sport were launching a probe into phone hacking and widespread illegality in newspapers. He said he had no idea of Jamie's sacking but he wasn't in the least bit surprised.

'There's no limit to their thuggish tendencies,' said Trevena. 'To not get be able to clear your desk and say goodbye is hard to get my head round. I still can't believe it.'

'My shoulder still hurts. How's the Mandy Dean story gone down in the Commons?'

'They seem to be relishing it. Three MPs approached me the other day and claimed they'd been on my side all along and wanted to see the tabloids liquidated. I felt a great emptiness and sense of anti-climax as I listened to them. I'd been a lone voice in the wilderness for so long that this new-found praise and back-slapping felt phoney and calculated. Their smiles and jokes made me sick.'

'At least politicians are finally taking it seriously. Is there a police investigation yet? I haven't been keeping up with news lately.'

'Lord, and I thought MPs were of touch! What have you been doing? Locking yourself up in your bedroom and twiddling those hundreds of tape recording knobs you've got piled up in there.'

'No, I've been sipping a bit of liqueur, doing some shopping and writing a few letters. I wrote one to Mandy's grandparents.'

'Don't think you would have done that a few years ago. I do wonder, how on earth, the police and social services failed on such a massive scale. Fitton's story was terrible but it pales into insignificance when compared to their inadequacies.'

'So what about the police then? Fitton in jail in a couple of years' time?'

'We can only hope, but they haven't even started investigating yet. Anderton doesn't want to look into this too much, for obvious reasons, but Grayson Black does... '

'Do you think Grayson Black's corrupt too?'

'I don't think so. I have met him – and he looks a decent sort. Although I said the same about Anderton. This is still going to take a long time. The hacking victims are starting to talk but the illegal payments are harder to trace. The police are notoriously slow when any of their own are involved.'

'Hope it's quicker than that; might get my job back.'

'... You'd want to go back there? Are you mad?'

'If Fitton and Danny left, the stables would be cleaned out – and we could make a new beginning.'

'You're being naïve. I would forget all about that paper. Its reputation is diminishing by the day. There's plenty of media jobs elsewhere.'

'I'm missing it more than I thought. A couple of mornings ago, I automatically put my shirt and tie on and only remembered I wasn't working there anymore when I started preparing my breakfast.'

'Sounds like you need a doctor... '

'You've already sent one: Noonan. That reminds me, did you know about his amazing story when he was a teenager? He survived a crash.'

'Never told me about it.'

'Hmm... '

Jamie picked up his notebook from the bedside table. He

quickly wrote down Noonan's name at the top, Trevena's underneath with WarFit on the third line.

'Just had a couple of ideas,' said Jamie. 'I need some freelance stuff, just to keep the tills ringing. I could do a piece on Noonan and maybe one on you too. Do a profile on how you never gave up.'

'Leave me out of it. A few papers have already requested interviews. I've passed. What was the story on Noonan anyway?'

Jamie paused and looked at his notebook. 'He had a heart problem and was flung out of an ambulance. He somehow survived. It's unbelievable, really.'

'Now that's an article I'd really want to read.'

'... And a lot of punters would also want an article on the MP with integrity who took on the tabloids and won.'

'Nothing has been won. There are no arrests yet, never mind charges. The court of public opinion has given its verdict but it's not the one that matters. I want you appear at our committee hearings and give evidence. You've got plenty of time on your hands now.'

'No chance.'

'Ditto, leave me out of your papers too. But, my freelance friend, one day you will be up before a committee, or even jury, and you'll have to wield the knife deep into the tabloid flesh so it never smirks so much again. Who else has the inside track? Who else saw the abuses? No-one – or they're too afraid of coming forward.'

'I'm afraid too...'

'Of what?'

'Having no job security. I don't know how to do anything else apart from journalism. It's in my blood.'

'If it's in your blood you'll make sure it's dark heart starts to pump properly. If not, more Mandy Dean's will suffer and that'll be a tragedy for all of us.'

Over the next few months, Jamie was alarmed at how many of his freelance queries and ideas weren't considered or just plain ignored. A couple of emails came back – one from *The People* features desk (not even the editor) and another from *The Mail* – with the former saying they had more than enough freelance copy and contributors up until Christmas and the latter saying only if he had something dazzling would they consider it. Jamie thought the Noonan story *was* dazzling but obviously not. It did cross Jamie's mind that some of the editors may have found out about Jamie's sacking and that he might have been blacklisted. If this was the case, the freelance game would be much harder to break into than expected. He'd have to up his game to win over those gatekeeping commissioning editors. Signing on was out of the question.

These minor setbacks led him to explore other avenues like websites, magazines and newsletters. He also realised he'd have to work 10 times as hard as he did in the newsroom. He had become lazy in the office. Most of the stories were spoon fed to him and he simply had to stitch them together. Now, more research had to be done and more angles had to be found, Names, dates and anniversaries were explored with surgical precision to extract story potential but, most of the time, they lead to dead ends and weak copy. Jamie quickly came to a conclusion: freelancing was no glamorous trade; it was lonely, daunting and intimidating.

One morning, Jamie was sitting on the sofa in his boxer shorts and t-shirt flicking through the meagre job ads in *Press Gazette*. The front door opened and closed; he knew who it was so he put his bare feet up on the table. He looked closer at a couple of ads for sub-editors. These cunts always had job opportunities. He should have trained as one. He looked up as the door opened. Tina walked in with a copy of Sunday's Daisies under her arm.

'Moping around isn't going to help,' she said. 'Heard the local paper might be taking someone on.'

'Must be joking if you think I'm going back to one of those sweatshops.'

Tina threw the paper onto the table and walked towards Jamie. She sat down on the edge of the sofa, facing Jamie with her hand on his knee.

'You were a bit vague on the phone,' she said. 'What reason did they give? Was it something to with that Mandy girl?'

'God no, that was Fitton's decision. I was dead against running the story. He got rid of me because he thought I was grassing to another paper but it wasn't me.'

'... I thought you were grassing to another paper?'

'Not on this occasion. It wasn't me.'

Tina rubbed Jamie's knee and got up. She walked to the door.

'CherishUs has gone into administration,' she said. 'Adam's going through a hard time right now. He said it was mainly to do with Lehmann Brothers going down but I think the papers had more to do with it. They got into people's heads.'

'You'll blame us if the whole global system comes crashing down. Just get me another can of Grolsch from the fridge, mum... '

Tina threw the copy of the Daisies in Jamie's direction. It landed on the carpet and he picked it up.

'Page 14,' she said. 'Is it accurate?'

Jamie flicked through the pages and stopped at Page 14. A short, six-paragraph story appeared with the headline: 'Sacked Reporter in Drugs Shame'. Jamie read the story in seconds and wanted to throw up immediately.

'Big deal,' he said.

'Did you take drugs?'

'Maybe, I have a lot of time to kill.'

'I thought Mark was one of your friends? He's quoted in that story. Some friend.'

'They must have paid him a good whack. We did go out, Larnell and Melvin Moon too. We just had a good night, that's all.'

'On speed and LSD?'

'You drink don't you?'

'It's not the same. Drugs are more dangerous.'

'So am I, please get me a drink. They're trying to destroy me.'

Tina sighed and put her index finger and thumb on the bridge of her nose.

'Just make sure you don't destroy yourself.'

Jamie told Larnell their friendship was over if he carried on hanging around with Mark. Larnell had no idea about the story but said that Mark had gone on a long holiday to Cape Town anyway. After five weeks, when he didn't come back, Larnell became more sympathetic to Jamie's side of the story. Jamie wrote to the PCC to complain and eventually received an acknowledgement letter. That was about all he expected. Hannah called and asked him if the story was true even though she was sympathetic about his sacking. Charming, thought Jamie, he'd left the paper what seemed like an age ago and hadn't heard a dicky-bird from her and here she was now grilling him over a drugs matter.

'Well, at least you've cleared that up.' said Hannah. 'Just a little fun night with the lads, nothing wrong with that. Did you try any coke?'

'No, but if we did, I'd ask an MP for tips on how to cope with it.'

'... At least you haven't lost your sense of humour. Wouldn't mind getting lost in some spacey drugs right now.

It's not going to happen for me. The Labour guy, Jim Ryman-Davies, is still respected around here and, no matter how much hustling and lobbying I do, it's not making much difference. He's already got a surgery set up in a plush little office where people can drop in. I've got a dingey little room in a youth club, it's not much of a contest.'

'I did warn you.'

'I'm a big girl. I can take it. I could do with some good PR though. He's got a good campaign manager already. They're getting their message across. Have you got another job yet?'

'No, I'm freelancing.'

'You could do some PR for me... '

'You must be joking.'

'Don't want to work for a woman?'

'It's not that; I just don't want get involved in all that spin and bullshit.'

'... As opposed to your spin and bullshit? It's okay, it was just a suggestion, me thinking out loud. Got to go now, anyway, have a meeting with the post office manager. Their branch might be shutting down so he's got a lot on his plate.'

Jamie wanted to talk for longer but she hung up abruptly. He may have been hasty in dismissing Hannah's PR proposal outright but there was no way he could put on the kind of performance, which is what it was, for 24 hours a day in a long campaign. But he had a more disturbing thought: he had desperately wanted Hannah to make it as an MP but now, with his own problems stacking up, he wasn't so sure.

Jamie was watching Grayson Black giving a press conference on TV while talking to Bill Marsden on his mobile. Jamie found Bill pretty boring but it was essential he knew about the legal issues about fighting a case against the Daisies. Bill said he could put him onto a solicitor but Jamie had made a decision: it would be messy, pointless and, most likely, a waste of time. He didn't have the energy, will or resources to go the distance. Whether the evidence was on his side too wasn't clear-cut. Bill was sympathetic to Jamie's position and Jamie used his generosity to ask him about jobs and freelancing. There wasn't much about, said Bill, because management were using the bank bailouts and financial crisis as an excuse to lay off more workers. Jamie felt more gloomy but also more knowledgeable after he got off the phone to Bill. He gave his full concentration to Grayson Black, who was flanked by the officer who would be in charge of the phone-hacking investigation, Marina Doodson. Anderton was nowhere to be seen. Black was asked why it had taken so long to get this investigation going and answered that it would take even longer to trawl through the hundreds, potentially thousands, of victims. They still didn't have enough evidence and witnesses; they needed more. They didn't have enough documents in their possession and some had already been shredded. Jamie imagined Danny and Fitton lighting bonfires in the car park by the swing. After the press conference, Jamie switched the TV off and headed off up to his bedroom. If his faith in the police was ropey before, Mr Black and Mrs Doodson hadn't done anything to restore it. He was exhausted already: being in it for the long haul wasn't a prospect he was relishing.

Jamie went in to see Dr Hobson because he was finding it difficult to sleep. The doctor asked Jamie about his circumstances and then prescribed 20mg of Amitriptyline. After four days, of taking a couple of tiny blue pills a day, Jamie's sleep patterns drastically improved – in fact, he was oversleeping. On the fifth lie-in day, Jamie's mobile rang and he reluctantly picked it up from the carpet to answer it.

'*The Fitton Well's* having its first series in America next February.'

'Sorry, I've just woke up. Miss Orange, is that you?'

'I'm now Miss Apple. I was made redundant. Luckily, I've landed on my feet. This company looks like it's going places.'

'Can you get me an i-Phone?'

'Bed's best friend? I'll see what I can do. Is he still running your paper? I'd have thought the bosses would have got rid of him by now, what with all the criticism.'

'They got rid of me instead.'

'Shit, no? How and why? That's obscene.'

'Didn't you read that story about me recently?'

'What story? I've been busy with all the work problems, relocating and everything... '

'Anyway, the bottom line is I'm gone and Danny and Fitton and everyone else are still there. How do you know about this show in America?'

'I've had to do lots of advertising research lately for my new job, particularly of American websites and media so we can use similar strategies over here. I came across this piece on a showbiz website.'

'There's been no news over here... '

'He probably wants to keep it quiet for now with all the shit he's been getting. Be interesting to see if he can pull in a better standard of guest.'

'Not interested. Look, I don't want to talk about this now. I'm grateful for this dazzling breaking news but I need to get up and fire off some desperate emails.'

'No breakfast or fag then?'

'I don't smoke.'

'I was reading about a trend the other day; people wake up and the first thing they reach for is their smartphone – because they need to do something with their fingers. Fags are dead because they've been banned in public places. The new FAAGs: Facebook, Apple, Amazon and Google are ready to take over the world, to become the new addiction. I ain't complaining because I've got a good job but you should, because along with cigarettes, your papers are going up in smoke. No-one will be reading them when I'm a granny.'

'Thanks for the early-morning lift – and the lecture.'

'You're welcome. Let's those fingers roam.'

Miss Apple hung up and Jamie looked at his mobile. It had very basic internet access. He fiddled about with it for a few minutes but then threw it onto the bedside table. He wondered if he'd ever be able to afford a smartphone – but really, he wanted a joint between his fingers.

Louise sent Jamie an email about Elliot. He had left journalism all together and opened a small art gallery in Oxford. After a couple of weeks of prevarication, Jamie decided to drive up the M40 to St Aldates in Oxford. It took almost an hour to find the gallery which was hidden away, between shops, through a heavy grey door and steep staircase. There was no shop front or display; it was unlikely anyone else knew it was there. Jamie climbed up the stairs and eventually reached a white door with the words 'Broom of Beauty Ltd' painted on the door in bright orange letters. Jamie found it difficult to contain his laughter. He walked in and there in front of him was Elliot, sitting down on a vintage armchair, drinking coffee and reading a copy of *The Guardian*. He was surrounded by framed pictures, haphazardly lying on the floor, resting against the wall, hung up and, even, stacked up vertically, although they looked as though they could topple over at any minute. There was a small counter where he presumably did business and some striking vases, pots and sculptures dotted around. Jamie's eye was drawn to one picture which showed pieces of a torn newspaper, like snow, falling on top of a huge crowd as they looked skywards in horror. Elliot was so engaged in reading the paper, he hadn't even noticed Jamie come in.

'The news bug is a hard one to shift,' said Jamie, walking towards Elliot. 'What the hell are you doing here? Even MI5 couldn't find this place.'

'It's precisely the reason I'm here,' said Elliot, putting the paper down on the three-legged table next to him. He got out of his chair and walked towards Jamie. He smiled as he shook Jamie's hand. 'The media world can do without me for a while. Who put you up to this? Louise, no doubt. She cares, I suppose, and that's all that matters. Want some coffee?'

'Surprised, you've got a kettle. No, I'm okay, unless you've got some soy milk. Black makes me sick.'

Elliot nodded. 'Have you got that sorted now? The lactose stuff?'

'Kind of,' said Jamie, with a smile. 'Now, I'm out of the newsroom, I can't be sent to dairy farms or cheese festivals.'

'What are you on about?'

'Don't work there anymore. Booted out.'

'Louise never told me.'

'... Well, you are on some sort of desert island here. Broom of Beauty Limited? Couldn't you come up with something better?'

Elliot walked away towards the counter. 'Thought it wasn't too bad, actually.' He picked up a scrawny-looking catalogue and handed it to Jamie. 'You're a martyr now, you should be proud. In the history books of this sorry saga, you'll be a whistleblowing hero.'

'Don't know about that,' said Jamie, taking the catalogue and sitting down on the vintage chair. 'Martyrs are the kind of guys who've just gutted Mumbai. Don't want to be associated with them.'

'Funny that, I was just reading about it. Paper covered it well.'

Jamie glanced up at Elliot. 'You're still missing it, I reckon.'

'Journalism? Not a chance. This is what I've wanted to do

for a while. I used to daydream while I was in the office. I could see giant canvasses in my head. I love it. I would never go back.'

'But where's the money coming from?'

'I have just enough to pay the rent. There's a website, mini-exhibitions and a thriving art community round here so I don't have anything to worry about. I feel freer than ever, certainly more relaxed than I was chasing stories. That wasn't for me anyway. I did an interview with a famous painter once and told him I'd dabbled in art and he said: "Are you just going to ask silly questions all your life or are you going to do something meaningful with it". That had a big effect on me.'

'Hmm, that kind of life's not for me,' said Jamie, flicking through the catalogue. 'If I think about internal things too much, I go mad. I'd rather talk to people, go out, cover their issues.'

'Like anything you see?'

Jamie looked up and smiled. 'Want me to be honest?'

'Be brutal.'

'They don't do much for me.'

'Sometimes, you have to look a bit harder and deeper. Enough about me, what are you doing with your time right now? Freelancing?'

'I wondered when we'd get round to me,' said Jamie, with a smile. 'You've talked about yourself a lot. I mean, I've heard about artists being up their own arse but that was ridiculous. You could blab on forever.'

'Keeping it brief is for tabloids.'

Jamie laughed and looked down at the catalogue again. He saw a sparse picture of a mountain with a solitary bike perched on the top of it. Jamie glanced up at Elliot.

'This what I think it is?'

Elliot walked up to the three-legged table to pick up his

mug of coffee. He took a sip and glanced down at the catalogue.

'It's part of my life,' said Elliot. 'I had to exorcise the guilt. It was eating me up. There was so much it was unbearable.'

'You with someone now?'

'Not seriously but, yes. One day, we might live together but that's a long way off.'

Jamie closed the catalogue and got up. He walked towards the canvas that had caught his attention as soon as he'd walked in. He picked up the landscape painting and looked closely at the expressions of the crowd as they watched the newspaper shreds falling onto their heads.

'You like that one?'

'I can see what you're saying with this one.'

'I've called it 'Pry in the Sky'. I'm really trying to say that no one is safe from the tabloid peril. Everyone is in danger.'

'How much are you charging for these?'

'For you, that's free.'

'No, come on, don't fuck around.'

'I'd usually charge about £150 for that.'

Jamie looked over his shoulder at Elliot. 'Things are a bit tight right now.'

'... And you ask me what I'm doing for cash! Who's the pauper now? Editors not giving you any commissions?'

'Something like that.'

Elliot walked over to Jamie and eased the picture out of his hands. He grabbed a large piece of brown paper, wrapped up the picture and handed it to Jamie.

'We've made a big contribution in improving the general health of newspapers, give or take the odd indiscretion,' said Elliot. 'We shouldn't forget that. They've taken our scalps... ' Elliot pointed to small bald patch on the top of his head. '... But they'll never take our dignity.'

Jamie looked at the picture and shook Elliot's hand. 'As I

said, artists are always up their own arse.' He smiled and walked towards the door.

'Just make sure you're tabloid-stained one is covered,' said Elliot. 'Plenty of dirt there to still clean up.'

25.

You've Been Framed

Noonan had been arrested – but released without charge after 36 hours. He called Jamie and asked to meet at the pharmacy. Jamie had inhabited these places a little too often recently and was reluctant to go but Noonan's surprising revelation swayed his decision. Jamie sat down opposite the doctor, who was without his hat, but sipped his regulation cup of camomile and honey tea.

'I hear you're on about 50 milligrammes now,' said Noonan, without looking at Jamie. 'How many times did I warn you of getting hooked on pills?'

'I'm not hooked. I didn't think that's why we're here. How did you know that anyway?'

'Your Dr Hobson is a nice man – but he's not trying to look after you. I am. He's interested in writing prescriptions and sending people to shiny hellholes like this. I'm interested in you not throwing your life away – and becoming dependent on drugs.'

'They're not drugs.'

'Anti-depressants are drugs. If you're not sleeping: meditate, read, or go for a walk.'

'Didn't medication save your life?'

'Who knows? A mother and son did. A heart operation also. Lots of things contributed to saving my life like my head hitting the wheel of car rather than the kerb. I'm sure some pills did too. Hell, there was a preacher on the sidewalk who claimed he'd said a prayer while I was flying through the air. Who could argue with him?'

'Look, I didn't come here for philosophical mumbo jumbo. I thought you were going to tell me why you were arrested. Looks like the overnight cell might have messed with your head.'

'No, I had a good night's sleep,' said Noonan, smiling at Jamie. 'I meditated, got seven hours at least.' He took another sip of tea and pursed his lips as though he was tasting some vintage wine. 'The interrogation itself was pretty cowardly. They only asked a few questions about Gordon and Fitton; it was mostly about my time dealing with film stars and what they got up to. One detective asked me if he could get Ray Winstone's number because his father used to drink in the same pub as him.'

'And did you?'

'I like his movies but don't have his number.'

'Should have gone all *Scum* or *Nil By Mouth* on him,' said Jamie, with a smile. 'Look Fitton's already smearing me with negative stories and, if it was up to him, you'd be locked away too. Don't worry about my odd little blue pills. They're nothing. They're just giving me a lift. I'll be fine. Please let's stay together on this one; we've still got unfinished business.'

'If you don't get off the pills, you won't have any business to finish. Have you sold any freelance articles yet? Apart from the one you were going to do on me.'

'A couple of websites took my copy. Fitton's ensured that I can't get my freelance career off the ground. I'm going to give it another month, then I need to find something else... '

Noonan paused and finished off his tea. 'How about you do a piece on my interrogation? The Fitton story is still live in the media so you could tie my arrest and release in with that. Surely, some two-bit editor will take that – and maybe from there you could establish yourself.'

Jamie nodded. 'Sounds good. If they don't want that, they're all corrupt.'

'One condition, though... '

'What?'

'No more pills.'

'We'll see. Bylines are the best anti-depressant there is.'

Jamie's interview with Noonan was published in *The Independent on Sunday* but none of the dailies took it. Jamie earned a measly £160 for the piece, nowhere near enough to keep the house running in a satisfactory manner. He would have to start earning regularly soon. He had a final blitz by sending a batch of query letters and emails to news and features editors containing a whole host of story ideas: a preview on Guy Ritchie's film *Sherlock Holmes*; the collapse of Iceland's banking system; an English farmer smuggling himself into Zimbabwe during historic elections; boy band Blue reforming after a split; terrorist attacks on sports teams, a feature on Prodigy's new album and a piece on potential Tube chaos leading up to the London Olympics. None of these were met with a positive response. He also spent a lot of time on Facebook and Twitter, taking verbatim quotes from celebrity pages, which was a difficult habit to shake off. It was a pathetically easy story to write. After another month of deep consideration and mild despair, Jamie called Hannah and was ready to accept her offer of PR bullshitter.

'I've hired someone else, sorry Jamie,' said Hannah. ''I had to do something because I couldn't cope on my own.'

'You could have fuckin' waited.'

'Calm down. It's been months since we spoke. Trevena kindly helped me out with a bit of money so I could hire someone decent... '

'Which I'm not obviously... '

'No, you would have been ideal with your years of experience in the media. But I did ask you – and you couldn't do it. I'm trying to be an MP, not a lap dancer. This is a serious business. There's a hate campaign running against me so I need some support. We've got no chance anyway because Labour have got the seat nailed. They've got an army of helpers.'

'What the hell are you doing it for then?'

'It's a good experience. I'm still young. I might be able to stand again one day. So I take it the job hunting isn't going so well?'

'You work day after day in this industry, extra hours, ridiculous deadlines, a hostage to newsdesk but once you're on a scrapheap, they don't give a shit. They'll have new trainees or shifters who they can prostitute for a good story. I'm just fucked off with the whole grisly circus. I don't want part of it anymore. I'll do something else, anything… '

'Like what?'

'I don't know but I'm all out of stories.'

After a badly-needed trip to the barber's because his hair was covering his ears, Jamie walked the short distance to Lavendales recruitment consultancy in Sycamore Road. He walked in and, as expected, Gemma was there behind her small desk, headset on, speaking into a mike, peering into the computer screen and briskly pressing the keys. She didn't see Jamie straight away but just as Jamie pondered whether to leave, she glanced up and Jamie had no option but to approach her desk and offer a strained smile. Jamie had to wait as Gemma continued to talk to a customer offering a range of employment opportunities. She finally ended the call and took off her headset and mike.

'Your mother's been calling me relentlessly asking me to help you out with job opportunities but really, you're a big boy, and you should be able to help yourself,' said Gemma. 'What kind of things are you looking for anyway? Not much glamorous media stuff in here.'

'Not even advertising and PR?'

Gemma looked at her computer. 'Thought you loathed them?'

'Something about beggars, choosers and losers… '

'Look Jamie, let's not waste each other's time. There's unlikely to be anything related to your field. I'm sure word of mouth is kingmaker in the media world. In the real world, not many firms are hiring due to the financial climate. If I'm going to help you, there's going to have to be a big readjustment on your part. You're probably overqualified for some jobs and underskilled for others. Do you want a full-time position?'

'Not sure, but I need something quickly, preferably local.'

'How about temping? If you start with that, you'll be able to tell if you can hack it.' Gemma smiled as she said the word. 'We know you're good at that. Are all your staff in jail yet? Hope so, after that dreadful piece on that pregnant teenager.'

'Me as well?'

'Did you try to stop it?'

'Yes.'

'Let you off.' Gemma looked at her computer again. 'Right, there's quite a few temping posts that you could get started on straight away. Most of the ones in this area are warehouse-based, packing, that kind of thing,' Gemma hesitated and looked at Jamie. 'Are you sure you're up for them?'

'I have to be up for anything,' said Jamie, grimacing as he rubbed the back of his neck.

'Are you all right?'

'Yeah, just had a haircut. They never fucking cover your neck properly.'

'No, I was thinking about your eyes, they look a bit droopy and lethargic.'

'Just get on with it.'

'Don't get funny with me, Jamie, I'm trying to help you.'

'What's the most local you've got?'

Gemma gave him a cold look and clicked the mouse on her computer. 'It's a company called First Frames in Bell Lane, they're involved in shipping frames to retailers.'

'I'll take it. When can I start?'

'It's shift work: six till two and two till 10... '

'Fuckin' hell, can't get up at six. The other one.'

'They've got an order for four months work initially. They've got a big batch to get out. If you do well, they might give you a permanent position.' Gemma picked up her pen and started writing on a Post-it note. This is the number of the guy who runs it. Give him a call – and you might be able to start Monday. Make sure you've got the usual things: NI number, bank details... '

'Yeah, yeah I know the score,' said Jamie, taking the note and putting it into his pocket without looking at it. 'When are you seeing my mother again?'

'Spoke to her a couple of days ago. They've adopted a 14-year-old girl from a care home. Should be living with them soon. Called Natalie, I think... '

Jamie nodded and walked away. His mother hadn't told him about Natalie; probably a good thing. The last thing he wanted was to engage with another damaged young girl who had the sharp-tongued ability to leave him defeated and exhausted. The scars of Mandy Dean hadn't healed yet – and perhaps never would – but another precocious girl flitting around would be impossible for him to bear. Total avoidance was the only strategy.

Jamie found his first day at work oddly exhilarating but it was nothing to do with his job description. Barry Weymouth, his supervisor, whisked through the health and safety drills, location of the toilets, nature of the job, company policies and much more in a half-hour tornado that left Jamie trailing in his wake. When Jamie did get started he found the work confusing and a lot harder than expected. There were four frame colours: walnut, cherry, brown and black and they had to be matched with boxes that had samples of those colours on the side. Once Jamie had identified the boxes' colour, his job was to gather six frames of that colour, stack them up neatly, place them in the box, seal it, put an address label on it and place it in the corner of the warehouse on a giant trolley with multiple wheels. The problem was, Jamie found it difficult to match the box colour with the frame: the walnut looked like brown and the cherry looked like black. Was he going colour blind? Was it the pills? The benzo's Melvin Moon had been slipping him? He didn't want to disturb Barry so he called over one of his work colleagues Richie Yallop who was wearing a headband, woolly gloves and had a closely-cropped beard.

'Yeah, it's wank isn't it?' said Richie. 'Don't fret over the colours. There's little sticker codes on the bottom of the box. Zero one for walnut, two for cherry and so on. It's piss once you know that.'

'Thanks a lot, mate. Appreciate it.'

'You new?'

'Yeah, just need some cash to keep things rolling.'

'Tell us about it. You done this kind of slavery before? Look a bit overdressed for this line of work.'

'First time, really.' Jamie paused and weighed up his next words carefully. 'Used to be a journalist.'

'Funny that, I heard on the radio this morning something about a newspaper bloke being arrested. Love, something… Davis Love?'

'No, that's a golfer.'

'Whatever, but do you know the bloke? You're all a bit cozy down there in London town.'

'Was it Danny Love?'

'Think so, yeah. The way I see it, all you toads have got your fingers in the tiller: bankers, journalists and now these dirty MPs as well… '

'MPs?'

'Don't you listen to the news man? What kind of journalist are you?'

'What about MPs?'

'Expenses mate, expenses. It was in one of the heavy papers this morning. My mum, for some strange reason, still gets it delivered. It's now all over the airwaves. Thing is, they steal money and then they ask for your vote. They need stringing up. Anyone who comes round my house during the next election could get hurt. I'm not joking.'

'… Were there any clean ones?'

'They're all corrupt but if a decent one emerged they'd win hands down.'

A week later, Jamie was sat in the tiny break room eating his ham and lettuce sandwich while slipping crisps from his bag of McCoys into it for more flavour. He followed up by drinking straight from the carton of soy milk. There were four plastic green chairs, a battered Sanyo stereo, a kettle, three dirty mugs and several slug-like tea bags in the sink. The door to the break room was also annoying in that it didn't close so everyone in the warehouse could see and hear what was going on. The stories had been confirmed: the MPs expenses story had well and truly blown up and Danny Love had been arrested. Danny's arrest came after a dawn raid at his house. His wife had complained of excessive force being used and their kids being frightened. Would the police come after him next? Danny said Jamie's name was on the invoice for the Leaver/Rocheman story but, equally, news editors were also the biggest liars on the planet. They had to tell more porkies than politicians, estate agents and US presidents put together. Jamie's mobile rang and Hannah's name flashed up.

'Sorry Jamie, bit chaotic right now,' said Hannah. 'Ryman-Davies was named in the paper a couple of days ago. He's got a second home and he's been flipping things around to pull the wool over people's eyes. He's out here today trying to reassure the public but some people are very angry. I've never seen them so mad.'

'I told you MPs are dirtier than hacks. What about old Leaver? Can't believe he did that.'

'Don't want to talk about him.'

'Claiming for a second home is one thing but claiming for a Napoleon hat, waistcoat and whip is shocking. Dirty old bastard. At least it'll bring him down a peg or two.'

'He's pretty resilient.'

'He'll need to be. There were some other funny ones too: moats and ducks ponds. Jesus, the most I did was for a fuckin' cab.'

'Are you sure?'

'If I'd done more I wouldn't be working in shitholes like this.'

'Look, Jamie I've got to go. The election campaign's still months, or even a year away, but it's as mad as hell round here. The local paper wants me to do an interview.'

'They'll probably back you all the way now: Hail Hannah the noble MP-in-waiting… '

'Not sure about that.'

'I am. I know how those lazy subs think. You'll win hands down now. Labour out of the way, the Tories are hated on the hospital, or so Trevena says. Hope you get in and poke the PM in the eye.'

'The former will do. See you Jamie… '

Jamie wanted to carry on talking but Hannah hung up. He got up and walked out into the main floor of the warehouse.

The boxes and frames were stacked up about 10 feet in the air. Richie was tending to a cut on his finger he'd got from folding a cardboard box. He was sucking the blood from his index finger.

'Was that your bird or a bastard MP?'

'Both, I hope. One day.'

Jamie finally got round to watching the American version of *The Fitton Well*. Danny had been charged with making illegal payments to police officers and unlawfully intercepting voice messages so Jamie wanted to see how his boss was dealing with the news. It was amazing to see the polished, smug-looking Fitton making wisecracks to a laughter-tracked audience while his lieutenant lost his mojo in London. Jamie did wonder how Fitton was managing to hold his job at the Daisies with all these TV commitments but Ben Fox-Tucker was probably taking up the slack as usual. Fitton couldn't help but make a joke about Don Leaver and his Whipping Dictator expenses claim. The show was similar to the British version, but with better guests: Ben Isaacs and Lisa T were both on and the music came from Mika. Jamie switched off before Fitton got to his Guest Wish slot. Jamie went to bed but couldn't sleep. He went downstairs for a pill and a glass of water in his boxer shorts and t-shirt. He walked into the kitchen and was stunned to see Callum Gordon sitting at his kitchen table, reading an old copy of the Daisies while smoking a Don Diego cigar. An umbrella lay on his lap.

'Thought I'd warm you up a bit,' said Gordon, taking a drag and blowing the smoke towards Jamie.

'What the fuck are you doing here? And how did you get in?'

'Keys, I did have a couple cut on the last occasion. Do you think I'm as stupid as Danny Love?'

'Yes, because you'll be inside as well. I'm calling the police. I'm not taking this anymore.'

'Have you seen that Mel Brooks film *High Anxiety*?'

'No, are you going to leave or not?'

'He's an overlooked genius, I think. Anyway, to get to the point, I'd say you, me, Danny and a few others are in a state of high anxiety right now. Danny has been charged and you're thinking "I'm next", am I right Jamie?'

'No, you're not. I'm just going out in the hall to call the police. Don't move.'

'Tap the numbers in, no security code needed.' Gordon smiled and flicked the ash from his cigar onto the newspaper. 'Do you honestly think the police are just going to be interested in me? I don't work for anybody but myself. You worked for the world-famous Daisies, a solid news reporter; a tasty scalp I'd say for the more predatory aspects of the Met.'

Jamie walked to the sink to pour a glass of water.

'... And that's before they ask about the drugs story in the paper,' said Gordon. 'Melvin tells me you've moved onto Benzo's and Dizzies, is that true?'

'Melvin talks a lot when he's stoned.'

'Quite. Let's not waste time on such non-entities like drugs. The reason I'm here is to say goodbye... '

Jamie stared at Gordon in a deeply sceptical manner.

'... You won't see me again – and I will not enter this house again without your permission. Next time, I'd want to be invited with a Mr Kipling lemon slice and a cup of PG.'

'Why do you keep lying?'

'Back to *High Anxiety*. I like watching it every couple of years. Danny may say things about me – incriminating things – but that's a long way from the Met maniacs bashing down my door. As I say, high anxiety nothing else. Yet that feeling is enough for me to give you one final revelation before I leave... '

'It's your revelations that have got me in this mess. Go now, I'm cold.'

'What's up? Mummy not giving you cocoa and a warm blanket anymore? Where is she these days anyway? Still married to that wussy soldier? Heard about that too. Terrorist funding, nasty business. More perish us than CherishUs, don't you think?'

'Fuck off. I've got work in the morning.'

'No, you haven't, you begin at 2pm. Break at six, finish at ten.'

Jamie picked up an empty plate and hurled it at Gordon's head. He ducked and the plate hit the wall and smashed onto the floor.

'The kitchen's got plenty more of those,' said Jamie. 'Don't use them; mainly eat takeaways now.'

'Would you like a cigar to calm you down?'

Jamie picked up a glass this time and shifted it side to side like a baseball pitcher.

'Of course, you've got the pills to do that,' said Gordon. 'As I was saying, high anxiety can do strange things to people so I'm saying goodbye to you today. I don't think I'm in any danger but I've always taken sensible precautions. If they come, they won't find a Callum Gordon and they won't find an address matching that name... '

'Your name isn't Callum Gordon?'

'Was Mel Brooks always Mel Brooks?'

'I don't fuckin' know. You're saying the coppers won't have your real name or address?'

'Something like that. It pays to have a number of fallback positions.'

'What is your name then?'

Gordon placed the house keys and his pack of Don Diego's carefully on the table. He walked up to Jamie and offered a handshake but Jamie blanked him.

'You can call me what you want,' said Gordon, picking his umbrella up and putting his hat on. 'But you won't see me again. The newspaper on the table is covered in ash. It'll never recover. It's finished.'

Gordon walked out of the kitchen and Jamie waited until he heard the front door close. Jamie walked to the kitchen table and sat down. He examined the pack of Don Diego's which still had three cigars left. He took one out and lit it up with a box of matches on top of the oven. He took a drag and sat back to try and relax. He looked down at the filthy copy of the Daisies. On the front page, there were three handwritten words: 'Regards, Callum Gordon'.

26.

Fly Me To The Moon, My Man

Jamie came home after meeting Gemma at Lavendales to discuss his progress at First Frames. As soon as he stepped in, he could hear Michael Jackson's *Human Nature* coming through the walls. Jamie went upstairs to his mother's bedroom and walked in. He saw his mother sitting on a chair by the bed, feet up, hands clasped round the legs, head on her knees. Jamie wasn't sure if she had tears in her eyes because his own vision was slightly blurred.

'He's dead mum, get over it,' said Jamie. 'Switched the telly off straight away last night when it was announced. Couldn't stand all that arse-licking.'

Tina looked up at Jamie and offered a mild shake of the head. 'When I got back in the car after Doctor Lawford had told me they'd made a terrible mistake, this song popped up straight away on the radio. I didn't move off until it was finished. The collars on my shirt were drenched.'

'Come on, mum, enough of that. It was ages ago... '

Tina wiped her cheek and eased her feet onto the floor.

'Gemma tells me you're doing okay but couldn't you find a better job? Is it the drugs?'

'I'm not on drugs. They're just helping me sleep. I have more brandy than pills.'

'For crying out loud, alcohol issues as well as drugs, I don't know what's got into you. A big-shot reporter rubbing shoulders with the stars and now you're packing boxes for a few quid an hour... '

'It's more than a few quid.'

'Course it is. Gemma says you missed a couple of days?'

'Jesus, she's not your daughter... ' Jamie walked over to the bed. He lay down flat on his back with his hands under his head, eyes looking up at the ceiling. '... but Natalie is. What's she like, this new daughter of yours? Has she even heard of Michael Jackson? Actually, better if she hasn't – with his form with kids.'

Tina picked up one of the pillows and smacked Jamie over the head with it. Jamie started laughing and hit back with his own pillow.

'You're a bigger rascal than he is,' said Tina, breaking into a smile. 'You're not fit to lace his boots.'

'Thought he only wore slip-on shoes,' he said, finding it difficult to get properly balanced on the bed so he could strike effectively at his mother. 'Even if he did, they're a good height for the kids.'

Tina struck a few more blows and then stopped, just as the chorus of *Human Nature* came round again. She eased the pillow towards her chest and held it tight.

'You didn't tell me about Natalie,' said Jamie, out of breath and finding the pillow fight tougher than expected.

'What can I say? She's into Shayne Ward and JLS, loves Waffles and spaghetti and likes wearing a cardy and jeans all the time. Adam's had more time with her because I'm still working and they seem to get on well.'

'Is she local?'

'She was at a care home in Margate. Ran away, registered missing for nearly a year, but then came back. She's a sweet girl and she's already telling me what clothes to buy when we go shopping. I'm falling for her.'

'... It was Adam's choice wasn't it? To adopt her?'

'So? It's also his choice that she doesn't come into this house yet, which I'm perfectly happy with. Judging by the state of you, it's probably a good thing. Natalie and me are getting on fine. We're learning as we go along. She's going to be the wonderful daughter I never had.'

Jamie sighed and got up from the bed. He walked towards the stereo and stopped the music.

'I have to get ready for work, mum.'

'Oi, leave that on. It's still my bedroom.'

'No, it isn't, I pay the bills and the mortgage. That makes it my bedroom.'

Tina picked up the pillow again. 'Do you want one of these in your face again?'

'Yeah, because it'll drown out the rubbish music.'

Tina got up from her chair, barefoot, and ran towards Jamie with the pillow ready for action. Jamie jumped over the bed and rushed towards the door. He went out of the bedroom and ran down the stairs. Tina chased him all the way down as he headed towards the front door. He flung it open and headed out down Stanley Hill. Tina rushed out too with the pillow above her head.

'I'll chase you all the way to the Old Town if need be,' she said.

Suddenly, Tina bumped into a man, wearing a beanie hat, a few yards from the house. She stumbled and the man helped her up. Jamie looked over his shoulder and put his head in his hands as he realised who it was. He came back sheepishly and ushered his mother away from the man.

'Looks like you're already on the Benzo's and Dizzies, Jamie boy," said Melvin Moon.

'I told you not to come round the fuckin' house.'

'Who's he?' asked Tina, wiping the dirt from the soles of her feet.

'Are we still on for a sesh, tonight?' asked Melvin. 'Larnell and his girlfriend are coming too. Got some specials for you.'

Tina walked into the house and Jamie lowered his voice.

'Course we are, but what the fuck are you doing here right now? That's my mum, if you hadn't already noticed. You stick out here like a sore thumb.'

'You said you'd get me sorted with a bit of work... '

'I don't remember that.'

Melvin smiled. 'You don't remember a lot of things. At this framing company or something. London's hard to find work, man. You said you'd put in a good word for me.'

Jamie rubbed his forehead. 'Jesus, must have been well gone.'

'The solar plexus.'

'Look, I've got to start work soon. I'll see what I can do – but you've got to disappear now. My mother's in a bit of a state and she might start on you if you're not careful.'

'Okay Jamie, thanks brother,' said Melvin, putting his hand on Jamie's shoulder. 'I was thinking tonight we could down our specials with a little tribute to Michael Jackson. Shamone... '

'FUCK OFF!!'

Barry Weymouth called Jamie into the break room as he didn't have an office. He asked Jamie to sit down but Jamie preferred to stand. Barry walked over to the sink and put water into the kettle. He turned it on and picked up his Stoke City mug. He examined it and dropped in two tea bags.

'Wanna brew?'

Jamie shook his head. 'You put two tea bags in there.'

'It's how I like it,' said Barry, turning towards him and folding his arms. 'You were off sick for a couple of days. What's the excuse this time?'

'I've got this condition, lactose intolerance... '

'I've got an intolerance too. I'm intolerant of slack, lazy workers who would prefer to get drunk or drugged-up rather than put in an honest day's work. Had a couple of Polish lads in last year: model pro's, no moaning, good workrate, reliable, efficient, a supervisor couldn't ask for more. I never asked for it but they always gave more.'

'Know all about them. I used to work for a national newspaper.'

Barry smiled and turned round to pour the boiling water from the kettle into his mug.

'I wouldn't boast too much about national newspapers right now. They're about as respected as the shit on my shoe – and believe me there's a lot of shit down there because I've worked in worse dives than this one.'

Barry opened the fridge and picked up a carton of milk. He opened it and smelt it while looking up at Jamie.

'Lactose, nice... '

'You shouldn't discriminate against people. One day you might be the victim.'

'Okay, super scribe. What made you so sick?'

'I'm not sure. There was a doughnut tray and a milkshake by the bed when I woke up a couple of days ago so it must have been that. I think a mate ordered it and might have spiked us, I don't know.'

'Some mate. You couldn't walk in a straight line when you came into work. Sure it wasn't the liqueur?'

'I like the odd drink but I don't go overboard.'

'Well, don't go overboard when I tell you this... ' Barry finished preparing his cup of tea. He turned towards Jamie and slipped his hands in his overalls. '... You might be the same age as my son, I don't know. I spend quite a lot of time trying to talk to him out of certain things too. He's already been in trouble with the police a few times. Thing is, Jamie, I haven't got any tolerance left for this runaround. I'm letting you go. You've only been here a few months and let us down too many times already.'

'Come on Barry, give me another chance. My work's been pretty good, hasn't it?'

'Yes, when you're here. But your absence and timekeeping are dreadful… '

'Truth is, I'm not getting much of a kick out of this work. It's too one-paced and repetitive. I used to have deadlines, there was a buzz and a bit of adrenaline but this is harder in a way… '

'… And you're getting your buzz and adrenalin from the drugs and liqueur?'

'I'm not taking drugs. One more chance, that's all I ask for… '

Barry took a drink from his mug. 'Who do you support, Jamie?'

'Watford.'

Barry showed Jamie his mug, making sure he could see the club crest clearly.

'This team are heading for Europe. If they ever go to Warsaw I'll nip in there and hire a couple of their lads.'

'Jesus, you'd have them all over here.'

'No, just the hardworking ones. Look Jamie, I've made my decision.'

'Yeah, and I'll make one too: this is a shit firm and Stoke City'll never play in Europe.'

Jamie headed for the door.

'PO Box Warsaw if you want a reference,' said Barry.

Jamie felt he could sleep for another week when he heard the doorbell ring. The previous night had been epic: dropping Benzos and Dizzies into multiple glasses of brandy had given him the kind of buzz he'd never experienced. Fuck exclusives, this was the real thing. A gorgeous cloud of marshmallow ease had devoured him; a woozy calm, a deep longing, an indestructibility. But the doorbell rang, rang and rang again. He got up and nearly lost his balance as he ambled to the window. Then the stones started hurtling into the glass. This may have felt mild in the days Jamie wanted to speak to a source but, today, if felt like a siege. Jamie peered out of the window and Gemma was standing there, her eyes meeting his, a pitying expression, a stripping away of his soul in seconds. He took another five minutes to go down and open the door. Gemma said nothing and walked in. She went into the kitchen and made herself a cup of tea. She sat down at the kitchen table and eased an empty bottle of brandy away to give her some space. Jamie pulled a half-eaten Cornish pasty from the fridge and started eating it immediately.

'Don't you dare come into our branch again,' said Gemma.

'All right... '

'You've embarrassed me a few times before, I know, but this is something else. First Frames probably aren't going to use our consultancy again to hire anyone because we send them wasters like you. I can understand it but it doesn't put me in a good position. My boss gave me a good grilling because he knows we have history... '

'Look Gem, I'm really sorry about it. I'm trying to sort things out... '

'Don't start that Gem stuff again. We have a league table at work and some of us try to guess how long certain temps will last. There was one who lasted only 48 minutes on one job so you're obviously not as bad as that but as a former hack you should have done better.' Gemma finally looked up at Jamie. 'You were always a stickler for time, what happened?'

Jamie drew up a chair on the opposite side of the kitchen table. He finished his pasty off in seconds.

'I'm missing it, that's all I can say to you.'

'Journalism?'

'It's stupid, I know, but up here... ' He knocked on his head with his hand. '... I've found it difficult. The change has been too quick and too wild. I haven't been able to adjust.'

Gemma paused and took another sip of tea.

'Wonders never cease. Is this Jamie being honest? You're probably still under the influence.'

Jamie smiled. 'Yeah, a manky Cornish pasty. Look Gem, can't you just get me in one more time? I've got to keep things rolling.'

'No, I'm through with you. Even if I wasn't, someone's taken your place at First Frames. A Mr Moon, I think.'

'Melvin fucking Moon?'

'You know him?'

'Er yes, no. I need a fucking drink.'

'Barry phoned me to say he'd been recommended by someone on the staff. So instead of having to look for another temp, we said okay. Saved us some work.'

Jamie reached into his trouser pocket and counted the money he had.

'Can you lend us a tenner?'

'What?'

'I'll give it you back. Just need a bit more to get my weekly shop done.'

'No Jamie,' said Gemma, getting up and heading towards the door. 'I can't lend you anything. I'm going now. You need to sort yourself out.'

'So marriage is totally out of the question then?'

'You need a doctor.'

'I've got the best and most famous doctor in the world: Alexander Noonan. If he can't straighten me out what makes you think you can? Go back to your decorated house, your dodgy cats and your dead-end job, Gemma. I made a mistake: I should have turned you over rather than Paul Markham.'

Gemma stopped by the door. 'What do you mean by that?'

'Nothing, see ya.'

'You turned Paul over... that usually means you dug the dirt on him.' Gemma paused and eased her back against the door, her hands behind her back and her head up to the ceiling. 'He was only in the paper once – for that story with greasy Holly Rivers... it was a lie wasn't it? You made that whole fucking thing up. I can't believe it.'

'Well believe it because everybody else did.'

Gemma glanced at Jamie and shook her head. She reached into her handbag for her purse and pulled out five ten pound notes. She walked over to the empty brandy bottle, rolled up the notes and placed them inside the bottle. She looked at Jamie and headed for the door.

'Don't leave Gem, I did it for you,' said Jamie. 'Because I loved you so fuckin' much – and still do.'

Gemma opened the door and left the kitchen. He picked up the bottle of brandy and pulled out the notes. He put the money in his pocket and wanted to smash the bottle on his own head.

Jamie lay in bed until 3pm. His clothes were piled up in the corner of the room needing to be washed. His silver-backed waistcoat was on top of these clothes and he wondered how it got there as he hadn't worn it since his newsroom days. The problem was, the waistcoat made him think of the silver fern emblem on the All Blacks rugby shirt which was one of his father's favourite tops. He knew he should apply for Jobseekers Allowance but why should he follow a similar path to Tom Parkes? Going on benefits was the easy way out. His father became an electrician for the Southern Electricity Board in the late 70s after a four-year apprenticeship. But only six months into the job, a householder claimed he did a faulty rewiring job which led to a small fire, hospitalisation and injuries for the resident's family. The story made it on Page 26 of the Daisies. The rest in the Tom Parkes story was down to Fiona Ashcroft. Jamie remembered his father celebrating with a bottle of Cognac and offering Jamie a drink the day before he jumped ship to New Zealand. Jamie was barely nine years old. He joined Fiona for the anti-apartheid protests against the Springbok tour and they eventually settled in Auckland. Jamie never remembered him having strong political views and he was a rare breed: a man who looked happy trawling job centres. Tina said he met Fiona there.

Jamie got up and went to toilet but only managed to cough up phlegm in the sink. His stomach was in knots, as though an army of mice were nibbling their way through it, and he desperately needed a drink. He went downstairs and raided the fridge for a can of Grolsch. He turned the radio on and, immediately, a deep, measured voice of ghoulish familiarity dominated the room. It was Anderton. Jamie sat down at the kitchen table and listened with as much focus as he could summon. The fucker had resigned.

'I don't believe I did anything wrong but I did accept hospitality from journalists. I can see how this could have been perceived as an inappropriate relationship. For that reason, I am stepping down from my post. I go with the best wishes of the Commissioner and most of my colleagues.'

No mention of Fitton. Again. Anderton's quote was recorded from earlier and the radio reporter followed up by giving details of the case. He said the Screws had given Anderton free lunches in return for access to criminal databases while the Daisies had also offered specialist media staff to the Met if they needed more PR. He was about to switch off when the reporter started talking about phone hacking in general and Danny Love's trial date which had been set for summer next year. It felt like an age away. They had plenty of time to come after him next. Jamie went out into the hallway and could see the post piled up against the front door. He ignored it and spent the rest of the day watching *Crank: High Voltage* and *State of Play* on DVD. At 10.30pm, Melvin Moon came to the door. Jamie answered it and, curiously, didn't want to beat the shit out of him.

'As a treat for you, my friend, got some juicy ones for you tonight,' said Melvin, opening his lunchbox and showing Jamie his range of Diazepam, Benzodiazepene and Ecstasy tablets. 'It's the least I could do after you hooking me up with some work. Thanks brother.'

'Fuck work, grab the glory. Get in here and let's get going.'

'You sorted for cash, man? I can help you out.' Melvin looked down at the floor as he came in. 'You got mail, as they say.'

'Leave it. Just junk anyway.'

'Safe man, this is the dog's bollocks I've got for you tonight. You'll never have experienced anything like it. Got a three month's supply too.'

'… Exactly what I need. Go in the kitchen and get prepared. I'm in the mood for ripping it up tonight. Got this new Editors album, something about light and evening, some top sci-fi shit on there… '

'Tune it up, man.' Melvin shook Jamie's hand. 'Once again, thanks for hooking me up with some pennies. My father was almost in tears when he heard I was working… '

'FUCK YOUR FATHER – AND MINE TOO. NOW GET IN THE KITCHEN AND LET'S GET RIPPING… '

27.

Publish And Be Grand!

Jamie's face felt like it was glued to the kitchen tiles when he heard the front door being pushed open. As he lifted his head from the dirty blue tile beneath him, he imagined a human head resting on each of the yellow tiles, peering at him and asking him why he was the only one on the blue tiles. Jamie knew he was hallucinating but the sound of the front door crashing open with an almighty thump was real. Before he knew it, a pair of black shoes, shiny trousers, a file and a mobile phone came into view. They were being carried by a tall man in the hallway. The man looked into the kitchen.

'Are you the homeowner?'

'Who wants to know?' said Jamie, slowly crawling towards the kitchen table and sitting down.

'Craig Sinton from Jackson and Alexander Limited. We need a payment off you, today.' Sinton looked at his file. 'The sum you owe is £4,475,22p. Can you get it? We have to act quicker these days. Lots of clients under strain.'

'How did you get in?'

'We've been here a couple of times before, there was no answer. We can't wait, forever, Mr Parkes.'

'I don't have it.'

'I can't leave until I have some form of payment.'

Jamie checked his pockets. 'I've got about 16 quid and 52 pence.' He put it all on the table. 'Here, you can take it… '

'Comedian, hey Mr Parkes? I need the whole sum today.

If you don't have it, we will have to take something else. Have you been smoking in here? Smells terrible.'

'I haven't got the money. Give me a couple of weeks… '

'We don't have a couple of weeks. What's it to be?'

'I'm not paying, now fuck off and get a proper job you fuckin' leeches.'

Sinton nodded and looked at his mobile phone. 'Perhaps the police will be interested in your substance-related activities, what do you think? I can give them a bell now.'

'I DON'T HAVE THE FUCKIN' MONEY… '

'So what can you give us then?'

'A fist – it's the only thing you understand.'

'Okay, I've given you ample opportunity to resolve this matter… '

Sinton walked to the door and came back with another two men, one with a stud in his ear and a back-to-front baseball cap, the other covered in tattoos with a fag in his mouth.

'Right, start in the living room,' said Sinton. 'I've already been in there: start with the TV and the sofa… '

'Oi, when did you go in there?'

'Stay off the drugs and you might notice things.'

'Okay look, please stop,' said Jamie, getting up and standing in front of the three men. 'I'll call my mother, she'll be here in 10 minutes flat. Trust me, we can sort something out. Here, I'm calling her now… '

Jamie called his mother. There was no answer and it went straight to voicemail. His mother deserved to have her phone hacked.

'No answer? What a surprise? Okay fellas, let's go… '

'NO STOP!'

Jamie came forward and tried to push the two men away from the living room but Sinton grabbed his arms and pinned him against the wall.

'Wimps like you are small beer to me,' whispered Sinton. 'I'd think very carefully about what you do next. Assault could be added to a drugs charge.'

Jamie could feel the tears welling up in his eyes as he tried to break free. He put his hands up and Sinton finally let go. Jamie couldn't bear to watch his living room being pillaged so he walked back to the kitchen. He closed the door, sat down and looked at £16.52p on the table. Enough for a few bottles of soy milk – and a spliff or two.

Jamie went up into his bedroom and took out a tape recorder from a shoe box under the bed. He listened again to the words of the young Prince as he peppered Larna Wilson's phone. Jamie was on his knees, literally, and this time there would be no turning back. Yes, it was hacked material but where else could Jamie turn now? He transcribed the quotes and began composing the story. It took nearly three hours, during which time he went downstairs for a glass of Grolsch laced with Skittles. The 1600 words were complete. He turned on his computer and typed up the completed piece. He printed it out, double spaced, sat on the bed and looked at it again. He made changes and printed it out again – and then a third time. The excitement was palpable. There was no point in waiting anymore. He took out his mobile and called the news editors at the Screws, the *Mail on Sunday* and the *Sunday Mirror*. Unsurprisingly, none of them were available. He emailed them. He waited for a response but none came. He was hungry and used his £16.52p to walk down to The Fish Bar in Woodside Road for his supper. He walked back home and got a text from his mother. She apologised for not calling sooner but she had to take Natalie to school because Adam had flu. She would call when she could.

Three days passed before the Screws got back to him; then the *Mail on Sunday* a couple of hours later; then the *Sunday*

Mirror minutes after that. The news editor at the Screws, in mild, gangsterish tones, asked a few searching questions about how Jamie got the story – and whether he could get Larna to speak on the record again – but he was more interested in guaranteeing exclusivity for the paper. The MoS wanted the same, ditto the Sunday Mirror. Jamie went back to the Screws. The news editor offered £50,000 for complete exclusivity. Jamie went back to the others – the *MoS* was prepared to match that but the *Sunday Mirror* dropped out. Jamie went back to the Screws saying the MoS had matched their offer so he upped it to 60k. It was the best Jamie was going to get so he accepted the Screws' offer. The only problem was, the news editor at the Screws was annoyed with Jamie because he knew the two other papers would unleash their dogs and be on the hunt for Larna Wilson right now. Jamie said she was in America and wouldn't be easy to track down. For that reason, the splash had to go in as soon as possible: this Sunday. The next morning, however, Jamie received a call, not from the Screws or his mum but from Larna Wilson. She was in Britain. Further, she'd been back here for years.

'There's press and photographers outside my house, Jamie, what the hell have you done?' said Larna.

'Where the fuck are you? I thought you were in America?'

'Things didn't work out. The film didn't happen. I didn't have enough money to stay over there – so I came back. Answer me? You've blabbed about Henry, yes? For a few dirty pieces of silver? How could you that? I thought we had an understanding?'

'We did – but I was desperate… '

'So you sold me down the river. I'm being hounded by these animals right now, my mother is really frightened. Usually, I can look right down the seafront and feel the giant tides swishing around but all I can see is a line of press and snappers staring at me and staking me out. It's horrible.'

'Look, I am sorry but I had to do something. I had no money...'

'What the hell happened to you? Did you gamble? How did you piss everything away?'

'Long story...'

'They always are with you – but this better not be.'

'Look, just hear me out. How about if you give me an exclusive interview tomorrow and lay everything out on the table: you, Fitton, the Prince? You'll get rid of all this press outside your house. How about it?'

'And what about if I drive all you lot in the sea? I'm not saying another word.'

Larna hung up and Jamie felt anxious about what would appear in the paper on Sunday given the subbing butchers he knew from the national tabloids. There was also a feeling of guilt that Larna was now under siege in her own house. But one thing was certain: the buzz was back – and no shit-kicking, artificial drugs could replace that.

Jamie never thought he'd see the day: his byline was on the front page of the Screws with a 'World Exclusive' boasting the ropey headline Sex Pest Henry A Quick Larna. *The Mail on Sunday* and the *Sunday Mirror* ran their own pieces but with quotes from 'friends' or 'insiders' rather than direct from Larna or Prince Henry. Jamie bought a copy of each paper from the local newsagent. He sat in his bare living room and spread the papers out on the carpet. There were supplementary pieces about Larna flying out to Afghanistan to join Henry on his tour of duty. Larna never told him about that. There were also a couple of pieces from bitchy columnists criticising Larna's looks, her dress sense and her taste for French food and culture. There was plenty here that was new to Jamie – whether it was true or not was a different matter. The Screws said the break-up came because Larna was seeing Fitton as well at the time and the Prince found out about it. The *MoS* claimed her 'dotty Gallic habits' sent the Prince crazy and he simply couldn't envisage having a long-term relationship with such an 'obsessive' woman while the *Sunday Mirror* said she was the one who broke off the relationship because she wanted an acting career. Jamie had his own theory but it would have to wait. His mobile rang.

'Morning Parkesy,' said Fitton. 'Congratulations on your scoop. Pity you couldn't come up with a few more on my watch but, hey, you're in a better place now.'

'I never thought I'd speak to you again... '

'... Or use quotes from hacked phones.'

'You can talk. It was only three or four lines, anyway. Most if it was from Larna. Are you in America or over here? Nobody seems to know these days.'

'The show's going very well... '

'Americans not familiar with the Mandy Dean case?'

'Come on, now, no low blows this early on a Sunday morning. That was a tragic event but my conscience is clear. I tried to help the girl.'

'She took her own life on a decision you made. How do you sleep at night?'

'Decent, no problems at all. But I'm not here to discuss Mandy; another girl is the talk of the town. Larna Wilson is booked in as a guest on my show in America early next year.'

'What the fuck are you on about? She's appearing on your show? Why would she want to do that? It's madness. She didn't want to do any media.'

'She wants to act and my show is a plugger's paradise. People want to hear what she has to say.'

'But you spent all that time trying to keep this affair quiet?'

'That was silly. I was a relatively young editor at the time. We'd had a relationship. I'd known her since school. She knew a few things about me – I didn't want those to come out.

Anyway, fuck that, let's get back to the real story… '

'Did you introduce Larna to the Prince? I mean, you were good friends at the time.'

'It's not me you've got to worry about, Parkesy. The Prince will be pissed about this and he won't think twice about putting the warpaint on.'

'Save your conspiracy theories. You're just pissed off because the other Sunday's have scooped you big time. Not to mention that your circulation's in the toilet and your news editor's going to jail. And why the fuck are you in America all the time anyway? Who edits the Daisies now? A monkey, judging by the shit that's in there.'

'Facts, Parkesy, facts. That's why you had to go. You had a loose relationship with them. I'm only in America for three months a year. I take no holiday whatsoever. I use all my quota to do the show in America. The wife and kids come with me sometimes. The other nine months, I'm here editing the paper. Fox-Tucker takes over the rest of the time. The paper is fine. Yes, we had to weather a storm but it's blown over now and my show has played a part in rehabilitating it. We've raised our brand awareness despite the problems we've had. That's the reality JP so make sure you tune in for Larna's World Exclusive interview early next year. You've been trying to get her to open up for nearly a decade. Not much of a reporter, are you?'

'Fuck off. You're the one who should be locked up, not Danny Love.'

'Danny overstretched with his coup d'etat fantasies. He's a middleweight and always will be. He should have known his limitations.'

'You shopped him?'

'Don't be silly. Anyway, must rush, got a few inspiring people coming round for Sunday lunch. We've got Unsung Britain soon so I thought I'd let them take the podium and make some suggestions. Goodbye, and make sure you get a telly in place for the show.'

Fitton hung up and Jamie's good mood disintegrated. How the hell did Fitton know about his television? There were too many questions – and it wasn't worth it. This was a time for celebration. A cool 60 grand was on its way to him so everything else could be given two fingers.

A cherry-brown leather sofa, a coffee table, a display cabinet and a 46inch plasma TV came into the living room to restore some sense of normality. Jamie was preparing to sit down on his new sofa with his meat lasagne and glass of brandy when his mother rang.

'Been thinking about that message for days, Jamie,' said Tina. 'I can come round today if you want. Natalie too. Adam doesn't mind. Why were you so hysterical? What happened?'

'Nothing mum, forget about it. Did you see the Screws the other day?'

'You know we don't read that filth. Adam won't have another paper in the house although I do sneak one in sometimes. What was in there? Anything interesting?'

'Nothing really. Look, you don't have to come round. I'm getting a few things sorted right now.'

'Like that job, you sorted? Gemma says you threw that away too. Can't you hold on to anything?'

'Oh that job. It's all done and dusted. I'm freelancing again, things should be a bit easier now.'

'Well, you're not going to make a success of freelancing by sitting on your arse. I know the media have been full of that Henry and Leena Wilson story… '

'Larna… '

'Yes, Larna story. I mean, somebody must have broke that story in the first place. You need to get off your arse and do some work. It's the only way freelancing is going to pay.'

'Yes, mum. Don't bother coming around. I've got work to do.'

'Don't you want to meet Natalie?'

'Some other time. Bye now.'

Jamie hung up and gawped at the 46inch screen. He smiled as he enjoyed the tastiest brandy he'd drunk in years.

Jamie was experiencing the twin benefits of Noonan trying to get him off drugs while a freelance career was beginning to take shape. Noonan called in at the house when he heard about the exclusive and persuaded Jamie that he would never have a better time to 'flush this poison' out of his body. But there was no detoxification process or cranky therapy – Noonan had his own methods. He wanted to stay at the house for a month and, initially, Jamie wasn't enthusiastic but after a trial run of a couple of nights, Jamie warmed to the idea. Melvin Moon was banned from contacting him. All drugs, drinks and prescribed medication were also banned for a month. Noonan liked to meditate in the mornings – and then tell Jamie how much he missed Jake every single day of his life. Noonan's words did have a clarifying affect. Yet it would be wrong to say this played the biggest part in Jamie's recovery-of-sorts. The simple truth was, the polite requests to news and features editors about possible story ideas were now being taken much more seriously. This was the main reason Jamie cleaned up and gradually got off drugs. Some of the successful stories he offered included a follow-up on the Prince and Larna saga (which was nothing more than a statement from the Prince's office saying it was all a long time ago and it was time to move on), a city trader who'd opened a new ethical bank, Hannah gearing up for her general election campaign, everyday superheroes connected to the film *Kick-Ass*, volcanic ash disruption causing chaos at airports and an obituary on Malcolm McClaren. These stories, published mainly in tabloids, got Jamie back on his feet. He also covered a media-related story on Louise Dorrans who won Reporter of the Year for her tireless work on tabloid ethics and the Mandy Dean story. Jamie was happy for her and sent her a text of congratulations. It was a long time since he'd felt like that. She texted him back to say he must make sure he becomes an NUJ freelance member, which he did immediately. Once Noonan left the house, Jamie eased back into a newsroom-style routine. Early breakfast, go to the office (the bedroom), make a few calls to sources, write up some stories, have lunch, do interviews in the afternoon (on the phone or in person), transcribe them, mess about on the internet for the last hour and finish at six. After dinner, settle down in front of the plasma with a couple of DVDs and small glass of Grolsch. Go to bed nice and early at ten so he would be fit and ready for another rollercoaster day tomorrow. It was official – Jamie was back; so was the adrenaline, so was the thrill, so were the stories.

28.

Sentences Aren't Our Thing M'Lord

Hannah was stood on a stage with eight others, all men, hoping to become MPs. Jamie stood in a small crowd in the school hall, watching them, waiting for the returning officer to reveal the number of votes for each candidate. Most of the hopefuls had their hands crossed in front of them but Hannah had hers behind her back. She was wearing a neat dark blue suit with slightly overlong, flarey trousers and a striking red shirt. She looked elegant and confident. How could anyone not vote for her? According to the polls, it was a straight fight between her and Ryman-Davies – the Tories and Lib Dems never did well here. She, because of Trevena's dedicated work and long-standing reputation in the town and Ryman-Davies, because this was always a safe Labour seat before Trevena hijacked it with his hospital campaign. Yet the polls suggested it was still too close to call – and that was probably why Ryman-Davies didn't look nervous. He was stood next to the returning officer, with a slightly bigger red rosette on his jacket than normal. Finally, the returning officer was ready to announce the results. Jamie inched forward and folded his arms. He was only interested in hearing Ryman Davies and Hannah's votes: Lib Dem, Tory, UKIP, BNP, Monster Raving, Green's and English Independents were unlikely to cause a threat.

'Ryman-Davies, Labour, 6,738 votes… '

'FUCK ME,' said Jamie, putting his hand over his mouth as if to apologise. Perhaps he'd underestimated the wrath of the general public.

'Michael Ronson, Conservative, 22,147 votes… '

'JESUS.'

In military terms, this would be a 'fluid' situation, thought Jamie. In media terms, it would be 'we're fucking useless at predictions'. The other candidates, in particular, the Lib Dems and UKIP posted some respectable numbers but it was down to an unexpected battle between the Tory Michael Ronson and Hannah.

'Hannah Rocheman, Independent, 23,164 votes… '

'GET THE FUCK IN!'

Hannah raised one arm up in the air and an almighty cheer went up across the school hall. Jamie ran as fast as he could, jostling through the crowd, trying to get close to the stage.

'I hereby declare that Hannah Rocheman has been elected as the member for… '

Jamie knocked the microphone stand over as he headed towards Hannah. The returning officer didn't look too pleased but this wasn't his moment: it was Hannah's. Jamie put his arms round Hannah who looked surprised but was laughing. Jamie jumped up and down and started celebrating football-style. What a night! The atmosphere was electric. Hannah Rocheman, MP, was ready to take her seat in the House of Commons.

Hannah and Jamie were sitting in the school cloakroom after most of the raucous crowd had melted away. Jamie felt this might be his moment. Why else would she bring him into this cramped, claustrophobic room almost immediately after one of the greatest nights of her life? She had taken him by the arm down the corridor and, as soon as Jamie saw her top button undone, he couldn't wait to reach their destination so they could celebrate the night in style. He couldn't wait to get his hands underneath that red top. Hannah looked slightly distracted as she sat on the wooden bench scrolling through the congratulatory messages on her mobile.

'Trevena wasn't here tonight for a reason,' said Hannah.

'Yeah, because he was angry at the expenses stuff.'

'Partly, but he's more angry at the hospital's main services are moving out of the town. They're going to announce it soon – and I have to tell my constituents... '

'But I thought Trevena had won that battle?'

'He had. But they're now using the excuse of the financial crisis. If they don't move, they go bust. They've got some crappy PFI arrangement – so they're in deep trouble.'

'... And you're the poor sap who has to sell this to the public that has just voted for you?' Jamie leaned back and folded his arms. 'Talk about celebrating a great achievement.'

Hannah switched off her phone and looked at Jamie. 'MPs have to make these compromises. I expected to make such difficult calls but not so soon. But I can take the criticism – I'm a tough girl.'

'Maybe not as tough as you think. That's why you've got me in here with you.'

Hannah nodded and put her phone away. She tapped Jamie's thigh with her hand and then used a coat hook to get up off the bench.

'Trevena's absolutely devastated,' she said. 'But he also sent me a text saying he was in tears when he heard I'd been elected. He gave me some tips on how to handle the fallout from all this. I'm going to need it.'

'Well, at least you won't have Don Leaver chirping at you in the Commons. He was smashed tonight. No more Napoleon whips for him.'

'Don't bet on it. There'll be plenty of his chummy mates there to remind me. I'm not worried about those idiots. I just hope the constituents don't turn on me.'

'Trust me,' said Jamie, reciprocating by putting a cheeky

hand on Hannah's thigh. 'You'll be fine. Once they look into those beautiful eyes, they'll be bowled over.'

Hannah walked towards the door. 'That's what I'm worried about. That people will be so bowled over that they won't listen to the issues.'

'… Sorry,' said Jamie, with a smile. 'What was the issue again?'

Hannah took off her suit jacket and flung it at Jamie's head. She did up her top button and left the room.

It was odd for Jamie to see two people he knew well – Fitton and Larna Wilson – appearing face to face on a chat show thousands of miles away in America. Larna was now obviously better known over there than she had been when she tried to make it as a writer and actress – and Fitton didn't take long to remind her of that fact. Yet, as Jamie sat watching the curious interview in his living room, he got the impression that Larna was in complete control.

'So on the trip to Kandahar, when you secretly met the Prince in a tea shop,' said Fitton. 'Did you ever wear a veil?'

'Yes, I wanted to respect local customs.'

'Even if Al Qaida didn't respect them?'

'I can't speak for them… '

'But you did when the war started? You didn't support the war in Afghanistan, is that right?'

'Yes, I didn't think it would solve anything.'

'How did that work with the Prince who was on a tour of duty there?'

'It never really came up. He was a gentleman about it.'

'American viewers might have a term for you, although they mainly used it for Iraq… '

'I hope it's complementary… '

'Er not quite. A cheese-eating surrender monkey. That's what they'd probably call you.'

'Well, you should know. You liked to grate the stuff onto your croissants in the morning... '

Fitton looked at the camera and offered a mild smile. 'Just to remind you, folks, Larna and I do have some history. We had a short, sharp relationship which ended when she fed me too many croissants... ' Cue audience laughter. Fitton looked pleased with himself. 'As you know, I really love the French.' Cue more laughter.

This kind of bizarre banter – a kind of *Fairytale of New York* without the music – was the dominant theme in the feisty half-hour interview. To Jamie, it felt as though Fitton wanted to talk less about the Prince's relationship and more about Larna herself. But Larna gave as good as she got. Why did Fitton do it? For ratings? Because he knew Larna? As for Larna, Jamie was still completely in the dark about why she wanted to appear on a talk show in America opposite someone she know so well. She hadn't spoken to any other British media about the affair with the Prince (apart from Jamie's original story) so a few of them were ready with their knives drawn to lay into her once the interview was over. Jamie would have liked to have done the same – but could only admire her steel and resolve. The knives would have to be long and deep to do any lasting damage.

Jamie decided against going to court in person for Danny Love's trial. He wanted to keep a safe distance away, as though he'd be influenced by some hacking vapour if he sat in the public gallery, so he followed it on newspapers websites and TV. The first few days did not seem to bring anything remarkable – Jamie had heard it all before – but when the first witness was called the game changed. It was Bernard 'Peeper' Wallace. The former copper said he worked for Danny Love on a flexible contract and landed bonuses if he came up with the goods on big-name celebrities, notorious criminals and sly politicians. Jamie expected most of what he heard in Wallace's evidence: the snooping, the hacking, the intimidation, the odd payment to an official but the real meat was in his dealings with the Met. Wallace claimed Danny had two coppers on his payroll plus Anderton – and that all their phones were hacked. He claimed he acted as a middleman paying the two low-ranking officers bribes of up to £2,000 in £20 notes hidden inside the travel supplements of a thick Daisies newspaper on a Sunday. He claimed he met those officers outside football grounds where they were on duty for a game. Anderton didn't take any money, he said, but still gave information to the paper in exchange for hospitality and gifts. Anderton also wanted a column in the paper which Danny agreed to but Fitton overruled. Each day, there was a new revelation. Anderton didn't give evidence in court but provided a statement. He admitted Danny's family had been dinner guests and also told of his disappointment that Danny had not become a proper police officer after finishing his training. Not once had Danny mentioned he trained as a copper. He claimed to hate them so much he never watched a cop show on TV although no-one in the newsroom really believed him. As the trial went on, Jamie was worried his name would come up – but it didn't. Other colleagues did. Jimmy Betson appeared as a witness and, then, amazingly, so did Fitton in week four of the trial. He claimed he knew nothing of Danny Love's antics and if he had, he would have sacked him immediately. He was asked if he sanctioned 'illegal activity' and created a 'culture of excess' in the newsroom and he replied that, in hindsight, he had given Danny Love too much responsibility. Changes had now been made on the paper to ensure nothing like that could happen again. The news websites covering the trial agreed that Fitton had given an assured performance although one broadsheet did label him a 'tabloid Houdini' who couldn't perform without an audience.

Jamie had read enough – it was wearing him out. There were more witnesses: a prison guard, an NHS official, a pop star-turned hacking victim but Jamie had lost track and didn't pay attention to the closing arguments. But when the day of the verdict came, Jamie had his radio tuned to Radio 5 Live while he tried to iron a shirt in his bedroom. The steam from the iron was already warming up his forehead. The verdict was in: guilty. Danny Love was going down. The days of asking reporters to take extra care with legal copy were over; for now. Strangely, Jamie turned the radio off immediately. He thought he would want to hear details, sentencing and all the rest, but it was the opposite: he couldn't help but feel something for Danny despite his bullying tendencies and power-grabbing delusions. There was also a nagging doubt that it had been a stitch-up with Wallace, Anderton and Fitton all ganging up on him. But it was too late now: he was facing jail. He had denied the charges to the bitter end and the vengeful mood of the public, media and institutions needed their tabloid scalp. They had one. Jamie hoped this trial, in Fitton's new buzzword, would offer 'closure'. If it was only the start, things could get very messy indeed.

Danny Love was sentenced a few days later – to three years in prison. Jamie imagined him sitting in his cell alone, isolated, in gloomy silence, with no-one to bark instructions at. He could make the walls of the Daisies reverberate with a lash of his tongue but the firm, filthy walls of a prison cell were probably less susceptible to his blistering vocal charms. However Danny coped it was time to forget about him and start thinking about what Hannah had proposed. She had hardly got her feet under the Westminster table and she was already aiming to sit on committees that looked into a range of a questionable activities. Unsurprisingly, the Home Affairs Committee's investigation into unauthorised tapping and hacking was in full swing and had caught her attention so, on the back of the Danny Love verdict, she wanted to invite Jamie to come and give evidence in front of MPs. She wasn't on this committee yet, or any others, but she did have her eye on easing into Trevena's vacant position. Jamie got back to her to say he would love to do her a favour but wasn't sure he could handle the thought of being grilled by a bunch of arrogant MPs. How could those who stole money from the nation during the expenses obscenity now pontificate to others about immoral and unethical behaviour? Jamie didn't give an outright 'no' to Hannah but giving evidence in this atmosphere felt like a witch-hunt.

The atmosphere also wasn't great in Hannah's new constituency. Trevena had organised a petition and a small protest outside Sparrow Hill hospital which had now announced it was moving its maternity services, A&E, children's services and stroke and cardiac units out of town, 30 miles away to a bigger hospital. A short item appeared in the local paper but the TV stations and national papers ignored it. Trevena had a good moan about this when he called Jamie. He'd also organised a sleep-in – inside the A&E department – and this was successful in getting a little more media exposure, although not as much as he wanted. When Danny Love was mentioned, however, Jamie realised how much Trevena now cared about phone hacking and the rest.

'That's saga's dead for me,' said Trevena, speaking from the foyer of the hospital while sipping a coffee from the vending machine. 'This is my only focus now. Who's going to care for these elderly people here? Most of them haven't got cars. How are they going to travel?'

'You must have felt a little bit of pride when Danny Love went down?'

'No, because Fitton was there with his smarmy grin. He's still around – and getting him inside will be nigh on impossible.'

'But there's still a chance that some of this stuff from Noonan, Vernon and Tristan Boyce might stick. If Wade and Boyce come out with a bit more, he'll be in trouble.'

'No, it's all about Callum Gordon. All the illegal payments went through him. If he's not around, nothing will stick on Fitton. As editor, he probably never hacked phones, although he might have authorised it, so you can close that down too.'

'But Callum Gordon's gone... '

'What do you mean 'gone'? Did you meet him or something?'

'Well, yes, he smuggled himself into my house a couple of times. Bit of an intimidating bloke.'

'What did he say?'

'Not much. "Goodbye", that was about the gist of it.'

'Well, if you don't see him again, it's also bye bye to any hopes of nailing Fitton. Enough about this: why haven't you ran a story about our sleep-in yet? I know you've got yourself back together with your freelance stuff – I read a good piece of yours on Alex Higgins' death recently... '

'You liked it? Yeah him and Jimmy White; old-style heroes of mine: fast and hard... '

'Yes, I read it – but now you must do me a turn. I've got a few pictures I can send over to you that one of our people took of the protest. We had to smuggle it out a little because the hospital doesn't allow pictures inside. Give us a good piece – and you'll do a great service for this town.'

'Look, I'll do the best I can but you know how it is. Editors are looking for a name or celebrity stuff. There's cutbacks too so they're being more picky with the freelance stuff they commission... '

'I'll tell you about cutbacks. The Trust who run this place have been cutting back for years – and that's when we had an economic boom. Now, they have a ready-made excuse with the financial crisis, so they're ready to rip everything up in the name of austerity. I've never liked that term 'over my dead body' but I swear on my father's grave, just a quarter of a mile away from here, that I'll put everything on the line.'

Trevena's story didn't run in any paper – despite Jamie's best efforts. The closest he got was when one features editor asked for a profile on the former MP but wanted Jamie to dig into his history to see if he'd fiddled his expenses. Jamie didn't file the story. But other stories were being commissioned: one on the late Norman Wisdom's connection to Albania and another on the film *Tron Legacy* exploring how computers had changed since the original movie was released in 1982. He was also talking to his mother more – and this led to him granting a request for Natalie (and Tina) to come over to the house for dinner. Adam had finally agreed to let Natalie meet Jamie even though he still had reservations. After the collapse of CherishUs, he had started writing a book about the tsunami and hoped he could gain the interest of a publisher. Natalie came in with Tina, carrying a supermarket bag of groceries, and they both rushed past Jamie to the kitchen where they started to prepare dinner.

'This is Natalie, Jamie, now budge out of the way,' said Tina.

Natalie smiled but Tina ushered her quickly into the kitchen. She said they were behind schedule so they needed to get a move on. Jamie walked in behind them as they started emptying the bags and then briskly began to cut cucumbers, wash lettuce and peel potatoes. Natalie looked over her shoulder and smiled. She then started to sing Florence and the Machine's *You've Got the Love* and Tina eventually joined in. They looked very content: a proper mother and daughter. He walked up behind them and picked a cucumber from the bowl. He eased the whole slice into his mouth.

'Don't put any milk or eggs in this will you?' said Jamie.

'She knows... ' said Tina.

'You've got allergies then?' asked Natalie.

'Sort of... '

Jamie looked at Natalie up close for the first time. She was quite tall for her age with short, spiky brown hair, swollen cheeks and a small nose. She was wearing a black t-shirt and ripped blue jeans: the holes around the knees were massive.

'Did you hack any phones then?' asked Natalie.

'Natalie!' said Tina, ripping open a bag of lactose-free pasta and dropping it into a pan.

'Some of 'em deserve it. Not Bjork or Bat for Lashes or anyone like that but, you know, people like Justin Bieber. Have you got his number? I'll do it for you.'

'No, I haven't got his number – and I haven't done any hacking.'

Tina glanced across at Jamie and offered a knowing smile.

'You did the Royals, yeah? Or so Tina says. Bo-ring. They're a bunch of freeloaders. Can I see your bedroom? Done a couple of poems so far. It might help us.'

'But I'm not a writer... '

'What are you then? You put one word after another. You make things up. I do that too. I could show you some of my poems later.'

'Maybe, let's eat first.'

'Won't be ready for a while,' said Tina. 'Go on Jamie, take Natalie upstairs. She's been waiting to talk to you since she first walked into our house.'

'Come on, what are you waiting for?' said Natalie. 'I want to see the famous Jamie's little pad. Never had my own bedroom so I spend a lot of time in them these days. Don't be shy, you're a star.'

Jamie couldn't remember the last time he blushed – but now he had a full-frontal red alert. To avert any more embarrassment, he headed out of the kitchen and upstairs into his bedroom. Natalie stepped in first.

'Wow, not bad,' she said, looking up at the front-page exclusives on the wall. 'But what are those?'

'Shorthand notes. I like to see how a story was conceived.'

'Looks like some shitty squiggles to me.'

'Mum thinks they look like something out of *The Shining*… '

'Stephen King, man, don't start. I'll be here all night. Adam bought me *Cell* and *Duma Key* because I was pestering him. Got through them both in a couple of weeks.'

'Haven't heard of those… '

'Because you're stuck in here all the time,' she said, with a smile. 'You'll end up like one of the crazy characters in his books.' She walked forward and started going through some of the tabloid papers stacked up in the corner of the room. 'All going onto the internet, isn't it?' She sat down cross-legged on the floor and flicked through one of the papers. 'My real mum tried to contact me a couple of years ago but not by phone or face to face but on Facebook, can you flippin' believe that? Told her where to go. If she can't look me in the eye and say what's on her mind Facebook isn't going to save her. Adam and Tina are better than that. They look me in the eye. They've given me my own bedroom. I don't know, it's stupid: I just like spending time in these places… ' She leaned back against the wall. '… they just feel secure and cozy, do you know what I mean?'

'Course I do, what about your real dad?'

'Never saw him. Left when I was two. He married another woman and they had so many kids I lost count. But he died and I don't even know how. I never tried to find out and don't really care.' Natalie stopped at a certain page in the newspaper. 'I heard something about this girl in the papers: Mandy Dean. I think the media has got a problem with young people. If it's not knife crime or hoodies, it's drink and drugs. I could sort some of that out for you. You've got a bad rep in the youth clubs. I could go down to some of these estates and talk to some of these people. I could make a difference.'

'Not right now, Natalie, I don't think that's wise.'

'Promise, you'll let me though?'

'We never promise anything: not even to Prime Ministers and Royals so I can't make an exception for you. I promise I'll try, that's all I can do.'

Natalie smiled and got up. 'I'm starving; haven't eaten in couple of hours. I like this room, but Adam's is better. He's got some poetry on the walls. Wilfred Owen, I think. He's got books too. Come on, let's eat.'

Natalie and Tina started to come round each month and, gradually, with Jamie's freelance output increasing, the order and stability had returned to his life. They didn't sleep over because Adam wanted them both to come home but Jamie didn't mind that as he slept better with no-one in the house. After the third of these visits, however, when Jamie was putting the bins out in the evening, he was sure he spotted a figure lurking just yards away outside his garden. Jamie walked forward and dropped the rubbish into the bin. No one was there. He couldn't blame the Benzos for this one, only his imagination. He walked back into the house, put the kettle on, waited a few minutes and then stepped out again. He walked towards the garden gate and, in front of him, just feet away, with the whites of his eyes clearly visible was Barnaby Bin prowling around like a giant cat sticking his paws into Jamie's bulging black bin liner. He instantly spotted Jamie and threw an empty can of beans at his head. Jamie ducked but it caught him on the side of forehead. Barnaby Bin ran and Jamie chased him as far as he could but a small cut developed on his forehead, leading to drops of blood falling into his left eye. Jamie stopped and watched Barnaby Bin fade into the black fog of the night. The fucking bastard – now he was snooping around his house. What next?

Digging into his friends and family's bins? Who was his employer now anyway? Maybe he didn't have one. Jamie walked back into the house and ditched the proposed nighttime cuppa. He looked in the cupboard for a plaster and applied it hastily to his forehead. He reached for a can of Grolsch, topped it up with brandy and necked it down as fast as he could.

29.

Bin Laden In Hackistan

Larna rang Jamie in the new year and said she was about to start shooting a film. British producer Richard Leeves had contacted her after seeing her play *The Princess Who Never Was* and her TV appearance on *The Fitton Well*. He felt a low-budget feature could do well during the period of the Royal Wedding. Larna wanted Jamie to come down onto the set in Hambleden and write a newspaper feature about the film. So Jamie drove down to the film set hoping he could get a 2,000 word piece out of it, at least. He got there and stopped a few feet away from the cameraman – a picnic scene with a maid and a Prince was being shot (although how you shot this kind of thing in winter and made it look as though it was a different season was beyond Jamie). Larna, in matching purple and pink scarf, hat and mittens, was kneeling down beside a man and woman giving instructions. There were about 40 or 50 people standing around (a few on mobiles), lots of wires and cables and a couple of cameras. After seven takes, Larna spotted Jamie and acknowledged him but she went on talk to a woman with a flip chart and a storyboard. Jamie hung around till 4pm – he had been there for five hours already – and they finally began to wrap up for the day as it was getting dark. Larna walked towards him and took off her hat, running her fingers through her straggly hair.

'Like the Tunisian revolution, I wanted to see this through,' she said. 'Sorry Jamie, we're on a ridiculous schedule. They want to get this out in cinemas by late April.

We'll be shooting for five weeks, then intense post-production.' Larna's mobile rang. 'Sorry, I've got to take this.' She walked a few steps away and answered the call. The call went on for at least 20 minutes. Larna looked apologetic as she walked back towards Jamie. 'Look, we're going down to the village pub for a drink to wind down, why don't you come? Meet some of the cast? Our lead Polly Simmons used to be a waitress at Beefeater. I think she's going to be a massive star; the next Kristin Scott Thomas... '

'Who? Doesn't matter, I thought it was you who wanted to be the famous actress?'

'It was nothing more than girl's talk and ego. Writing the screenplay to this and looking at the rushes has given me the creative bug. It's unlikely to let go. So what's it to be? The Stag and Huntsman in a lovely little village or a cold, early night back home in Amersham? Be quick, because I hear the pub's closing for refurbishment soon... '

Jamie looked at the crew wearily ambling away with their booms, cameras, props and generators.

'Hope you've got some better lines for me than the Tunisian revolution?' said Jamie.

'Why? It's one of the most important events in the world right now. It's wrongfooted everyone – even the French president, which I admit is easy to do. I hope it spreads.'

'Not sure about that. Arabs seem to like their dictators.'

'So do we. You worked under one for nearly a decade.'

Jamie laughed. 'Yeah, Fitton was worse! At least I didn't appear on his show.'

'Hey look, that got me more attention and exposure than I'd had in the previous years in America put together. After the hysteria of me being the Prince's love interest died down, they started taking my work a bit more seriously.'

'... But it's only been picked up because of the Royal Wedding, yes?'

'I think we'll have a good film in the can. Richard, our producer, may think it's all connected to the wedding but most producers think like that; I don't care.'

'Have you changed it much from the play?'

'It's totally different; much better.'

'Autobiographical?'

'Hack alert! Pub needed. Beer down your throat, wine down mine. Come on... '

Larna put her hand on Jamie's shoulder and ushered him away.

'Maybe I don't want to spend a night with thesps and ego-driven actors?' said Jamie.

'Tough. A whole article on me is out of the question.'

Jamie reluctantly walked away with Larna to join up with the other crew members. He had more than enough copy for the feature anyway, nearly all on Larna. She *was* the story; the thesps and performers were just filler.

Jamie had been right to go to The Stag and Huntsman. He had a wonderful night and more quotes than he could handle. After three days of knocking the story into shape, he offered it out and the response was phenomenal. But he did wonder why there weren't more press at the film shoot? Had the media pack been told Larna was writing and directing her own film? Larna had kept an embargo on all PR and press releases until after Jamie had visited. Jamie hadn't realised this at the time; he naturally assumed other media would be there before and after this visit. Jamie was grateful to Larna for this kind gesture. It landed him some very nice cheques and further, supplementary articles in papers, radio and specialist film and celebrity magazines. But it was while he was basking in the success of one of these pieces that he caught sight of a small story in the Squires (byline, Louise Dorrans) about Hannah and the news that her father had died. Jamie called her immediately. It went to voicemail. She called back about three hours later.

'I've just come back from the funeral,' said Hannah. 'I'm sorry, Jamie, that I haven't been able to call you. Things just happened so fast. He had a stroke and I couldn't get there in time. I was helping open a new pharmacy in my constituency and a nurse phoned me but when I got there, he was gone... '

'You don't need to say sorry to me. When did it happen?'

'A couple of days ago. I was getting round to inviting you to the funeral but then I was forced to go down to the local hospital and show my face at that sleep-in. It's chaos down there, and things are getting ugly. I got a couple of eggs thrown at me.'

'Is Trevena still down there?'

'He was – but he also came to the funeral. I don't blame him. I agree with him – but some of the protesters think I'm the enemy.'

'Look, if there's anything you need me to do... '

'Well, there is something – a couple of boxes with dad's things still need to be picked up from the care home. I'll be in tomorrow night, if you can drop them off. If you can't, no problem – I'll probably get them next week.'

'I'll go round this afternoon. I think you need a break.'

'No, I had mine in the school cloakroom with you. That was my honeymoon period – lasted all of a few minutes. I can't talk any more now – my throat hurts. See you tomorrow night.'

'Wait on, I know it's not the right time but what about that hacking committee? Do you still need me at the hearing?'

'Shit, forgot about that. See what you can do... '

Hannah hung up. Jamie thought about the way Ted's tremor had delivered an electric current into his body and made him develop a conscience. Jamie had to be thankful of that. Now that conscience would be tested at the MP's

340

committee hearing in the summer. Jamie didn't want to go but he felt sorry for Hannah after she'd lost her father. It was the least he could do for her.

Jamie delivered the two boxes to Hannah's house but she looked absolutely shattered when she came to the door. She stood on the doorstep in her tracksuit bottoms and t-shirt and gestured for Jamie to open them immediately while trying to suppress a yawn with her other hand. In the first box it was standard stuff: slippers, toothbrush, vests, nighttime hat and earmuffs among other things. But in the other box, Jamie pulled out two pictures: nicely framed paintings with images that looked strikingly familiar.

'Shit that's us,' said Hannah, putting her hand over her mouth. 'The nurse said he was enjoying his dancing and painting but I didn't think he was so involved.'

The first picture was of Hannah and Jamie sitting on a park bench underneath a tree, eyes down, heads forward, big smiles, reading a newspaper together. The other was of Ted and Ellie ballroom dancing: hands tenderly on each other's shoulders, eyes swivelled towards the invisible camera. Jamie handed the pictures over to Hannah but she slumped on the doorstep and began to cry. Jamie sat next to her and put his arm round her.

'These are unbelievable,' said Jamie. 'You should be proud.'

'I am, but I should have been there for him.'

'I like this one… '

Jamie put the 'park bench' painting onto her lap. Slowly, the tears turned to mild laughter.

'Destiny, don't you think?' said Jamie.

'You wish,' said Hannah, wiping her cheeks with one of Ted's vests. 'These days, I never smile like that when I read papers. They're laying into me all over the place.' Hannah got up and shifted one of the boxes inside the house. 'Come on, get the other one,' she said. 'If I don't sleep in the next ten minutes, I'll combust.'

'Just don't make me combust at the hacking inquiry... '

Jamie picked up the other box and put it in the hallway.

'I'll be gentle,' said Hannah. 'But I'll abide by the journalistic rule... '

Jamie shrugged his shoulders.

'I can't promise anything,' she said.

Tina phoned to say Adam was seriously thinking of abandoning his book project because of the Japanese earthquake and tsunami. He was distressed about the event itself but also that it might have a knock-on effect on his own book of the 2004 tsunami – and perhaps not attract any publishers or agents. He had written 80,000 words already and become quite depressed about it. Jamie wondered why he got so worked up about something like that. His lost his wife at the age of 33 for God's sake.

One person who wasn't getting worked up was Trevena who called to say he was disappointed Jamie couldn't get a piece in about the protest but wasn't going to give up because the hospital wasn't going to move its services for another 18 months at least. The camp had been suspended and all the protesters (17 of them) had gone back home. The local paper said this was because police were about to move in and arrest them but Trevena claimed this wasn't true. It was more to do with a handful of patients at A&E, concerned that they didn't have enough parking spaces because some protesters had camped their tents there. Trevena listened and felt it was better to move on – and reconsider their tactics for the next wave. Jamie concluded that Trevena had been down the road of negotiation, etiquette and diplomacy (in true MP style) and it hadn't worked. He had no option but to step up his tactics to another level. He had self-belief of a kind Jamie had never seen or experienced before. Jamie admired that – but was frustrated that none of it had rubbed off on him.

Natalie was so angry about the hysteria surrounding the forthcoming Royal Wedding that she dubbed it the WillyKaM wedding. When asked how she'd come up with this term (something Jamie would probably find in the *Daily Sport*), she said she'd heard a Year 9 pupil say it at school and thought it sounded good. She came round to stay for a week when Tina and Adam went on holiday to Istanbul. It was one of the most enjoyable weeks Jamie had ever had. It flew by as they went to watch Watford at Vicarage Road and the film *Source Code* at Cineworld in High Wycombe (she was obsessed with Jake Gylenhaall). She also got hooked on pizza at Zizzi in Denmark Street and Jamie returned there three times in a week. During this time, Natalie talked a little more about the care home she lived in for most of her life. She claimed it wasn't too bad – and also talked about how good a dad Adam was. There were also a couple of friends in London (Zack and Howie) who she liked to visit from time to time (with permission from Tina and Adam). At the end of this week, Jamie heard the news that police had arrested three senior staff at the Screws. His mood wasn't quite the same as it had been earlier in the week. He knew the Screws and the Daisies were on the police's radar. It was going to be a long summer.

The Princess Who Never Was got a slightly bigger release than expected. It opened at 46 screens across the country and received additional funding from Canada, Ecuador and Spain. Larna didn't even watch the Royal Wedding and spent most of her time doing satellite interviews to film critics in America and preparing the cover design for the DVD. Jamie secretly wanted to see the film at the cinema but had no-one to go with: Larnell and Mark would rather have watched *Fast Five*, Hannah was still mourning her father and Natalie had made her views on the WillyKaM love-in pretty clear. The film became a slow-burning success and ran before, during and after the Wedding that had supposedly gripped the nation. One editor wanted Jamie to go and watch the film and do a vox pop afterwards to discover what all the fuss was about. Jamie didn't like to say no to gatekeepers but it was taken out of his hands anyway. Late one evening, he was having a shave when the doorbell rang. He got to the door but couldn't see anyone. He looked further down the road and spotted Barnaby Bin walking briskly, carrying a black recycling box which consisted of Jamie's old newspapers, magazines, junk mail, pizza leaflets and squashed Amazon boxes. Jamie felt he'd been given a thousand cuts at once. Barnaby spotted him and started to run, looking totally absurd with the recycling box awkwardly in front of him, the lid balanced hastily on top, the white district council symbol glowing in the dark. This time Jamie was determined to nail him. Jamie sprinted out of his house and caught up with him within minutes. Surprisingly, Barnaby stopped and put the box down on the pavement. He was sweating and out of breath. He put his foot on top of the box and his hand on his chest. He finally looked at Jamie and raised his hand, warning him to keep his distance.

'Bin Laden's dead, people aren't gonna call me that anymore,' he said.

'What? I thought everyone called you Barnaby Bin?'

'They did, but they also called me Bin Laden – and I didn't like it.'

'Yeah so? What's that got to do with stealing from my house? Again.'

'It's not stealing; it's borrowing. That's what we all do, hackistan. Banks, punters, governments, it's why we've got a crisis. Borrowing's all the rage – so I wanted a piece of the action.'

'What the fuck are you on about? Who sent you? And don't you dare go through my papers and bills.'

'Why? Summat I should know about? You were cleaned out a while back. Took your furniture, did they?'

Jamie launched forward at Barnaby but he quickly picked up the recycling box and smacked it hard against Jamie's legs. The lid from the box flew off and the bills, papers, magazines and flattened cereal packets poured out dangerously onto Stanley Hill as the few cars which were on the road at this time of night, swerved to avoid the harmless debris. Barnaby picked up as much of Jamie's mail as he could, particularly envelopes, and stuffed it into his pockets. He then ran as fast as he could towards Chequers Hill and Jamie chased him. Barnaby had a curious running style, he hardly moved his arms or his head, but still managed to navigate the bends with ease. It was clear where the alternative bin man was going – to the station. But Jamie was well up with him. He could smell the tumble-dried rubbish from Barnaby's hair and body: the mouldy milk, bad eggs, the sickly onions, a whole fucking waste recycling plant going up Jamie's nose, making his eyes water. Jamie was inches away now and aimed to grab his neck. It was a skilful move: Barnaby buckled and ended up on the pavement. But almost at the same time, Jamie's eyes were almost blinded by a set of car headlights. Jamie was on the ground when the car parked up and the headlights were thankfully turned off. He could see a woman's legs walking briskly towards him. Did Barnaby have a wife or girlfriend? Not with shoes like that.

'This mail… ' she said, carrying a wad of brown and white envelopes. '… some of it ended up on my windscreen. It's got a Stanley Hill address on it. I saw you down there, is it yours?'

Jamie's loosed his grip on Barnaby's neck. The woman handed him the mail.

'Er yeah, gas bills and stuff. Always too high. Thanks for that.'

'Do you need some help? Shall I call the police?'

Before Jamie could answer, Barnaby Bin had slipped away, looking over his shoulder, heading towards the train station.

'There's no need for police,' said Jamie, looking down the road as the Other Bin Laden vanished into the station like his deceased namesake had once slithered into a cave. 'They'd probably arrest the wrong man, anyway.'

30.

Bedknobs And Big Sticks

Jamie prepared rigorously in the days before MPs' hearing on phone hacking. He rehearsed his answers on a dictaphone, watched how Al Pacino performed in front of the Senate in The Godfather Part II and read up on some of the more spikier MPs on the committee to ensure he wasn't caught out. The whole hacking saga had reached fever pitch and just when he thought things couldn't get messier, a bombshell was dropped by the Screws. The paper was about to close after 127 years of a rollercoaster existence. Jamie felt the shudder in his bedroom. What now for the rest? When the dirtiest organ is forced down, how do the rest of tabloids survive? Yet it might be a stroke of luck for him that the Screws' big boss was in town. The world would be watching hoping the tabloid tsar got some of the treatment he had been dishing out to others for decades. In this climate, Jamie hoped he could nip in front of the Culture Media and Sport Committee, give his evidence and quietly slip away. This could have happened if the Danny Love verdict had gone another way. Not now, MPs were keen to show the tabloid menace was rampant across many papers not one. They had a point but to compare the Screws' illegal behaviour to the Daisies was ridiculous; it was like comparing an abusive father to an errant child. Yes, the Daisies behaviour had been bad but for God's sake they were only aping the masters.

Jamie was ready. He wore his best River Island suit: a pinstriped, dark blue concoction with a sky blue shirt and maroon tie. He got a call from Larna on the way to London but couldn't take it because he was on the Metropolitan Line to Baker Street. He walked right out of the station to call her back. She said she was already shooting her next film and hoped to get a big nationwide release of 600 screens-plus on the back of the success of *The Princess Who Never Was*. She was vague about the story of the new film but said it was media-related. She was also delighted at the Screws' demise. The call was important for Jamie's confidence: it eased his nerves. The problem was the call went on for longer than expected – and Jamie was 10 minutes behind schedule. He got off at Westminster and walked briskly towards the House of Commons, flicking over the pages in his notebook to ensure he had his stock answers ready. He had been to the Commons on a couple of stories before so it wasn't completely alien to him but the beady eyes would now be trained on him now rather than the other way round. He went through the Cromwell Green entrance and knew the session would already be underway. Perhaps his name had been called already? Hannah hadn't told him anything. After the security checks and a few strange looks (when he offered his name), Jamie took his seat in a hushed, reverent committee room with a firing squad of MPs in horseshoe-shape around him, examining him with the odd tut, smirk and folding of arms. He counted the MPs, nine of them, including Hannah who looked as stern as the others, second from the left, hands crossed on table, hair tied up. As Jamie settled into his seat and took a sip of water, he wondered how many press and members of the public were behind him. Couldn't have been more than a dozen; there were a lot of empty green seats. The bastard MPs prolonged the silence to increase his discomfort. Finally, the chair of the committee, Stephen Lassiter, opened his mouth.

'Mr Parkes, thank you for honouring this committee with

your presence. Much appreciated. We are slightly behind schedule so we'll crack on with proceedings… '

Jamie switched off as Lassiter began to waffle on about the background to the hearing. He looked at Hannah and offered a mild smile: nothing, she didn't even make eye contact. Lassiter must have gone on for 20 minutes, at least. Jamie had a headache already and drunk some more water. He looked at his notes and wondered if they'd be any good at all. He was so relieved none of this was under oath. Finally, Lassiter shut his mouth and opened it up to his colleagues. He looked directly at Hannah. YES! It may have been a stitch-up but at least Hannah would get first dibs before the fat fuckers on the right butted in with their awkward questions. Jamie deserved a gentle introduction.

'Mr Parkes, why did you hack phones?' asked Hannah, poised and upright like some modern Cleopatra.

'Er hold on… ' Jamie looked at his notes and then leaned back in his seat.

'Little boys can't do without their notebooks, is that it?'

'No, that's not it.'

'Can you answer the question then, please?'

Jamie closed his notebook and looked up. 'Better than working for it, wasn't it?'

'Can you elaborate?'

'Well, access is our currency and we had gold coming out of our ears, it's all I can say.'

'So it was all about access?'

'It's our lifeblood, if we don't get it, we shrivel and die.'

'Which is what part of your industry are doing right now.'

Hannah looked down at a piece of paper she had on the table.

'Did you ever pay people for stories?'

'Never.'

'But you worked closely for Danny Love, yes?'

'He was my news editor… '

'So you never offered money to sources?'

'I was never in charge of that side of things. That was all to do with Danny and Fitton. We had to get permission from them.'

'What did Pubs A and E mean?'

'It was just a term an old reporter called Lenny Calvin came up with. He used to meet sources in Pubs A, B and C and so on. He liked to be discreet.'

'… And you carried this on?'

'Yeah, it was convenient.'

'What kind of sources did you meet? Drug dealers? Criminals?'

'Those – and a few others… '

'Kiss and Tell girls?'

'Sometimes… '

'What did you call them?'

'KATS; Lenny's name not mine.'

'Did you ever agree to pay any of these women?'

'I'm not getting into that.'

'Why?'

'… Because you might get into trouble.'

Hannah leaned forward and rested her knuckles on her chin. 'Oh, how so?'

Jamie couldn't believe how aggressive Hannah was. Did she want Jamie to reveal that she'd been paid 60k for the Whipping Dictator story? She may have had a strong moral case – and it may not have been illegal – but she still took money from a paper.

'Mr Parkes, would you answer the question please?' said Lassiter.

'I have nothing to say about that.'

'Okay, maybe we'll come back to that again later. Mr Richmond?'

It was one of the fat fuckers on the right. Jamie couldn't remember if he was Labour or Tory, even though he stayed up half the night swotting up on them. He might have been Lib Dem because he had a funny-looking yellow shirt beneath his suit. Whichever way he rolled, he'd obviously been fiddling his expenses with a belly like that.

'I'd like to go over some of the history with you, Mr Parkes, if I may... '

Oh for fuck's sake, this was going to put Jamie to sleep. He began by asking Jamie when he started working for tabloid newspapers and it was downhill from there. When he finished, a Labour MP took over and he wasn't much better. In all, Jamie was questioned by another five MPs for about an hour and a half. He was exhausted, tetchy and miserable. His brain was scrambled and he found it hard to come up with coherent answers. And then Hannah came back with all guns blazing.

'Aren't you ashamed of tabloid culture, Mr Parkes?' she asked.

'No, it's given us a good living. It's part of this country's DNA, like fish and chips.'

'But the things they do: demeaning women, paying police, never apologising. They're just a rogue industry, out of control. Don't you agree?'

'You probably think that because they're after MPs. The man on the street loves them.'

'... But not the woman on the street?'

'Them too.'

'Were you sorry to see Danny Love go to jail?'

'A little... '

'He did a lot of illegal things.'

'Yes, but a few good ones too... '

Hannah picked up another piece of paper from the table. 'I've got some evidence here from a Louise Dorrans. Do you know her?'

'I worked with her for a few years.'

'She claims there was culture of bullying at your paper… '

'It was probably harder for her than for me.'

'Why?'

'Well, when she started she was one of the few women in the office. Obviously, there's loads more now but she ended up doing some of the low-end jobs.'

'Low-end jobs, what do you mean?'

'Sort of humiliating ones. Posing as a host at a Swingers party, dressing up as Wonder Woman, being told to go to a mosque in a low-cut dress… '

'… And she did all those things?'

'Some of them.'

'Were you bullied?'

'Not really, I'd say it's more like giving orders than bullying.'

'Like the army?'

'Not as bad as that but the pressure to get stuff before your rivals was intense.'

'Which meant you had to bend the rules?'

'No, I just wrote stories and made deadlines. I fed the news editor what he wanted.'

Hannah nodded and crossed her hands on the table.

'Do you see yourself as a whistleblower?'

'Not really. I didn't see the job through.'

'Didn't or couldn't.'

'Couldn't. As you know, I was sacked. But I suppose the Danny Love stuff has vindicated what I was saying… '

'Agree with that. You've been incredibly brave.' Hannah uncrossed her hands and fiddled with her hairclip at the back of her head. 'What about the tabloid papers attitude to sex? What do you think about that?'

Jamie was annoyed with Hannah's haphazard line of questioning. Ted's death had affected her much more than Jamie expected.

'Don't really have a view on the sex stuff,' said Jamie. 'It's always there.'

'Did they go too far?'

Hannah's words hung in the air.

'Er, no, I don't think they went too far.'

'So you think words like 'busty bimbo', 'curvy' and 'lick-worthy Lucinda' are acceptable do you?'

'No, I don't know. Not sure what you mean.'

'I mean, are those words acceptable?'

'It's harmless, a bit of fun really... '

'A bit of fun?'

'No, sorry didn't mean that.'

'Did you ever write anything like that?'

'I don't know, can't remember... '

'If that was said about your girlfriend, what would you think?'

'I haven't got one, I don't know... '

'Wonder why? Please answer the question.'

Jamie was finding the pace and intensity of questioning extremely taxing. The sweat was pouring off his forehead and dribbling into his eyes. He blinked a number of times, trying to keep his eyes on the formidable Hannah. She was roasting him alive: kicking him, beating him, stripping him of any dignity he had left.

'It if was my girlfriend,' said Jamie. 'I'd say sorry to her on behalf of the paper.'

'Yes, but what action would you take?'

'Action?'

Jamie's mind went blank. He had no answer. Hannah had defeated him and, if she continued in this vain, he'd have to beg her to stop. It had been a disastrous decision to turn up.

'If you don't take action,' said Hannah. 'Extinction is the only course.'

'Extinction? The Screws may have gone but the rest won't be so easy.'

Hannah looked at the other members of the committee and smiled.

'It started with the Screws... ' she said.

They all laughed and Jamie could feel the chuckles of breath behind him, invading his neck muscles like a thousand razors. He had to get out of this hellhole: now.

It was like some fantastic dream. Hannah had booked one of the Commons rooms, which she used for lobbying business, and wanted Jamie to meet her there immediately after the session. She had texted him and asked him to wait in the Central Lobby. When she arrived, she walked briskly ahead of Jamie and they stepped into a room with a leather chair, desk, fireplace, painting on the walls and too many other posh items to mention. There was no-one in there. Did she just want a chat? Jamie's heart pounded as she kicked off her heels and she was onto him before he knew what was happening.

'So you still don't want to talk about sex?' she said, putting her hands round his neck and flinging him to the floor. 'I don't have time to fanny about like we did in there... '

'What are you doing?'

She put her finger on his mouth as he lay on the floor. 'Got another appointment in five minutes... '

She lowered her head and kissed him to deliver a blistering headrush of pleasure. She unbuttoned his suit and loosened his tie. All the tension and anxiety Jamie felt was magically cured by her heavenly hands. The bottom half even quicker – the old KAT hadn't lost her touch. He was naked now, apart from his socks, and she kissed him all over; the warmth and intimacy of her mouth giving him the type of Rock Hudson he thought he never possessed. She took her shirt and bra off and Jamie was desperate to get those supple, heaving breasts around his lips but she had pinned down, primed for action. She slipped off her skirt and knickers and laid into him. Whoosh! The gorgeousness of her being electrified his body. It tingled and vibrated as she powered in, riding, sinking, fucking. She speeded up and Jamie begged she'd never stop. If she wanted to put this on expenses it was fine by him. She carried on until Jamie eyes watered and he could thrust no more. He was suffocating and out of breath, a joyous corpse of death-exhilaration. He'd run his course and opened his eyes to look at the high ceiling. She eased out of him and smiled. She bent down and kissed him before getting changed.

'So what's the headline for his story?' she asked.

Jamie was so exhausted he could hardly speak. 'Kiss and Tell boy romps with MP... '

'How much would you get for it?'

'50k easy.'

Hannah laughed and walked up to Jamie. She used her foot to lift up his boxer shorts and then caught them in her hand. She threw them down on his body.

'Nice little lobby you've got there,' she said. 'But 60k? Give us a break... 50p maybe.'

Jamie looked up and grabbed Hannah's leg to make her trip over. He managed to get on top of her and started kissing her haphazardly. She was receptive and turned him round again to get in control. Fuck her appointment, she was punctual enough as it was. No headlines needed; no stories, no words. This was a real session – unlike the previous one.

Jamie stayed up till three in the morning, playing 'Guess the Story' with Tina and Natalie. This was the teenager's idea – she wanted to go through back copies of the Daisies and find non-bylined stories that Jamie had wrote. There were lots of them and Jamie couldn't remember which ones were his. Truth was, he was still dreaming of Hannah's gorgeous legs and found it hard to go to bed without her. But Tina and Natalie's company, a homemade lactose-free pizza and a couple of cans of Grolsch were an adequate consolation. Jamie was happier than he'd ever been. He felt so good he called Hannah from his bedroom just before trying to turn in. It went to voicemail and he considered leaving a racy message but decided against it. He would call her tomorrow. He couldn't wait to reverse the action in the Commons room. After that, a relationship – and, possibly, marriage; he had waited long enough. These thoughts ravished him all night, until he got to sleep at about 4.30am. The dreams were even more exuberant; among them Hannah as Prime Minister and Jamie as her special adviser. But they didn't last long. A monstrous thud blew them all away.

It came just before dawn. Jamie thought part of the house had been blown off. Big booming sounds reverberated round the house making the walls shake. Rough shouting, thudding boots and crashing noises ripped into Jamie's ears. He sprung out of his bed, half asleep, his eyes stitched together, stumbling into the bedside table for the first time. The shouts got louder and closer: sounds of cups smashing into walls, glasses breaking, pots and pans clattering, weapons bashing against doors. A wrecking crew were destroying the house and he was in his fucking boxer shorts. He thought about Tina and Natalie sleeping in their beds but it was too late – his bedroom door flew towards him like a slab of deadly polystyrene. He managed to avoid it but couldn't sidestep the helmeted brutes rushing towards him with their ant-like faces, dark glasses, shiny weapons and bone-shuddering demands. Jamie put his hands up in the air but it made no difference; the sci-fi army were onto him in a flash.

'GET ON THE FLOOR, YOU FUCKIN' TWAT. NOW!'

He was already on his knees but that wasn't enough. He was flipped over ferociously and smacked his nose against the floor. His eyes watered and his arms were jolted behind his back. Jamie heard his arm crack and shrieked in pain. He could see the bedroom being poked and trashed: tapes ejected from recorders, wires ripped out of devices, computers, monitors and phones confiscated. His body, so erotically charged just minutes ago, was emptied of its energy and felt savagely numb and listless. But this was just the start – the screams from Tina's bedroom hit his ears like a fatal RTA.

'Get out of my fuckin' house now,' she shouted.

Jamie closed his eyes as he imagined her being pulled out of her bedroom. Handcuffs clicked onto his wrists. He struggled for a few seconds until he realised it was pointless. He was lifted up and ushered out of the bedroom. He saw three armed coppers in his room, strutting around, dripping in uniform-ego, tooled up to the eyeballs. What the fuck did they want with him? Weren't there any terrorists to catch?

'Leave my mum alone,' said Jamie. 'There's a young girl in there too, if you touch her… '

'Or what paper boy?'

'Just leave her alone, she hasn't done anything.'

Jamie could see Natalie on the other side of the landing, struggling with an armed copper in her t-shirt and shorts. Another copper had to help out and she was dragged downstairs. He followed her down, a gush of wind was blowing into the house after the front door had been smashed down. The steps were so cold, Jamie couldn't believe it was his own house. He must have woken up into a nightmare. The coppers led him out of the house and bundled him, nastily, into the van. He had a craving for breakfast; warm soft-boiled eggs and luscious toast. A few minutes later, Tina and Natalie were also strongarmed into the van. Jamie looked down at his bare feet. His nipples were erect and his neck stiff. He was shivering and folded his arms, rubbing his biceps on each side vigorously. He didn't dare look at Tina and Natalie. Even Hannah's heat couldn't warm him up now.

31.

Nat's No Way To Behave!

Jamie wasn't questioned for at least nine hours. Nine fucking hours in a shitty little cell, head in hands, staring at walls, wondering if his mother would ever look him in the eye again. He only had one conclusion: this was Old Bill getting its own back, trying to cover up for its own impotence by throwing hacks into the fire; grilling them and burning them, using the harsh criticism they'd suffered to pummel an old friend, give them a good kicking they'd remember. Jamie knew the dawn raid was excessive but (apart from Tina and Natalie) would anyone else care? The armed cops may have acted like a pack of wild animals, running and flailing, tearing strips out of whoever got in their way, relishing collateral damage even if it got them a nugget of evidence, but journalism was still more in the dock than Old Bill, it always would be even if the Met commissioner turned out to be a serial killer.

Jamie was close to breaking point when he finally stepped out of the cell into the interview room; not because of his own predicament but that of his mother and Natalie. Where were they? To think of them locked up in a cell was unbearable. Jamie demanded that the well-groomed copper, DC Andy Connor, tell him where they were before he started the interview.

'They've been released,' said DC Connor. 'Now sit down and take your time. We need clear answers. Do you want some water?'

'What about a solicitor? Don't I get one of those?'

'You will. But we want to try it this way first.'

DC Connor was clean-shaven with short blonde hair and a fair, freckly complexion. One of his fingers had a nail missing. There was a copy of the Screws and the Daisies on the table. Jamie noticed the Screws' copy was its last ever edition. DC Connor flicked through the copy of the Daisies. He didn't turn the tape recorder on.

'You see, the problem with this investigation... ' he said, not looking up at Jamie. '... is that most people who've been hacked don't want their dirty washing to be aired again for a second time. They've been snooped on once... ' He looked up at Jamie. '... and they don't want to explore that grubbiness again.' He licked his finger and briskly went through a few more pages. 'Do you see our problem?'

'Yeah, but what's it got to do with me? And why isn't this being recorded?'

DC Connor looked at Jamie and closed the newspaper. He crossed his hands on top of the paper.

'When asked by an MP if you'd ever hacked phones you said "it was better than working for it", what did you mean by that?'

'Is that what this is about? Some fucking MPs' hearing that no-one watches or cares about? You smashed into my home at dawn, terrified my mother and my sister... '

'Your sister?'

'My mum adopted her... '

'So she isn't really your sister... '

'Not technically, no, but we're close enough. The point is they were scared. So was I. There was no need for that. I would have come in voluntarily. Is that what you do to journalists now? Point guns at their heads while they're sleeping? I thought this was still a democracy.'

'So is hacking phones better than working for it?'

'It was a joke.'

'Didn't sound like a joke.'

'It was. She was pushing hard.'

'Who was?'

'The MP... '

'Hannah Rocheman?'

'Yeah.'

'Do you know her?'

'Suppose so.'

'She had a fling with Don Leaver and you did a story on it, yes? The Whipping Dictator story. Was that from hacked material?'

'No.'

'Are you friends with Miss Rocheman?'

'Sort of... '

'She's come a long way... '

Jamie shrugged his shoulders but his heart was beating rapidly.

'I want to get onto the story about Larna Wilson and the Prince,' said DC Connor. 'Our sources say you got that from hacked material... '

Jamie wanted to throw up – and the freckles on DC Connor's face didn't help. 'Look, I can lend you a tape recorder if you want. Might be a bit bashed up though.'

'Nice attempt. Look, we know you've done pretty well in recent years to try and clean up newspapers. We've spoken to Mike Trevena, Elliot Broomfield and a few others. Louise Dorrans said that you led the charge from within; great, but if you've done something illegal, we can't treat you any differently. Now, how did that Larna Wilson story come about? Where did you get those quotes from the Prince from?'

'Have you been in touch with Larna?'

'Yes, but let's just say she – and the Prince – don't want any more legs in this story. They've had enough. As I said before, many people don't want their private conversations dredged up for public ridicule, again. Yes, some want compensation but those two, I'd say, don't need it. Anyway, they are not our sources for bringing you in.'

'Who is?'

'Unlike your mob, we don't mind revealing our sources if it gets a result: Warren Fitton and The Coby brothers. The company who runs your old paper are co-operating with us. They've given us your name.'

'FITTON? You fucking believe him?'

'Keep your language under control.'

'It's not being recorded so I won't. He's more bent than most of your department.'

'He says he stopped you running that story on a number of occasions. Is that true?'

'It's not the point… '

'Is it true?'

'Yes, but he's the one you should be after not me. Why haven't you raided his house? Thrown a gun into Grace's mouth? Frightened her kids?'

'Because we don't have enough evidence on him. People have come forward with allegations but they haven't been substantiated. Yes, he's been hung, drawn and quartered in the media but so have bankers and company bosses – and they're hard to pin down too. He said the quotes you used for that story came from Larna's Wilson's phone… '

'I don't see why I should answer that when you've got a criminal editor running a paper, doing all sorts of illegal things. Has he got friends in the Met or something? Given you some gifts? Coby Brothers meeting the Met chief for dinner later?'

'Stick to the question.'

'No, Danny Love is in prison and you've locked me up. How many more are going to suffer before you get the man who pushed us to do all these things?'

'Did you hack Larna Wilson's phone?'

'No, I didn't hack her phone – and you can ask her if you want.'

'So how did you get the Prince's quotes?'

'Larna gave them to me… '

'Just like that?'

Jamie didn't answer.

'If you're lying, you'll definitely go to prison.'

'Without a tape recorder or a solicitor present?'

'With or without it… '

'Compared to the Coby Brothers and Fitton, I'm a saint. They can fuck right off.'

DC Connor sighed and looked down at the two newspapers in front of him. He picked up the Daisies and laid its masthead right underneath the Screws. 'I've never liked copycat crime. It's a hard one to crack.'

Jamie was released without charge which didn't surprise him. Terrorists, protesters and now, reporters could be added to coppers' fishing expeditions which were growing as their workforce shrunk. They didn't have the resources anymore, so they brought 'suspects' like Jamie in to give them new leads. Jamie had lost count of the number of times he'd seen 'released on bail pending further enquiries' for other hacks caught in the nasty beak of Old Bill. He was relieved he wasn't one of them but when he got home and looked at his front door lying the garden, a sea of glass in the kitchen and his bedroom looking like a bomb site, he knew there was no release from the deep psychological scars of the last 48 hours. He walked into Tina's bedroom and walked out immediately; her wardrobe was upside down, cupboard drawers were on the carpet and a smashed bottle of gin lay on the ironing board. He hadn't spoken to her or Natalie since the raid and Adam would probably see to it that they never came here again. Jamie didn't linger too long over this depressing thought: he called his mother immediately.

'You're out, thank God,' said Tina. 'That's all that matters. Tell me straight, what did you do?'

'Nothing. Fitton's out to get me, he's got the Coby brothers onside too, so it's the whole company.'

'But you were sacked – they've already got you?'

'I think they're under the pump too, so they're looking for a fall guy. Anyway forget that, what about Natalie? How is she doing?'

'How would you do if you get a gun up your arse at six in the morning?'

'Don't start mum. I didn't bring this on.'

'Who did then? The Dalai Lama?'

'Look, I knew you'd be like this so I'll just get on with finding a firm who can fix our door and stuff and we'll speak later… '

'No, no you're not getting away that easily. Let's get one thing straight: you *did* bring this upon yourself. You put your mother and sister in great danger and we could have been killed. Natalie was so hysterical in the station, she started to punch one of the officers. In one way, he was quite lenient with her in the end because he let us both go, but she's been traumatised by this. She says she's having nightmares and can't sleep. I've taken her to the doctor already for some mild sleeping pills. She's had to take the whole week off school too. As for me, you don't have to worry, I'm surprisingly fine even though our house is destroyed. It's Adam you've got to worry about because he's pissed big time. He's banned Natalie from going there permanently – or talking to you – so you can forget about her now.'

'I'm not forgetting about her. We got on well.'

'Well, you won't be getting on at all from now on, so put her out of your mind.'

'… Can you say sorry to her from me?'

'Already have, Jamie. You don't know the half of it. I apologise nearly every day on your behalf. I've had enough. Adam always said a reporter's family are fair game for a story and you've just proved it. I think you were up to no good, hacking someone's phone, otherwise the police wouldn't have gone in so hard.'

'The police do that all the time – to a lot of people. They're up to their necks in this as much as reporters are. That's why they're going over the top. They're wounded… '

'You could have fooled me. I could see who the wounded ones were and it wasn't them. Anyway, I've got to go because the brewery want an explanation for why I've missed work for the last couple of days. It's unlikely you'll see us over there again for a very long time… '

'Oh come on, mum, don't say that. You grew up in this house.'

'I mean it. Adam's a caring man and this has hurt him bad. I'd stay away from him for a while. I hope you've got the message because I don't want things to get any worse than they already are… '

'Loud and clear. Adam's all yours.'

'It's not the time for sarcasm. Oh and make sure you get my bedroom exactly the way it was looking before. See you, if Adam lets me. Bye… '

Jamie put his mobile in his pocket and headed downstairs. There was a pile of junk mail, newspapers and magazines by the wall. Jamie looked underneath them and picked up the Thomson Local directory. Jamie sat down and leaned against the wall. He looked outside as a waft of cool air brushed against his warm face. He would eventually fix the front door but how would he fix his family again?

A few light repairs had been carried out round the house but

Jamie had to find a reliable local firm to come in and do the heavier, trickier stuff for a decent, cash-in-hand price. His freelance routine was harder to revive: the letters and emails were longer, the copy was harder to write and the phone calls to sources were brief and abrupt. He was finding it hard to get excited about stories – any stories. It was as though he'd acted a part in the biggest one ever. How could he top that? He couldn't resist a bit of brandy and Grolsch to get him going but even this wasn't enough. But late one evening, after he'd taken a three-day break from all news stories to give his brain a rest, he was watching the news on TV when one of those special journalistic moments popped up which could help him get back into the swing of things. If he couldn't get excited about this then he should stop being a reporter all together. The burning images of the riots from London, Manchester and other big cities gave him the kind of journalistic electric shock that was badly needed. What the fuck was happening here? Old Bill were being overrun and smacked around. Why were people so angry? Didn't matter because Jamie was enjoying the spectacle of frightened coppers cowering behind their shields like little children. Aw, the poor darlings, if they didn't waste time smashing into innocent people's homes, they might have more resources to get a grip of situations like this; serves them fucking right. Even though it was late, Jamie started to call round a few of his local contacts to see if anything had kicked off in sleepy South Bucks. Quiet, as usual. He then called Larnell and Mark and had a story in mind about which brands were the most attractive to steal for the rioters. Larnell thought Nike, Mark went for Samsung. The next day he wrote up the story and could feel a rush of momentum; the adrenaline was back. But at about 4pm, he got a call on his mobile.

'Don't tell Adam but I'm in a manky police station,' said Natalie. 'Come and get me now.'

'Natalie? What happened?'

'Got caught in the riots, didn't I? Met a couple of friends in London. Copper pushed us around so we lobbed a couple of traffic cones at him. The uptight bastard arrested me and Zack. Howie got away though. Come on, get down here. It'll be one-one between you and me. You owe me this favour.'

'I don't fucking believe this. How the hell did you get caught up in that madness?'

'Police treated me bad in your house so I don't really care about them. What did I do wrong? Nothing but they still put me in a police van. I told my friends about this and Howie got really angry. He thinks the police hate young people. So when these riots started, we just wanted to go down to see what was happening. Just have a bit of fun. We didn't want to cause trouble but the police pushed us around.'

'Have they charged you with anything?'

'Don't know, they were talking about bail or something.'

'Jesus, a 14-year-old girl involved in the riots. Papers'll go mad for a story like that.'

'Is that all you think about you scummy hack? Come here now or I'll call your mother. She cares about me more than you.'

'Do you know what Adam will do if he sees me with you?'

Natalie paused and took a drink from a can which she threw away after she'd finished.

'I miss Grandad,' she said. 'He used to call me Nat Queen Cool but I didn't even know who he was on about. I was thinking about him when we walked into this gutted antique shop, which had loads of furniture, and there was this old woman sitting there listening to the radio. She looked so sad… '

'Did you steal anything?'

'No, course not. I don't steal – and never have.'

Jamie cleared his throat. 'Right, this is what we're going to do: I'm going to pick you up and take you home to

Beaconsfield and then I'm leaving. If I bring you here, I might not be around for much longer to write stories. Adam will see to that. So wait there, I'll be down in about an hour, which station are you at?'

'Are you gonna tell Adam?'

'Don't know, probably not, but he'll find out anyway.'

'Promise you won't tell him?'

Jamie rolled his eyes but felt partially guilty about Natalie's predicament. The dawn raid meant she was not totally responsible for her actions. Jamie was also guilty – the least he could now was lift her out of the fire that was threatening to engulf the whole country.

Jamie dropped Natalie off in Beaconsfield Old Town. She was more chirpy than Jamie expected and acted as though she'd just come back from a panto rather than a riot. She had been bailed to return to the police station in three weeks. He did consider doing an interview with her in the car – it was a dead-cert commission for virtually all the papers – but felt it was insensitive. He needed a break. He went home but couldn't relax. He wondered how Melvin Moon was doing at First Frames. Barely three hours later, his mobile rang.

'I know a youth worker called Lars in Norway,' said Adam. 'He's a good man but even he still wants people like Breivik to burn in hell. I really don't care who I compare you to now, you're taking a chance with a young person I dearly love and cherish. Be in no doubt, what I'll do if she comes to any harm.' There was a pause and long sigh. 'You won't be seeing her again.'

'I'm sorry about the raid, Adam, I really am. But I don't take responsibility for anything after that. If you're such a good dad then why did she call me and not you to pick her up? Scared of you is she?'

'No, she probably panicked. Most adults have treated her

abysmally throughout her life and she still sees you as an adolescent with your playful tabloid tales. She told me so herself. It's been a lot for her to take in. First, the armed raid, then the riots; that's a few days of hell for an adult right there, never mind a young girl. And anyway, a small amount of fear in parenting is a good thing. Perhaps, your father wasn't too good at that and that's why we have the problems we do.'

'Leave my father out of it... '

'Yes, leaving is his speciality. I hope I've made myself clear. Don't talk, speak or be in the presence of Natalie again. I bet you had a story prepared on her too... '

'No, I didn't.'

'It didn't cross your mind when every other journalist is in a frenzy about the riots?'

'No.'

'Not a very good journo then, are you? Stay away from her. If you think London's been burning recently it'll be nothing compared to the damage I can cause... '

'Don't threaten me.'

'It's not a threat, it's a pledge. I love Tina and Natalie more than anything in the world. They felt those armed coppers were like rapists, did they tell you that? No, because they knew it might end up in a newspaper somewhere. It's great your industry is finally destroying itself but I won't let them go down with you. Never. Hope you've got the message.'

'She's my mum too, you don't own her... '

'No, but I care for her, there's a difference.'

32.

Fuck Leveson, Give Me Hutton

Natalie was charged with stealing a CD worth 99p – of Nat King Cole. It had been lying in a box of hundreds of cheap CDs in the antique shop. Jamie knew the public mood was bloodcurdling and a difficult appearance before a magistrate was in store for Natalie. He sent her a text of support but got one back from his mother telling him not to interfere. The magistrate gave her a referral order, which was excessive – a caution should have been enough – but Jamie felt more responsible now than when the so-called riots had taken place. Up to now, his sleep patterns hadn't been disturbed too much by the raid but on the day the verdict was announced, everything changed. He woke up in the middle of the night and was certain his house was crawling with armed coppers. He went downstairs: nothing. He went outside the front door: peace and a sweet gush of wind. He dropped a couple of aspirins in a glass of brandy and went back to bed. But he couldn't sleep: the image of scowling, barking coppers tearing his house apart kept his mind ticking over and his body flipping right and left on the bed to get comfortable. He stayed in bed till 2pm – and there were already a couple of messages on his phone: one from Trevena, the other from Miss Apple. He called neither. Trevena called him when Jamie was shopping online for groceries. Going to the supermarket was heavy-going: too busy, too many kids and he was certain he saw Paul Markham in there on the previous occasion.

'The papers have accused me of being an Occupy

member,' said Trevena, with a laugh. 'Can you believe that? It's the broadsheets too, not just your mob.'

'Sorry, I haven't been keeping up.'

'No, my apologies, I should have been more sensitive. It's not everyday your house is raided. I hope they've apologised to you and your mother.'

'No, not to me anyway... '

'Sadly, we've had some of the same treatment. After the sleep-in at the hospital, police tracked down seven of our group and arrested them.'

'When did that happen?' said Jamie.

'You didn't know?'

'No.'

'Your freelance career will be long and fruitful. Anyway, they've all been released now but one of them came to me later in a terrible state; having panic attacks and clearly traumatised. He's now having mental health problems. I had encouraged him to join us in this campaign. I felt guilty about his plight. I can do no more – my race has been run. The campaign will go on but without me... '

'But that was your whole life, what are you going to do?'

'Who knows? I used to watch my father play the organ at Sunday service for all those years, I've been thinking about that a lot lately... '

'Sons shouldn't always follow dads. Anyway, what about the hacking stuff? Did you hear about my stint at the Commons select committee?'

'That's another game that's run its course but the difference is we've won it. Look at all the arrests, apart from yours of course, the Screws closing, Danny Love jailed, journalists giving evidence, the Leveson inquiry... all these are indications that we've won the battle.'

'But Fitton's still around... '

'Stop obsessing about him. He'll pay for his sins.'

'Jesus, you've already started with the religious stuff… '

'That was always the problem with you, Jamie, you have no belief or faith in anything. Chasing stories, yes, a few drinks, yes, football, perhaps, but what else? Find something before it's too late.'

Jamie wrote a story on the death of Steve Jobs after Miss Apple agreed to be quoted anonymously that some employees were asked to meditate during the three minutes' silence. She was on terrific form but it was the last time he heard from Miss Apple because someone at Apple towers got wind of her mole-like tendencies and she never returned Jamie's calls again. She would have been interested to hear about the Daisies' newsroom being raided by police with boxes, computer disks and files being taken away. A leaked story claimed computer hacking was now being investigated too. Fitton hadn't been arrested and was co-operating with police but he was due to appear at the Leveson inquiry. Jamie hadn't been asked to give evidence and wouldn't want to in any case. Well, only if Hannah turned up to ask the questions.

He was desperate to see her but she was ridiculously busy with MP surgeries, Commons business and preparations for London 2012 which included numerous visits to hockey clubs, youth clubs and schools. Jamie tried to take his mind off her by renting the DVD of *The Princess Who Never Was* which was better than he expected. It was an eye-opening tale of a futuristic reality TV show in which a bored Prince created a series of tasks for future brides including learning to wave, appropriate dress and accent training. The arrogant, smarmy Prince voted them off if they weren't up to the mark but meets his match when a former maid takes part and gets revenge on the family that treated her so badly. It was one of the strangest films Jamie had ever seen (but so was *The Full Monty*) and he was amazed it had made so much money. He sent her a text to say he enjoyed the film. She didn't reply for two days and didn't talk about the film at all but said she was looking forward to Fitton's appearance at the Leveson Inquiry. Jamie wasn't; the grisly parade of journalists at inquiries, committee, police stations and even prisons was affecting his health. He went back to see Dr Hobson who agreed and put him back on 20mg of Amitriptyline. The pills made him eat more, piss less and have more constipation. It also didn't help that the likes of DC Connor called his mobile at 8am when he was clamped to the toilet with stomach cramps and a stone-like bowel. However, on this occasion, there was a pleasant surprise in store.

'I don't think it's right for journalists to be arrested in dawn raids like that,' said DC Connor. 'If they're involved in major criminal activity, yes, but phone hacking, no, we should use armed police for more serious operations.'

'Why are you telling me this now? You nearly killed my family with shock, never mind the brutality. You're just a bunch of thugs.'

'I'm not speaking for anyone else here, just for me. Doesn't mean you're innocent, it just means that I don't agree with the heavy-handed way we're targeting reporters. We don't get the best results that way. The rift gets too big.'

'You got that right,' said Jamie, pulling his pants up and flushing the toilet despite their being nothing in the bowl. 'The rift is so big we have nothing to say to each other.'

'I've said my piece so we'll leave it at that. I did have something to discuss but I don't see much mileage in it so let's keep it civil.'

'Come on, who are the corrupt cops? Name names… '

DC Connor smiled. 'Good try. You're freelance, yes?'

'Rather be staff, but yeah… '

'I've got quite a few contacts on the nationals but they're always looking for heavy stuff.'

'So am I. Make some sense, I've got stomach cramps.'

'Well, there's an 84-year-old woman called Sheila Rix. We're throwing a surprise party for her in a couple of weeks. She's given us information on so many burglars, domestics and dodgy motorists that we thought we better honour her before she knocks off. Thing is, she's never wanted any press attention. We don't care; she's going to get it in a week or so. She's a great woman, simple as that. She has no family left; we are her family.'

'Have you given this to any other papers?'

'No, you've got some decent form behind you – you're not all bad – so I thought I'd lob it over to you. The police press office would just do a general press release and fuck it up.'

Jamie walked out of the toilet and headed downstairs.

'Can't see any harm in it,' he said. 'Sheila's not going to come after me with a rolling pin is she?'

'No, but she might come after me – and a few of my colleagues.'

Jamie got downstairs and realised he would have to go straight back to the toilet again as the cramps became worse.

'Can I ask you a question?' said Jamie.

'Loads – if they're about Sheila.'

'No, forget about her for a minute. Why are you doing this – giving me this story? You've had me in a cell and now you're being all lovey-dovey.'

'You've tried to have some sort of moral compass in an industry that's, frankly, full of shit – that's the reason. I've interviewed quite a few journalists now, for this hacking business, and you'll be the only one to talk to the wonderful Sheila, get the picture?'

'Sort of... I've just got to go to the toilet again.'

'Haven't you just been? I heard it flush.'

'Bit of constipation, I'm afraid.'

'You'll get on grand with Sheila.'

*

373

The Sheila Rix story was a hard sell to the nationals, as expected, so Jamie had to settle for trying to flog it to agencies and the local paper. Yet even with this story he couldn't shake off the image of a gang of coppers keeping an eye on him. Were they watching him now? Keeping hacking reporters close would allow them to pounce much quicker. Jamie realised a lot of this was irrational but bashing into someone's house while they were sleeping was irrational too. But that didn't matter now, he had been left alone to deal with it. The house was too quiet and the rooms too big. There was too much space and not enough voices: Hannah, Tina, Natalie, even Adam, he needed someone or something to fill the void. There was only one big bang that could drown out the sickening sound of the armed raid: a Melvin Moon special.

He came down straight after his shift at First Frames. Jamie was staggered to learn that Melvin had been made supervisor after 'Two Bags' Barry had left to live in Estonia. He was dressed differently too: the beanie hat and hooded top were gone. It was now a white shirt, grey trousers, shoes and a neat side parting with too much Brylcreem. Jamie knew he had to go easy. Hannah had finally agreed to dinner at her house and he needed to be on top form for her, particularly after her performance last time.

Melvin sat down at the kitchen table and pulled out a tiny silver and black tin of anchovy fillets. Jesus, was the fucker shopping in Waitrose now? No, the tin didn't have any fish in it but was, according to Melvin, full of the 'tightest, purest Benzo pills' he'd ever seen from a new internet supplier in India. Melvin didn't waste any time: he necked one down with a glass of water and offered another to Jamie. There were a couple of days till he met Hannah so there was plenty of time for it to wear off. He slipped one into his glass of brandy. The reaction came after about 45 minutes: gorgeous, gooey and soothing. The seething images of coppers scowls and flailing boots magically numbed into a hopeful, euphoric state. Melvin took out his smartphone and switched on its music player. He laid it on the kitchen table and turned the volume up. He got up and stood on the table.

'What the fuck are you doing?'

Melvin put his fingers on his lips. He closed his eyes and looked at the ceiling. Marillion's *Sugar Mice* started to play on his smartphone and he sang along to it. After a couple of minutes of gawping, Jamie had a startling realisation: he didn't know Melvin Moon at all. No matter, Jamie needed to forget, banish and exorcise the morning nightmares – and Melvin gave him what he needed. The coppers had been purged from the house.

Jamie had fallen asleep at four in the afternoon and didn't wake up until eight when he heard his mobile bleep. It was a text from Hannah. Dinner – white rice, chick pea curry, naans and pine nut salad – was being eaten by herself and he could 'fuck right off' if he had any designs on coming to her house again. Jamie groggily got up and called her on the way to the bathroom. He filled the sink up with ice-cold water and stuck his face down into it. He came up when he heard Hannah answer; his mobile was drenched. Why hadn't he just put it onto speakerphone?

'Sorry Jamie, this next summer's going to be one of the busiest for me with the Jubilee, the Olympics and God knows what else. I can't afford to deal with wasters, which I'm sorry to say, is what you've become… '

'I'll be over there in less than an hour,' said Jamie, trying to dry his mobile with a towel. He finally put it in on speakerphone and rested it on the side of the sink. 'Thought, we had something. You were like some fucking Han Solo in the Commons. You can't do that and now call me a waster.'

'That's mild, believe me. Have they called you to the Leveson Inquiry?'

'No, but Fitton'll be there.'

'Yes, I know that. I just don't understand why they haven't called you. You're one of the few reporters who used to be naughty but turned nice. They should be gagging to interview you… '

'I was arrested, maybe that's the reason.'

She smiled. 'Maybe they've just got too many dirty hacks to get through… '

'Oi, watch it, between me and you, we know who the real dirty one is… '

'Hmm, talking of dirty tricks, a Tory MP approached me the other day and wanted me to defect and join their party. He talked about the riots and how someone like me with my working class, comprehensive school background could inspire young people. He sent me a card and wanted dinner too. Said I could be a cabinet minister in three years.'

'Thought you hated career politics?'

'I do. But I can't get anything done in the Commons. Trevena warned me but I thought I could do better. But he was right: no-one listens to an Independent. I stood up at Prime Minister's Questions and got the shortest answer ever back from the Prime Minister while other MPs were making snide, sexist comments.'

'For God's sake, don't defect to the Tories. You're not part of that world. Leaver'll have the last laugh, if you do.'

'My father was a Labour voter and said the same. He used to call Thatcher the most evil woman in the world. I was only a kid and laughed about it but now I can see how men deal with women with a bit of power. They tear into them.'

Jamie rolled his eyes. He was sympathetic to Hannah's plight but felt his mood dip whenever the spectre of sexism was raised.

'I think you haven't got over your father's death,' said Jamie.

'You really have pushed your luck tonight. No child ever gets over their parents' death, what's your point?'

'Doesn't matter. What are you going to say to that Tory?'

'Probably what I'm going to say to you now... '

'Go on, my head's hurting.'

'Do one.'

The line went dead and Jamie threw the mobile into the sink full of water. He watched it float around for a few minutes and went to bed.

It was the first story Jamie read on his new phone. The BBC News website was reporting that seven Daisies' staff, mostly former employees, had been arrested on suspicion of phone hacking and a list of other things that hurt Jamie's head. He had to read the list of names twice to make sure he hadn't made a mistake: Ben Fox-Tucker, Jimmy Betson, Chris Reeves, Angie Octavia, Will Mackenzie, Maxine Cort and Louise Dorrans. Louise? No fucking chance – and where was Fitton? Jamie called Louise immediately. Her phone was switched off. Two days later Jimmy Betson and Chris Reeves were charged with making illegal payments to sources. Jamie called the Squires' newsroom: she hadn't come back to work. Jamie was getting worried about her. Two weeks passed: she hadn't been charged but there was no news of her release either. The rest had been bailed pending further enquires. Fitton was due to appear at the Leveson Inquiry but Jamie didn't care about that anymore. The editor had shot himself in the foot by being overheard at a dinner saying 'Fuck Leveson, give me Hutton'. It was all over the papers the next day. He managed to defuse the criticism; he always did. Here was the editor almost revelling in the Leveson hysteria while some of his former (and current) staff were being dragged from their beds and banged up in cells for hours. The day he appeared at the hearing was the same day Louise, as she often did, turned up at Jamie's door unannounced. Jamie stepped forward and hugged her before she could say anything.

'Well, you have missed me,' said Louise. 'What's wrong with your eyes? Been skinning up?'

Jamie let go and ushered her in. 'Been worried sick. Where have you been?'

'Wait on, we're having a Fitton-free zone today, okay? I couldn't stand to see his face while I'm here.'

'But he's at Leveson... '

'Yes, and I was nearly in prison. Which will it be? Me or him? I want a news blackout if I come in.'

Jamie smiled and closed the door behind Louise. 'My stories have dried up so you've got no problems there.'

Louise put her hand on Jamie's shoulder. 'I'm not joking, Jamie. If I hear, read or sniff a story today, I'll smash the house up.'

Jamie realised she was being deadly serious. He put his arm round her and they walked into the house. He made her coffee and offered her some lactose-free sponge cake. She sat down and ate the cake but only drank a third of her coffee.

'Been away for two weeks with Martin,' she said. 'We went to the Lake District. Sort of a holiday, I suppose, but Martin didn't want to go. He wanted to have it out with the coppers at the station.'

'How the fuck did you get caught up in this? It's obscene. I mean, I can understand why they roughed me up, even though it was evil, but you? You never did anything wrong, you never hacked phones, made payments, did anything; Jesus, I don't think you ever made up a quote either so why? I just don't understand it.'

'I didn't either. When I was being questioned, I was thinking: why have these bastards got me in here? Is it because the Squires needed taking down a peg or two? Or is it because of some minor thing in the past at the Daisies. Coppers said it was wholly to do with the Daisies but they were really vague about it. I didn't know what they were talking about. But the other day, after my release, it became clear. Martin reminded me that in 2002, when we took a break in Sri Lanka, I lent my mobile to Angie because hers had conked out. She'd ordered another one but it was taking too much time to get the Sim activated so she asked if she could borrow mine while I was on holiday. I didn't mind because I hated the fucking things – and still do – so I was glad to have it away from me while I enjoyed the holiday. The rest is showbiz, as you know; Angie and the others got loads of stories through hacking so that's the only explanation I have. I called her a couple of days ago but she hasn't replied yet. Haven't spoken to her in years, anyway; probably won't do again.'

'What are the Squires saying?'

'They're supporting me. They think the timing's suspect, with Fitton appearing at Leveson. Ran a story about it already.'

'Did the coppers raid your house?'

'No, I was asked to report into the station.'

'FUCKIN' BASTARDS!'

Jamie picked up a plate and threw it against the wall.

'Steady Jamie, this is what they want. I know what happened to you but you have to keep it together or they'll have you in again.'

Jamie walked to the fridge and picked up a can of Grolsch. He opened it and took a long, lingering swig. 'Do you want one?' he asked, wiping his mouth with the back of his clenched fist.

Louise shook her head. 'I may work for a broadsheet now but I can still see what's happening. Journalists are being hunted and humiliated and I've never seen anything like it.

The fear's spreading across all the tabloids. Some have shut down and some are so fucking paranoid they'll do the job themselves. We were lucky to get out of there when we did.'

'I don't feel like I'm out of there… '

'You're freelance, you should be. It's your state of mind, Jamie, you're still a red-top at heart. That'll never change. How are you doing with stories? Writing enough to make a living?'

Jamie shook his head and took another drink.

'I want to see Fitton at Leveson. I want to see the fucker squirm.'

'We did a deal. News blackout while I'm here.'

Jamie finished his drink and threw the can in the bin.

'I've had a news blackout for months already,' he said. 'The freelance lark's too much for me. I miss the buzz of the newsroom; the banter, the crack, the wild chase for stories… '

'… Even though some of it was illegal?'

'Sad to say but, yes. Anything is better than being cooped up in here trying to flog crap to editors who won't give you the time of day.'

'What happened to the cash from your Larna exclusive?'

'It's running out – and if you don't work it runs out quicker.'

Jamie walked to the door. 'I'm off to watch Fitton. I want to see his face, his short tie and his crap glasses. I want to see him grilled the same way we were by the coppers.'

Louise got up from the table. 'See you then… '

'Oh come on, don't come over all lofty and broadsheet on me now. I just want a bit of a lift by seeing this fucker get his just desserts.'

'You're so fucking naïve. He'll run rings round them you idiot.' Louise brushed past Jamie and walked out of the kitchen. 'You worked with him for so long but you know nothing about him. This is exactly what he loves: the whole world watching him, being the centre of attention, playing to the gallery. It gives him a reason to live. He'll come with a smile and leave with one.' Louise walked into the hallway and towards the front door. 'Thanks for the coffee. Oh, and you've repaired this house pretty well, considering. Pray for the other jailbirds.' Louise opened the front door and left the house.

Jamie looked at the front door for a few seconds and then decided not to watch Fitton at the Leveson Inquiry after all. He went upstairs and opened Melvin Moon's magic tin of anchovy fillets. He took out a pink little pill and swallowed it with a small amount of water. He lay down on the bed and imagined himself rather than Fitton giving evidence at the inquiry. He'd be on blistering form, letting it all out, not holding back, thrilling the gallery with his stunning, breathtaking revelations. Fitton was a pipsqueak; he was the main event. The great Jamie Parkes: the ultimate whistleblower.

33.

Hop, Skip And A Running Jump

The pink pill was a ripper; a mind blower with limb-sapping tendencies and a marathon drowsiness that made Jamie want to sleep all day and all night. He spent weeks waking up extremely late and doing as little work as possible. The stories had dried up and so had his mouth – it needed a glass of brandy each morning to lubricate it and make it work. After this kick, the story ideas did return but they generally bunched into two categories: the Jubilee and the Olympics; his brain didn't have the capacity to think of anything creative. The pink pill, however, came at a cost as he realised when he finally got round to checking the messages on his phone. There were 163 of them. Surely there weren't that many bleeps? His ears had been ringing anyway. As long as Hannah's name didn't pop up, he didn't care. He finally pushed himself to get on the computer. Louise's news blackout had worked well for him in the last few weeks. It was liberating and soothing; a quiet joy. It emptied the mind of all the shit swimming in there from red-top headlines to burka-wearing woman screaming at the TV. But it didn't take long for the wonders and horrors of news anxiety to return. Jamie checked all the news websites just to check if it was true. He had already known that Fitton would have few problems at the Leveson Inquiry and that's how it turned out, but what was this? Most of the news outlets were running a story concerning 'The Fitton Tapes' and Jamie couldn't read the stories quick enough to find out what the fuck was going on.

It was clear Larna Wilson was a major part of this story. After reading just one, Jamie called her immediately. Jesus Christ, this was unbelievable.

'Larna, it's Jamie, why didn't you tell me about this? You've been hanging onto this for about a decade and now you give it to all the other rags but not me, what's going on? Why didn't you call? I don't get it.'

'Calm down, Jamie, I'm on set. Have you checked your messages? I sent at least four... '

There was a pause on the line as Jamie checked his inbox.
'Well?'

'I've been a bit busy. Forget that, I want to know about these Fitton Tapes. How the hell did you pull that off? I knew he was a bastard but even by his standards, this is eye-popping.'

'I can't talk about this now: I'm on the sixth take with this tricky scene. All I can say is when I saw him at the Leveson Inquiry lying and lying and lying again, I decided enough was enough. All those years, I've wanted to protect everyone's reputation: mine, the Prince's, and yes, even Fitton's so that we wouldn't be dragged through the media but, at Leveson, he went too far: the level of deceit was astonishing. You've read about the first series of tapes – but there's more to come in the next few weeks.'

'What the fuck? There's more?'

'Yes, but I can't talk now. If you want to meet, come down to the set. Some press have already tried to get me to say more – but that's it now. I'll only be talking about my films in the future.'

'I'll be down straight away, just need a drink to perk me up. I read the first piece in the Squires, are they serialising this?'

'Yes, Louise Dorrans called me to ask for my views on Fitton at the inquiry. I wasn't interested but then she told me she'd been arrested by police which made me quite angry. It shocked me that some of his staff were in cells while he was grinning away at the inquiry.'

'So you've got a price like we all have?'

'You can see it that way – I see it as the only way to bring Warren Fitton down: through the medium he believes he controls. The law don't have enough on him, but I do. And no, I didn't get paid for it. Some people prefer money to sense, I don't want to be one of them. Come down if you want, but be quick, we're packing up in a couple of hours.'

Jamie felt good as he drove down to the film set in Farnham Common but was desperate to know more about the 'Tapes' to come. The first tape was juicy enough. Jamie already knew that Fitton and Larna had been childhood sweethearts but these revelations went much further. The main narrative was one of infidelity and abuse. The couple were engaged just after Fitton got a job as showbiz reporter on the Daisies. Larna moved up from London from the south coast but found it hard to adjust. Fitton started drinking and Larna was convinced he was seeing other women. Then Larna saw a photo of him with TV soap star Kitty Marina in *Heat* magazine and, from the way she looked at him, Larna knew he was having an affair and subsequently confronted him. He gave her a torrent of abuse and told her they shouldn't have got engaged in the first place. He started coming home late – or not at all – and it was then that Larna decided to find a couple of his old tape recorders and start recording their conversations. Jamie thought some of these were lines were better than any of the hacked material the Daisies had got from celebs. Ever.

'Fuck off back to LarLarLand, if you can't hack the big city.'

'I fancied you rotten when you were at school, what happened to you?'

384

'I slept with her, yeah, I'm in a different world from you now, why can't you understand that?'

'If you don't stop nagging, I'll slap you one, I really will.'

'I should have dropped you in the English Channel.'

'Showbiz reporters stay out till dawn, you're lucky I come back at all.'

'Put some make-up on, these London girls piss all over you.'

'You want to be an actress? I know some real ones, you're light years away.'

And so on. There were at least 60 other quotes – and this was just the start. Jamie felt a certain glee that Fitton had been diminished in this manner. But was it enough to do him terminal damage? He had already put out a statement claiming that it was all 'a long time ago' and he was 'young and stupid' and that he had apologised to Larna many times before. He also pointed out that he wouldn't have invited Larna onto *The Fitton Well* in America if they hadn't already patched things up and become friends. But there was already feverish speculation about his future. Some reporters cited anonymous sources in America saying producers were already getting nervous about Fitton's chequered history. Columnists also claimed his editorship at the Daisies depended solely on the company's business interests and whether shares in Coby News were holding up or plunging. At the moment, shares were steady and the Coby's still believed in the Fitton 'brand'.

Jamie got onto the set which was a disused garage on the outskirts of the village. Larna, who was wearing a baseball cap and dungarees, acknowledged him and flashed 'ten' minutes with her hands. The garage had been turned into some sort of cellar or basement which was adorned by Christmas lights. A father was showing his son how to turn them on. Finally, the crew packed up. Larna made it clear she wanted everyone to leave so she could be alone with Jamie. Larna slumped on the chair and took off her shoes. She wiggled her toes and rubbed the soles of her feet.

'Punishing work this,' said Larna. 'But if I don't do it, who will?'

'Bit dark in here without the lights,' said Jamie, sitting down on the straw chair opposite Larna.

'Don't think so. Some good natural daylight coming through that garage door. Are your eyes okay?'

'Yeah, yeah, don't worry, just seeing a few more colours than normal. Anyway, back to business: I wish I could be as creative as what you did to Fitton. Reporters would die for those kind of quotes.'

'It wasn't planned. He just drove me to it. Moving to London like that, as soon as he got that big showbiz job, was a jolt for me. I found it very hard. I had no work, family or friends, all I really had was him. We had known each other for such a long time that I thought he would cover for those things, but things went the other way… '

'I can't believe he said some of that stuff… '

'There was worse. But I suppose you have to remember that he was under pressure too. Sometimes, he worked in the day and in the early hours, that's a lot of stress but he wanted to get on… '

'To be editor?'

'Yes, he felt the paper was losing its way – and he could increase circulation.'

'So come on, what other knockout blows have you got in store for the next few weeks?'

Larna's mobile rang and she apologised by raising her hand – but she still took the call.

'Sorry Jamie, I've got to go, the producer wants me to talk to some of the extras who are getting cold feet. We'll have to turn this into a quick tabloid chat rather than a broadsheet one.'

'Are filmmakers always this busy? Be amazed if you get time to piss.'

She smiled and put her mobile away. 'See, I haven't even got time to answer that question. Let's move on. I hope you've got a strong stomach for the next bit.'

'It's been rumbling a lot lately but go on... '

'I became pregnant while all this was going on. I didn't tell Fitton because I was emotionally confused and vulnerable. I agonised about it but then decided to have an abortion at 11 weeks. A couple of months later, we were invited to a charity dinner where all the celebrity bigwigs were: Henry was there too. Fitton introduced me to him and then went off to mingle with his glamorous group by the buffet. We got talking and the Prince seemed to take a liking to me. I didn't think anything of it but a couple of days later I got a beautiful handwritten letter in the post from him. He knew I was engaged but said I looked totally miserable. He wanted us to meet again and I agreed. We saw each other for about 8 months and Fitton didn't have a clue about it. The Prince was wonderful but that life wasn't for me: the restrictions, the lack of privacy, the protocols, so I broke it off... '

'Wasn't old Princey upset?'

'Yes, but I don't want to get into that. He's more mature now and won't have any problems finding someone else. As for me, this is my life, right here, on set, it's where I'm happiest.'

Larna put her shoes back on and got up from the chair.

'Not much of a life if you can't give an old friend a few minutes of your time... '

'Your currency is column inches – and I've given you acres of that over the years.'

'All right, is there anything else major apart from the abortion?'

Larna raised the peak of her baseball cap and looked down at Jamie.

'It's rather a seismic event in a woman's life, Jamie, you almost sound disappointed... '

'No, you're the one who's brushing over things. So? Anything else?'

'He took cocaine for about 2 years while he was still working at your paper. There was a group of showbiz reporters from the tabloids who met at a certain club every Thursday to shoot some of the white stuff.'

'Jesus, he's fuckin' finished... '

'The bullying and abortion obviously weren't enough then?'

'Well, yeah but the Americans are insane over drugs. They want their celebs and stars to be squeaky clean. The bullying? Every tabloid editor's a bully. It's in their nature.'

Larna walked over to Jamie and put her hand on his shoulder. 'I think you know more about this subject than you're letting on. I lived with a heavy drug user night and day for two years. Don't you think I can tell?'

'Don't know what you're talking about, Larna.'

Larna bent down and hugged him. 'For all these years you've worked so hard to get Fitton on his knees. I've served him up on a plate. Don't let it all go to waste now.' She got up and walked away towards the garage door.

'Wait, don't leave,' said Jamie, suddenly feeling drowsy and rubbing his forehead. 'Can't I come with you? I just want to talk a bit more. Don't want to go home yet.'

'Not right now, maybe later, when the film's wrapped up. I'll make sure you get to see the premiere this time. Think you might like it.' Larna pulled down the garage door. 'Oh, one more thing... '

'What?'

'There was a guy rummaging through my bins a few days ago. Looks like he was from your world... '

'What did he look like?'

'Gangly, unshaven, chipped tooth... do you know him?'

Jamie sighed and shook his head. The drowsiness disappeared in an instant.

This time there would be no compromise. Jamie had phoned around for three days to track Barnaby Bin down. He had used Callum Gordon's best blagging voices and outright lies to get the desired result. Barnaby changed mobile numbers more than most but Jamie wanted to ensure the slithery sneak didn't slip from his grasp on this occasion. He called his new number.

'Er Mr Barnstable, I'm an old business friend of your father Jack. Can you just tell me where you are? We need to meet urgently.'

'Yeah, but what's the rush, major?'

'He started a business a few years ago – but left due to personal problems. Despite the financial crisis, it's doing unbelievably well now. It's made thousands of pounds worth of profit. Tell me where you are so we can talk about this.'

'Hold on, hold on, I've just got to jump out of this skip.'

'A skip? Sounds nice. Whereabouts?'

There was a long delay.

'Whereabouts?' said Barnaby. 'Where-fuckin-abouts? You don't sound like a business friend of my dad's. Parkes, it's you isn't it? Only someone as common as you would use 'whereabouts'. I've got nothing to hide. The skip's in Latimer Street by the Federico's Chippy. Come down, if you think there's unfinished business between us. If not, then fuck off.'

Jamie turned into Latimer Street and saw the graffiti-covered green skip immediately. Barnaby was stood in the centre of the skip, eating from a tray of chips, examining the poorly cut spuds and throwing them through a discarded toilet seat like a lazy darts player. Barnaby flung a batch of chips towards

Jamie as he approached. One of them hit Jamie's eye and it began to water; the salt stinging so much he thought his eyeball was about to pop out. Jamie climbed into the skip straight away and went for Barnaby. It was about a quarter full with discarded chairs, carpets, metal poles, rugs, wooden boards and a punctured football. They rolled over a couple of times until Jamie was on top, hands round Barnaby's neck, the power seeping through his fingers. Jamie grabbed the metal pole and prepared to smack it round his head.

'This one's for Larna Wilson,' said Jamie. 'Can't you leave anyone alone?'

'Why, you fuckin' her, you dirty bastard? You're no better than me. We're in the same game; we fuck over the same people.'

'WE'RE NOT THE SAME!'

Jamie raised the pole back over his shoulder and aimed at Barnaby's head but he managed to narrowly avoid it.

'WE ARE IN THE SAME GAME! I'm just at the dirty end, the sewage, the shit, the shameful end. You lot would be nothing without me.'

Barnaby broke free and scrambled to the other side of the skip, falling over and shrieking in pain as one of his hands pushed into a nail sticking out from a dusty rug. Jamie picked up a chair, with its seat missing, and threw it at him; then a cushion, an ironing board and a hammer. Most of them missed – or he fended them off – but the hammer hit him on the shoulder and he grabbed it with both hands while letting out a cry of anguish. Jamie punched him in the face but felt as though he'd nearly broke his own hand. Barnaby's lip was cut and his nose was bleeding. Jamie picked up the hammer and threatened to strike him on the shoulder again. There was little resistance: Barnaby kept both hands on his shoulder, mouth open, eyes up to the sky, head shaking vigorously.

'That's for coming into my house without permission,'

said Jamie. 'I've been waiting to do that for a very long time.'

Barnaby didn't reply and Jamie eased the hammer away from his shoulder.

'Your boss's game's up too. He's been fucking people over for too long, he's forgotten what it's like to suffer. Well, he's certainly doing that now.'

'Don't know what the fuck you mean.'

'Fitton; don't you read the papers?'

Barnaby gave Jamie a wild, incredulous look. He paused and then started laughing. Jamie picked up the punctured football and squashed it against Barnaby's face.

'SHUT THE FUCK UP OR I'LL SUFFOCATE YOU WITH THIS RIGHT NOW!'

'Man, you've got the wrong end of the stick,' said Barnaby. 'Or the hammer as it were. Fitton ain't my boss, not in a hundred years... '

'Who are you working for then?'

Barnaby gestured for Jamie to come closer.

'I'm keeping my distance, you dirty bastard,' said Jamie.

'Okay, Kleenex,' said Barnaby, sitting up and moving towards Jamie. 'I'll tell you who I'm working for... '

'Who? Which tabloid is it?'

'It's not a tabloid... '

'Can't be a magazine, they wouldn't employ you, so who is it?'

Barnaby inched closer to Jamie and pointed to his lip. He gathered a gobful of phlegm and propelled it viciously onto Jamie's face and eyes. Jamie felt the sticky, smelly liquid rip into his eyes and combine with the salty texture of the earlier chip-weapon to induce temporary blindness and a terrifying falling sensation. A speedy migraine developed as he frantically blinked and tried to clear his eyes with his fingers. Finally, a blurry passage of light opened up and he saw Barnaby jump out of the skip, still clutching his shoulder with both hands. He looked over his shoulder and smiled at Jamie.

'This was personal, not business,' he said, as he slithered away.

Jamie eyes finally cleared and he felt an overwhelming tiredness which made him lie down in the skip. At least he made Barnaby bleed, he thought. A victory on points. He was a bastard and so was his dad. Fuck them. Jamie lay in the skip for another five minutes until he noticed a man on the corner of the street speaking into a mobile while peering into the skip. Time to leg it; the coppers would love to snare another hack – the smell in the skip had become unbearable anyway. He climbed out of the skip and grabbed the punctured football. He stood on the pavement and rubbed the panel where Barnaby's blood had dropped onto the leather. He put the ball under his arm and headed home.

34.

Raiders Of The Lost Parkes

Fitton's cocaine revelations were published in most national newspapers and American producers, as Jamie had expected, didn't take too kindly to his antics, no matter how much he'd cleaned up his act. They axed repeats of *The Fitton Well* and said they wouldn't be commissioning another series. Fitton said he was 'sad' and again claimed it was a long time ago but was less defiant than usual in tone and delivery, particularly in TV interviews. He also said *The Fitton Well* would be back on TV screens within two years but didn't say where; the Coby brothers had long-stated ambitions of breaking into the UK TV market so that may have been on Fitton's radar. It was also probably the reason the Coby's didn't sack their editor immediately after the cocaine-heavy 'Fitton Tapes' were plastered all over the media. They gave qualified support to their Daisies' editor and wanted assurances from him there would be no more disturbing revelations. It looked like Fitton was about to get away with it until the firestorm on his paper started to rage again. Five former staff were charged after their second visit to the police station: Jimmy Betson, Chris Reeves, Angie Octavia, Will Mackenzie and Maxine Cort. Jamie was gobsmacked: Will and Maxine were probably only there for about two months. The media criticism of the Daisies, particularly in the broadsheets, was now personal, vicious and relentless. The Coby's, Fitton and the staff faced a daily barrage of attacks, innuendo and wild speculation. It took another staff member, Ben Fox-Tucker, to be charged with perverting the course of justice to push the Coby's into decisive action. They watched Fox-Tucker give an interview on TV saying he was innocent and Fitton had asked him to burn boxes of evidence. The Coby's finally sacked Fitton when rumours began to swirl that the paper was about to shut down. Jamie drank multiple cans of Grolsch and listened to Prodigy's *Firestarter* extremely loud on this stereo numerous times. The elation he felt that Fitton had been dismissed was so powerful that he danced manically all night. But there was also a tinge of sadness about the reporters in the dock – and the rumours about the paper's closure. Despite all the ups and downs, he still loved the Daisies. The paper had been his life for so long that seeing it go under would be hard to bear. Jamie finally slumped into bed at 6am after the wonderful news about Fitton. Six. They'd charged all the reporters on the paper so why did he think the coppers would be back for him? It was all over: he was cleared, some had been charged; the end, he could relax. But no, the crashing sound of the dawn army lurked within. They'd come for him again; he was sure of that.

The joy had come at a price: more drinking, more Benzo's and more rejections from commissioning editors. Jamie felt he had no stories left to offer; the ideas had dried up – and it was so fucking quiet in here too. The Jubilee had come and gone and he could only think of Sex Pistols' stories – epic fails. The Olympics was his only hope: a security breach story was always a good fallback position. He searched online and found a company called G4S was in charge of recruiting Olympics guards. Amazingly, only a few weeks before the big event, they were still recruiting people, although Jamie was sure this was an error. He applied anyway, to fill in a boring afternoon if nothing else, and 36 hours later, a woman got in touch asking him to come down to a recruitment centre in London for training. Jamie didn't ask too many questions, sobered up and travelled down there. When he got to the centre, he thought he was back at college studying for a BTec National: most of the recruits were very young, listening to music, chatting and paying little attention to the security trainer who was struggling to be heard. The next day, Jamie slipped a kitchen knife into his bag and walked into the centre without any checks. If Bin Laden were alive he'd have loved it here. Munich 72 all over again. Jamie was hired after just four days of so-called training. He was told uniforms hadn't arrived yet and would be handed out closer to the opening ceremony. He had a vague of the layout of the Olympic Park, his security duties and what to do in an emergency or a terrorist attack but most of the staff seemed to be disinterested or there for a laugh. Some of them simply didn't turn up. At this rate, they'd have martial law at the Olympics. Jamie went home and started to compile the story: it felt like a big one. When it was completed, he sent it out to the Squires, *The Times* and *The Guardian* as well as *The Sun*, *The Daily Mirror* and *The Daily Mail*; but not the Daisies. A Sunday paper wasn't immediate enough for this. Three days later, Jamie's heart sank. The G4S 'security shambles' story was all over the TV news, from an unidentified whistleblower, and the next day it was all over the papers too: no sign of Jamie's byline anywhere. Did they steal his idea? Or did they simply want a civilian rather than a hack telling them about this story? It didn't matter; he felt sick and frustrated. Fuck G4S and fuck the Olympics. He didn't want to write a story again for a long, long time.

Trevena organised a special service at Broad Street Church – and a talk at the community library – to commemorate the 61-year-old history of Sparrow Hill Hospital which had now been broken up. He posted Jamie information about these events as well as a long letter saying the fight was now over. He was retiring to play the organ at Broad Street, go on safari with his daughter and listen to Tommy Steele and Dusty Springfield records. He did mention Hannah's 'brave but ultimately futile' efforts to stop services being moved out of town and Jamie sensed there was some friction between them but she was at both events so things couldn't be that bad. Jamie imagined himself sitting down in the church playing the organ with Trevena. They could play Prodigy tunes while no-one was watching. They could reminisce about how they – and Elliot Broomfield – were the real superheroes who exposed tabloid wrongdoing rather than MPs' committees, Leveson or the broadsheet media. This would all be wonderful – but Jamie couldn't do it now. He needed a bigger kick than that. The only faith he had was in Melvin Moon.

Hannah had booked tickets for the Olympic hockey game between Great Britain and Japan at the Riverbank Arena. She wanted Jamie to come but in true politician-style she had her eye on other benefits rather than the sole enjoyment of Jamie's company. Chief among these was another two tickets for Tina and Natalie in the hope of encouraging Natalie to take up hockey in which she'd shown a mild interest. Jamie hadn't realised how close the three women were; they told him nothing these days. For his part, a little less intoxication might have helped. Jamie was desperate to go, mainly, because he didn't want to disappoint Hannah again. He was flattered to be invited; he thought he'd burnt his bridges. He phoned his mother to clarify the arrangements. Did Adam know about all this? How would he react when he found out Jamie was sitting next to Natalie, munching a hot dog while mumbling *God Save the Queen*?

'He doesn't know about it yet,' said Tina. 'He's more concerned about all these soldiers being called in to do security. He's got some old friends who've been drafted in. He thinks it'll be a total shambles and switches off when I mention the Olympics.'

'Cheers mum, makes me feel much better. If he doesn't kill me, his army pals'll lay me to waste in east London.'

'Stop it, you idiot. This is Hannah's idea anyway. She's been talking to Natalie quite a bit recently… '

'Since when did you become close?'

'We're not close, but she speaks sense. She got in touch with us because she knew Natalie was involved in the riots. She was doing some research and trying to help young people in the area. We thought it'd be a good idea that Natalie spoke to her because they were from similar backgrounds.'

'She didn't tell me… '

'That's because you've been frying your brain with booze and pills. Didn't you tell me to get a grip once? I think I know who needs to pull themselves together right now.'

'It's nothing serious, mum, if you're gonna be like this at the Olympics, I'd rather not go. Should have got tickets for the football, anyway. I'm not too keen on women's hockey.'

'You will go. Hannah's got a surprise for you. I want to see you – and so does Natalie. I'm going to tell Adam that you'll be there – and he'll be fine with it. He just doesn't want you and Natalie alone, that's all. And anyway, he can't stop a mother from seeing his own son, can he?'

'No. What's the surprise?'

'Wouldn't be a surprise, would it? Where do you want to meet? Beaconsfield Station or Stratford?'

'… In the stadium.'

'You won't get into the Olympic Park without a ticket. I'll get Hannah to send it to you. This is going to be a fresh beginning for us. Natalie's completed her referral order and she's ready to turn over a new leaf. You need to do the same. We can be a family again.'

'That'll never happen with Adam around… '

'You never used to be this paranoid, what happened to you?'

'I'm bloody scared of the ex-military bastard, that's what? Has he never knocked you about?'

'Enough, Jamie. Be outside the relevant entrance at the Riverbank Arena at about 6.30. If not, we've all got mobiles.'

'What's the surprise again?'

'I'll ram a hockey stick up your arse! And don't come in with a Japanese flag. Bye.'

Tina hung up abruptly and Jamie quickly switched his phone to the internet browser to check the Olympic schedule. The game was on a Sunday – but what was the surprise? An engagement? Moving in together? Here was a chance to redeem himself and get in Hannah's and Tina's good books. He could even see Natalie again without the threat of violence from Adam. What wasn't to like? He felt energised, strong and replenished. He chucked a full packet of Skittles into a beaker of Grolsch and settled down to watch *Watford FC: Classic Cup Encounters*. Stag nights weren't for him but if he ever had one, he imagined a solitary affair with a beer and a DVD like tonight. No-one could then rib him if things didn't go to plan.

Jamie watched the Olympic ceremony on his own at home and went to bed at about 1am. The broadcasters ruined some of it by talking over the images but generally he felt Danny Boyle had done a good job. But it wasn't as good as *127 Hours* – he'd never top that. Jamie woke up the next morning and shopped for groceries online before checking his Olympic tickets – sent to him by Hannah. The tickets: Riverbank, Orbit and Travelcard didn't interest him; a four-line handwritten note hidden at the bottom of the envelope did.

This is the real beautiful game
Be there for me
She talks about you a lot (Natalie)…
She's not the only one.

He folded the note and put it into his pocket. He slipped the tickets back in the envelope. He took a shower and imagined Hannah in with him, warming him up, kissing him tenderly and telling him how she'd balance her life as an MP with his freelance career. He stepped out of the shower, had a shave and went downstairs for tea and biscuits. He sat at the kitchen table to read about Fitton's divorce with Grace in the Squires. His mobile rang before he got to end of the piece. It was a voice he didn't want to hear today.

'Enjoying the Olympics?' said DC Connor.

'Haven't really watched them... '

'Listen Jamie, it's highly unusual for me to do this, but I have to tell that you're going to be rearrested. They're likely to come for you tomorrow and it won't be pretty.'

Jamie took a sip of his piping hot tea and burnt his lip. His head started spinning. The dirty sweat of the bathroom whistled up his nostrils to create a sick feeling in his stomach.

'But I was cleared; what now? What the fuck now?'

'Obviously, there's more evidence than last time – and I tried to ensure you were asked to report in to the station but no, they prefer to do it this way again.'

'What evidence? I don't believe you. The same as last time?'

'I don't think it's wise for me to discuss that now. There'll be time for that when you come in.'

'So why the fuck did you call then? To tell me I'm going to be terrorised in my own house again? To be stripped and humiliated? To have a gun waved in my face?'

'You deserve prior warning that's all. My neck will be on the line too because of this. I feel we've got it spectacularly wrong in alienating the media with these kinds of raids, that's why I've called. I feel you can be well prepared; the shock and surprise may not hit you as hard if you know they're coming. Perhaps, have an early breakfast... '

Jamie nearly choked as the tea dribbled out onto his mouth and neck. He cleaned up with a tissue and started laughing to alleviate the numb feeling his body. 'Don't believe this shit. I thought you were trying to help me not have me put behind bars again.'

'I'm deadly serious. Raids work primarily because of their shock value. Suspects don't know they're coming; they're usually asleep. If you're up and absorbed in a task at the time, maybe ironing or preparing breakfast, you won't feel the same impact.'

Jamie felt weak and unable to speak. The hot tea had roughed up his throat. 'Thanks DC Connor, I'll get the eggs ready early in the morning.'

'Sarcasm will not help you now, strategy will. Take this advice from a friend… '

Jamie couldn't listen anymore and hung up. DC Connor rang back a couple of times but Jamie ignored him. His head was swirling with wild thoughts and horrific images. What would they do this time? Coppers never liked to see the same faces again. They would really smack him around this time. And the sound? That fucking sound of screaming coppers, flailing weapons, crashing dishes and flying furniture was emerging again in Jamie's brain. Thudding black boots and brutal, barking beasts. A ripping, tearing noise that he thought he'd banished. Tinnutus with a torpedo. A bewildered, shaking body. Cries and shouts at dawn. He couldn't take that again. Never.

35.

A Page In The Times of Our Lives

Jamie got up at 4am after spending most of the night thinking the ceiling was shrinking. He went downstairs into the kitchen and reached into the cupboard for a shiny strip of Amitriptyline. He took three pills with a glass of brandy. He made breakfast, got dressed and checked his Olympic tickets for the small details. He couldn't read them properly. Did he drop a Dizzy or a Benzo the night before? He couldn't remember. Most the pills looked the same. Before leaving the house, he printed out some of his old exclusive stories (from the internet) and hung them up again on the bare bedroom wall, to replace the old ones that had been destroyed by the previous raid. He looked up and touched them with the palm of his hand. He got to Amersham station and was desperate to get on the Metropolitan Line as soon as possible. He was sure he spotted Paul Markham on the platform opposite. His heart fluttered but, generally, he couldn't feel it at all. He got on the Tube train and thought about all the people who were out to get him: there were more of those than there were in the carriages. The police, MPs, Callum Gordon, Markham, Warren Fitton, Barnaby Bin, his dad, Peeper Wallace, Adam Solent; the list was endless. There was a story in there somewhere. By the time he got to Marylebone he was desperate for the toilet but didn't have the 30p in change required. He had £45 in notes and a few coppers. The machine only took 20p and 10p. It would have been better if he'd realised this before he was a few feet away from the cubicles. Fucking agony. He walked back towards the departure boards – and headed into WHSmith to buy a copy of the Daisies. He looked at the splash of a possible cyber attack at the Olympics and thought it was flimsy. He got his required change, tucked the paper under his arm and went to the toilet. On his way back, he walked past a couple of patrolling coppers. They were giving directions to a man with a rucksack and a map. Jamie was relieved to get out of the station. Less than 45 minutes later, he was in Stratford. Where was all this transport chaos he'd read and heard about? Jamie nipped into the Gents once more to check his tickets and rehearse a few exchanges. He walked out and could feel his sweaty hands loosening their grip on the tickets as he approached the volunteers and guards.

'Enjoy yourself, you'll remember this event forever,' said one volunteer, in her violet and pink top, waving a foam hand-pointer.

A high-five from another volunteer lifted Jamie's spirits as he reached the security area and could see lots of soldiers milling around. They were mainly young, well-groomed and up for a chinwag. Jamie entered the tent and started to empty his pockets into the tray. His mobile rang and he looked up at the ginger-haired soldier sheepishly.

'Bugger when that happens,' said the soldier, looking down at Jamie's newspaper. 'Is that the wife or the editor?'

Jamie shook his head and stepped back. He answered the call as more soldiers stared at him.

'Jamie, give yourself up, don't fuck about,' said Tina. 'The police have called us. They say you weren't at the house. Now they've got some sort of macho manhunt going on. For God's sake, stop this madness.'

'I wasn't going to wait to be humiliated again... '

'... Better than being in jail for years. Why did you flee? They only wanted to question you. You'd have been freed again just like the last time.'

'No, the coppers want to nail as many reporters as possible. And they want as many headlines as they can generate. It's a witch-hunt – and I'm not waiting to be lynched.' Jamie looked at the soldiers watching him and smiled politely. Their uniforms were impairing Jamie's vision. The dusty beige patterns felt brighter than usual. 'Look, I'm at security now, Mum, I'll be in the Olympic Park in a few minutes… '

'DON'T GO IN THERE, PLEASE, I'M BEGGING YOU. THERE'LL BE A MAJOR INCIDENT. THE OLYMPICS'LL BE SHUT DOWN.'

'Why aren't you here by now, anyway? I thought we had four Orbit tickets. Hannah's not here yet either. Have coppers told her about the raid as well? I don't care, I'm going up it.'

'Please don't go up there, Jamie, just come home. – or at least come to Beaconsfield. We were told not to go into London yet so… '

'Because of me?'

'No, no, I had Natalie to think of as well. That's the problem with you, Jamie, you never see the bigger picture.'

'Did they trash the house?'

'I honestly don't know. Please don't go into the Olympic Park, get the Tube back. I'll be here, Natalie's here… '

'But no Adam?'

Tina didn't answer.

'Where is he, mum?' Has he left or something? Always knew he was a bastard.'

'He's on his way to London now. He went straight to Amersham when the police told us they wanted to question you. He wants to help you, Jamie, don't forget that.'

'He's the one that needs help. Goodbye Mum.'

'JAMIE, NO, DON'T GO IN… '

Jamie hung up and emptied the final items from his pockets: coins, pens, two C60 microtapes and a packet of Skittles. He walked forward and, after a few more nods and winks from the youthful soldiers (mainly because of Jamie's choice of newspaper), he was through security and entered the Olympic Park. He looked at the strange, winding tower in the distance and felt the Orbit ticket between its fingers. The curious longing to go up the tower had been heightened rather than diminished by his lack of companions. If they were too chicken, fuck them. At least his mother had called; what was Hannah's excuse? They couldn't feel it the same way he did, anyway. They'd be too busy pointing and talking. He'd let the experience wash over him: a calm, woozy feeling from 900 feet. A natural high to complete the set. He walked forward and headed towards the red-blooded tower which felt like a twisted organ within his body. It was deformed and protruding; something that wanted to escape its own surroundings. But what was that above it? A helicopter? They were coming for him. Bring it on, boys, if you want games, I'm the ultimate Olympian. I've got five magic rings in my head and I'm in orbit already.

Jamie waited for the lift and looked at the giant trumpet-like shape above his head. He wanted to shout extremely loud to see what kind of sound was created but there were other visitors preparing to go up the Orbit too so he had to keep his composure. That was difficult with the red, criss-crossing bars surrounding him like pumping veins; they were more alive and potent than the ones inside him. They were suffocating him and making him breathe a little faster. He started to feel dizzy and mildly sick. The eyes watered and the stomach cramps began. He flicked open his newspaper and was desperate for the lift doors to open quickly.

'You okay sonny,' said a man from behind, wearing a Team Australia t-shirt.

'Tip-top,' said Jamie. 'Just feeling a bit queasy.'

'Look, I know the feeling. My wife didn't want to come up

today; felt a bit funny too. The army stuff and terrorism fears have got her going a bit.'

'Not much terrorism around now,' said Jamie.

'You wanna come from outside here, mate; the riots and all that, even our Aboriginal brothers wouldn't have gone that far.'

Jamie could feel his blood pressure rising and his heart beating faster. He rolled up his newspaper and tapped it on his opposite palm. He wasn't sure he wanted to go up here anymore. Finally, the lift door opened and people started to walk in. Jamie hesitated and let the Team Australia man walk ahead of him. Jamie cocked his head up again. He felt calm and reassured. Oh beautiful trumpet, swallow me up and take me as high as you can – until there's nowhere to go.

Jamie looked through the small circular window as the lift went up. The bruising clatter of steel bars and red veins were relentless with tiny pockets of east London emerging in the distance. He came out of the lift and was ushered to a balcony which was already full of people looking out at views of the city. He felt his legs weren't as stable as usual. What would happen if this whole tower collapsed? He walked forward and nipped into a gap vacated by a young couple wearing matching orange shirts. He was about to ask them for a spliff but thought better of it. He settled down on the platform and looked through the viewing window: the Velodrome mattress, ice-rack tower blocks, part of the Olympic stadium and spaceship Basketball arena were prominent – because he was familiar with them; the rest was a blur. He looked up at the sky and searched for the helicopter. Where was it? Nothing. Would they have one out for him anyway? Was he that important? He walked round the platform to the other side and his mobile beeped. It was a message from Hannah.

Sorry about Orbit, had to cancel at short notice. Please
don't do anything silly. Luv U and See
U at the beautiful game!

The last line gave him a lift but she hadn't turned up; case closed. Seven PM was an eternity away. It was colder up here than Jamie expected. A waft of cool air kept coming from the lifts. He looked into the curved mirrors and could see himself upside down (or was that the people behind him?). The wobbly reflections were making him dizzy and familiar faces kept popping up even though he tried to move away: Fitton, Markham, Gordon, Barnaby Bin, they were there looking at him with their feline poses and blank expressions. Jamie felt violently sick and fell to his knees. He tried to vomit on the floor but nothing came out apart from dribbly mucus from his throat. He'd never felt pain like this: his stomach felt as though it had been pulverised by the giant, intimating red veins surrounding him. A volunteer came over to help. He put his hand on Jamie's shoulder. Jamie glanced up at the mirror again. He saw a figure wearing a v-neck jumper he recognised. He thought he was going to pass out.

'Come on, I'll get you some help,' said the volunteer.

Jamie was about to answer but felt a hand on his shoulder. He looked up and saw Adam.

'Don't worry, I'll take care of things from here,' said Adam.

'Are you sure?' said the volunteer. 'I'll get you some water anyway.'

Adam nodded and the volunteer walked away.

'Where's my mother?' said Jamie.

'I have her ticket,' said Adam, handing Jamie a tissue for his damp mouth and trying to help him up. 'You shouldn't have fled, it just causes more problems. The police are angry enough as it is these days.'

'Don't try to help me up. I feel so dizzy my head's going to fall off… '

'Just rest your head on my arm then. We've had our differences but now's not the time to dwell on them.'

Jamie hesitated and then reluctantly eased his head onto Adam's arm who was now sat down beside him. He could see the volunteer coming back with a bottle of water. He handed it to Adam.

'Look, are you sure he doesn't need any medical help?' said the volunteer. 'Unfortunately, we've got health and safety considerations too because we've got a lot of people up here. If he's okay, can you just move to the side a little? If not, we'll get him all the help he needs.'

'He's fine, we'll be quick, don't worry,' said Adam. 'I have a bit of experience in these situations. Come on Jamie, up you get. We're in the way here, let's move away from the mirrors. I know that's been hard for you in the past… '

The volunteer smiled and walked away.

'Fuck the jokes, why are you being so nice to me now?' said Jamie.

Adam sighed and reached into his pocket. He pulled out a familiar 16-page pamphlet which made Jamie shudder.

'When the police called us,' said Adam. 'I went straight over to Amersham to see what had happened. After the raid, the police allowed me to go into the house, I don't know why, I don't think it's normal but then dawn raids on reporters aren't normal either. Anyway, I checked all the rooms and came across this in your bedroom, lying on the floor next the bed… ' He handed it over to Jamie. It was The Soonami Times.

Jamie held the mini newspaper between his fingers and looked through its pages again. The drawings of Mo's deceased parents and destroyed villages were too much to bear. Jamie was in tears almost immediately.

'Why didn't you tell me about this?' said Adam, inching

closer to him. 'This was under your pillow for years and you kept it a secret. You cared so much but you buried it away. Why didn't you show it to me before? We could have avoided so many things.'

'It was too raw to share,' said Jamie, sobbing and wiping his chin with the tissue. 'I was angry with Mo for coming into my room – but when I saw the little newspaper he'd made it just blew me away. I've never felt like that before. Our papers are good at dealing with the superficial things but not stuff like that. It was a window into someone's soul.'

Jamie handed the little newspaper back to Adam.

'Mo was like a son to me and he gave us this wonderful gift,' said Adam. 'We're going through a fraction of what he'd been through, don't forget that. He knew us better than we knew him.'

Jamie put his hand over his face. 'It's strange but he feels like one of my best friends.'

Adam nodded and offered his hand to Jamie to help him up. As Jamie sat up gingerly, Adam noticed the bigger newspaper by his side for the first time. 'Why did you buy that rag again? Won't you ever learn? You're bigger than that now.'

'Bigger than that, what do you mean?'

Adam opened the bottle of water and eased it towards Jamie's mouth.

'Tina says there's a film being made about you; that Larna Wilson girl who's been in the papers a lot, her new film's about you.'

Jamie felt a momentary surge of exhilaration and then a savage pain to the right side of the head. He remembered the scene in the disused warehouse of a man with his son trying to get the Christmas lights to work. That man was his father; the son was him. How could she do such a thing? He couldn't bear to see his father being portrayed on screen. It would be wrong whatever was shown. The light from the camera was enough to improve his image.

'Did Tina know about this film?'

'No,' said Adam, taking a swig of water himself. 'It's based on the whistleblower stuff that you were involved in with that MP and other reporter. You should be grateful; only a few people get their life stories put up on the big screen.'

Jamie shook his head put his head in his hands.

'All you need to do is come out of here in one piece,' said Adam. 'Then we can get down to the station, get the questioning overwith and get you released. The film will help with all that because you'll be seen as a victim treated horribly the police. So come on, get up and get yourself together.'

Jamie still felt a sick, swirling feeling inside his head and a stabbing pain in his stomach. He sighed and looked down at the Daisies by his side.

'Stop reading that shit, will you, and let's go home?' said Adam.

'Headline: Former hack's biopic the topic of new film, what do you think?'

Adam stood up. 'I think it's over. You won't be seeing headlines like that ever again.'

'What are you talking about?'

The lift opened and a couple of pages from the Daisies started to blow away across the platform. Jamie tried to stop them.

'Leave them, Jamie, the paper's closing. It was announced in the last couple of hours that today was its last ever edition. They're not even having one next week. Gone, kaput. No goodbye parties. Staff left high and dry.'

Jamie felt a sharp pain just below his heart, a burning, searing sensation that he'd never felt before. His arm became numb and he tried to speak but nothing came out. Falling, suffocating, sinking. His eyes became droopy and he tried to grab Adam's hand but it was weak and listless. The pages swished and floated across the platform; the front page landing under an old man's feet, the back going into the lift. Hundreds of stories, hundreds of tales, hundreds of broken dreams. It was time for Jamie's own page. He wanted to write it with a crayon.

ACKNOWLEDGEMENTS

The Author wishes to thank:

David Rallis for his inspired choice of beverage for Jamie Parkes' character.

Steve Cohen for giving me my first break in journalism without which none of this book would have been possible.

The team at Troubador, ably led by Jeremy Thompson.

Helen Lewis at Literally PR.

Pukka Pads where I wrote initial drafts of the novel in longhand.

Tabloid newspapers for their wit and wickedness.

Shabina, Liyana and Mikail for dragging me through to the end.

RESEARCH MATERIAL (selected)

Tabloid Girl: A True Story by Sharon Marshall
All The President's Men – director Alan J Pakula (1976)
Hacks – Channel 4 (first broadcast Jan 1 2012)
The Leveson Inquiry 2011-2012
Stick It Up Your Punter: The Uncut Story of The Sun
by Peter Chippindale and Chris Horrie
The Front Page – director Billy Wilder (1974)
Flat Earth News – Nick Davies

nasserhashmi.com
nasseronmars.com